SEVEN DAYS
❧ IN MAY ❧

SEVEN DAYS ❧ IN MAY ❧

A Novel of the Lusitania
Inspired by true events

KIM IZZO

HarperCollins*PublishersLtd*

Seven Days in May
Copyright © 2017 by Scarlett Ink Incorporated.
All rights reserved.

Published by HarperCollins Publishers Ltd

First Edition

HarperCollins books may be purchased for educational, business or
sales promotional use through our Special Markets Department.

HarperCollins Publishers Ltd
2 Bloor Street East, 20th Floor
Toronto, Ontario, Canada
M4W 1A8

www.harpercollins.ca

Library and Archives Canada Cataloguing in Publication
information is available upon request.

ISBN 978-1-44342-249-9

Printed and bound in the United States of America
LSC 9 8 7 6 5 4 3 2 1

For my great-grandfather Walter, who survived to tell the tale.
And for his daughter Muriel, my grandmother, who kept his story alive.

In wartime, truth is so precious that she should always be attended by a bodyguard of lies.

—*Winston Churchill*

The RMS Lusitania *arrives close to port, circa 1912. Photo courtesy the Mike Poirier Collection.*

1915

JANUARY 4

Sydney Sinclair, New York City

It was half past nine in the morning when Sydney stepped out of the taxi wearing her most drab topcoat. It was plain boiled wool in a dark rust colour that provided a comforting camouflage amongst the worn-out browns of the tenement buildings and bustling pushcarts of Orchard Street.

She picked her way through the maze of foreign languages being shouted about her. Italian, Hebrew, Polish and other unfamiliar tongues swirled around her, the speakers no doubt haggling over the price of potatoes and root vegetables, of articles of clothing, perhaps even of the live birds and rabbits on display. She glanced at the scrap of paper in her hand. The tenement she sought was directly across the street. She crossed cautiously, the heels of her lace-up boots squishing into the dirty snow.

They were expecting her. She followed a small woman wearing a tartan skirt up five flights of stairs and down a hallway, stopping at a black door marked 5C. There was no ceremony upon entering the flat. No one to greet her with deference or offer her a seat, tea or even a glass of water. That she was a young woman of independent means from one of New York's wealthiest families meant nothing here. Well, not entirely.

"You must be Miss Sinclair?"

The tartan woman who had led her inside had swiftly disappeared into another room, leaving Sydney alone by the door. Sydney smiled at the woman who spoke now. She was young, at least young enough to still be considered pretty, which was saying something considering the dour nursing uniform she wore. The cap wasn't especially flattering either.

"Please call me Sydney," she said, and offered her hand but the nurse shook her head.

"We don't shake hands in here. It's not sanitary. I'm Gretchen."

"You worked with Margaret Sanger?" Sydney asked.

Gretchen nodded. "Still do work for Margaret, if you ask me. What we do here is all because of her."

Margaret Sanger was a notorious and controversial advocate for women's reproductive rights; she was also Sydney's heroine, and someone she wanted to emulate, which had created a bone of contention between Sydney and her sister, Brooke. Tension between them was nothing new but it had risen substantially since Brooke had become engaged to an English aristocrat, Edward Thorpe-Tracey. Even the name was pompous to her. Several bitter arguments over Sydney's politics, which conflicted with his traditional views, had resulted. And this was before she'd even met the man. Edward wasn't due to arrive in New York until the end of April to escort his fiancée and her only remaining family to England for the wedding. Of course an American wedding wasn't grand enough for Brooke. So Sydney was travelling overseas to stand with her sister as she wed Edward on his estate, Rathfon Hall. The only silver lining for Sydney was the opportunity to meet with Sanger, now exiled and living in London, having broken too many laws in America.

Gretchen led Sydney through the flat. In its previous life it would have been a family home with three rooms. Two for sleeping and one for living. But now it was a makeshift hospital. Bed after bed took up most of the floor space. She counted three nurses including Gretchen; the others were occupied with inventory and cleaning. Despite the activity there were only two patients. One sat up reading a novel, a very ragged and dog-eared copy of *Anne of Green Gables*. Sydney got a closer look at the girl reading it. *She can't be older than fifteen*, thought Sydney, who was only twenty-one.

"She's recovering nicely," Gretchen whispered, and walked well out of earshot of the patients. "She had a nasty infection after her procedure. Whoever did it used a crochet hook."

Sydney tried desperately not to react. Squeamishness wasn't what was needed here. "Who did this to her?" Sydney asked, not sure if she wanted the name of the back-alley abortionist or the cad who had impregnated the child.

"She worked in a garment factory. I think the man was her boss, poor thing," Gretchen said as though reading her mind. "I don't think she went to a doctor but she wouldn't tell us. Whoever did it butchered her insides getting rid of the fetus, that much we know. We don't need her telling us *that*. But she'll be fine."

Sydney looked at the woman in the next bed. She had her eyes closed and her forehead covered with her arm. Her hair was tangled and dirty.

"Has she been here a long time?" Sydney asked, indicating the other woman by a nod of her head.

Gretchen sighed. "She tried to abort the baby herself." Sydney winced. "She succeeded in the end but she turned septic. We're not sure if she'll make it. And if she does, she won't be able to bear any more children."

"How awful for her."

"It's not too awful," Gretchen said coldly. "She already has nine children at home. Catholic, you know. Husband won't leave her alone."

Sydney didn't want to stare at the stricken woman and turned again to the young girl reading *Anne of Green Gables*. The girl turned a page and giggled.

"Will she return to her job in the garment factory?" Sydney asked.

Gretchen shrugged. "What choice does she have?"

Sydney felt light-headed. It was very hot in the flat. She staggered a few steps. "I need water." She swooned.

Gretchen took her by the arm and led her to one of the beds. Sydney lay down and closed her eyes. She heard a commotion not far from her and then Gretchen was back with a glass of water and a cool cloth for her forehead.

"I didn't really faint," Sydney said, and struggled to sit up.

"Stay put," Gretchen ordered. "You're not the first visitor to react this way."

Sydney sat on the edge of the bed and Gretchen left her alone a moment. When she was able to focus she looked up and saw the young girl staring at her. Sydney looked away, feeling self-conscious.

"Hello, Miss. I'm Mary," the young woman said. "Did you get rid of your baby too?"

Sydney looked carefully at the girl. She was so young. Her cheeks still had the rosy glow and baby fat of childhood. Yet her eyes lacked all innocence. To think this child knew more about the intimacy between man and woman than she did.

"I did not, Mary," Sydney said simply.

"Better to wait until you got here," Mary said. "They know what they're doing."

Her words made Sydney wonder. "How did you come to be here?"

Mary smiled. "The man who got rid of my baby, well, when he saw the blood he went crazy. Practically carried me all the way. I was lucky someone was here. Almost died." She stopped smiling and went silent.

"You'll be fine, Mary," Sydney said, knowing full well she had no idea if that were true.

Minutes later Gretchen walked with Sydney down the steps to the front door. "So will you help us? We could use the money."

Sydney was surprised by her boldness. In her world people didn't speak of money so nakedly. But she nodded. "I will send a cheque," she said.

"Cash," Gretchen said bluntly. "We can't have any records, for obvious reasons."

They had reached the front door. She still smelled the antiseptics from the clinic. Then again maybe it was Gretchen who carried the odour with her.

"I will see to it you get cash," Sydney said. "Goodbye."

Back on Orchard Street the aromas from the pushcarts wafted up to her and rescued her senses. She lifted her chin to take in the soothing smells. The scent of smoked meat and roasted potatoes was more pleasing than iodine and other hospital chemicals. Sydney had stayed longer than she had realized. But it was difficult to walk away from such a place. She pulled on her gloves and headed north, as fast as she could under her own power before hailing a taxi. She was expected at home any minute. It was a bad habit of hers to be late, especially when it came to meeting her guardian. But her guilt only went so far. *He's well paid to put up with me.*

Isabel Nelson, London

sabel stood staring up at the old Admiralty Building. It was an intimidating three-storey U-shaped structure complete with columns and an imposing archway. The building stood on Whitehall and was one of the power centres of the British government and yet she, of all people, was standing on its threshold working up the nerve to cross it. She'd been in London but two days and already she felt sure the city would eat her alive. The crowds, the filthy streets and the fumes in the air smelled unlike anything she'd encountered before. How did people stand it? But she had come for a fresh start and that must be enough to put up with any amount of discomfort. The first week of the New Year was especially cold and a thin veil of wet snow billowed down from the grey murk above. It suited her mood.

Isabel straightened her felt hat and took a deep breath. She was early. It was a habit of hers formed in childhood by a mother who arrived everywhere thirty minutes ahead of schedule. Being late was a sin in the Nelson household. Mind you, she'd since been guilty of greater crimes than tardiness. Why else was she standing in the freezing damp in the capital? She glanced at her wristwatch and felt a familiar panic rise up from her belly. The time had come and she would go from being early to late if she dawdled any longer. She imagined that naval officers agreed with her mother on tardiness being a grave sin. With gritted teeth Isabel stepped forward and marched into the Admiralty.

You must be Isabel." It was Mrs. Burns, who was in charge of all the women typists, clerks and stenographers, who spoke to her, with a stern and assessing gaze. Several other young new hires stood shoulder to shoulder alongside Isabel in the small space that was Burns's office. She was a stout older woman with a few errant whiskers on her chin and grey frizzy hair poking out of its bun.

Blimey. The government isn't too fussy about appearances, thought Isabel. She had taken great care to dress, first impressions and all that. While the other young ladies painted their eyelids and cheeks with pots of colour and stained their lips to have that "bitten" look, Isabel had forgone this fad and instead used only a translucent powder. And unlike these other girls, who wore their hair in chic chignons with wisps or loose waves softly framing their faces, Isabel's hair was drawn severely off her face and imprisoned in a tight bun guarded by a dozen bobby pins. Her skirt, blouse and jacket were plain but clean and tidy. Not that she was against prettying herself up; that morning she had stared at her lipstick and pot of rouge on the vanity at the boarding house in Kentish Town. But pretty was no longer her role to play. London was a fresh start to be launched with a fresh face.

"Cat got your tongue?" Mrs. Burns was staring at her.

"No, ma'am. I'm Isabel Nelson, from Oxford."

"Is that so?" she asked. "And what did you read up in Oxford then? Ancient history? Latin?"

The other young ladies stifled giggles. Isabel hated Mrs. Burns.

"I didn't say I went to the university, ma'am. But the house where I worked was in the city centre."

The older woman pursed her lips, not even bothering to try to hide her disdain. "All right, ladies. It's time for a tour and then you will go to your assigned offices."

"I heard that she's nice enough once she gets to know you," one of the girls explained to Isabel.

She shrugged. "I don't plan on knowing her." The girl raised her eyebrows in surprise. Isabel quickly changed tactics. "I mean I'm here to do a job, an important job for the war effort. As we all are."

"I think we're here to type and file," the girl answered, and walked away.

Mrs. Burns gave the newcomers a tour of the old Admiralty Building, which was full of history as expected and had the added distinction of having had the body of Lord Horatio Nelson lie in repose there the night before his burial. Lord Nelson was of no relation to Isabel. She had checked, of course. There was no noble blood in her veins. No heroic ancestors to lay claim to. Yet she wasn't the only one who made the connection.

"Are you related to him, then?" asked one of the girls a little too loudly for comfort.

Isabel hesitated. "I'm not sure," she answered quietly. She hadn't denied it outright. But that wasn't the same as lying. Unfortunately Mrs. Burns heard their exchange and rolled her eyes for all to see.

"What would the great-granddaughter of Horatio Nelson be doing typing and filing at the Admiralty?" the older woman rightly pointed out.

The group's next stop was the Admiralty Board Room. Mrs. Burns took great pride in pointing out a wind dial above the fireplace. "It's operated by a metal vane on the rooftop," she'd explained to the bored faces that stared back. "It's from the original 1695 building." That didn't impress them. There were also elaborate carvings of ancient nautical instruments around the fireplace. But it wasn't until Mrs. Burns brought their attention to a diagram that Isabel really paid attention. The diagram itself meant nothing to her. It was only when Mrs. Burns spoke the word *telegraph* that her interest was piqued. "It's a shutter telegraph," she explained to her captivated audience of one. "The Admiralty sent important messages to signalmen who were stationed throughout the country. Think of it as the wireless of the eighteenth century."

"I prefer not to think of it at all," whispered one of the other girls into Isabel's ear. Isabel shunted her off with a disapproving glare. Telegraphy was an interest of Isabel's. In Oxford she had had the opportunity to listen in as amateur radio operators intercepted foreign messages. She had begun to learn Morse code too but there hadn't been time to become fluent . . . and now she was here.

That had been the morning gone by. Now she tried her best to appear confident as she made her way down the corridor toward her assigned post—Room 40 OB. Isabel was not at all impressed that the room she was given to work in was so inconveniently located from the main entrance. It was on the main floor but hidden down a dimly lit hallway and tucked in a corner. *You'd think they didn't want to be found*, she grumbled to herself. When she arrived at her destination the door was closed. She stood and waited. For who or what she didn't know. *How stupid I must look, standing here staring at a door.* But for some reason she was afraid to knock.

"You lost, Miss?"

Isabel turned to see a young man, about her age, behind her. "I've been assigned to this office. I'm a secretary." Isabel held out her written assignment letter as proof she was in the right place. The man skimmed it quickly.

"I'll take you in then."

He opened the door. Isabel stepped inside and was immediately transfixed. For one thing the room was smaller than she expected. Though perhaps it wasn't the actual square footage that made it seem so, rather it was the fact of its being cramped, as though the men who occupied it had been stuffed inside an envelope and sealed, its creases bulging against the pressure. Paper was everywhere. Neat piles on a table. Haphazard stacks on the floor. Willy-nilly mounds in a corner. There was no obvious order, no apparent system. Nestled inside the mess were several men seated at a table laden with enormous books and still more masses of paper. The men were as silent and intense as seminary students studying for their ordination. None of them looked up at her.

"Do come in, Miss." The young man spoke again, jolting Isabel from her paralysis.

She took another step when there came a crash that made her jump. A loud "Oh!" escaped her lips. Then she saw the source of the crash; it was a tray into which several metal tubes had clattered from a pneumatic system. It was a startling sound but the others seemed accustomed to it.

"So what's your name, then?" the young man asked.

Isabel smiled and shook his hand. "Isabel Nelson."

"I'm Henry Phillipson."

"You're not in the navy?" she asked him quietly.

He shook his head and smiled. "Just a civilian volunteer."

Isabel saw that there were a few other girls in the room. They looked about her age but unlike her these girls wore fashionable clothes and cosmetics and styled their hair. They were clustered around several typewriters on one side of the room. Underwood No. 5s, to be exact. She had learned on the same model in Oxford. These machines were things of beauty to her. Like musical instruments that could play prose and poetry (or spew vile remarks if one gave in to impulses), in the right hands, beneath the right fingers, they were freedom and power.

One of the girls walked by with an armload of files and stopped when she saw Isabel. She studied her in a friendly way. "You're the new girl, aren't you?"

"My name is Isabel," she said.

The girl hugged her load and reached out her hand. "I'm Dorothy." She gestured to the other two girls. "That's Joan typing and Violet's the one filing her nails. She shouldn't do that in here. Anyway, welcome aboard."

Henry returned to her side as Dorothy scuttled away. "I'm to take you to Commander Hope," he said.

Isabel followed Henry to an isolated desk that was set up on the far side of the room. Seated on a simple wooden chair was Commander Hope. He looked up as she was introduced and without a smile said, "Miss Nelson, welcome to Room 40. We perform a vital job for the Admiralty and for the war effort." Isabel nodded, too nervous to speak. She felt Henry touch her arm. She looked at him and he winked. Then he was gone and she was left alone with Commander Hope. "How much have you been told about our work?" he asked with no hint of his own friendly wink being forthcoming.

"Not a thing, Commander, sir," she said. It was true. Mrs. Burns had been incredibly vague about her assignment. The other new girls had been told in front of the others whom they would work for and in what department, and were free to ask questions. When it was her turn Mrs. Burns had handed her an assignment sheet that only listed the room number. When Isabel asked for more information Mrs. Burn had replied sternly, "You will know soon enough."

"Glad to hear it," Commander Hope said, and seemed to relax his posture somewhat. He reminded Isabel of a professor. "What goes on inside these walls is a secret. I trust you can keep a secret?"

"Yes—yes, sir," she stammered, unsure why he'd ask such a thing of her.

"When we're through here, I've asked Alastair Denniston, he's my second-in-command, to instruct you in the details of your job. In the meantime you're required to sign this . . ." He handed her a government document. Isabel quickly scanned it.

"The Official Secrets Act, sir?" she asked, as if she needed confirmation.

Hope raised an eyebrow. "Is it going to be a problem for you, Miss Nelson?"

Isabel shook her head furiously and, grabbing a pen off the man's desk, she scrawled her name in the space given and proffered the paper to him. He studied her closely, her sudden eagerness no doubt off-putting to a man accustomed to well-trained sailors and naval officers. "Thank you," he said. "I cannot overemphasize how seriously we take discretion, Miss Nelson. Nothing that happens within these walls must ever be spoken of outside of them. Now please go find Denniston. Good luck."

"You're welcome, Commander Hope," she declared, and with a surge of optimistic energy saluted him. The inappropriate gesture made him smile, but only slightly.

She found Alastair Denniston waiting for her. He wasn't a tall man, but was rather good-looking. Judging by his heavy eyelids he hadn't slept in days, though his suit appeared freshly ironed. Beside him was an ashtray overflowing with discarded cigarettes. A few empty whisky tumblers dotted the table but there was no evidence of whisky.

"Are you any good at math?" he asked her.

"Math, sir?"

"Do you speak German?"

Isabel felt flustered. "I can do basic arithmetic. But I don't speak German." Her answer seemed to disappoint him.

"Very well" he said. "I always like to ask new recruits."

"I do know some Morse code, sir," she said, grasping at anything that might impress him. It worked.

"Well, then. If you have a knack for that sort of thing we may have to train you beyond secretarial duties," he said.

"What is it you gentlemen do here exactly?" she asked, and looked around the room at the men, pencils in hand, scrawling madly. "Are you writing a book?"

"What makes you ask that?" He laughed.

"All the paper, sir," she said. "Though it doesn't seem very organized." As soon as the words had left her mouth she regretted them. Who was she to critique the Admiralty? Fortunately, Denniston smiled. "That's why we need you and the other ladies," he answered, and lit another cigarette. "But if you would like to be in on the great mystery, the holy of holies, I can tell you."

Isabel's eyes narrowed. Was he teasing or mocking her with such an odd expression? "Yes, I would."

Denniston exhaled a ring of silver smoke. "Cryptography," he said with a sly grin.

She had never heard the word before. "We decipher code," he said as though that explained everything.

"Throughout the country there are amateur ham radio enthusiasts whom we've enlisted to intercept wireless transmissions from the enemy via our Hunstanton Coast Guard Station in Norfolk. These men are supplementing the work being done elsewhere by the Post Office and Marconi operators."

Isabel knew this only too well. Her employer in Oxford, George Chambers, was one such man. She had worked for him as a housemaid and he had written her a letter of reference and sent it personally to the Admiralty. Isabel and another girl named Mildred Fox had been let go at the same time for very different reasons. She didn't know what had become of Mildred. But she felt certain now was not the time to mention Chambers or the letter of reference. What had happened to her in Oxford was as secret as anything in Room 40.

Denniston continued. "All of these various groups send the intercepted German messages to the Admiralty. We have men here who take down the messages, which were encrypted and encoded by the Germans, and send them to us through the pneumatic tube system. Then we find the key to the code, decipher the messages and translate them. As you'll soon learn that's why so many of us are linguists, we knew nothing of code breaking when we began last autumn. But Fleet Paymaster Rotter was able to find the key and decipher the encrypted messages. From what is intercepted we can track every movement of the German High Seas Fleet. Are you following me?"

Isabel nodded and he went on. "Most messages are fairly routine, dull you might say. But we've found that when organized and compared they often reveal information of vital importance. Indeed we've grown so accustomed to the routine messages that when ones arrive that are not routine we pay close attention. This has proven to be useful."

"Yes, sir," was all she could manage to say. Her mind was whirring with all this startling information.

"Now where you come in is that each message is typed up and copied and logged. It's soul-destroying work, I grant you. But it's our orders from the First Lord of the Admiralty himself. Then Commander Hope interprets the messages from the naval standpoint and passes them along to the Director of Intelligence, Captain Hall, then up the chain of command. Our work is so secret only nine men know of our existence in the whole of the British Empire."

It was a lot to take in. She looked at Denniston expectantly, but he seemed content to wait for her to ask questions.

"Oh," was all she could manage. He seemed disappointed and she couldn't take that so she quickly added, "How do you break the codes?"

Denniston grinned, satisfied by her curiosity. "Follow me." He crossed the room to where three great books lay; one was more massive than the others and had covers made of lead. There, Fleet Paymaster Rotter and another man, a Mr. Curtis, were introduced to her. They were hard at work on something and after a swift how-do-you-do their heads were bowed over the papers in front of them. Denniston seemed to look at the books as though they were religious artifacts. He ran his hand across the lead cover of the largest.

"This is the *Signal Book of the Imperial Navy, Signalbuch der Kaiserlichen Marine*, or the *SKM*," he told her. "It was captured by the Russians and given to the Admiralty in October. It took us a while to understand how it worked."

At this Rotter lifted his head from his work. "It was easy." He grinned in such a way that made it obvious it was anything but.

"Don't let him fool you, Miss Nelson," Denniston continued. "Rotter was a real hero. He broke the cipher last November."

Rotter appeared self-conscious. "Don't listen to a word he says," he said modestly. "We're a team here. I got lucky."

"By guess and by God," Curtis added.

Denniston explained at length the difference between codes and ciphers. To send messages in code the codebook was required by both the sender and recipient. To send a message in cipher no book was needed but instead the plain language, or *en clair*, was enciphered by substituting letters from a key that both parties had access to. Another method was transposition or scrambling of letters; again a key was needed to descramble. Sometimes both methods were used. He explained how the *SKM* was no use on its own because messages weren't just coded but were also enciphered. "But we were fortunate to intercept enough numbered messages to realize how they were doing it and now we can be quite accurate."

She took shorthand notes but most of it was too confusing to grasp in one afternoon. By four p.m. another man, by the name of Norton, arrived to begin his shift. Denniston nodded in his direction. "I'm going to have Mr. Norton finish with you. He's a naval instructor by trade so he'll be able to explain the rest."

Norton seemed perplexed by his new order. "Should we waste our time teaching the girls?"

Isabel flinched. Denniston glared. "Yes, Mr. Norton. Teach Miss Nelson to know as much as the others do so she can properly understand her role and how to perform her tasks."

Norton threw his coat on a chair. "It's not like they're going to be breaking codes."

"Mr. Norton, one day you may find women doing the same job as you and more. They work as hard as any of the men and complain half as much, if at all."

"If you insist," Norton said.

"I do." Denniston turned back to Isabel. "I'm going home to get some rest."

She watched him move slowly, a mark of his exhaustion, to the closet, where he grabbed his overcoat. He didn't say goodbye. She looked to Norton. There was no point in trying to make friends after his outburst. If he wanted no-nonsense then she would oblige.

"Shall we continue?" she asked him bluntly.

Norton grabbed another of the enormous codebooks and gave it to her. It was heavy and well-used, its cover ragged and dirty. "This is the *Handelsverkehrsbuch*, or *HVB*. It fell into our hands along with the *SKM*. The Germans use it to communicate with merchant ships but we've discovered that U-boat commanders use it as well, though they've come up with more complex ciphers to try and prevent us from knowing where they're going."

"Do the Germans know we have these books?"

"Indeed they do. So far they haven't issued new codebooks. But look at these monsters, that is a massive undertaking." He then picked up the third book. "And finally this is the *Verkehrsbuch* or *VB*, the *Transport Book*. They use it to communicate with their naval and military attachés, embassies, you know, diplomatic Intelligence."

"So that's the most important codebook?" she asked.

"They all have their purpose," he said. He crossed to a bureau on one side of the room and picked up a folder full of handwritten transcripts. He handed it to Isabel. "See to it these get typed up by the end of your shift."

He might be done with her but *she* wasn't finished yet. She noticed a large tin on the table that had the letters *N.S.L.* printed on it in black letters. "What goes in there?"

Norton snorted. "That's for all the codes and messages we can't break. The letters mean 'neither sent nor logged.'"

"I see."

"Let me show you another riveting item," he said, and took her to an enormous closet. He opened it and she saw that inside were shelves loaded with paper.

"What a mess," she said, panicked that its organization might fall to her.

"Stuff."

"Stuff?"

"Yes. Messages that were intercepted and translated but have nothing to do with the navy. Though I did hear that some Jerry sent a very good strudel recipe over the wireless to his brother who's stationed on a destroyer. And I think Mr. Anstie uncovered that one of the kaiser's top admirals is having an affair with his secretary. Those types of transcripts we call *stuff* and we stuff them in here."

"Understood," she said.

"Now be a good girl and type those up," Norton said, and tapped the pile of transcripts in her arms.

"Excuse me, Mr. Norton. I have one question," she said.

Norton looked at her, his patience wearing thin. "Yes?"

"I understand that Room 40 is run by Commander Hope and Captain Hall. Mr. Denniston mentioned a First Lord of the Admiralty. What is his name?"

Norton straightened up like his head was attached to a pulley. "That's none of your concern."

She swallowed. "I didn't mean any disrespect, sir. I thought it would be good to know the names of those in charge is all. I want to do a good job and Mr. Denniston made mention of there being only nine people in the Admiralty who know of Room 40."

"I won't tell you all nine. But those who matter most are Chief of Staff Admiral Henry Oliver, who presides over Captain Hall, director of the Intelligence division, and you've met Commander Hope already, he runs the day-to-day of Room 40. They all report to Jacky Fisher, the First Sea Lord. But the First Lord of the Admiralty runs the show. He's a civilian and a dandy in every sense of the word. I mean that with all due respect, of course."

"Of course," she repeated. "And his name?" It was her turn to be impatient.

Norton picked up his jacket from the back of his chair and removed a package of cigarettes. It seemed to take an eternity for him to light the damn thing. He took a drag and blew smoke into the air, waving at it casually so it didn't drift into her face. He grinned slyly.

"Winston Churchill."

Sydney

"Your sister will be the ruin of the both of you." Mr. Garrett's pronouncement of impending doom was spoken with unwavering confidence. "Not that you'll fare much better, Sydney. Making me wait until half past four. No doubt you were at another of those godforsaken rallies for the women's vote."

Sydney looked out the window of the second-floor sitting room, the one with the peony chintz drapes, to the bustling street below. She smiled when she answered him. "We are both difficult in our own way. But wouldn't it be dull if Brooke and I felt the same about everything? And I was not at a rally this afternoon."

Mr. Garrett smiled, relieved. Then . . .

"I was at an abortion clinic," Sydney said. "I'm giving them a large donation."

Mr. Garrett sputtered but composed himself quickly, fully aware which side his bread was buttered on. "Politics aside, you are a grounded, albeit headstrong, girl. Your sister, however, lives in a world that seems to be governed by plots from romantic novels. And given that it is my responsibility to manage both your inheritances, I must go on the record as saying I do not advise this scheme of hers."

Sydney turned away from the window of her family home, which stood at the corner of Fifth Avenue and East Sixty-Fourth Street. It was a Georgian brownstone that might have co-existed elegantly with its neighbour's façade had it not the added distinction of fire-engine-red shutters on its top-floor windows and an equally vibrant red door. Its number—828—was emblazoned in gold (what else) and set inside a bronze rectangular plaque that had turned verdigris since being affixed, in 1883, onto the wall facing Sixty-Fourth Street. Three stone-arched windows imparted a gothic air. Within the walls of number 828 were five floors of living space designed to impress even the most discerning Gilded Age millionaire. There was a vast parlour on the main floor, what the family preferred to call a "salon," and it was painted a slightly less garish red than the shutters and door. On the second floor were two additional sitting rooms, smaller than the salon, both with fireplaces and one more feminine than the next. The kitchen and staff rooms were in the basement. The other floors were the family's bedrooms. One floor per daughter, the younger on the third, the elder on the fourth, and the fifth, with its uncompromised view of Central Park, was the domain of Mr. and Mrs. Augustus Sinclair. The top floor had sat empty for some time. Mr. Sinclair, who had accumulated a vast fortune in California oil during the 1880s (thus building on the already extensive fortune his own father had amassed during the California gold rush of 1848), had passed away at the ripe age of sixty-seven, during a snowstorm in the winter of 1914. His wife's death had predated his by sixteen years.

Sydney crossed the room and took a seat on the lavender silk divan beside Mr. Garrett. He was normally stern, practically despotic, now he acted like a nervous grandmother. She reached over and placed her hand on his arm.

"We agree on that much," she said. "She's read too much Jane Austen. But she is the eldest and perhaps is even more headstrong than I." At this she removed her hand and sat upright, smoothing the creases in her forest-green dress before folding her hands in her lap.

"It was a mistake not sending you to England last fall," Mr. Garrett said darkly. "Perhaps things wouldn't have happened so quickly, so carelessly. You could have talked some sense into her."

"I'm not my sister's chaperone," Sydney answered sharply. "Brooke wanted to secure a title and she has done so. Well, at least once the wedding takes place. She will be Lady of the Manor and that suits her sensibilities. Besides she'd scarcely have listened to me; you know she and I aren't as close as some sisters are. We lead different lives. Now she will move to England and lead an even more different life."

"But neither of us have met this man!"

"*Gentle*man," Sydney teased. The situation required levity. "He will one day be Sir Edward Thorpe-Tracey, a lord, the third earl of Northbrook, making my sister Lady Northbrook." With that said, Sydney laughed. It was so absurd to her.

"I can't abide the thought of handing over every last penny of Brooke's money to some—some—*Englishman*. I don't care if he's the Lord Almighty himself. What would your father say?"

"Our father is dead," Sydney answered solemnly. How she missed him. "You can imagine, as I can, he wouldn't like the idea one bit. He was American, through and through, and the thought of his money leaving the country would not please him. Perhaps we can be thankful he's not here to see it. But in the end he would want Brooke to be happy."

"Happiness? Is that what she's after? I'd say it was status and notoriety. She has always courted attention. And now she will have more than enough. Brooke Sinclair, the last of America's Dollar Princesses," he said. "In your mother's day it was practically common for New York's first families to marry off their daughters to Englishmen in need of money. I thought that time had passed. I was wrong."

Sydney understood what Garrett was implying. Brooke's marriage might be considered somewhat gauche. All the young ladies who ran in the Sinclairs' circle were raised to be above whispers and sideways glances, yet each of them lived to hear and speak such things about one another. This love of gossip began when they were very young, their drive to tittle-tattle fed by a natural competitiveness formed during horse shows, tennis matches and piano recitals. During these pursuits there was always one girl who stood out by being the prettiest, cleverest, most accomplished at whichever activity her parents had insisted she develop an expertise in. For such a girl it went one of two ways. Either she was admired (often due to her wealth) and imitated by the others, or she was secretly ridiculed owing to the petty jealousies of her competitive peers. Sydney knew that she and her sister were initially granted immunity from this social skewering because of their dead mother. Sympathy trickled down from their friends' parents rendering any whispering about them in "poor taste." But as the group of contemporaries grew into sparkling debutantes and later were shipped off to college—Smith, Bryn Mawr, Radcliffe, Vassar—their critiques of one another morphed from how one sat a hunter to how much attention one received at a ball (and more to the point, *why*) to how far one went with a beau or what's more, how many beaux one had.

At this juncture in their young lives, the Sinclair sisters' immunity was revoked for different reasons. Both were Vassar girls but their characters had developed distinctly. Brooke required that any girl who wished to remain in her inner cabal be appropriately deferential—she was simply accustomed to being treated with kid gloves. Most devoted followers of fashionable people (particularly the fashionable people themselves) knew that she was the sort of girl who wished only the best for her friends, as long as their best didn't outdo her own. Fortunately for her temperament, the Sinclair wealth was such that it was a rare occurrence for another girl to have or do something better than what Brooke had or did. Marrying a future earl was one step further to cementing this status.

Once Augustus Sinclair passed away the young men of New York had rallied around the sisters and offered their help, the use of their servants or motorcars and one had even offered his hand (on separate occasions to both sisters, which made the offer easy to turn down). But when Brooke learned of her closest friend Lillian Crane (one of a dozen such closest friends) sailing to England to land a title it was as though angels (or her mother) were speaking to her from heaven. It made perfect sense. There was even talk that several of the spurned young men the young women had left behind were placing wagers on what title each girl would wind up with. Though in the end, Miss Crane had returned home empty-handed (which her mother blamed on her thin lips). But Brooke had become engaged to the most attractive, kind and respected, and yes, nearly bankrupt, young aristocrat who was presented to her. All New York agreed: What was her money for if not to help her marry the best sort of man?

Sydney, in contrast, wasn't exactly a loner, but she didn't thrive on the company of her peers either. She was more inclined to have tea with a Vassar professor than with another student, or to attend a lecture in Greenwich Village rather than a dance on the Upper East Side. Then there was the matter of her political views. Views she never hid from society. Again, the Sinclair fortune was a sort of talisman against being outcast for having opinions and activities that weren't *acceptable*. Instead her kind looked upon her with sympathy and even pity, for it was obvious to everyone that Sydney's wayward interests had grown out of not having a mother, and having a father who was too busy to notice his youngest daughter's inclinations. Or if he did, he didn't have the strength (poor man) to rein her in.

It was accepted that the sisters were polar opposites, yet after their father passed and they were able to think (and spend) independently both were uniformly admired, feared and criticized in equal measure. Still, it must be said that no one in New York had the poor sense to be on the "outs" with either. One never knew when a Sinclair would be needed.

Sydney stood up and focused her gaze on her guardian. "Enough, Mr. Garrett. You've said your piece. We both agree that Brooke isn't being very prudent. But what's done is done. She's engaged to this Edward person and that's that. No matter how much we might dislike the idea of him or his classist attitude, he will be my brother-in-law and he will spend my sister's money any damn way he pleases."

They both chose silence as their next retort. Mr. Garrett sulking. Sydney knowing that everything he said about Brooke and Edward was completely true.

"And when is the wedding?" he asked, seemingly resigned to his fate of not protecting the Sinclair girls from ruination of either the financial or moral kind.

Sydney crossed the room to the window once more. She opened the drapes and peered outside. On the street below she watched her sister getting out of a motorcar, her arms burdened with packages. Sydney closed the drapes.

"The fifteenth of May. We are to set sail on the first."

The sound of the front door opening, the servants scurrying and the unmistakable flutey voice of Brooke drifted up to them. Mr. Garrett stood and moved to the door of the sitting room. "I can arrange passage," he said glumly, a defeated man.

Sydney shook her head. "Edward has seen to it already. We sail on the *Lusitania* on the first of May."

Old Mr. Garrett had best watch his tongue. The nerve! Complaining about my engagement behind my back," Brooke snapped.

Sydney sat on the bed and watched as her sister stomped around her bedroom, furious and indignant.

"He's looking out for us. It's his job."

Brooke tore open one of the many packages she had brought home. Inside was a silk dress the colour of amber with delicate pale pink roses embroidered on the neckline. The elegant beauty of the garment immediately soothed her mood and she smiled, holding the dress up to her.

"What do you think?" she asked, Mr. Garrett forgotten.

Sydney smiled. A pretty dress could always be counted on to improve her sister's mood. "It's lovely."

"Glad to hear it. I bought it for you," Brooke said as she laid the dress over Sydney's lap. "It's time you stopped wearing dark things. Our mourning period has been over for nearly a month. And I thought the colour suited your hair."

Sydney touched the dress, ran the silk through her fingers. It felt cool and decadent. She touched several honey-hued strands of hair that fell about her face, framing it in soft swirls. The dress did suit her; even she knew that. She adored dressing up in elegant clothes like any woman. But fashion no longer had a place in the world she wanted to inhabit. Her future lay in practical shades of black, ivory and grey, like the typeset print of a newspaper, direct, no-nonsense, right and wrong.

"Thank you, but you know I won't wear it." She carefully placed the dress beside her on the bed and regarded it as though it were a mounted butterfly in a museum.

Brooke smiled. "Darling, I know you miss our father but you have to live your life." She sat down beside Sydney, carefully moving the new dress aside as she did so.

"It's not about Father," Sydney said. "I miss him, of course. But I do not worry about being alone. You have to not mind me so much. Once you are married, you will be on the other side of the Atlantic and I will lead my life my way."

Brooke sighed. "Not more of that New Woman business. I thought we had agreed it was a fleeting interest. When are you going to grow up?"

Sydney was the indignant one now. "We had no such agreement. Women's rights are a very grown-up cause. And I wish you and everyone else would let me be." She inhaled slowly, resolved to calm herself. An argument would not be won on this topic. And given that she had her own fortune, there was nothing her sister could do. But if only Brooke could see things as she did.

"I do not need the vote," Brooke announced as if reading her sister's mind. "That's what my husband will be for."

Clearly Brooke would never see things as she did. Despite a forced calmness, Sydney's heart was beating so hard she worried she might burst out of her corset, or more likely faint. She must look into one of those new brassieres; a woman's freedom could begin with her undergarments, couldn't it? She slowed her breathing and smiled. "You could try to understand me a little better."

Brooke was staring at the floor. "I'm sorry. I shouldn't have criticized you. But I do worry about you. What sort of life can you have marching in protests and making people uncomfortable with your independent ideas?" she asked. "Will you at least reconsider moving to England with me? With your beauty you would be the belle of any English ball. We could have so much fun. And if I can't find you a duke or baronet to marry I can at least buy you any horse you want."

Sydney giggled. She couldn't help it. Brooke's solution to everything was a purchase and she knew her weakness for horses too.

"I have my own money, I can buy myself a hunter."

"Oh but the finest hunters are in England. Even you must admit that."

"I'm perfectly happy with an American Thoroughbred. And besides, what would I do in England? They are at war and I'm afraid women aren't much use in a war."

Brooke's expression turned serious. "I hate this war already and we're not even in it. What it's done to English society. Most of its men have joined up and no doubt most will die and for what? Because some silly archduke got his brains splattered all over Sarajevo."

"Another reason for you to postpone the wedding until it's all over. When peace comes then you can celebrate victory alongside your new-found countrymen and *women*," Sydney pleaded, but it was futile.

"How many times must we go over this? Edward is to be given a commission as a lieutenant and will ship out to France in June. That's why the wedding must take place as soon as possible." She forced a smile.

"So you'll get the title even if he's killed?" Sydney asked dryly. She saw at once her words had stung Brooke.

"Don't be mean. And yes, as his widow I think I would. Besides, I like Edward and don't want anything to happen to him."

Sydney bit her tongue. Who wants to only "like" her husband?

Brooke took her silence for acquiescence and smiled sweetly like she'd won the argument. "Let's not have war talk here. Not now." She stroked the gown lovingly. "If you won't wear the dress then I'll give it away to a more appreciative girl."

Sydney looked at the silky confection on the bed. It would make her sister happy and she hated to argue especially when soon they'd be living apart with the whole of the Atlantic between them. "No. I'll keep it. I'm sure one day it will be exactly what I need."

FEBRUARY 12

Isabel

The winter gloom clung to the windows like a slimy film. Outside, the panes were edged with soot-tinged snow, while inside condensation beaded down the glass and formed small pools on the wooden ledge. Alastair Denniston wiped a window with the sleeve of his jacket, leaving a wide streak to peer through. There wasn't much to look at. The desolate courtyard was flanked on all sides by Admiralty buildings and contained several tracks of footprints but no evidence of who had made them. Night was falling and there was still so much to do. With the outdoors providing little distraction he turned back to the room.

Several feet from the window the code breakers of Room 40 sat together around the larger of the desks. A couple of them had cigarettes dangling from their mouths, the smoke settling into a silvery-blue halo above their heads. With the encroaching darkness the room retained a yellow glow from the lamps, making their faces appear jaundiced. The men were exhausted. Many eyes were traced with dark circles. One man rested his head on top of the table, another had the nerve to put his feet on the same table, not bothering to clear a space but dirtying several piles of paper with the bottoms of his boots. And yet, despite, or perhaps because of the state of weariness, an argument raged on. Isabel, Dorothy and the other girls tried not to look like they were listening but one by one they stopped their work, riveted to the conversation.

"We can't have another Dogger Bank. The admirals already thought we were a useless lot before that."

"How were we to know it would turn out that way? I'm a German teacher not a naval officer."

"We did our part. The rest is up to *them*."

"Exactly. The problem is with how they dispense our work. It isn't given directly to the men out on the ships, is it? We give it to Hope who gives it to Hall who gives it to Oliver, then it's on to Fisher and Churchill. It's them who directs the navy."

"They misinterpreted the transcripts, the bloody fools. I heard that Jellicoe wanted to send the entire Grand Fleet but Oliver and Fisher said no, so only Beatty went with a few destroyers and one squadron to meet the whole of the German Fleet."

"He's right. That fiasco wasn't on our heads."

Denniston pulled out a chair and rested one foot on it. "It wasn't their entire fleet. And our boys still managed to sink a German ship," he said, lighting a cigarette. "We suffered few casualties and lost no ships. I'd say we can claim the Battle of Dogger Bank a win for the British." The other men looked to him as though his words were the final thoughts on the matter.

Isabel sat organizing her desk like it was a battle plan. In her month on the job she had learned much about the men in Room 40. For one thing, they were nearly all civilians. The common denominator was that they could speak, write and read German. In fact linguistics and an ability to understand the Germans' way of thinking was as crucial to the cause as deciphering code. Dorothy had told her that Denniston was a German-language instructor and had studied on the continent, which explained why he had asked her if she spoke it. The other men were Fleet Paymaster Rotter, the naval officer, Norton, who had grown less caustic with her over time, Anstie, Curtis, Parish, Laurence, Bullough, Montgomery, Lord Herschell, who was a baron and, of course, Henry

Phillipson. He was the only man in Room 40 she called by his Christian name. Henry seemed younger and more naïve than the others and she liked that in him. He always had a smile and an offer to help the secretaries when he wasn't busy. But he seemed partial to Isabel. Not in a romantic sense—she wouldn't allow that anyway—it was more brotherly. No matter her personal rapport with one or the other, all these men relied on her. Isabel had proven herself to be accurate, swift and clever, even catching the occasional error in the transcripts.

Who knew such clerical skills would be the turning point in her life? In Oxford they had seemed a silly waste of time. The house where Mr. Chambers lived and where she worked was on Banbury Road near the old parsonage in the city centre. He was an attractive man of about thirty-five and seemed to take a particular interest in Isabel. He would often smile at her and ask if she'd read the papers and if she had, what she thought about the news. It was enormously flattering, especially given the boyish grins that accompanied his inquiries. He made her blush often.

And as if she wasn't busy enough keeping the house clean for him and his wife and wee boy, he had insisted on expanding her talents. 'The world is changing, Isabel. You'll waste your life as a maid unless you do something about it.' He'd said it many times until she relented. Part of her hesitation had been Mrs. Chambers. She was an imposing woman who stood nearly six feet tall and therefore towered over her husband who was only of average height. She lived to entertain the various professors and administrators from the university. Playing social hostess to the Oxford intelligentsia gave her distinction. Allowed her to rise above her station. That's what the lady of the house had written to her sister (Isabel had only glanced at the letter, honestly). She disdained the hoi polloi though. Once a young tutor had shown up at one of her dinners without a proper invitation, which was of course very poor form of him, but she had dressed him down in front of the other guests, including a visiting dignitary from Cambridge, and it was Isabel's firm belief that this showed even poorer form on the part of Mrs. Chambers. Yet it proved that she was not to be trifled with. And for Isabel to take a typing and shorthand course in the evenings was reckless in this regard. Should she have been discovered by Mrs. Chambers, there would have been hell to pay: a severe reprimand—"Such an indecent activity for a girl in my employ"—if not outright dismissal. In hindsight that would have been far more desirable than what eventually transpired. Oh well, it didn't do her any good to dwell.

She hadn't known what lay in store for her at Room 40. But now she wanted to learn to decipher code. As well as her rudimentary knowledge of Morse code she had a knack for seeing patterns in things—numbers, letters, the design in a Persian rug or floor tiles—and she saw patterns in the ciphered transcripts that Rotter and the others were decoding. She only had to find a way to spend more time with the codebooks and she could teach herself. Then she'd be indispensable.

"Isabel, type this up for me."

It was Rotter. "Of course," she said, and inserted a clean sheet of paper into her Underwood. Violet, Joan and Dorothy came back to life as well and stood admiring Isabel's typing skills, which had become legendary.

"She sounds like a machine-gun operator," Violet quipped.

"I've heard slower tap dancers in the West End," said Joan, impressed.

"I wonder if she can play ragtime?" Dorothy giggled.

"You know I can hear the three of you." Isabel's eyes never wavered from her task but her lips curled up in a smile. She was pleased to be passing muster so early in her job.

"I'm surprised you ladies can hear a bloody thing over that racket," said Curtis as he placed a fresh pile of handwritten transcripts beside Isabel.

"That's a bit rough, Curtis," Violet chastised gleefully. "She's only just been here a month. You'll have her fingertips bleeding by the end of her shift."

Curtis watched Isabel tapping like a mad thing and nodded approvingly. "We all have our bit to do for the war effort. Carry on."

The girls groaned as he walked away. Isabel continued unabated.

"Stop showing off, Isabel," Joan said, and took up at the desk next to her, feeding a piece of paper into her typewriter. "I can't keep up."

"I'm sure you possess skills that I do not," Isabel offered.

"Sure she does," Violet teased. "Just last week she gave the First Lord a letter to her beau instead of the official letter from the War Office."

The girls burst out laughing. "Churchill was no doubt thrilled to have such expressions of love and devotion from one of his employees."

"Could have happened to anyone," Joan defended herself. "He's a scary sort. I became all thumbs and mixed up the letters."

"He does generate a heap of correspondence," Dorothy admitted.

"Is he really such a terrifying person?" Isabel asked, at last stopping her typing. The sudden hush that fell upon the room was disconcerting. Rotter and the other men looked up as though something was the matter.

"Keep typing, Isabel," Joan whispered. "We don't want the gents to know we gossip."

Isabel launched back into her work and waited for the girls to answer.

"He's a gentleman," Dorothy explained. "But he's firm. Serious."

"And a bloody bore," Violet shot back.

"His house is just beside this building," Joan added.

Isabel wasn't sure that it was right of them to discuss the First Lord in such a manner. It smacked of impropriety let alone insubordination. Besides, after all she'd been through she wouldn't let a man, even one with such a title, ever intimidate her again. Before Isabel had finished the typing the transcript Captain Hall entered Room 40.

He wasn't a tall man, and he was mostly bald, but what hair remained stuck out in tufts from beneath his cap and darted in all directions. He had a stern but handsome face with a cleft chin and a long nose that formed a sharp point at its tip. He had a tic whereby he blinked all day long and for that he acquired the nickname Blinker. When he spoke everyone listened and not only because he was the Director of Intelligence; he was also charismatic and charming. Yet you got the feeling that if you proved inadequate or made a grievous error he'd never let you forget it. The men seemed to have a blind devotion to him.

It was his custom to head straight to Denniston and Commander Hope to go over the day's transcripts and discuss the contents. Only this time he made a beeline for the typing pool. The girls stopped their work and waited to learn why they should be so honoured.

"Ladies, I need one of you to pick up a letter from the First Lord's secretary," he ordered.

"Speak of the devil," Violet whispered.

Perhaps Isabel should have hesitated a moment, just for appearances. Instead she stood up and chirped, "Let me, sir."

He seemed surprised by her eagerness. The girls stifled their giggles. "Thank you, Miss Nelson, you are to bring it straight to me. It's of vital importance," he stated. Then he walked over to the men and became immediately immersed in conversation.

"You're a keen one," Joan said.

"I just want to prove myself," Isabel said, feeling self-conscious.

"Go on, Isabel," Dorothy said encouragingly. "Don't mind Joan. She's upset she's missing out on the chance to pass another love note to Churchill."

Joan ripped the paper out of her typewriter, screwed it up into a ball and threw it at Dorothy.

'm here for a letter for Captain Hall," Isabel said to the secretary, an older, round woman who barely looked up from her desk.

"I haven't got it," she said, then peered over her eyeglasses and gave Isabel a thorough going over. "You'll have to go into his office and get it."

Isabel's eyes widened. "In there?"

"Well, his office isn't outside on the Horse Guards Parade now, is it?"

Isabel shook her head and, smoothing her hair, marched through the doors behind the secretary's station. She found the First Lord at his desk riffling through a mass of paper. He barely looked up when she entered. He held out the letter and spoke three words. "Here it is."

Even though she'd been told enough times that the First Lord was no giant, he was smaller than she expected and he looked younger than his forty years. He came from money, that much was a fact. His suit was a stitch above the usual expensive custom-tailored suits that all the government officials who shopped on Jermyn Street wore. There was something finer about his, the fabric and fit, the colour of the shirt, the pocket square; the whole ensemble was as fashionable as the finest ladies who took tea at the Dorchester. What had Norton called him? A dandy? She couldn't imagine being married to a man who dressed better than a woman.

He was still holding the letter, only now he was staring at her, waiting. She took a deep breath. There comes a time in every ambitious young lady's life when she is bold enough to engage with her superiors as an equal. This was such a moment for Isabel. She lurched forward, practically snatching the letter from him. Then she stood at attention in front of his desk as though awaiting further instruction. After a few moments it became clear to both parties that unless more words were exchanged she wasn't moving. If he was annoyed it didn't show.

"Was there something else, Miss . . . ?"

"Nelson, sir," Isabel said. "Isabel Nelson. No relation to Horatio, sir."

He appeared taken aback by this revelation. "Neither am I," he said at last, and scrutinized her further. She sensed disapproval. Perhaps she should have lied or at least hinted there might be a familial tie to the war hero.

"I work in Room 40," she explained unnecessarily.

His expression softened and a hint of a smile creased his cheek. "Yes, I would assume so, given I requested someone from Room 40 pick up the letter and deliver it to Captain Hall."

She could feel the heat of humiliation rising through her. *My face is red. I probably look as though I've had a glass too many of claret. He must think me a simpleton.*

"Of course, sir. I wanted you to know that I'm committed to the war effort and the top secret work that we do." She hoped such a display of patriotism would save the moment.

"Yes, well, glad to hear it." Churchill returned to his papers.

Her moment had ended with a whimper. "Will there be anything else?"

"No," he said, slightly amused by the blushing secretary. "Thank you."

Once she was safely in the hall and marching back to Room 40 she began to feel unwell. Her nerves were acting up. All she had wanted was to have a proper conversation with the man. To show how much she'd learned and could be counted on and, more important, to prove she wasn't afraid of him. Was there anything wrong in that? Yet now that she had met him, she had to admit that the girls had been right to say that Churchill was scary. He was frightful without even trying. Mr. Chambers had never frightened her (which proved her downfall). Neither did the other men she worked alongside. The way Churchill had stared at her. It was as though he could see right into her and know what she was all about.

She was so consumed by such thoughts she was nearly back at Room 40 when she remembered the letter in her hand. She knew it was classified and that her task was to hand it to the captain. Isabel didn't know what possessed her but she found herself slipping into an alcove and removing the letter from its unsealed envelope. It was dated today and addressed to Walter Runciman. Isabel hadn't heard the name before, but according to the address he was the president of the Board of Trade. It was wrong to glance at it, let alone read it. Yet there it was, open in her hands. *I signed the Secrets Act, didn't I?* Isabel skimmed it quickly. It was about the ongoing British naval blockade and the German submarine threat in retaliation and how it would affect trade. Much of the letter was dreadfully dull. But a particular passage sent a chill through her. She immediately regretted reading the letter. Panicking, she had begun to fold it up when Henry appeared out of nowhere.

"Isabel, I called your name twice," he said with a smile. "What's got you so captivated?"

Isabel shoved the letter behind her back. "I didn't hear you. What is it?"

"I saw you hiding in this nook," he said. "Reading. Is it a letter from a beau?"

"Not at all. I felt a bit faint," she lied. He looked worried. "I'm perfectly fine now. I must get back to work."

As she stepped forward the envelope slipped from her hand. Henry picked it up for her. Damn his gentlemanliness. She froze. Henry wasn't daft. He'd see the name of the sender marked clear as day.

"What are you doing with this?" he asked.

"Delivering it to Captain Hall. The First Lord gave it to me himself."

He shook the envelope. "Just the envelope, then? What happened to the letter?" She remained silent, hoping he'd leave her alone. "Isabel?"

"The envelope wasn't sealed."

Henry's face was stricken. He grabbed her elbow and led her down the hall away from Room 40. They reached the Admiralty Board Room. Henry looked inside. It was empty. She followed reluctantly and shut the door, clutching the doorknob in an attempt to prevent anyone from coming in.

"I hope Churchill's letter wasn't what I saw you reading in the blasted hall," Henry said. "You could get the sack for it."

Isabel stood her ground. She'd been sacked before. "I don't know why I did it. I suppose being around all you men and your top secret messages, it seems like second nature now." She held out the letter. "Part of it is rather disturbing."

Henry shoved his hands in the air. "I can't," he said firmly.

"Fine, I'll read it to you," she said, and cleared her throat. *"It is most important to attract neutral shipping to our shores in the hope especially of embroiling the United States with Germany . . ."* She paused to assess his reaction. The stern look had been replaced with an intense expression that she assumed was alarm. She continued. *"For our part we want the traffic—the more the better; and if some of it gets into trouble, better still."* She saw that Henry was gnawing on his lower lip. "I'm guessing that you also find it troubling."

Henry raised an eyebrow at her. "We need to get back to the office now."

To her dismay he was headed for the door. "But Henry! Does this mean what I think? Does Churchill want the Germans to target a neutral ship just to get the Americans to join the war?"

Henry stopped, his hand on the doorknob. He turned to face Isabel.

"I'm sure whatever he means isn't your business. You need to deliver that letter to Captain Hall and let's both pretend this never happened."

Isabel was crestfallen. "If you really think that's best. But are you sure we shouldn't ask one of the others—"

"Absolutely not!" Henry snapped. Seeing her flinch he took a deep breath to calm down. "War is a complex machine. Who are we to make sense of it? That's for Churchill and the others to do."

"But our work is about uncovering secrets," she insisted.

"My job is to decipher code, yours is to organize it. We are absolutely forbidden from analyzing the messages or passing them along to anyone but the very few who have clearance. And we are certainly forbidden from reading correspondence from our superiors and questioning their motives. Do I make myself clear?"

Isabel knew he was right, of course. "You won't tell on me, then?"

"I should," he warned. "But I won't. Only because you're fairly new and a woman. Just for heaven's sake don't snoop on anyone ever again unless they're the enemy."

FEBRUARY 24

Edward Thorpe-Tracey, Somerset, England

Rathfon Hall sat in the valley like a sleeping giant. Formidable yet tired. The oldest part of the house had the year 1632 etched above its door as if to remind residents and visitors alike that it would outlive them all. The newer parts of the house were completed in 1740 and 1813 respectively. There had been a fire at one point and nearly the entire 1813 wing had been destroyed. The rumour was arson. An irate farmer angry over taxes, or a mistress gone mad with unrequited passion, depending on who was telling the story. By the time the Thorpe-Traceys got hold of the estate in 1836 it had fallen into disrepair. The first Lord Northbrook had seen to it that the whole of the house and its lands were brought up to modern standards. An ambition that each successive Lord Northbrook had taken upon himself to continue, including the current one—until his debtors had caught up with him.

Now it was up to Edward to ensure the legacy continued in spite of his father's poor management. Because of this, his father had allowed Edward free rein to take over the estate in the hopes it could be saved from financial ruin. Edward accepted the responsibility, knowing what it meant: that his life's work would be bringing Rathfon Hall into the twentieth century and making it thrive, and to do so he could not marry for love. Indeed he had settled on Brooke Sinclair for her fortune and for Rathfon Hall's future. The work on the estate would wait until after the war. Though he suspected that his soon-to-be wife, with all her money, would initiate a slew of innovations immediately after the wedding—even while he was on the Western Front and even without his direct input. Electricity, telephones, each room with its own toilet and bath. Brooke had made it very clear—in her sweetest American voice—that she desired, nay, expected, all the conveniences of New York to be in working order at Rathfon Hall. "Whatever makes you happy," he had responded good-naturedly. Having witnessed his parents' countless arguments during his twenty-eight years he knew for a fact that it was wisest—not to mention peace-inducing—to allow one's wife the luxury of final decisions in matters of the house.

His mother, Lady Northbrook, however, did not herself enjoy the reputation of peacemaker. When informed of these ideas she had seen fit to hire a local man to draw up plans for the additional bathrooms. "I will be the judge of what an English bath will look like," she had said. "The way Americans throw their money around they probably bathe in solid-gold tubs!"

Edward had smiled at his mother at the time. They were alone with tea and cake by the fire. A couple of days a week they managed to steal some time together to discuss matters freely. Lady Northbrook was a graceful woman, but had a hard edge that stood her in good stead in times like these: her eldest son to be married off for financial gain and then sent to fight in a war; an invalid daughter with no hope of marrying; and a husband with a gambling problem that had nearly cost them Rathfon Hall.

"Careful, Mother. You don't want to start off on the wrong foot with your daughter-in-law," Edward reminded her. "She was your first choice after all."

"She presented well," his mother responded. "At least in the beginning."

"And her oil and gold money certainly helped in those early presentations," Edward pointed out wryly.

"But once that garish ring was placed on her finger she became so . . ." She paused, searching for the perfect word to sum up all the disappointment that was sure to come with her future daughter-in-law. "American."

Edward couldn't help but laugh. His mother would not let go of the fact that Brooke had rejected his grandmother's delicate diamond-and-sapphire ring—it wasn't overly large but was a treasured and elegant family heirloom—for a modern emerald-and-diamond square-cut affair that was designed and set in New York. And in the end, the local man never got the chance to bring the bathrooms to light for he was called up the next week and sent to France, leaving the future of Rathfon Hall's lavatories in jeopardy.

"What will become of us once it's *your* time to fight and Brooke is left to her own devices, and worse, to her own taste," Lady Northbrook fretted.

"I think you can be confident that she wants to please you as well," Edward said reassuringly, though in truth he wondered whether, once the wedding was over, he wouldn't find more peace at the front than in his ancestral home.

"Very well. I mustn't fuss so. Brooke will grow on me eventually. I only hope she grows on you."

Edward hoped the same thing but he had his doubts. Brooke was unlike any woman he'd ever met before. For one thing she was more regal than her American counterparts, and talked less too. She also understood what he and his family did not—finance.

Her father had apparently insisted that both his daughters understand how to manage their incomes and how to invest. Brooke wasn't afraid of money, wasn't afraid to talk about it, spend it or make it yield to her wishes. During her visit she had shocked many people with such forthrightness. Edward had secretly cheered her on one occasion when she boldly suggested to a financially weakened baron—who minutes before had openly criticized Edward's father for mismanaging Rathfon Hall—that he could double his income if he converted a portion of his country estate into suites for members of the paying public. The baron nearly crushed the brandy snifter he was holding in his hand.

Yet there was a coolness to her that didn't exactly inspire Edward to write poetry, and that depressed him. For he was a romantic, albeit a reluctant one.

"I'm proud of you for making this decision," Lady Northbrook said, her words bringing him back to earth, and tea. "I know it's what I wanted. What your father needed. But it wasn't easy for you. To sacrifice yourself in this way."

She was smiling at him. He sensed pity. He hated it. "The war is a sacrifice," he said. "Marrying Brooke is my duty. But you're right in thinking my life's ambitions did not involve a marriage of convenience. I had thought more of world travel, exploring South America perhaps, learning to fly an aeroplane, even entering politics."

"Not that, surely," his mother teased.

"I do hold out hope," Edward said, trying to convince himself, "that Brooke and I will one day love each other. I'm not the worst sort of man, you know, she may grow rather fond of me." He grinned and sliced another piece of cake.

That conversation over tea had taken place before Christmas. Now it was the end of February as he sat at the breakfast table with his mother. His April voyage to America to bring Brooke and her sister, Sydney, to England was drawing near. Edward fought hard not to resent it, but the best he could manage was resignation—he was the family's only hope for financial recovery and there was more at stake than the walls of Rathfon Hall.

His little sister, Lady Georgina, whom he loved dearly, with her chestnut hair and soft green eyes, was a bright and effervescent girl of eighteen who undoubtedly would have attracted many a suitor had she not been crippled in a riding accident five years earlier and condemned to life in a wheelchair. Edward often worried about what sort of life she would have. Unlike her friends there would be no coming out during the season in London. No dancing. No possibility of children. Her future: destined to play the role of maiden aunt to his offspring. There were worse fates. But crippled *and* impoverished was a double wound that Edward couldn't bear to inflict on her if he could prevent it, and it gave him added motivation to ensure that Rathfon Hall would always be here for Georgina to call home.

He abandoned these dire thoughts and decided on a more lighthearted topic. At least that was his intent when he made the suggestion to his mother that he drive his new motorcar—an extravagance he had indulged in once the engagement was settled—to the docks in Liverpool.

"Edward, you can't be serious," Lady Northbrook said, her butter knife savagely spreading jam on a crumpet. "*Drive* to Liverpool? *Yourself?* Have you asked your father?"

He was about to respond when his father entered the room. "Asked me what?" Lord Northbrook said as he sat down. He unfolded his newspaper and was immediately served tea by a servant.

"I intend to drive the car to Liverpool," Edward explained. "But I don't think mother agrees with me."

"It's reckless," she added, and turned to her husband. "What if there's an accident? And—"

"And I don't live to marry Brooke Sinclair and get all her money?" Edward teased as he took a mouthful of scrambled egg.

"Don't accuse me of being unfeeling, Edward," she responded. Not that her son was completely wrong. "Though to be frank, with all this German high-seas warfare going on I'm not sure you should be sailing at all. Let her come to you."

Edward was shocked. "Mother, you can't be serious? It's fine for the Germans to attack Brooke as long as I'm not with her?"

Lady Northbrook stirred her tea furiously. "What do you say, Duncan?"

Lord Northbrook had a large dark moustache and a receding hairline. He wore spectacles that magnified his blue eyes, his best feature and one he had handed down to his son. As though it was a contemplative aid, he removed the eyeglasses and produced a cloth from his jacket pocket and began to clean them. A manservant came to his side with another cloth but Lord Northbrook waved him off.

"About what? The German threats, our naval capabilities or driving to Liverpool?" he asked.

"Driving to Liverpool," Edward said quickly, cutting his mother off before she could speak.

"I think it's a splendid idea," his father said. Then, satisfied with the clarity of his lenses, he put them back in their place and picked up the newspaper. "Rolls-Royce built it as a touring car and so it should tour."

Edward grinned. Lady Northbrook shook her head in defeat.

"I suppose this means that Maxwell will ride beside you?"

"Unless I tie him to the roof I can't see another way," Edward said cheerfully.

"Valets should know their place," she insisted even though it was a losing battle. "At least let him drive part of the way."

"Maxwell will enjoy the rest," Edward insisted jovially. "He will be run off his feet once we arrive in New York and must keep pace with all those Americans and their way of doing things."

"If only the Americans would see their way into the war," Lord Northbrook announced, snapping the page of his newspaper as he turned it.

"We will win it without them," Edward said proudly.

His father didn't look up from his paper. "That is doubtful. But mark my words, the Americans will get pulled into the conflict and soon. It's only a matter of time before the kaiser does something to anger Wilson."

"And what might that be?" Lady Northbrook asked.

"I don't know, my dear," he answered gravely. "But we will know it when it comes."

"Then we shall be glad to have them," Edward said.

His father grunted, too buried in his paper to utter anything further. His mother smiled, but it was a forced smile. Her son was getting married and going to war. The latter was a thought that plagued many mothers all over England and across class lines; it was enough to make any parent wish to remain in bed until it was all over. She inhaled deeply as though the air of Rathfon Hall itself would save her.

MARCH 10

Isabel

Spring had come. The spindly tree boughs grew fat with buds. London parks were still the colour of straw but a few crocuses poked through the deadness. Birds were noisy and squirrels thin, but they and every other creature came to life at the first hint of warmth in the air. The gentler breezes also softened the city's human inhabitants. Women strolled unhurriedly, socializing outdoors and out of earshot of whomever they might be gossiping about. Men wore lighter topcoats and doffed hats at less ferocious speeds than frigid February winds had forced them to. The war was still on the minds of England's citizens but there was no keeping the freshness of a new season from lightening their hearts.

Isabel sat on a bench beneath a large oak tree on the Mall. She was excited to see spring melt away the sourness of winter. London might be less grey and less lonely in the coming weeks she decided. Her new London life was quite satisfactory. She had grown almost fond of her small but pleasant room in Kentish Town. Mrs. Ogilvie, the landlady, was a stickler for decorum and tidiness. Isabel understood the virtues of both although sometimes she chose to ignore them. But her transgressions were slight compared to those of some of the other girls in the house, who worked in shops or offices, except for one spirited redhead who was a seamstress. They led frivolous existences and smoked cigarettes, drank

gin and could be found flirting in public houses. The redhead even short-
ened the hems of all her skirts above the ankle and offered to do the same
for the other girls. Everyone had agreed except Isabel. In truth she envied
them a little. She missed frivolity.

But she had her work and that sustained her, that and her colleagues.
She admired the men of Room 40 and enjoyed her friendships with the
women. Henry occupied a special place however. They rode the bus
together nearly each night. He lived in a room in Camden Town. Spending
so much time together at the Admiralty and on the trip home they
became friends, yet never once did they discuss the letter incident. He
had been good to his word. She was happy to have a real friend again but
was wary of trusting anyone too much. He could still rat on her if he
chose. It was a possibility she tried her best not to give much credence
to. After all she couldn't fathom what would prompt such a betrayal on
his part.

By far the most thrilling part of her life was the hours after her shift
that she spent helping Rotter and the other code breakers to decipher the
wireless transcripts. She had expected more resistance from the men
when she first broached the subject of learning. But her basic understanding of Morse code gave her an edge and they certainly needed all
hands on deck.

The jumble of numbers and letters were a mess of gibberish at first. It
was daunting when she looked at the paper that contained only row upon
row of ciphers. She learned that certain letters stood for specific things.
Compass bearings, for example, all began with a capital X, time was noted
with a Y, and the letter Z was used for locations. So many of the transmits
contained an X, Y or Z.

It was painstaking work to refer constantly to the three codebooks. But
eventually she would remember certain keys and her keen eye at seeing
patterns had proven useful. When she'd first asked Denniston if she
could learn more about code breaking he had waffled due to his concern
over how it would be perceived by the naval officers, particularly

Commander Hope and Captain Hall. Whatever he told them must have allayed any fears about a woman in the role for whenever either man saw her studying the codebooks he made no mention of it.

The code breakers seemed to appreciate another set of eyes. In her mind this extra work made her more than a secretary; she was a junior code breaker (not that she dared refer to herself that way in public). It far exceeded her expectations for meaningful employment; it was Important. Not even George Chambers could have foreseen that his letter of reference would play out this way.

When she returned from the Mall, Rotter seemed relieved she was back. "Isabel," he said. "I need you to help me with this transmission at once. It's just come in." There was an unexpected urgency in Rotter's tone.

She quickly scribbled down one segment of the cipher onto a notepad and began. She was no match for Rotter; he was so fast. It was her goal to be as skilled as he was one day. He was a very patient teacher and not condescending or put off by her ambition to learn. When she'd started he'd given her a few old transcripts as a test. It had taken her several days but eventually she had done it. It was an achievement unlike anything she'd ever experienced. The men were astonished that she'd done it at all but they seemed pleased, even proud of her. Rotter and the others had bought her a pint at their local pub, the Coach & Horses. She had sipped whisky, a drink her days in Oxford had made her partial to, and basked modestly in the knowledge that she belonged with them.

Isabel focused on the cipher. It was only part of the message but she wanted to get it to Rotter as fast as possible. She had developed an ability to tune out the buzz of Room 40 and hardly took notice of the clang of the typewriters, the conversations between the men—some of it in German. Today was no different from any other, the rush of excitement Isabel got each time she unlocked one letter of the cipher making it a step closer to *en clair* . . .

"Tea time already?" It was Parish who spoke first when the tray of sandwiches was brought in but soon enough all the men were clamouring. Isabel had her back to the door, busy with her work. She heard only the scraping of chairs on the floor as Rotter, Anstie and Norton, as well as Parish and Henry, moved toward the server who had brought the food.

"Egg mayonnaise, again?"

"That's devilled ham, Anstie."

Isabel was famished. Mrs. Ogilvie didn't approve of her working so late and refused to leave any leftovers from tea. She stood up, eager to grab a sandwich, when Henry spoke out.

"You're new, aren't you?" he said.

Isabel saw her then. A very pretty girl with black hair stood by the tea tray. She carried herself with a confident elegance that Isabel thought inappropriate in a servant. One thing was certain; she was the last person on earth that Isabel had ever wanted to see again.

"Today is my first day," the girl said in that familiar husky tone that Isabel always suspected was put on.

"What's your name, Miss?" asked Rotter, who appeared smitten. So they all did. Surrounding the girl and grinning like fools as they tore off bites of sandwich.

"What have we here?" Dorothy whispered to Isabel and Violet who had gathered to watch the men fuss over the new tea girl.

"Mildred Fox," Isabel said, and crossed the room toward her. The men opened their circle to her as though they could sense unfinished business. She saw at once that Mildred was as startled as she was. The two women stood in silence, each waiting for the other to speak first. It was Mildred who cracked, allowing an artificial smile to lighten her expression, grinning at Isabel like they were long-lost friends.

"Why it's you, Isabel. I hardly recognize you." Mildred examined her face closely. "You aren't wearing lipstick and you changed your hair. It's so *respectable*."

The other secretaries had gathered around as well.

"Isabel wearing lipstick?" Violet questioned. It seemed unthinkable.

"I don't know what you're talking about," Isabel said to Mildred.

"Oh don't be that way," Mildred said, then addressed the others. "We both worked at the same house in Oxford."

"Oooh, the famous Mr. Chambers," Henry teased, hoping to break the tension.

"So you must be an expert typist too?" asked Curtis.

At this Mildred's wide smile closed tightly and she looked at Isabel. "I'm afraid I don't know how to type. I didn't receive the same special attentions that Isabel did." An uncomfortable silence fell over the room. There was a code between women that not even the cryptographers of Room 40 could decipher.

Isabel looked at the tray of sandwiches with a sniff. "There's nothing here I want."

"If you tell me what you'd like I could go down and see if the cook could make it for you," Mildred said sincerely.

Isabel crinkled her nose. "I'm not very hungry at that."

"Go on, Isabel," Henry teased again. "You have enough appetite for two men."

The men laughed, which horrified her. Mildred stood stone still, the tiniest of smiles on her beautiful face.

"I must get back to work," Isabel said brusquely, and marched away, nearly knocking over Violet.

"I take it they aren't close," Isabel overheard Violet comment to Dorothy.

It wasn't long before the others resumed their duties. Isabel returned to her cipher, her back to the room and her head buried in the codebook next to Rotter. She refused to turn around again, even as Mildred continued to chat up Henry rather outrageously (in her opinion). It was distracting her from the code. She had to triple-check one line because of it. What a stupid boy he could be. How easily a pretty face beguiled him. *He should be working like the rest of us.* After what seemed an eternity, though in fact was less than ten minutes, Mildred left the room.

With her gone Isabel felt a rush of panic. How had she found work at the Admiralty? There was only one possible explanation. Mrs. Chambers. Not that it mattered now. The fact was, Mildred Fox was in the same building, working the same shifts. The girl couldn't be trusted and she despised Isabel as much as Isabel despised her. *I'd rather go toe to toe with a German than risk Mildred spreading gossip.* No, it wouldn't do having Mildred around. She was a distraction in too many ways. Isabel left Rotter and cornered Henry at the filing cabinet.

"Be careful, Henry. Mildred is not what she seems," Isabel warned.

He gave her a puzzled look.

"Go on, don't be so mysterious. Is she a murderess?" he joked. Isabel rolled her eyes. The fool wasn't taking her seriously. "What then? A mistress?"

Isabel didn't have the chance to answer because Commander Hope and Denniston entered the room. They had been gone much of the afternoon in meetings with Captain Hall and Admiral Oliver. Henry and Isabel each raced back to their duties.

"What have we missed, gentlemen? Other than tea."

The mention of tea made Isabel twinge all over again. She could see from the lengthy handwriting on the notepad that Rotter was nearly finished decoding the message. A cigarette hung from his mouth, the ash so long at the tip it threatened to fall onto the papers he was concentrating on. Then in the nick of time he flicked it into the ashtray.

"Have you finished that bit I gave you?" he asked.

"Very nearly," she said, feeling stupid for letting Mildred distract her. She had managed the first few letters before the unwanted interruption. There were only a few more to go. She could tell Rotter was anxious for her to be done. She hurried through, so much so that when she was finished she doubted her accuracy. "This can't be right. I must have made a mistake." She gave him her notepad. His eyes widened.

"I will double-check." He pored over the portion of the message he had given her. Isabel felt terrible about messing up. All because of Mildred

Fox. Rotter scribbled out the words on another pad of paper. She admired his mind's ability to do the job with such speed.

"I'm sorry if I got it wrong," she apologized but he wasn't listening to her.

"Commander Hope, sir." Rotter, his voice urgent, stood waving the handwritten transcript in his hand.

The commander walked over to him. "Anything interesting, Rotter?"

"This just came through. It's a list of suggestions for the U-boats."

"Suggestions?"

"Targets."

Targets? Isabel felt a sudden shiver as though the warm spring air had been sucked out and replaced by ice.

"They've been taking aim at some Dutch ships," Denniston interjected.

"Bloody Jerrys can't think they'll do their side much good by hitting neutral ships," said Parish.

"The first message is about two British merchant ships, sir. The *Khim* and the *Omrah*," Rotter said. "It's telling the U-boat commanders the two ships will leave London on March 12." He paused, as though wanting to avoid the truth of what he had to say next. "It's not just them, Commander Hope, sir," he continued. "There is a second report to the U-boats directing them to a key target." Rotter handed the transcript to his superior. "Isabel helped decipher it."

Isabel was too occupied with the horror of what she'd decoded to notice he had given her credit so publicly. She wasn't the only one. Everyone in the room studied Commander Hope's expression as he read the report, searching for a clue as to what it contained. But it was no use. His was the face of a seasoned naval officer and showed no emotion.

Commander Hope held it in front of Denniston so he could read it. Denniston nodded that he'd finished reading it. But Isabel knew what the report said. She exchanged alarmed looks with Rotter.

"Isabel, type up Mr. Rotter's transcript and have it delivered to Captain Hall at once." The commander held the paper out to her. Isabel jumped to her feet. This was as serious as she thought. Her decoding was accurate and what it revealed was horrifying.

"Shouldn't we alert Cunard, sir?" Rotter asked.

"The right people will be alerted, Mr. Rotter, as usual."

The commander's words didn't seem to satisfy Rotter, who grabbed his jacket and cap and abruptly left the room. The rest of the team looked to the commander for direction.

"Back at it, gentlemen. There's a war on you know."

Isabel was shaking when she returned to her desk and sat down. She slipped a fresh piece of paper into the typewriter carriage, ready to type, and quickly glanced at Rotter's handwriting. She always read the messages at least once before she typed them, that way there were no surprises and she could assure her accuracy. She saw once again the words she had decoded. She thought back to Churchill's letter to Runciman. Perhaps the First Lord would get what he wished for.

A sense of unease settled in the room. The usual chatter had ceased. Everyone was working in silence. Isabel caught Dorothy's eye. Dorothy took the hint and moved to stand over her shoulder. Isabel's fingers, normally so nimble as they punched the keys, were clumsy now and slipped, making at least three spelling errors. She ripped out the paper. Dorothy handed her a fresh page. Taking a deep breath Isabel slowed her keystrokes and her breathing and carefully typed out the message without a single mistake. It was a short transmission. Finished, she stared at the sentence that the Germans had broadcast to every submarine commander in their fleet. Then she looked up to Dorothy, whose own features were drawn and serious.

Fast steamer Lusitania *leaves Liverpool March 13.*

When she was done she rose from her desk. The hush in the room was startling. Her throat was so dry she swallowed. But with Rotter gone who else would speak up about it?

"Commander Hope, sir?" Isabel said, her voice raspy. There wasn't a set of eyes not turned her way, including those of the commander, who stood with Denniston. "She's a passenger ship, sir," Isabel pointed out needlessly. There had been no other civilian vessels on the Germans' target lists that she knew of.

The commander looked about to reprimand her but seeing how closely their exchange was being watched he took a great breath instead. "The *Lusitania* and her sister ship, the *Mauretania*, were built for peace *and* war," Commander Hope explained. "The British Admiralty was heavily involved in the funding and design of the ships. Not only are they the most luxurious and safest transatlantic passenger liners in the world, they also have the capacity to become the fastest and most powerful armed cruisers in the war, should the need arise." Commander Hope continued, "It's no secret that the *Lusitania* has twelve gun mounts on her decks but so far she hasn't been outfitted with actual guns."

"And given Germany's policy of unrestricted submarine warfare," Denniston added, "the *Lusitania* could be considered a proper military target."

Isabel looked down at the paper once again. If she didn't know these facts she wagered few of the passengers did either. She looked to Dorothy and Violet; they didn't seem any more reassured than she did.

"Last summer while at sea she was painted battleship grey to hide her from the Germans," Norton said. He looked at Isabel as he spoke. "Then the government decided that as a passenger ship she wasn't in danger. Besides, she can outrun any submarine, so Cunard was instructed to return the *Lusy* to her company colours."

"But shouldn't we tell Cunard then? As Mr. Rotter suggested?" Isabel asked. Even if what they said was true that didn't mean the shipping company shouldn't be told of the transcript.

"The numbers speak for themselves," said Commander Hope. "Where is the records book we keep about ship crossings?"

Isabel was sure the men were glaring at her, thinking her silly. Yet the commander and Denniston seemed willing to explain things to her.

"It's here, sir," Dorothy said. She grabbed a file from a drawer and handed it to him. The commander flipped through it as the rest of them waited for whatever it was he was going to say next. "Since the threat began in February, out of more than thirteen hundred ships leaving British ports, only eleven have been attacked and only seven have sunk," he said with authority and a certain amount of patriotic pride. "And none of them could touch anywhere near the *Lusitania*'s speed of twenty-five knots. Submarines are slow things. They just can't get to her."

APRIL 15

Edward

A heavy mist hung about Rathfon Hall like a soft blanket draped atop a sleeping giant's back. It was the morning of Edward's departure. The dreary weather wasn't enough to postpone the journey or to prevent Lady Northbrook from seeing him off. Edward looked up from inspecting the automobile's back seat, full of his trunks, to see his mother descend the stairs wearing a white fur stole as though she was going to a ball.

"Mother, you didn't need to come outside," he scolded her softly, and kissed her cheek.

"My dear boy, I wouldn't let you leave on such a long voyage without at least one of your parents bidding you Godspeed," she said with a small smile. "Though since you're sailing on the *Lusitania*, speed you shall have."

"To think I shall be in New York on the twenty-fourth," he marvelled. He looked at his mother. She was always so sad lately, as though the weight of the world not only rested on her shoulders but also within her soul. It was just a house, Rathfon Hall, but it meant everything to her and to him; it was a passion they shared, one of the few things they held in common. "I will return safe and sound with my bride-to-be," he said.

"Yes." She sighed. She stroked the automobile's hood. It was so smooth and polished, like a ballroom floor. "I'm so looking forward to having her live with us."

"Smile, Mama," he said. This elicited an artificially wide smile from her but it would do.

"Edward!" came a shout. It was Lady Georgina. The butler gently pushed the girl's wheelchair outside so she could get close to her brother. Her red hair flowed over her shoulders and she wore no coat, too anxious not to miss Edward to bother with hairpins and warm garments.

"Georgina, you will catch your death," Lady Northbrook admonished her.

Edward leaned down and they embraced. "I've made this for Brooke," Georgina said, ignoring her mother, and held up an embroidered scarf. "I hope she will like it. She remarked on my needlepoint skills when she was here."

Edward smiled. "That is very kind of you. I'm sure she will adore it. Now promise me you will behave yourself while I am gone."

"I promise." She giggled.

"You're my best girl. Always remember that." He smiled and kissed the top of her head.

This pleased Georgina, who clasped her hand inside her mother's as they watched Edward and a groundsman start the motorcar. The engine turned over immediately, its sound a powerful purr that startled the birds enough that they fled to the nearby hedges. He climbed inside, Maxwell, his anxious-looking valet, beside him, and waved once more before driving off.

Georgina and Lady Northbrook remained on the drive watching the silver automobile disappear into the fog.

"I can't wait for the wedding," Georgina said. "It will be so glamorous and beautiful."

Lady Northbrook sniffed. "It will be an absurd extravagance."

"Oh, Mama, don't be so negative. Who doesn't love a wedding?"

Lady Northbrook avoided looking at her daughter's useless legs. What man would have a cripple as a wife? Especially when children weren't possible. Yes, Edward's wedding would be the only such event at Rathfon Hall for a generation, let Georgina enjoy it.

APRIL 25

Sydney

It had been a very good afternoon to start with. The placards had turned out exactly as planned. The slogan "No Gods, No Masters" was painted boldly and the wood the placards were affixed to was sufficiently light-weight for ease of carrying. The gathering had drawn much larger num-bers than expected; many new faces joined the ranks of the movement and marched alongside and many more remained on the sidelines nervously observing. Then there were the men. And the police. Both appeared on high alert. It was a noisy affair. There was chanting. Shouting. And even-tually the shrill call of a police siren.

Sydney marched up and down Washington Square with the others, calling upon the state to allow a birth control clinic to operate legally in the city. *I'm marching to make social change*, she told herself, proud to be part of the demonstration. She believed vehemently that birth control was as much the key to women's advancement as the right to vote was. It would give women freedom, help them escape poverty and control their health. It wasn't enough to read about these theories in books and maga-zines; she had to put her own feet on the ground for the cause.

But secretly, she found it thrilling. Nothing in her life before had made her feel this way. Dinner parties, balls, the opera and every other fashionable activity of her social sphere were pleasant enough pastimes yet they could also be dull. The only thing that came close to the exhilaration of taking part in this rally was when she galloped toward a jump on the hunt. Danger was a rush, an intoxication, a glorious sensation that made her feel vital and alive. Life should have more of this.

"Shame! Shame!" came the call.

Sydney was startled to see several women hissing at her. "Shame!" they repeated once they'd caught her eye, their faces contorted with hatred. She kept marching. *I mustn't engage such women. I must let the rally and the placards speak for me.* But she was too proud, too sure of her beliefs to do anything but stare back at the hissing women, all of whom were of a certain class, namely hers. She observed that the poorer women who dotted the crowd stood silent as sentries.

It was then that one of the protesters began to argue with a man in the crowd. Sydney wasn't close enough to hear their words but she was well within range of the first stone that was thrown. It hit her square on the back of her head. She felt the sting of the blow and staggered more from shock than injury. She touched her velvet glove to her head and examined the tip. Blood. She looked up and saw one of the hissing women waving her fist. Another rock visible in her hand. The woman threw it toward Sydney but this time it missed and crashed to the ground. What happened next was a blur. The chanting had been abandoned in favour of outright shouting. More stones and other items were thrown at the women and the peaceful rally descended into madness. Sydney was shoved and she shoved back. Someone grabbed her hair and tore off her hat. The placard she was carrying was knocked from her hand and stomped on. When she bent down to pick it up someone kicked her to the ground. She might have been trampled in the rush if a large brutish police officer hadn't seen her go down. Stupidly not recognizing her saviour in the moment, she slapped him; that ensured her ticket to the police station.

The women from the rally were lined up at the police precinct like common criminals. The room where they were held smelled like sweat and urine and, strangely, of smoked meat. It was uncomfortable squatting on the floor like a child. It was the better part of two hours before Sydney was called into another space, a cramped room with several desks arranged in a line, each with a police officer manning it. The processing room they called it. She sat down where she was told and was asked to give her name and address.

"Sydney Sinclair?" The police officer was a sergeant with a handlebar moustache and sideburns that could use a trim. "You're father wasn't—"

"Yes, he was," she answered swiftly. If her surname wasn't enough to end this silliness than nothing was. The whole thing was ludicrous.

"He died, what, a year ago?"

"Fourteen months."

The sergeant examined Sydney's face. She touched her cheek. How dreadful she must look. Hair askance, clothes torn and dirty. She assumed there was dried blood on her face to add to the picture. Thank heavens the sergeant knew who she was and was sympathetic.

"Your father was a fine man. And I have no doubt that if he were still alive he would be very disappointed in you, Miss Sinclair."

That wasn't the reaction she'd hoped for. She sat as straight and high as she could on the wooden chair that was far lower than his. "I assure you, Sergeant, that my father allowed me to be independent."

He didn't look up from his paperwork. "Did he allow you to spend the night in jail?" Sydney's eyes widened. "That independent enough for you?" he said with a smirk.

"You can't be serious?" she asked. "I have to be at my sister's engagement party at the Plaza this evening." He gave her a look. "I've broken no laws. I'm sure you're aware of the First Amendment, Sergeant. I was only exercising my rights."

"Was it your right to strike an officer?"

Sydney looked down at her gloves. The index finger was stained with her blood. She was the one who had been hurt, not some tough-talking policeman who didn't know to stay out of the way. "That was a mistake."

"Yes, it was."

Looking around at the ashen faces of her fellow rabble-rousers she grew fearful that perhaps the sergeant was serious.

"Okay, Miss Sinclair," he said authoritatively as he put his pen down. She thought this meant he was finished with her so Sydney stood. "Sit down." She sat.

"You will have to miss the party," he stated. "You can send a message if you like. But you'll have to pay for it."

"Send for a messenger, please," she said. "Then you will soon see that I won't be staying the night."

He eyed her. "Money buys freedom, does it?"

She didn't dare answer him.

When Mr. Garrett fetched Sydney from the police station he was already dressed in his evening clothes. She was out of jail but she felt like a prisoner nonetheless.

"I have been resigned to your marching in protests, Sydney. But to strike a police officer?" Sydney made to answer but he waved her silent. "I'm taking you home to change. Your maid Sarah is there to help you with your hair and anything else you need." He looked her over. "Perhaps a bath. Then you will arrive at the Plaza in time for dinner. You'll be too late for the reception."

Sydney swallowed. "Was Brooke very angry when you told her what happened?"

Mr. Garrett exhaled. "She was not happy. You've embarrassed her."

Sydney said nothing further. For the remainder of the drive she pictured Edward, the tall, thin and stiff-looking man from the photo Brooke had shown her, standing at the reception, impressing all their friends with his Englishness. She imagined him acting like a trained dog in a circus, dancing for his supper, performing Englishman tricks for Brooke's fortune. Yes, missing such a spectacle was a disappointment.

Edward

The Plaza Hotel's lobby was a crush of Manhattan's finest young men and women come to meet the future Lord Northbrook. Edward knew he had been talked about incessantly before he'd even set foot on American soil, his title and family history dissected and his financial status analyzed by every single person whose hand he now shook. To his face at least the swarm of bejewelled ladies and gentlemen were polite, even deferential, their curiosity forcing any judgments to be concealed beneath their corsets and tailcoats.

"Of course they are charming to you," Brooke answered when he had remarked on this. "Every last one of them wants to be assured a weekend at Rathfon Hall."

He found her opinion of people harsh. Although this tendency seemed to spill into other areas, including him. Since his arrival yesterday their time together had been strained. He had talked about his voyage. She had asked after his family. He inquired after the wedding plans (as Georgina had instructed him to do, so he'd appear modern) and she had caught him up in every detail. She questioned him on Rathfon Hall and he obliged. Then they had run out of conversation. Was there really so little in common between them?

He then asked about the guests for tonight's engagement party—which was planned to be as ornate and elaborate as money (a lot of money) could buy—and Brooke had obliged, running through the guest list and going into intimate detail on every person's financial status, their taste in fashion (or poor taste according to her) and any whiff of scandal that may have touched them. He heard every word she spoke but he didn't really listen, his mind drifting to the news of the war he'd read on the ship's papers and upon his arrival in New York. On April 22, mere days ago, the Germans had unleashed a new weapon on the battlefields of Ypres, Belgium—chlorine gas—a yellow cloud of poison that in forty-eight hours choked, tortured and killed thousands of British and Canadian troops. He knew no one in New York and initially turned to his fiancée to talk about these developments. She listened for a moment then quickly changed the subject back to the impropriety of one of her school friends.

It occurred to him, over a luncheon at the Fifth Avenue brownstone, that in their twenty-four hours together, without the distraction of family and social engagements, he had learned the path their marriage would take. It wasn't a path of twists and turns, of surprises and discoveries; it was straight and narrow and would run its unyielding, expected course through to its end.

Yet despite all of this, there was one subject where he found Brooke remarkably silent: her own flesh and blood. It surprised him when Sydney wasn't at the pier with Brooke to receive him. And Brooke's dismissal of it was absurd. And at lunch today, the young lady was mysteriously absent. The sour-faced guardian-banker, Mr. Garrett, had also been oddly laconic on the matter and mumbled something about Sydney having a prior engagement.

And now here he was, the reception nearly over and dinner soon to be served in the Grand Ballroom and he had yet to lay eyes on her. Was she really such a troll? He began to imagine Brooke was hiding something. Perhaps Sydney was the family idiot or was disfigured or obese. Or more likely, Sydney disapproved of the marriage and was boycotting all this fuss and bother. He told himself that such thoughts were lunacy: he was reacting to being very tired after the long voyage.

"It's such a shame your sister is so delayed," he whispered to Brooke between endless introductions to her friends and acquaintances.

"Isn't it, though? She can't help these migraines," Brooke said.

Edward saw her look at Mr. Garrett, who stood nearby. Edward had met with him that afternoon to discuss Brooke's fortune being signed over to him pending the marriage. The older man had been very clear that he was no fan of the scheme. Edward had been gracious as he listened to Mr. Garrett lecture him on the importance of preserving wealth and investing properly and not spending the Sinclair fortune on anything as ridiculous as maintaining a pile of stone such as Rathfon Hall. Edward didn't appreciate the man's attitude, even if he understood it. And now, seeing him and Brooke exchange looks, like they were co-conspirators, made him uncomfortable.

"This must be Edward!" The loud woman shouting at him was festooned with feathers and diamonds like an ornate rooster.

"Emily, darling," Brooke cooed, and tugged his arm. He bowed and took Emily's hand. The women began to chatter about some nonsense involving the hotel décor when out of the corner of his eye Edward spotted the loveliest girl he had ever seen. She was tall and regal, her elegance in manner and adornment stood heads above the other creatures in the room. Then she smiled at someone and it lit her face with such warmth that he couldn't help but smile himself. He was unaware that he was just standing there, staring and smiling, and had ceased to participate in the décor conversation until he felt Brooke yank his arm.

"Ah, it looks like my sister is feeling better," she purred, and to his amazement—and alarm—led him in the direction of the young woman, who, upon seeing them, projected her smile onto him. As they approached he was drawn to her full lips and to her eyes, which were not the pale icy blue of her sister's. Indeed once he was standing face to face with Sydney he saw that her eyes were a fetching shade of hazel, a further touch of warmth that nature had bestowed on her. The two women bore little resemblance to each other.

"Mr. Thorpe-Tracey, at last we meet," Sydney said, and took his hand. To his surprise, and apparently hers, he bowed and kissed it, eliciting uncomfortable laughter from both women. "My, Brooke, you didn't tell me how charming your fiancé is."

Brooke gave a thin smile, her blue eyes glistening like the ice that had seeped into her tone. "I thought such things would be trivial to you, my darling. So glad your headache is gone."

"Yes, no more pain at all," answered Sydney.

He picked up on the tension at once. "I'm afraid charm is not my forte," Edward said cheerfully. The sound of his voice caused the women to stop glaring at each other and look at him instead. For a moment he was a trapped mouse between two lynxes. "I'm rather shy. But good manners always win the day." He smiled though his words seemed to fall on deaf ears.

"Don't be absurd, Edward." Brooke laughed artificially.

"And how do you find New York so far?" Sydney asked him. "Do you mind if I call you Edward?"

"Please do. And I hardly know yet," he said, getting the feeling she wasn't really interested in his opinion. "This hotel is lovely."

"It is," she agreed. "Though it must seem rather small compared to Rathfon Hall."

Brooke laughed again. "She's teasing you, Edward. Sydney, perhaps you and I should go see about the first course? You don't mind, darling?"

He couldn't fail to notice Sydney's well-arched brow and the slightest flare of her nostrils as Brooke took her arm. They hadn't gotten far when . . .

"I see you're no longer in handcuffs, Sydney." It was Thomas Van Buren. Edward had met him earlier and thought him a simpleton with too much money. Sydney smiled as Brooke scowled at Thomas, who continued on like he was telling a very amusing story. "My driver happened to be near the police station when you were being taken inside."

Edward stood paralyzed with shock, certain this was more incomprehensible American humour. He expected Sydney to respond in the only way a young woman of her class should, with cool denial or a lighthearted laugh. Instead . . .

"What of it?" she asked.

Edward felt his eyebrows fly upward. "I thought you had a headache?"

Sydney and Brooke looked about the room, everywhere and anywhere but at him. He'd been had. It seemed that women the world over were incapable of telling the truth. Thomas grinned as he backed away from the fire he'd set. "I seem to have let the cat out of the bag. Beg your pardon," he said, and returned to the party.

Sydney turned to Edward. "It was all a misunderstanding. Now if you'll excuse me, I must check on the first course."

He was astounded by her lack of apology, contrition or any justifiable explanation. He had never known any man, let alone a woman, to dismiss such a social blot as an arrest so blithely, and while wearing evening dress. Edward was beyond astounded. He was in awe.

"Sydney is rather different from you," he said to Brooke, understatedly, as Sydney's lithe figure disappeared into the throng of guests. He was desperate to know the truth but at this moment he didn't trust Brooke to speak honestly. He had learned patience as a boy and knew when it was time to step back. The return voyage would give him enough time to unearth the mystery of Sydney Sinclair's arrest on his own time, in his own way.

"She is rather different from most young ladies," Brooke admitted. "We used to be close when we were little. The death of our mother hit her especially hard because she was so young. When we grew up we developed separate interests; hers are not to everyone's taste. But we have an understanding."

"What sort?"

"That we will never understand each other." Brooke smiled and placed her hand on his arm and led him into the ballroom.

Sydney

Dinner was an eternity. She had performed the part of the dutiful sister. Brooke had seen to it that the hotel had gone all out with the meal—five courses including the oysters—and they must have emptied a dozen bottles of champagne. But now the baked Alaska sat on its dessert plate melting into a mess of sodden meringue. Sydney felt sick. The headache that Brooke had invented seemed to be taking hold for real. She touched the back of her head where the stone had hit; there was a sizeable bump.

She observed Edward across the table during the meal. He wasn't what she expected. He had a pleasant face. It was perhaps a bit long to be considered classically handsome and with a jaw that jutted out a bit more than it should. His dark hair was thick and had a slight cowlick in front.

But the whole of him was attractive. She had presumed him to be polite, well-mannered and dressed in well-tailored clothes and he was all of those things. He was of course educated and had read all the books one would expect a lord-in-waiting to have read.

But when the dinner conversation inevitably turned to the European war, he had spoken about the politics of it with such passion and authority that the other men at the table seemed like fools next to him, their American isolationism a quaint yet dangerous idea when set against the terror of Germany and Austria and the impact a victory for the kaiser would have, even for the United States.

"You must have heard about the German warning that they may sink any ship in the North Sea?" one of the men asked Edward.

"Of course. All of England read about the threat back in February and about the American response. Your president Wilson all but threatened the Germans should they attack an American vessel or should any Americans lose their lives," Edward said. "If I recall, his exact words were that the United States would hold the Germans to 'strict account-ability' if such a 'deplorable situation' should arise."

"Well, another British merchant ship was sunk last week by a subma-rine. Over a hundred people died," the other man said. "One of them was an American. But did Washington declare war? No! So you see, Edward, we are not the solution to your country's problems. Europe must stand on its own feet if it's to survive."

Everyone at the table looked on in silence. The guest was clearly trying to provoke Edward. Brooke fiddled with the last of her baked Alaska, trying to hide her desire to pounce on the man. Sydney knew that the man, a Mr. Curry, was apt to drink too much and talk even more when out in pub-lic. "That man on the ship took his life in his hands, sailing a British ship through a war zone," Sydney spoke up, aware that as she did everyone stared at her, yet only Edward seemed interested in her opinion. "Why would our president send troops to defend the foolish actions of one man?"

She reached for her water goblet. Edward was smiling at her. "Indeed he would not. I dare say it will take more than that unfortunate incident to bring your country into the fight. But I hope that one day they will join in."

Sydney kept her gaze firmly fixed on Edward. "We are a brave country, Edward. When and if we feel it's the right thing to do, you will see Americans on the battlefield." They continued to look at each other despite the uneasy silence that followed their exchange. Mercifully, Mr. Curry was distracted by the sudden appearance of port.

Had the conversation drifted to more innocuous topics the evening would have been considered a success. So it wasn't her fault that Edward chose to continue down another path.

"Do all American women converse so readily about the war and politics?" Edward asked casually. "On my journey here, I read about your Margaret Sanger, who fled to England after jumping bail on obscenity charges."

Brooke glowered at Sydney. Like she had somehow willed him to say Mrs. Sanger's name. "That vulgar woman," Brooke said to appease Edward. "It's good she's left America."

"Yes, but now England has to cope with her," Edward said with a smile.

Dutiful sister was one thing, but Sydney couldn't resist making a calmly spoken observation; no one could object to *that*. "It seems to me, and perhaps you can clarify the matter, Edward," she began, knowing her sister's wide-eyed stare was intended to get her to shut her mouth, "that England must be very progressive if Mrs. Sanger thought it the place to escape? Are women free to choose in your part of the world?"

The way Brooke clasped the dessert fork Sydney thought she was going to stab her any moment. Edward, however, seemed reasonably unshaken by her question.

"London has its liberal factions," he agreed. "And I am certain that many English girls who find themselves in unfortunate circumstances do find solutions there. But as far as what Mrs. Sanger teaches, I am only too glad that my sister is confined to the country."

Sydney felt her temperature rise. The arrogance. The chauvinism. "Brooke told me that your sister is bound to a wheelchair?"

"She is."

"And yet you wish her confined to a rural existence as well? Is that some sort of aristocratic banishment?"

"Sydney!" Brooke snapped.

She had gone too far. The other guests stared at their plates. She could see that Edward's respect for her opinion had melted faster than the baked Alaska. "My apologies, Edward. I was only trying to suggest that modern views on women's roles in our society would benefit all women. Even those with challenges such as your sister's can still lead a fulfilling life."

"Lady Georgina will be fulfilled playing aunt to our children," Brooke said with a tight smile.

"I meant that in a city such as London she could find a job that suits her, be independent," Sydney continued. "I didn't mean to suggest she march with Margaret Sanger."

"No," Edward said brusquely. "Marching isn't possible for her."

Sydney wilted. Edward continued to finish his dessert as he began a chat with his neighbour about the quality of fox hunting in Westchester.

Brooke set her jaw. "Thank you, Sydney. You can always be counted on for lively words."

The sisters sat in the back seat of the motorcar on the way home. Even though it was after midnight the air was warm and light, though the same could not be said of the air between them.

"I know you think everyone is interested in what you have to say," Brooke said. "But in truth you embarrass yourself."

"You mean I embarrass you," Sydney said, and stared out the car window at the streets, the yellow light from the lamps streaming past.

Brooke squeezed Sydney's hand. It was meant to be conciliatory but it pinched. "I know my engagement must be difficult for you to understand. But the marriage will make me happy."

Sydney wasn't convinced. "Are you sure about that? Edward seems so serious."

Her sister laughed. "That he is. I suppose we didn't talk much about the war and politics when I was in England. It was all dances and parties. Reality wasn't part of the routine."

"And now?" Sydney implored her.

Brooke bit her lip. "How can anyone know that for certain?"

"It's not too late to call it off."

Brooke's eyes narrowed as though Sydney's words were an insult. Sydney knew the look well. Despite the moment of warmth between them, her words had angered Brooke all over again. Not that that stopped her.

"You really have no more ambition than to have a title and live in England like a fairy-tale princess?" Sydney asked. "Our father would be livid."

"Not this again," Brooke said impatiently. "Father would have hated it, but our mother would have adored it." Sydney softened at the mention of their mother. Brooke stared down at her gloves. "Besides, I am twenty-six. It's time for me to get married, I won't risk easing into old-maid territory. And I've decided to marry Edward," Brooke said. "And until I do you are going to promise he never finds out about your hobby."

"Hobby?" Sydney objected.

"Yes, hobby. It's a controversial one but it's a hobby. He's not to know until after the wedding, if ever."

"I can't hide who I am. And I won't," Sydney said.

"We'll see about that," Brooke said, and turned away to stare out her side of the car. "We sail in a week and I am going to insist you keep away from Edward until we board."

"And then what? Lock me up in the brig?"

"If that's what it takes," Brooke said.

APRIL 30

Isabel

Room 40 was in a state of heightened awareness. Captain Hall had been working closely with Lieutenant Colonel Drake who operated MI5, the domestic Intelligence agency, and together they had made the Germans aware of a plan—through a deliberate and elaborate web of espionage—for the British to invade the northernmost part of Germany, known as Schleswig-Holstein. The plan was entirely false but the hope was that it would draw German forces out of France. But to keep up the ruse the Admiralty had halted shipping traffic across the channel on April 19. On April 25 the code breakers intercepted a message that several U-boats were to be deployed to patrol the waters with the goal to attack transports, merchant ships and warships should this attack take place.

Isabel had watched the plan unfold with a mix of awe and fear. The German Admiralty, known as the Admiralstab, had continued to broadcast the schedule of the *Lusitania* to its navy since March. There had been no incidents to raise her concern but each time the *Lusitania* sailed out of port Isabel kept a keen eye on the incoming messages for any mention of the ocean liner. Ever since she had transcribed the ship's name on the target list she felt responsible for it. Isabel knew that was a silly notion, yet it haunted her that the British Admiralty knew what those men, women and children who booked passage on the *Lusitania* didn't—that the enemy was targeting the ship and would attack it if given the chance, with no concern for the innocent souls on board, and that Churchill would use it to lure the Americans into the conflict. Somehow in Isabel's mind she thought that if she intercepted a message at the right time then she could prevent tragedy. What was the purpose of breaking codes if they couldn't be used to save lives? And tomorrow the *Lusitania* was to sail from New York once again. This made the repeated messages from the German submarine U-20, reporting its coordinates throughout the day as it sailed across the North Sea, impossible to hear without her raising the alarm to someone.

"The U-20 has transmitted its location at least ten times so far," Isabel whispered to Rotter. He studied the latest message she had given him. "Its commander has been ordered to the Irish Sea."

Room 40 had intercepted orders sent to the submarines a few days earlier, including this specific directive to the U-20, which was commanded by a Captain Walther Schwieger, who was in charge when the U-20 fired at a hospital ship in January. He missed but it gave him the reputation as a brute, although according to British Intelligence, Schwieger was a career seaman who was popular with his crew and came from a well-to-do family in Berlin.

Rotter placed a rudimentary map of the British and Irish coastline in front of them. "Depending on his speed he could be in the Irish Sea in a matter of days."

"Exactly," Isabel said. "As will the *Lusitania*."

Since starting her job Isabel had learned that Room 40 had amassed knowledge of each German flotilla, including submarines, knowing their location and state of readiness, and when a vessel left port and where it was going thanks to these incessant broadcasts by the German coastal stations. But unfortunately U-boats couldn't transmit past a certain point at sea and they would literally vanish for days. It was then anyone's guess, including the Germans', what their exact location was, beyond a general area.

Due to the Admiralty's desire for complete secrecy, the men of Room 40 were further thwarted by not being allowed to keep a chart of British and Allied warships, so there could be no precise way of knowing what ship could intersect with what threat. It was all up to Oliver, Fisher and Churchill ultimately.

Since the letter incident Isabel had been more frequently in Churchill's company, acting as a runner between his office and Room 40. These notes were not confidential and she would see his trademark red pen scribbled across transcripts with such directives as *Watch this carefully*.

She had to trust that despite the contents of the letter, Churchill would protect the *Lusitania* and alert Cunard and its captain of the U-20 heading toward the Irish Sea.

Isabel lit a cigarette. She had joined the men in smoking and drinking whisky. She told Dorothy it was due to the stress of her work and all the extra hours she spent learning codes, but that was only part of it; in truth she enjoyed both vices immensely. If she was to be honest it wasn't only her job that pushed her to indulge in bad habits. It was Mildred. They ignored each other. Or more accurately, Isabel ignored Mildred but they couldn't avoid each other altogether. Isabel gave Mildred the cold shoulder whenever she entered with tea and sandwiches, though it was possible that this approach was doing more harm than good. Earlier on Mildred had made a few attempts at conversation but Isabel had turned her back, refusing to engage her. This had caused the girl some embarrassment. Dorothy had asked Isabel why she was so rude to the tea girl. Having Dorothy disapprove was very unsettling. She didn't dare explain to Dorothy why she disliked Mildred so much. She had made a feeble excuse about being too caught up in her work to have time to chat. When Dorothy had pointed out that Isabel chatted with the Room 40 staff constantly, she had accused Isabel of being a snob. It was a ridiculous accusation. But she had no rebuttal. Mildred had no right to be there. The Admiralty was Isabel's world. Her job. Her second chance.

These days Mildred scarcely looked at Isabel. To further complicate matters and force Isabel to reach for yet another cigarette was the fact that Mildred was stepping out with Henry. He hadn't even told her himself; Dorothy had run into them one night at the Coach & Horses. Their romance complicated things in Isabel's mind. She had lost sleep and her closeness with Henry had dropped off. The thought of the two of them sitting cozy in some pub was terrifying. What if Mildred told Henry the truth about Oxford? Surely that would ruin all she'd built in Room 40. And conversely, what if Henry told Mildred about the letter? She shook such a thought from her head. Surely she could trust Henry about that?

MAY 1

Sydney

It was the mob that caught Sydney's eye. Then came the sound. The racket reached through the motorcar and shook her. All over the sidewalk, spilling onto the street, men and women clamoured and shouted with the heady gaiety of a carnival. Yet the manner with which the crowd parted for the vehicle and gaped at its occupants had the predatory air of a Tudor execution. Sydney was startled by this unexpected commotion at the pier.

"Were there this many people when you sailed last fall?" Sydney posed the question to Brooke who was seated beside her.

"It's possible that a lot of them have come to see us off. After all, Edward is who he is. What he is," she answered eagerly, her eyes roaming the scene outside the car window; she had a way of appraising people like she was examining jewels for imperfections.

"And you're you," Sydney answered, with a slight tinge of sarcasm. She was still smarting from their terse exchange after the engagement dinner a week ago. They had done their best to make polite conversation ever since but the truth was they were both angry as hell. Any words beyond a cursory *How are you this morning?* or *What time is the dress fitting?* resulted in bickering. The voyage was either going to smooth things or increase the tension. No matter which way it went, it wasn't a journey that Sydney was looking forward to. Though in the case of the present crowd she had to admit there was a real chance that Brooke was right that her wedding would attract a lot of attention. Edward was travelling in a separate motorcar, coming directly from his room at the Plaza. Brooke had arranged to meet him on board at the ship's Grand Entrance. It now seemed a wise choice. They'd never find him in this fray.

Sydney furrowed her brow. Hordes of New Yorkers waiting on a drizzly morning to catch sight of her sister and her sister's fiancé gave Brooke's obsession with her sailing outfit credence. Sydney recounted the dozen dresses that had proven inadequate that morning. Her own trunks packed the evening prior, she had quietly observed Brooke fuss and fret over colour and texture. The winner was a sunflower-yellow silk dress with matching cape and feathered hat that coordinated identically with the paint of the motorcar, virtually guaranteeing maximum visibility on the pier. Sydney ran her hands over her own charcoal skirt and removed her gaze from the dazzling sun seated beside her.

"I wonder how many of the newspapers sent reporters?" Brooke asked.

"I'm sure they all did," Sydney answered. "All the papers have reporters on the docks. After all, there is a war on and this is a British ship heading into the war zone."

Brooke patted her skirt so hard it rustled. "But we're in America and we are not at war," she said. "People are tired of reading about death and politics. A society wedding is a happy diversion. It only makes sense that the papers would send reporters to get pre-wedding quotes from Edward and me," Brooke continued.

Sydney watched as Brooke wrinkled her nose at the unidentifiable faces. She knew what her sister was thinking: the crowd was too unseemly to be here for *her*. Too restless and vulgar. Not the send-off her *sort* would stage.

"I can't imagine what's got them so worked up," Sydney said as the car pushed through the thickening crowd. She fought the bubbling sense of alarm rising from her stomach. She had had enough of rowdy gatherings. How quickly a crowd could turn on itself, even turn violent. She looked to the front passenger seat at Mr. Garrett, his face buried in the dailies, oblivious to all but the latest news on the stock exchange. She guessed that he was avoiding being drawn into their conversation by pretending not to hear their "lady chatter," as he referred to it.

"Mr. Garrett?" Sydney asked directly. The older man started at the sound of his name. He twisted around and peered over the top of his spectacles at his beautiful young charges in the back seat.

"Yes, Sydney?"

"Why are there so many people at the pier? Surely they can't all be passengers?"

Mr. Garrett surveyed the scene unfolding outside. He smiled. "There's always a fuss when the *Lusitania* is in port. You see those archways?" he asked, and pointed upward to the immense steel archways. "That's the Chelsea Piers, which White Star and Cunard call home whenever their ships are in port. They're the work of architects Warren and Wetmore, the very same firm responsible for the new Grand Central Terminal on Forty-Second Street," Garrett explained.

Sydney had read several articles on the building of the new train station; it was the subject at many parties she had attended, though often brought up solely by male guests who were taken aback by her interest in such matters. Indeed both structures had the world talking of their opulence and efficiency, and local denizens debating if they were indeed everything expected of them and more, for to be considered a success in New York anything or anyone must be more. What was beyond debate was that the piers and the train station were the hubs of America's East Coast and, for many, the doorsteps into Manhattan, where residents and visitors alike could begin their love affair or their heartbreak with the city. "But don't you feel that the designs are too much of a tribute to old Europe?" Sydney asked, amused by the look of amazement on Garrett's face. "I would have thought that as a young country we'd be anxious to build more modern buildings?"

Her opinions always mildly shocked Garrett, who chose to ignore her this time. The car continued its push through the chaos. "See how close you can get the car to the porter's station," Garrett ordered the driver.

Sydney watched, fascinated, as the crowd let them pass. The motorcar drew in behind a long line of taxicabs and horse-drawn carriages whose passengers barked at porters to take care with their luggage. Sydney waited for the driver to open her door; through the fray she caught sight of a moderately dressed woman hurrying a young girl of about ten years through the mass of people. The woman was quite stout, with thick ringlet curls that would better suit her child. But the girl was dressed very well. A gold ribbon tied deep brown hair that shone like mink. The woman must be her nanny. She watched them vanish beneath the archway.

The driver opened the door. Sydney saw immediately that within the swarm of people were a slew of reporters and photographers guarding the entrance to the pier, a fact not lost on Brooke whose face lit up as though she had swallowed a sunbeam.

"I knew they'd want a photo," she gushed. "How do I look, Sydney? Be honest. These photos will appear all over the world."

Sydney studied her sister. It was a handsome face with a sharp nose and square jawline, dark hair and pale blue eyes that compelled everyone to stare; her relationship to their father could not be denied. Sydney took her features from their mother: upturned nose, heart-shaped face, lips like a Christmas bow and just as red, and the honey-blond hair that seemed the perfect accompaniment to her hazel eyes. She was the duplicate of Constance Sinclair; photographs and one imposing portrait enforced this view, as did the voiced opinions of her parents' friends. Many had come frequently after Constance's passing but gradually retreated into their own lives, leaving their father and a succession of nannies to raise the two girls.

"Why are you looking at me? Is it my hair?" Brooke demanded.

"You're beautiful," Sydney said simply, causing her sister to grab her hand with delight.

"Thank you, darling. Well, I best not keep them waiting," she said with a pout. "Now you get out first and stand over on the sidewalk so the cameras have full view of my dress and the car."

"But it's raining. Surely you want the driver to shield you with an umbrella?"

"It's a lovely mist! Besides, an umbrella would cover me too much. Now be a dear and step away."

Sydney sighed; the single moment of kindness between them was washed away as swiftly as the rain fell. She stepped onto the pavement. The drizzle flecked her face and she wiped her cheek as she took a few steps and stood where Mr. Garrett was waiting impatiently.

"Well, what do you think?" he asked her, a hint of exhilaration in his voice.

Sydney was so occupied with the mob and Brooke's frippery that she hadn't noticed. At his prompting she turned her attention from the sideshow on the street and at last saw *her*. The four black funnels that rose above the pier shed, the white bridge and decks that gleamed against the grey skies, the black hull with its sharp bow that curved to the heavens. Launched in 1906, she was immense and exuded strength and marvel but also grace and beauty. The *Lusitania* was like a goddess come down from Olympus. A glorious example of engineering and glamour united into one perfect object.

"Gorgeous," Sydney breathed, a wide smile brightening her complexion. "Such a marvellous and *modern* machine."

"She's more than a machine. The *Lusitania* is very much a woman—beautiful, comforting and temperamental," Mr. Garrett said as he scanned the crowd, as though seeing them for the first time. "This is quite a ruckus even for a celebrity like the *Lusy*. Let me see if I can find out what's behind it."

Sydney watched him disappear into the thick of it. The crowd had increased tenfold since their arrival. There must be a thousand. She caught sight of several people waving newspapers about, pointing and gawking at something in its pages and speaking animatedly to one another. She turned back to find Brooke had at last alighted from the automobile and stood posing, as though she were waiting for a curtain call.

"My, what a lovely day for a voyage," Brooke exclaimed good-naturedly to the crowd. She was perched on the vehicle's running board, a golden statue, arms stretched out, her biggest and brightest smile, putting on a show for the audience. But no one took notice of her. Whatever had gotten the crowd worked up it wasn't her sister's upcoming marriage. Sydney felt embarrassed for her. But Brooke appeared unfazed and strolled to her sister's side like they were on a Sunday picnic in Central Park. Sydney saw that the maid Sarah had arrived with the luggage in a separate car. Sarah was the same age as her, and had been with them only a short time.

"My, there are a lot of people here," Brooke said, loud enough to be heard above the din.

"They've come to see the doomed liner," a man tossed off ominously as he passed by.

Sydney shuddered. "Why would he say such a thing?"

"Don't pay him any attention," another man's voice said assertively. The man who spoke was a member of the Cunard staff. "The British Admiralty will take mighty good care of the ship. We will be escorted through the war zone by navy cruisers."

"That's very reassuring. Thank you." Sydney smiled even though she felt anything but reassured. The Cunard staffer nodded politely before hurrying toward the ship. As they stood on the sidewalk other bits of conversation floated by: "The kaiser wouldn't dare!" . . . "I told my husband we are not boarding come hell or high water. And in this case it may be both." . . . "Damnable scare tactics. They underestimate the English."

When Sydney turned to her sister she could see from Brooke's expression that she'd heard it all too. Then Mr. Garrett was back, his face as white as the *New York Times* he held in his hands.

"This is what's turned the pier into a madhouse." His tone struck the same serious note that he normally reserved for high finance. "I didn't see it when I was reading the financial news this morning."

"What is it?" Brooke asked.

"It's a notice from the Germany Embassy." He unfolded the paper and held it out so both women could read it. At the top of the page was the Cunard advertisement for the *Lusitania*, giving the date of departure: Saturday, May 1, 1915, at ten a.m. Directly below was something else entirely.

NOTICE! Travellers intending to embark on the Atlantic voyage are reminded that a state of war exists between Germany and her allies and Great Britain and her allies; that the zone of war includes the waters adjacent to the British Isles; that, in accordance with formal notice given by the Imperial German Government, vessels flying the flag of Great Britain, or any of her allies, are liable to destruction in those waters and that travellers sailing in the war zone on the ships of Great Britain or her allies do so at their own risk.
IMPERIAL GERMAN EMBASSY
Washington, D.C., April 22, 1915

"My God," Brooke said.

"Are they intending to sink her?" Sydney asked as Mr. Garrett composed himself. He never enjoyed managing female hysteria.

"I'm sure it's military posturing, my dear. The Imperial German Navy has more sense than to target a civilian passenger ship, especially, I might add, one that is carrying so many prominent Americans."

His words were enough to mollify Brooke who turned her attention to adjusting her wrap.

"Should we sail on another ship?" Sydney asked, still distressed.

"Don't be silly," Brooke said. "You heard Mr. Garrett. It's just a German ploy."

"You'll have an escort of several of the Royal Navy's best battleships," Mr. Garrett explained soothingly. "I wish I was sailing with you. It's quite an exciting time to be on the North Atlantic. Enjoy the adventure," he said, and touched Sydney's shoulder gently.

"Very well, Mr. Garrett," Brooke said, not seeming to care if she ever set eyes on him again. "You've done a fine job for us over the years. I thank you. We thank you."

"You're still managing me," Sydney interjected. Mr. Garrett smiled at her.

"Indeed I am," he said. "I will be here to greet you upon your return. Safe travels!" With that he disappeared into the swelling crowd, one more black bowler bobbing amongst the many that clotted the pier.

Sydney watched him go. "Do you think he's glad to be rid of us?" She was surprised by a wave of sadness over the banker's departure. He had been a steady presence since her father's passing.

Brooke evidently shared no such sentiment. "Sydney, let's quit this dawdling. We must find Edward," Brooke said urgently as she began to make her way toward the pier. "Sarah, make sure the porter is especially careful with the green trunk. It has my wedding clothes in it."

Sydney followed as Sarah trudged along with a porter behind her, his trolley stacked as high as his head. "Yes, Miss," answered Sarah.

Brooke placed a comforting hand on Sydney's arm. "Now let's get a copy of the passenger list as soon as we board. I want to see who we might know and who we want to know."

Sydney smiled and shook her head. Not even the German Imperial Navy could squash Brooke's anticipation of a grand social event. She kept her head low as she moved closer to the throng of reporters at the gate. She imagined the German threat made good copy. The papers were full of the war, even more so since February when Germany announced it would no longer stop and search an enemy ship before blowing it to smithereens. She imagined that a boatload of English and American passengers sailing through the war zone after the printed warning was the human-interest story to end all human-interest stories.

"Miss Sinclair?"

It was a booming voice, difficult to ignore but the sisters tried.

"Miss Sinclair?" the man shouted, and stepped directly in Sydney's path. Sydney stopped and stared at the reporter with his pad and paper held ominously.

"Are you speaking to me, sir?" she asked cautiously.

"I thought it was you," he said with a wry smile. "You probably don't remember me."

"Should I?" she asked, certain she'd never laid eyes on the man in her life. Oh, wait . . . Brooke had heard the man call her name as well and was glaring at the reporter as though he were a beggar. "And who are you?" Brooke asked. Sydney wished she hadn't.

"My name is Johnny Matson," he said proudly, and stuck his hand out, but when neither of the ladies deigned to shake it he quickly withdrew it. "I'm here interviewing the passengers, you know, in case the Germans make good on their threat."

"We have nothing to say about it," Brooke snapped. "It's very rude of you to ask. Are you trying to frighten everyone?"

"Hold your horses. It's Miss Sydney Sinclair I was interested in. I was down at the rally last weekend, you see, and I saw what happened. What you did. Quite impressive." He chuckled. Sydney and Brooke did not. He stopped. "Care to comment on it?"

Sydney was mortified and she could almost feel the arctic chill from Brooke's stare. This man had single-handedly brought all their bad feelings to the forefront once again.

"No I wouldn't," she said firmly.

"You sailing to get away from the scandal?" he persisted.

"There is no scandal," she stated as placidly as possible.

He whistled. "Well, Miss Sinclair, I beg to differ. One of society's youngest and brightest debutantes getting down and dirty with the suffragettes? Birth control, no less. That could be front-page news just as much as the *Lusitania*. How about you give me an exclusive?"

"Get out of here!" Brooke shouted, and stepped closer, towering over him.

"I can write a story about you too," he said to Brooke to appease her. "About your upcoming wedding to Sir Eddie." Brooke inhaled sharply at "Eddie." Matson smiled. "Our readers love a romance. In fact I can run the two pieces side by side. 'The Sinclair Girls: Sugar and Spice.'"

"Did you not understand me? Or do I have to call a police officer?"

"I can take a hint." He backed away and doffed his hat. "Bon voyage."

When he was out of sight Sydney let herself exhale. But her relief was short-lived.

"This is exactly what I was afraid of. You and your politics getting in the way," Brooke said, her voice not its usual singsong flute, but deep and hollow, like a gun barrel. "If that man writes such nonsense, what will Edward think?"

"Be reasonable, Brooke. Had the man and his photographer snapped you getting out of the car a few minutes ago you would not be as upset as you are now. Besides, even if he did write about me, by the time the story made it to England you would be married." At least she hoped that was the case. There was always the chance that some enterprising newspaperman would see fit to send the story over the wire to print in a local paper before they even reached England. "I think you're overreacting. If he loves you he won't care about your 'wild' sister," Sydney insisted.

"What makes you think he loves me?" Brooke asked bluntly. "My marriage isn't based on feelings as you well know. If something scandalous happens it could ruin everything. My reputation is very much tied to yours. It's only by our discretion and sheer luck that Edward hasn't learned the truth about your incident with the policeman."

Mr. Garrett had paid off the various newspaper editors to prevent the story from hitting the pages. It had been costly too as there were more than a few very striking photographs of Sydney in handcuffs. Strangely Edward hadn't brought up the subject of her arrest since the party. She supposed that was one of the advantages of so-called good breeding. Though she suspected his silence on the matter was more about his wanting to keep his hands in the Sinclair purse than gallantry. She noticed Sarah standing off to the side chatting with a handsome young man in a Cunard uniform. Being a member of the working class had merit, such as freedom to socialize with whomever one pleased.

"Now I must meet Edward on board," Brooke said. "You make your way to our Regal Suite. It's on B Deck, the Promenade Deck on the starboard side. Sarah will take care of the bags. I can't bear to look at you a moment longer."

Sydney flinched like she'd been slapped by her sister's gold kid glove. It was the final indignity and more than she could take. "If you're that worried about my presence upsetting Edward's opinion of you, then why don't I travel separately? I can book myself into third class and save you the humiliation of my views," Sydney stated.

Brooke's face was red as though her cheeks were on fire. "Don't be ridiculous. All I'm asking is that you stop being a stupid headstrong girl for the next two weeks. Is that too much to ask?"

Sydney felt the sting of another imagined slap across her cheek. She was old enough, and had her own fortune; she didn't need to succumb to Brooke's wishes. Her sister belonged in a world that was fading from fashion only she was too immersed in it to see it. The European penchant for titles and class was on the edge of collapse; the war was going to see to that. Spending one's life consumed by place settings, dress designs and social registers was not the real world for most women, certainly not when choices were finally opening up.

"It is too much to ask." Sydney turned to the porter. "There's been a mistake. I've been booked in first class but I want to travel third. Those top two cases belong to me. Please find another porter to escort me to the ticket desk so I can straighten this out."

The porter nodded. "Yes ma'am."

She turned back to Brooke. "There. It's done. I will be a threat no longer."

"Third? Why not second?" Brooke asked sarcastically.

"Because third is the farthest away I can get from you," she said, and turned away, hurt.

A second porter arrived and took Sydney's monogrammed cases from one trolley and placed them on another. Everything in order, she marched away from Brooke, fully expecting her sister to come to her senses and call her back. She was quite sure this would happen. Beneath the curved archway she went, the smell of the Hudson River filling her nostrils with dread. Alone inside the pier shed she began to panic. With each step drawing her nearer to the ticket counter she strained her ears to listen for Brooke's voice but no words came her way; instead the hectic drone of the crowd enveloped her until she was standing in the third class line.

"Anyone waiting to purchase a ticket?" a Cunard employee barked into the mass. Sydney raised her hand like a schoolgirl.

"Very well, come with me." The Cunard man escorted her away from the line of people waiting to board the ship and to a ticket agent. She presented her first class ticket.

"The first class entrance is down yonder," the man said, and pointed.

"I want to exchange this for third class," she said.

He looked at her as though she were mad. "I can't refund your money," he said brusquely.

Sydney exhaled loudly. "Then sell me a third class fare. You can do that, can't you?"

The man didn't answer. He scanned his booking sheet. "We're fairly booked. Not many cancellations despite the German warning."

She nodded. What was the German navy compared to the wrath of Brooke?

"I will have one ticket please."

The transaction complete, she and the porter went to the back of the third class line as it inched along toward the gangway where Cunard officers were checking each passenger's identification and inspecting luggage. She stared at the first class entrance that was orderly and far less crowded. *I will make the best of this.* At last she emerged from the shed and was able to take in the sheer majesty of the *Lusitania* once more. She smiled up at her. *You look like a headstrong girl too. I think we will get along just fine.*

Edward

Edward had reluctantly agreed to meet Brooke on board the ship rather than going around to collect and escort her, as a proper fiancé should do. Perhaps it was her American independence. That was certainly the case with her sister, Sydney. He had spent far too much time thinking about her since that night at the Plaza. She had what his mother would call "wild spirit." He wondered how his mother would react to learning her newest relation was an American outlaw. It made him laugh. The papers had been surprisingly quiet about the alleged arrest of the younger Sinclair girl. He pledged to be equally silent on the matter, especially when it came to describing Sydney to his mother. For certain, his future sister-in-law was beautiful and opinionated. Her comments regarding Georgina were especially pointed. Harsh. And he hadn't stopped thinking about what Sydney had said ever since. Lady Northbrook would be sickened by the idea of her daughter living as Sydney seemed hell-bent on doing. He hadn't broached the topic with Brooke either. It was best to pretend it hadn't happened and assume that she would be able to control Sydney, at least until the wedding was over and the latter was safely back in New York.

Edward was relieved when the taxi deposited him outside the Cunard entrance at Chelsea Piers, having fought its way through the crowd. As he stepped down from the cab he drew his coat tighter and adjusted his hat. The drizzle had turned to rain and the wind had picked up speed. There were few things more unsettling than to begin a transatlantic crossing a drenched man with a bare head. Maxwell supervised the porter with the luggage before taking his place behind him.

Once set to move onward Edward and Maxwell watched in amazement, their sensibilities under attack from all angles as the throngs of people crashed into one another with excitement, their words loud and indecipherable.

"It's quite the sight, isn't it, sir?" Maxwell said, a note of caution in his voice.

Edward gave a disapproving nod. "What in the devil is this about?"

Edward and Maxwell pushed their way through the crowd to the arch-way. A smallish man in a bowler hat thrust a camera in front of Edward and snapped his picture. Before Edward could react the man smirked. "Well, if anything happens, we've got your photo!" Then he disappeared into the crowd.

Maxwell very nearly tore after the man, but Edward called him back to his senses. "Let him go," Edward said. "We have more important things to attend to."

"Very right, sir," Maxwell said, and straightened his jacket.

"Are you sailing on the *Lusitania*?" It was a reporter who asked.

Maxwell shoved himself between them. "Get away, you!"

The reporter shrugged him off. "I'm Johnny Matson, writing for the *Post*. You're Sir Edward Thorpe-Tracey, the English *aristo*. I just spoke to your fiancée, Brooke Sinclair, and her sister."

"Is this about my engagement, then?" Edward asked impatiently. He now understood why Brooke had asked to meet him on board. What a circus the pier had turned into. It was perhaps proof that his future wife was going to be thoughtful and considerate of such things and this pleased him.

Matson rolled his eyes. "Yeah, your wedding has practically caused a riot," he said sarcastically. "But no, Your Highness, this ruckus is about the last voyage of the *Lusitania* and I'm a newspaperman, so sue me."

"What in heaven's name is that supposed to mean?" Edward demanded.

Matson smiled in mock shock. "This, Your Highness." He held out the clipping of the warning from the morning paper.

Edward snatched it away. He read the notice quickly, then passed it along to Maxwell. "Is that what all this fuss is about?" Edward asked Matson as he eyed the swelling crowd.

Maxwell, now a shade or two paler than usual, handed the paper back to the reporter.

"Sure is. People love a tragedy, especially a shipwreck," Matson said with a grin. "I was here three years ago when the *Titanic* survivors came in. You couldn't stop the crowds then either." He shrugged but was quickly losing interest in Edward. "So you got anything to say? Any last words for your loved ones in case this steel lady becomes your coffin?"

Edward glared at the man. "Don't be ridiculous."

A wall of noise erupted nearby as the crush of people parted. Edward watched as a tall and exceptionally well-dressed and elegant man stepped out of a private car. He was wearing a pinstriped suit with a pink carnation in his lapel and had a trail of servants, including his valet, behind him bearing luggage.

Suddenly Matson grew as excited as the rest of the horde. "That's Alfred Vanderbilt! Gotta run!" he said to Edward before getting swallowed by the swarm.

"Are you acquainted with Mr. Vanderbilt, sir?" Maxwell inquired.

"I have not had the pleasure." Edward smiled slightly. He couldn't take his eyes off the man. To have his wealth was to be free. Free to do whatever you wanted and with whomever you wanted. It was not the sort of freedom that Edward had ever known and he was instantly jealous at the sight of it being flaunted so flagrantly and in such excellently tailored clothes. He forced himself to look away and to face Maxwell, a far less intimidating soul. "But I shall seek him out on board. Brooke is well acquainted with him. He was unable to make our party last weekend. I understand he is a fine horseman too."

"Then you will have much in common," Maxwell said encouragingly.

It wasn't long after boarding that Edward saw Alfred Vanderbilt again. He was standing on deck posing for photographers with two other men. The first Edward knew as the *Lusitania*'s captain William Turner, an imposing man he had had the experience of dining with on his voyage to New York. Turner was no gentleman, but a hardened sailor from the old school, and took no pleasure in socializing with passengers. Edward found him gruff but capable. The other man was shorter and rotund, very animated and stood with a cane. The way the reporters were fawning he must have been of some importance. Edward passed by without anyone's notice and made his way to his cabin on the starboard side.

The Grand Entrance, with its elegant Corinthian columns, wrought-iron elevators, plush carpets and marble fireplace, was the conduit to everywhere else that mattered on the *Lusitania*. Edward watched Brooke enter the space, her trim figure encased in bright yellow like a canary. Her arrival caused a stir amongst the other passengers and she basked in the adoration. He did not. But he smiled when she kissed his cheek.

"This ship is like a floating palace," Brooke gushed. "As fancy as the Plaza."

"It is all that," he admitted. "Where is Sydney?"

"She's got a headache," she answered. "Confined to the suite already. Poor poodle." Brooke frowned playfully.

"Is this the same kind of headache she had prior to our engagement party?" he asked, and watched Brooke's throat as she swallowed. He shouldn't tease her; he would get to the bottom of their charade soon enough. "I'm playing with you." Brooke smiled with relief. "Does she get them often?"

He began to walk, his hands clasped behind his back. Brooke glided at his side, gawking at everything and everyone like she'd never been out in society before.

"Did I say headache? I mean seasickness," Brooke said breezily.

"That is serious," he said mockingly. "Sydney must have a very sensitive constitution if she can get seasick without yet being on the sea."

Brooke smiled and fidgeted with her hair. "Let's not talk about my sister. Let's walk toward the front of the ship and wave at people on the pier."

Sydney

The tugboat pulled away from the *Lusitania*, leaving her pointed downstream on the North River and headed to open water. The mountainous shards of concrete, steel and glass silhouettes that formed the Manhattan skyline began to fade from view like a mirage. Soon it would vanish from sight entirely. A booming sound signalled the start of the engine turbines roaring into service deep within the ship's core, sending a series of vibrations rippling upward. The ship's foghorn blared a farewell to New York. But it was also a sonorous announcement to the encroaching seas that she was coming.

Four levels below the first class Promenade and one level above the cargo hold and engine rooms was F Deck, which housed the baggage room, storage shelves, mailroom, food and wine cold stores as well as many crew cabins. F Deck was not by any means a glamorous counterpart to what existed several decks up. It was, however, where Sydney found herself after boarding the ship. For in addition to its other functions, F Deck also held several, but not all, of the third class accommodations.

She appeared to be the only person in her assigned cabin, for which she was thankful. The berth had one bunk bed and Sydney laid claim to the lower bunk just in case another passenger arrived before the ship sailed. She was thankful the space had a wash basin; she had read about the dormitory-like conditions of steerage on other ships, but clearly the *Lusitania* was much too grand for that. Still, it was a small room, much smaller than the ensuite bathroom of her Fifth Avenue home. *Yet this will be my home for the next eight days.* She felt a quiver of remorse that she'd taken things as far as she had.

Sydney made her way to the Saloon Deck and the third class dining hall near the bow. It lacked opulence to be sure. The furniture was sturdy and solid with tables and chairs made from polished pine. *It looks designed to withstand a military invasion.* An upright piano took pride of place at one end. Passengers were milling about hoping for an early snack. She took the staircase to the Shelter Deck, one above the dining saloon where she discovered the men's smoking room on the port side. She peered inside long enough to note yet more polished pine but withdrew swiftly upon receiving the glares of several men offended by her presence. *Exactly what I aim to change!* Not that smelling cigars and brandy was so important to the battle of the sexes. She walked to the starboard side where the third class ladies' room lay out before her. *Let me guess*, she wondered, *will there be polished pine?* She opened the door and swept in.

"Ah! Pine it is," she said gaily. A handful of women stared up at her, puzzled by her outburst. She quickly exited the ladies' room and proceeded to stroll along the third class Promenade, which was partially enclosed.

Continuing to walk along the Shelter Deck she watched children run and play as small gatherings of men smoked and spoke loudly of the German threat. There seemed to be more than a few single woman travellers too. One older woman had broken out her knitting and seemed content to let the afternoon pass by using her progress to mark the passage of time.

There seemed to be none of the illicit strangers or dirty immigrants that she had been told were common in steerage. The diseases and filth she'd read were found amongst the lower classes seemed ludicrous. There was nothing to fear. These people were no different than she was. She tried to imagine her friends' faces if they could see her now. They wouldn't be caught dead in third class. It made her smile.

Sydney watched a young couple at the railing gazing at the New York skyline. The woman was simply dressed but even with her modest clothes it was easy to see she possessed a voluptuous figure. Her hair was pinned up loosely in the Gibson girl style that had been the height of popularity a few years before. She gazed at her companion with such affection it gave Sydney pause. He was attired in a suit of cheap wool and his brown herringbone-tweed cap appeared as though it had seen more than its share of seasons. Yet he bore the confidence of an elder statesman who owned things—railways and oil fields—the type of man who belonged in her father's class. Perhaps it was love. Sydney could find no other excuse for the couple's obvious state of contentment and she noted dryly how different they seemed compared to Edward and Brooke. Now there was a man who puzzled her. There was something about him that she couldn't pin down. Partly it was the way he looked at her, as if she were a painting he was thinking of buying. Partly it was how he had listened to her at the engagement dinner when the other men seemed poised to dismiss her opinions. He asked what she thought and paid attention to her words—at least until the subject of women's rights came up.

Sydney continued her walk until she reached a locked Bostwick gate and was prevented from going farther. She spotted a seaman on the other side and beckoned him to her. Reluctantly he marched over.

"Yes, ma'am?" he said politely.

"What is this gate about?" she asked.

The seaman grinned. "It's to keep third class in its section of the ship, ma'am. Third class aren't allowed above C Deck, which is where we is," he explained, then looked her up and down. She followed his gaze, which roamed over her simple but well-cut dress sewn out of an expensive silk-and-cotton weave. No doubt he could also smell her Guerlain perfume—Vere Novo—the same fragrance her mother had worn. It was from Paris and one of Sydney's few extravagances. "Are you on the wrong deck? You need me to escort you out of here?"

She smiled. "That won't be necessary. I'm where I'm supposed to be."

His expression said he didn't agree but he tipped his hat and walked away. Sydney removed her tickets from her little purse and held them in her hand, first and third. Opposites. She stuffed them back inside and retreated along the third class Promenade to the staircase and down the countless steps to F Deck. She would be fit as a racehorse after this crossing. She had nearly made it to her cabin when a scuffle of footsteps and a shrill voice made her stop.

"Hannah! Where are you, child?" The shrillness grew louder. "Hannah!"

Then Sydney saw with some surprise the stout woman with the ringlets she had seen on the pier, now scampering toward the baggage room.

"Do you need help?" Sydney asked. "Are you looking for your charge?"

The woman, huffing loudly from exertion, swivelled on her sensible shoes and glared at Sydney.

"My charge? I'm looking for my *daughter*. She's run off," the woman snapped, then eyed Sydney carefully, assessing her like the seaman had done moments earlier. Then without a further word she brushed by and clambered up the stairs.

Sydney continued on. She had turned the final corner to her cabin when she nearly fell over something. Recovering just in time she saw that the object was a little girl squatting on the floor.

"Good gracious!" Sydney remarked. Then straightening herself she smiled. "Are you Hannah?"

The girl with the dark mink hair smiled up at her. She was a beautiful child. Sydney found it difficult to believe she was the offspring of that coarse woman.

The girl nodded. "My mother wants me to play piano. I don't want to."

"I see," Sydney said, and knelt down so she could meet her gaze. "I don't think you ought to be playing now anyway. The ship has just set sail. It will be dinnertime soon."

The girl shook her head fiercely. "Not now, not ever. I don't want to play piano. I want to sing and dance."

Sydney studied her face; the young girl was very serious and determined. "That is a problem," she admitted with a smile. The girl nodded emphatically. Sydney stood up and offered Hannah her hand. Reluctantly the girl took it and together they climbed up the flights of steps and back to the Shelter Deck to search for her mother. The wind had picked up so that the drizzle blew in their faces.

"I've found her," Sydney called out when she saw the mother stomping about, checking under blankets and deck chairs.

"Hannah!" the woman shouted at the sight of her child. She rushed over and snatched her from Sydney as though she was in the hands of a convict. "Where did you get to? Annoying this nice lady?" The woman smiled at Sydney. "Apologies if she did."

Hannah remained mute. "She was in the passageway. I believe she was lost and was frantically looking for you," Sydney offered. Hannah stared at her, thoroughly impressed.

The mother's eyes narrowed. "Is that true, child?"

Hannah nodded. "Yes, Mother."

The mother exhaled. "Thank you. I'm Gladys MacGregor. You've met Hannah. We live in Brooklyn."

"I'm Sydney. Sydney Sinclair."

"That's a boy's name." Hannah giggled.

"Don't be rude," Gladys snapped.

Sydney only laughed. "You're right, Hannah. It was my mother's surname before she married my father," she explained. "I think they hoped I'd be a son."

"Well, it is unusual. Nice to meet you, Sydney," Gladys said, and held out her hand, giving her the once-over again. They shook hands. "Time to get changed, Hannah. She has to practise her piano."

Hannah gazed up at Sydney, resigned to her fate, and followed her mother back into the ship. Sydney grinned and moved to the railing, taking in the disappearing skyline of New York.

Edward

As Brooke walked along the deck Edward was aware he cut a grim figure by her side. Now that the start of the return trip was here it pierced him like a bayonet. In eight days he would be home and then the wedding would take place. This voyage was the last of his bachelor days. His final moments of freedom and possibility. There was no denying he had made his bed and for the good of his family he would lie in it. Besides, there was always the possibility of dying on the battlefield to save him from a loveless marriage. Even if he were to perish in the trenches his family would still benefit from the Sinclair fortune and that was of some comfort. Brooke reached for his arm. He stared down at her hand; her touch felt foreign and limp.

"This Promenade is divine," she cooed. "It's a seaworthy Peacock Walk."

"A what?" Edward asked, having never heard the phrase before in his life.

"A public place where you stroll in your best dress and everyone can see you head to toe, silly," she explained, exasperated.

"You mean like a—a parade?" he stammered.

"I hope I've packed enough clothes," she said, not listening to him.

Edward examined her face hoping to see even the slightest hint of true attachment. He found only respectful deference.

They passed a group of men singing "The Star-Spangled Banner," which delighted Brooke. "How lovely to hear an American song on a British ship," she exclaimed.

"I'm happy you're pleased," he said, though in fact he much preferred "It's a Long Way to Tipperary," which the orchestra was playing so beautifully up on the Boat Deck.

Edward's attention was diverted by the sight of Alfred Vanderbilt strolling toward them with the same large man walking with a cane that Edward had seen posing for photos with Captain Turner. The pang of jealousy he'd experienced earlier rushed back. Vanderbilt was rich beyond imagination and handsome too but the money and good looks belied the darkness beneath the finely cut pinstriped suit and carnation. Edward knew the facts and the rumours and didn't bother to separate the two. Vanderbilt's first marriage to Elsie French had broken off due to his affair with a married woman, Agnes O'Brien Ruiz, who was the wife of a diplomat. The scandal shook all of East Coast society and when it wouldn't abate, the poor woman had committed suicide. The newspapers were full of the story for months. Alfred had sought asylum in London for a time, and after his return to the United States, eventually he remarried. A lovely American woman named Margaret Emerson. Even though the events had occurred a few years prior they were of such a scandalous nature as to leave unimaginable scars—emotional and social. He must be in constant torment, thought Edward. Brooke apparently didn't share his view of Vanderbilt's secret suffering for she smiled brightly and extended her hand in greeting.

"Alfred, *mon cher*," she said cheerily.

Vanderbilt returned her smile with a shine as blinding as her own. "Brooke, a pleasure to see you again."

"Alfred, may I present my fiancé, Edward Thorpe-Tracey," she said proudly. "The future earl of Northbrook." Edward extended his hand and the men shook. He thought he caught a trace of disapproval in Vanderbilt's eye. Not all men of character have your millions, Edward wanted to say but every drop of blue blood in his veins ensured such an outburst would never occur. Vanderbilt smiled politely. "My apologies that I wasn't able to attend your engagement party last Sunday. Mr. Thorpe-Tracey, it's a pleasure. I've heard much about you, of course."

"Oh call him Edward," Brooke said with a light laugh.

Edward shifted his weight from foot to foot. "As I've heard of you—"

"I'm afraid the Vanderbilts do get their fair share of press," Vanderbilt injected, his face the picture of calm assurance. He then turned to the larger man with the bushy eyebrows. "May I introduce Mr. Charles Frohman," Vanderbilt said.

Brooke lit up once more. "I know who you are," she said excitedly. The man blushed slightly at her eagerness. "Edward, darling, Mr. Frohman is a theatrical producer. He produced *Peter Pan*. Isn't that divine?"

Edward extended his hand.

"Guilty," Frohman said with a chuckle, and shook Edward's hand.

"I saw a production in London," Edward said. He had taken Georgina to the West End play not long after her accident and the fantasy had raised her spirits immensely. "It was delightful."

"Good to hear," Frohman said. "Now if you'll excuse me, I'm travelling with friends and I must go find them. It's almost cocktail hour."

"Oh but you must tell us who your friends are," Brooke insisted. "Anyone famous?"

"Brooke." Edward attempted to chastise her but she was having none of it.

"Don't worry, Edward, Americans aren't as fussy about simple questions as your people are," she explained, and laughed.

Vanderbilt looked uncomfortable. But Frohman was accustomed to female fans gushing over actors and actresses; his business depended on it.

"That's the truth," he said with a grin. "To answer your question, Miss Sinclair, my friends are George Vernon, Charles Klein the playwright and Rita Jolivet the actress."

Brooke closed her eyes a moment at the thought. "Rita Jolivet. I adore her! Will you introduce me?" she pleaded with a flirtatious tilt of the head.

Edward watched, slightly mortified. An actress and a playwright. Artists were to be admired and their work enjoyed but the notion of socializing with them seemed impossible to fathom. He looked to Vanderbilt for a shared sense of dismay but found none.

"Of course I will," Frohman said good-naturedly. "We'll be in the lounge before dinner. Come find us then." With a tip of his hat the man left them.

Brooke turned to Vanderbilt. "And will we have the pleasure of your company at dinner?" she asked.

"I'm afraid I've made plans with another acquaintance," he said, then seeing her disappointment he added, "Another night for sure. By the way, where is Sydney? I thought she was sailing with you?"

"Of course she is. I wouldn't get married without my sister to stand up for me," she said.

"Splendid. I look forward to seeing her too," he said cheerfully. "She's always game for lively conversation."

Edward couldn't tell if this was meant to be flattering or not. But Brooke seemed satisfied. "You know Sydney," she said with a laugh before changing the subject. "What part of the ship are you staying in, Alfred?" she asked. His attempt to answer was cut off by Brooke's enthusiasm. "Let me guess. It's the other Regal Suite, isn't it? I bet you're the one to blame for reserving the port side too, you devil. I was desperate for it. You know it's decorated just like the Petit Trianon at Versailles." At this she turned to Edward and said as an informative aside, "Marie Antoinette used it to escape the drudgery of the royal court."

Edward was astonished that she would think he wouldn't know his European history. He had gone to Cambridge! His baffled expression was not lost on Vanderbilt who obviously was trying to conceal a laugh.

"I'm afraid you can't blame me for that," he said, straight-faced. "I'm in a Parlour Suite on this deck, starboard side."

It was Brooke's turn to appear astonished. She recovered enough to say, "Well, then we are neighbours as I have the Regal Suite on the starboard side."

Vanderbilt nodded politely. Edward could practically feel the man squirming to leave their company.

"Now, if you'll excuse me, I need to check in with my valet," Vanderbilt said, and with a slight bow strolled back in the direction he had come from.

His abrupt departure made Edward wonder if he should be insulted. He didn't really blame him. A lengthy discourse on one's cabin décor was tiresome for even the most indulgent man. For her part, Brooke appeared not to have noticed.

"This promises to be an unforgettable voyage," she said. "I think I will go rest before dinner. I want to look my best when we make our debut in the dining saloon."

"I will see you to your stateroom," Edward said, relieved to have the last of the afternoon to himself.

Edward had been given a tour of the starboard side Regal Suite on his voyage over. It had been unoccupied and he was delighted to see inside. It was opulent, despite lacking the Marie Antoinette flourish, and was outfitted with two bedrooms and its own dining room, parlour, bath and water closet. It was an ideal layout and space for the sisters, affording them privacy as well as being a physical embodiment of their standing in society, which was of particular importance to Brooke.

They reached the Regal Suite and Edward grasped the door handle to open it for her, which seemed to alarm her.

"Oh don't bother," she said, and tapped his hand until he let go. "No need to constantly fuss."

Edward was stunned. He wasn't accustomed to being shooed away. Before he could respond Sarah opened the door unexpectedly, causing Brooke to lose her balance. But Edward grabbed her hand and righted her before she could tumble.

"Sorry, Miss, I didn't know you were out here," Sarah said in alarm.

"Why would you?" Brooke asked, her voice a sharp trill. Sarah seemed frozen to the floor. "Well, what are you doing? Have you finished unpacking already?" She looked down at what the girl was carrying and bit her lip. Wrapped in tissue paper was the amber silk gown that she'd bought for Sydney.

"I'm taking this to Miss Sydney," Sarah explained. "In case she needs it."

Edward tilted his head quizzically. "Taking it where?" he asked.

Brooke glared at Sarah until the girl nearly shook with fright. "I meant I'm taking it to be steamed," Sarah said breathlessly. "Miss Sydney is lying down and I thought it was good timing to leave her."

Brooke smiled, her lips pressing together grimly. "Why of course. Good idea, Sarah. Now off you go."

The maid darted past them and down the passageway. Brooke crossed the threshold and turned to Edward.

"Now be off, please. We don't want to wake up Sydney," she said, and forced a wide smile. "Shall you fetch me at six o'clock?"

"I will fetch both of you," he answered.

"That is if Sydney is up to making an appearance. She may prefer to take her meal in the stateroom," Brooke cautioned.

Edward's raised eyebrow was the only detail that belied his trust. But he would be a cad to press the issue any further and he wanted to avoid being cast as a villain so early in their relationship.

"Let's hope for a speedy recovery from her seasickness," he said kindly. "Have a good rest, my dear."

"Thank you, Edward," she said, and gently closed the door on him.

Isabel

The wireless transmissions from U-20 had ceased. The submarine was out there, miles below the surface, slowly marauding its way toward the Irish Sea. There was no way anyone could know its exact whereabouts any longer. Isabel counted the cigarette butts in the ashtray beside her typewriter. Fifteen. It was scarcely noon. She had barely smoked two a day before coming to Room 40.

She and Dorothy had gone to the picture show last night. Dorothy had insisted it would cheer her up. The screen stars smoked and drank a lot too. Only when they did it, it looked glamorous. Isabel hadn't felt glamorous in a long time. Perhaps that was for the best.

There was a birthday party tonight at the pub. Parish was the man of the hour. It would do her good to have a few drinks and laughs to celebrate. But Isabel was exhausted. She had been pulling sixteen- and eighteen-hour shifts. Denniston had ordered her to go home early to rest and not to return until Monday. But the impromptu birthday party had given him reason to relent. If it were up to Isabel she would skip the party and man Room 40 on her own. It was a ridiculous idea of course. What could she hope to achieve? The submarine was out of signal reach. The *Lusitania* was still thousands of nautical miles away. Tonight was one of the few nights she could relax and enjoy.

"Isabel?" It was Henry. "Are you coming tonight?"

She could guess why he was asking but wanted him to say it. "I could stand to get out and have a drink," she answered. "There isn't a problem, surely?"

"Of course not," he said, and paused. She reached for the cigarette pack. Then thought better of it. "I was going to bring Mildred."

Isabel snatched the pack and clawed a cigarette out of it. Henry waited for her to light it and take a drag.

"What does that have to do with me?" she asked. She could see she was making Henry uncomfortable but she didn't care.

"Nothing, really," he said. "You two don't get on. I just wanted you to know."

"Is that all?" she asked. Her fingernails pinched the end of the cigarette.

"Yes. That's it," Henry said, and smiled. He seemed relieved to have their exchange over.

"I hope you two have a lovely time," she lied. Henry nodded and walked over to the table with the codebooks.

"Isabel, please type these transcripts up." Curtis placed a load of new paperwork beside her.

"Of course," she said. She stamped the cigarette to smithereens and violently stuffed a sheet of paper through the carriage. Her fingers smacked at the keys so hard the tip of her index finger jammed between the *j* and the *h*.

"Blasted machine!" she yelped, and pulled her finger out slowly. The tip of the nail was torn clean off.

"Careful, luv," said Violet who had only sat down at the typewriter next to Isabel's a moment before. "We aren't meant to do battle with it."

Isabel forced a smile. "Do you have a nail file?"

Violet opened a desk drawer and handed an emery board to Isabel.

"Thanks." Isabel gently ran the coarse file across the edge of her tattered nail. Now she would have to cut all the others to match. *Damn Mildred. She ruins everything.*

Sydney

The ship rolled up and down and side to side like a demonic carousel horse. Sydney lay in her berth, willing the motion to stop. They had been at sea a couple of hours and her stomach wouldn't settle. When she stood her body swayed, when she walked it wasn't in a straight line. She had never been drunk but she had witnessed plenty of drunkards staggering on the streets of the Lower East Side. Maybe if she knew how to be drunk she wouldn't feel as ill from the ship. The thought of eight days at sea only made the nausea worse. Then there was a knock on the door. She didn't even attempt to get up.

"Yes?" she called out, wishing she was less polite and could say *Go away* instead.

"It's me, Miss. Sarah."

"Oh," she answered faintly. What did she want? No doubt Brooke had sent the poor girl to pack her things and bring them and her upstairs. Well, there was no way she'd let that happen. "Come in, Sarah."

The door opened and Sarah tentatively emerged from behind it. She found Sydney stretched out on the berth with her complexion an odd shade of green. "Miss Sydney!" Sarah gasped. "You don't look right. Should I get the ship's doctor?"

Sydney exhaled deeply and managed to sit up just as a fresh wave sent the ship falling deep into the water. She swallowed. "I'm terrific. What makes you think otherwise?" Sarah stared dumbfounded. Sydney forced a smile. "I'm teasing, Sarah. How did you find me?"

"I asked a steward, Miss," Sarah explained. "He said you were down here." The maid was doing her best not to examine every last detail of the berth. "Miss, this is the lowest deck on the ship. It's not right that you're here. *My* berth is two levels up!"

Sydney forced a smile. "Then you must enjoy the advantage."

Sarah studied Sydney's face and bit her lip. "You don't look well."

"I don't feel well," Sydney agreed. "*Mal de mer*, they call it. I asked."

"*Mal de mer?*"

"Seasickness. It's all the rage," Sydney said, and pointed to the parcel in Sarah's hands. "Is that for me?"

Sarah nodded and unwrapped the tissue, revealing the silken fabric. Sydney's eyes widened at the golden dress.

"I thought you might need it for dinner," Sarah said.

"I'm not sure third class passengers need to dress in silk," she replied with a faint laugh.

"I suppose not," Sarah answered glumly. "But I thought you should have it in case you change your mind."

"About?"

"About staying down here. You don't belong here, if you don't mind me saying so," she said as forcefully as a lady's maid could get away with.

Sydney laughed despite herself. "What? You don't think I can tolerate a mere week in steerage?" She stared at the girl until Sarah gave in and shook her head. Sydney sighed. "You underestimate me. As does my sister."

"I think she's upset," Sarah explained. "You should have heard her before. Telling her fiancé that you were napping."

Sydney exhaled impatiently. "I was napping. I take it she hasn't told Edward where I'm staying?"

"No, Miss. He expects to escort you and Miss Brooke to dinner this evening," she explained. "From the Regal Suite."

"Does he?" Sydney grinned. "That certainly puts Brooke on the spot. But to be honest even if I did want to make up with my sister I'm not sure I feel up to food and frivolity."

"That's what she told him."

"Well, then she won't be lying, will she?"

Sarah continued to stand there, awaiting instruction. Sydney stroked the gown. "It is beautiful," she said.

"It's gorgeous," Sarah agreed, staring once again at Sydney's green pallor. "You know, my uncle was a seaman."

"Is that so?" Sydney wanted nothing more than to be left alone to be sick in peace but the girl seemed determined to overstay her welcome.

"And he used to say that if you were seasick it would be better to be on deck, facing the bow, so your eyes can see the motion of the ship, as if you were the one steering. It tricks the mind."

Sydney contemplated this. Anything would be better than the constant swaying sensation. "It's worth a try. Thank you."

"I can assist you onto the deck," Sarah offered.

"Yes, that would be helpful," admitted Sydney.

Edward

The ocean's surface was whipped up into froth. White-capped waves cascaded into each other, their foamy lather dissipating just as another wave formed, like an endless parade of mermaids performing a high-seas dance. Edward watched the water repeating its pattern over and over, yet each wave was unique, an indefinite number of possibilities, like snowflakes. His thoughts drifted to Rathfon Hall. As a child he had played in its great rooms, hid in its many nooks and alcoves, fallen off his pony in its fields and had his first kiss in its garden (with Lady Amelia Clarke who went on to marry a duke). It seemed his destiny that Rathfon Hall would be his only love. His time in New York had not yielded much optimism that he and Brooke would find happiness beyond surface appearances. Marrying her would save the estate but not him. It was the right decision but he couldn't completely bury his true self for the sake of his family. Passion was what he wanted. Maybe after the war, if he survived, he would find it, if not in the arms of his wife, then in reviving the estate. Yet it would be nothing like the life he had dreamed of when he was a boy. No trip to the Amazon. No daredevil flying. But what did a boy understand of duty? As a man he knew all too well. His mother had been right to ridicule his dreams. And second thoughts about Brooke were a luxury he literally couldn't afford.

When he'd had enough of self-pity—deeming it unfitting for a man in his position—he climbed up to the Boat Deck, the highest deck on the ship, where the lifeboats hung, one level below the bridge. It was less crowded than the Promenade because of the lifeboats blocking so much of the walkway, making it harder for pedestrians to navigate. He strolled along to the farthest point forward until he was overlooking the forecastle. Stretched out ahead of him was nothing but an undulating carpet of ocean.

He caught sight of a lone woman on the bow below. She walked to the far end of the forecastle, and stood still as a statue, staring out at the sea. He couldn't see her face but there was something familiar about her—how she moved, her carriage. Edward was transfixed. She wore no hat and her hair had fallen out of its confinement of pins and was cascading down her shoulders where the breeze lifted it up. Then with her hands gripping the railing she tilted her head back, which loosened more of her hair. It was a bold display of wanton freedom. Edward had read about modern women who travelled alone but he knew no such beings within his own circle. As he continued to watch her he thought with amusement how the future Lord Northbrook conversing with such a feral creature would scandalize his mother to no end, which was no doubt partially responsible for his walking down the staircase and toward her.

Sydney

From her periphery she saw the man approaching. Sydney had been happy to discover this unoccupied portion of the deck and was relishing the solitude in case she needed to be sick overboard. Fortunately Sarah's uncle's advice had helped; she felt much better. But the last thing she wanted was a stranger attempting to get acquainted. She fixed her gaze on the shimmering waves, not wanting to avert her eyes, thankful for the veil the few loose strands of hair provided. Perhaps if she continued to stare ahead he'd pass by. No such luck. The man stopped a couple of feet from her and was staring out to sea alongside her. How irritating. Sydney was determined to ignore him. Then he spoke . . .

"Do you sail often?" the man asked pleasantly in an English accent.

Sydney looked straight ahead and answered coolly, "This is my first voyage."

"The *Lusitania* is the finest ship of her kind," he continued. "You've picked a very good first go at the North Atlantic."

He took a step closer so that she had no choice but to face him. She turned and gasped.

"Edward!" she exclaimed.

He stood wide-eyed and slack-jawed. "Sydney!" he returned, and offered his hand in greeting.

"I didn't know it was you," she said, and they both laughed. "I must admit I'm relieved. I thought you were some shipboard Lothario on the make."

Edward stopped laughing abruptly. "I saw you out here alone," he said, instantly formal in his address. "I was worried for your safety."

Sydney smiled. "But you didn't know it was me?"

"Not at all. Your hair . . . it's rather wild at the moment," he said, and gestured to her head.

Her hands went up and felt the loose hair. She was horrified to find so few pins remained; they must have come out when she was lying down. Edward continued to watch her and she felt self-conscious. He seemed to be expecting her to fix her hair, to put it in its rightful place so that all was in order, neat and tidy. Instead she was gripped by an overwhelming urge to show Lord Muck what an independent American girl was made of.

"Oh these pesky pins. I thought I'd gotten rid of them all," she said, and pulled the remaining ones out, allowing her long blond hair to blow freely in the wind like she was a girl of ten. Edward appeared stunned by her lack of propriety.

"They must have loosened when I was lying down this afternoon," she continued. "I wasn't feeling well earlier."

"So I hear," he said. His composure restored, he gazed out to sea, which despite the rolling waves was a much calmer view.

An awkward silence fell between them. He looked melancholy. Either that or he was also inflicted by *mal de mer*. "Did you enjoy your week in New York?" Sydney asked.

He smiled politely. "It is a spectacular city. Very exciting, even more so than London, I think," he said. "I can see why you love it."

"It's home," she said. "I wouldn't dream of living anywhere else."

The silence fell again. Then . . . "I'm fortunate that Brooke doesn't feel as you do," he said.

"That would make for a cold marriage," she said. His expression darkened. She had said the wrong thing. "I mean it would be unbearable to be away from the person you love for long periods of time."

"Yes. It would," he agreed, the darkness lingering over his face. "Since you're well now I take it you'll join us for dinner?"

Should she risk telling him her decision to travel in third class? The revelation would only elicit more questions. He had a severe opinion of her already after the engagement-dinner-party disaster. "I prefer to dine alone tonight."

"That is too bad. Brooke will be very disappointed, as am I," he said. "The dining saloon is of the highest standard. All the passengers are anxious to make introductions and connections. Your sister is looking forward to making an entrance and I'm sure you are too."

Sydney bristled. What an assumption to make. He knew nothing about her. Which was why she chose not to take offence, or at least, not too much of it. "To be honest, Edward," she began, "I've little interest in parading around in first class to be appraised like a prize show horse. That's Brooke's domain, not mine."

He stepped back like he'd been shoved. She despaired that a week at sea, let alone a lifetime, would be long enough to bring this uptight Englishman around to see her point of view. "What I mean, Edward," she said warmly, "is that we are very different women."

"So your sister tells me," he said curtly. "May I give you a piece of advice?"

Sydney scowled a little. "If you think it necessary."

"You should consider wearing a hat when on deck," he said sternly. "To prevent your hair becoming so unkempt. It's not becoming."

Then he bowed slightly and marched away. Sydney covered her mouth with her hands, trying to stifle a giggle. But it was no use. He hadn't gone more than a few steps when she burst out laughing.

Isabel

The backroom at the Coach & Horses was spilling over with Room 40's usual crew: Denniston, Rotter, Curtis, Parish, Norton and about half a dozen others as well as several of the women. Their solemn work left behind in the Old Admiralty Building, the group had turned boisterous and was singing out of tune and swaying side to side, drinks in hand.

"For he's a jolly good fellow,
For he's a jolly good fellow,
For he's a jolly good fellow,
And so say all of us!"

The end of the song brought rapturous applause as the object of the crowd's affection bowed his head in an exaggerated gesture of gratitude.

"Hear! Hear!" Norton shouted. "So how old are you today, Parish?"

Parish smiled. "Why, I believe I'm thirty-two."

Dorothy and Isabel sat at the farthest corner of the table and sipped whisky. Lately Dorothy had developed a favouritism toward Alastair Denniston. He had situated himself at the opposite end of the room but now and then could be seen to sneak a glance in Dorothy's direction, and when caught, smile attentively.

Isabel had observed all of this and while she didn't disapprove exactly, she cautioned her friend on the pitfalls of a romantic entanglement. "I see the way Denniston looks at you, Dorothy. And you, him," she chided. "Take care. You don't want a reputation."

Dorothy laughed. "Isabel, you are like a headmistress."

"I want you to be cautious," Isabel warned affectionately. "You are a dear friend and I would hate to lose you."

Dorothy squeezed her hand. "You're a lovely girl, Isabel. But you really ought to try and loosen up a bit. You can have fun and be respectable."

Isabel knew that was a sweet lie that Dorothy and the other girls told themselves. She'd heard it said often enough that the war would change things for society and for women. But Isabel fretted that if such changes came at all they would be too late for her.

The team had an arrangement with the publican that no one from the general public would enter this part of the pub while they were there. It was one further assurance that their top secret work remained just that. It did mean that when more drinks or food were needed they had to fetch it for themselves when it was ready at the bar.

"Mind if I come and join you, Isabel?" Rotter asked, and moved toward her. Isabel felt a shyness wash over her and into her cheeks.

A fact not lost on Dorothy who whispered, "You look quite pretty when you blush. Now try and have fun. Mr. Rotter is a handsome devil."

Isabel focused on her whisky. Rotter sat opposite her and Dorothy. She did find Rotter attractive, not only his good looks but his mind. She admired him more than she desired him.

"Mr. Rotter?" Isabel asked.

"Yes?"

"Will the Admiralty tell the shipping company about the U-20?"

Dorothy kicked her under the table. Isabel flinched but her gaze remained steady.

"Which shipping company?" Rotter sipped his whisky.

Isabel took a sip of hers. It burned her throat, a sensation she enjoyed because it meant she was tough enough to take pleasure in manly activities. His question was worrisome. He had been as concerned as she was. Now he acted like it was a thing of the past. Or was he telling her to keep such thoughts to herself? She wasn't about to oblige.

"Cunard."

The word punched the air between them and Rotter sat back against the chair as though he'd been hit by it. "Oh yes, quite right," he said dismissively. "We passed the message along as is our job."

Isabel was gripping her glass tightly now. "But will they give it to the right people? Will the ports at Queenstown and Liverpool be told? And Captain Turner: Will he be informed?"

Rotter rolled his whisky glass between his fingers and stared into the amber liquid as though the answer lay inside. "It's not up to us, Isabel. We have to trust those in charge. You know that."

Isabel knew it was useless to push. As had been explained on her first day in Room 40, the so-called charter that Churchill had written was to be upheld day in and day out by each of them, and in it he stipulated that the cryptographers could not interpret the information from the transcripts themselves, nor decide who should be given that information. They were to decode, catalogue and pass it up the chain of command, nothing more. The reminder made Isabel want a cigarette.

"The ship has made the crossing to New York and back to Liverpool three times since we learned she's a target," Dorothy said reassuringly. "The Germans wouldn't dare."

"But she set sail from New York today," Isabel said urgently. "And we know for a fact that the submarine may be in the area she will be sailing through in a matter of days."

"We will keep as close track of U-20's whereabouts as we can," Rotter said soothingly. Isabel was deflated. If only Rotter and Dorothy knew about the letter, then they would also doubt that the Admiralty would do the right thing.

Dorothy rose and crossed the room with Violet and began smoking near Denniston. So obvious!

"Do you have a cigarette?" she asked Rotter.

"Of course," Rotter answered, and held one out for her.

"Ta," she said, and took it. She leaned forward as he struck a match and lit it for her. The smoke filled her lungs and soothed her nerves. Isabel reminded herself to be happy. She looked around the crowded room. These men and women were her colleagues, they were doing great things and she belonged with them.

Back in Oxford, Mr. Chambers had been the first to encourage her to think and learn and have ambition and she was thankful for it. He had changed her life; he was the reason she was here now. Isabel indulged in a few moments of fond recollection. *When George smiled at me, when he spoke to me, I felt like the only person in the world who mattered to him.* Of course he had also been to blame for all the bad that had occurred too. She'd worked bloody hard to put the past behind her. To do a good job and gain recognition for it. She lifted her whisky to her lips and took a large sip. The drink was still finding its way down her throat when she saw them enter. The sight made her choke and she coughed and sputtered like a street urchin, regaining her composure just as Henry and Mildred took up residence near Dorothy and Denniston.

Isabel stared at Mildred, who seemed to relish the acknowledgement for she smiled and waved. *The nerve.*

Then to her dismay, Mildred walked over. Isabel noted the swivel of her hips.

"Good evening, Isabel," Mildred purred. "Mind if I join you?"

And in that instance several weeks of avoidance were obliterated by social pressure. Mildred was challenging her. Isabel wouldn't make a scene in front of her men. The girl plunked down where Dorothy had been. Mildred looked down at Isabel's empty tumbler. "You want another?"

"You don't have to wait on me here," Isabel said cuttingly.

"Oh don't worry, let me buy. Isn't it time we let bygones be bygones?"

Before Isabel could object Mildred had walked to the bar. She considered leaving. It was nearly ten and it was a long bus ride to the boarding house. But everyone would notice a quick departure and she didn't want to draw attention. She couldn't risk it. She finished the cigarette and pounded the butt into the ashtray. Rotter was engaged in a serious football chat with Curtis. She had no one to turn to for distraction.

"Here you go, love," Mildred cooed, and plunked the glass down. "Enjoy. Whisky's too strong for me. You were always the tough one."

Isabel wanted to toss the drink in the girl's face but why waste a good glass of whisky? "What are you doing here tonight?" she asked instead.

Mildred appeared puzzled by the question. "What do you mean?"

"I mean you aren't part of the team," Isabel said coolly. "This is a team party."

Mildred showed her offence by snatching the whisky tumbler from Isabel's hand. "Give me that back!"

Her words were loud enough that several of the men within earshot glanced over, including Rotter. Isabel stared her down, unmoved by the outburst. Mildred, aware a scene was unfolding and she was a star player, gently put the tumbler to her lips and emptied its contents in one gulp. She smiled at the others.

"I thought you didn't like whisky?" Isabel said.

"I lied."

"Of course you did."

The others returned to their own conversations. Mildred leaned forward and whispered, "You know what I really don't like?"

"I haven't the foggiest," Isabel said, trying to instill the perfect note of boredom and condescension in her voice.

Mildred's eyes narrowed. "You. I don't like you. Showing off your fancy skills and parading around the office like you're one of the men. But they don't know the truth about you, what you did, who you really are, do they? This show of yours with the schoolmarm hair and dreary dresses? Ha!"

The threat unnerved Isabel. But she didn't want the girl to know she was afraid. After a moment of silence Isabel laughed. "You've always been amusing," she said.

"Is that how you want to play? I've had enough of you," Mildred warned. "We'll see how you feel come Monday."

"You're being ridiculous," Isabel said sternly. She didn't appreciate being threatened.

"Am I? You'll see," Mildred responded brusquely, and stood up so fast her chair tipped over. Parish picked it up and looked at them. "Everything okay, Isabel?"

"Perfectly," she answered, and watched Mildred stalk over to Henry.

She was glad to be rid of Mildred for the night. Her life had moved far along from when they knew each other. The less she had to do with her the better. But as she watched Henry fawn over her it disturbed her more and more. Isabel needn't be insecure. She had a place here now and she didn't see it ending anytime soon, for despite what people had been saying at Christmas, the war showed no sign of being over.

Sydney

Back in her cabin Sydney took care to ease the brush through the tangles. Her hair was fine and she didn't fancy losing great wads of it due to her carelessness on the deck. She had been shocked when she'd finally looked in the vanity mirror and saw the dishevelled mess. A smile spread across her face: the untamed mane, her body unadorned by jewels, the drab clothing. She was far from the ideal sister that Brooke had hoped to present to her future in-laws. No doubt Edward too was wondering what impression she'd make on his family.

As much as she wished to laugh at the situation, in truth her father would have been horrified to see her acting this way, and the thought made her feel a pang of humiliation. To make matters worse, when she'd returned there was a note shoved under the door. It was from Brooke.

My dear Sydney,

I feel that I've indulged your whimsy long enough. You must end this charade once and for all and return to our suite. Edward is expecting to escort both of us at 6 p.m. this evening. I won't take no for an answer.

Brooke

The missive didn't generate its intended guilt. The fact of the matter was she wanted to be by herself and not deal with Brooke's hysteria over her having an opinion on things deemed impolite or unfeminine. She scribbled an answer on the back of Brooke's note and stuffed it in the envelope, scratching her own name out and replacing it with *Regal Suite—Starboard*. Sydney finished pinning her hair. Satisfied that she once again resembled a civilized woman she made her way to the third class dining saloon. But as she climbed the staircases the pangs of seasickness took hold again. She found a kind steward standing outside the dining saloon and handed him the envelope.

"Please deliver this as soon as possible," she said, her voice quavering.

"Are you quite all right, ma'am?" the concerned steward asked. He glanced at the envelope. His eyebrow raised at the sight of *Regal Suite* scribbled on it.

"I thought I was better," she explained. "But the seasickness has come back."

"Try eating a bit of bread. It helps," he said, and watched her slowly make her way to the saloon entrance. He tapped the envelope on his thigh and shrugged.

She was at the doors when the sound of a piano drifted toward her. It was Beethoven's *Moonlight Sonata*. She had attended her share of recitals as a girl, and listening to the player now she thought he or she sounded too regimented, too precise, lacking the warmth of feeling that a true pianist, a true artist, had. Still, it was preferable to listening to that insufferably cheery war tune the ship's orchestra had felt compelled to play earlier.

When at last she entered the dining saloon, she hesitated. She didn't know what to do. Dozens of people were jostling around finding their assigned seats. Fortunately the chairs each had a numbered plaque on the back to make this easier. The passengers were lively and the sound was nearly drowning out the piano. She was so accustomed to being treated deferentially that the concept of communal dining was utterly foreign. Here one had to fend for oneself. For a moment she reconsidered her decision and wanted to chase after the steward to retrieve the note. But another lurch in her stomach changed her mind. Bread was needed immediately or else she would be sick all over the carpet or, worse, other passengers. She found her seat beside an elderly couple and another single woman. They smiled at her as she sat down. Her nausea rose and fell along with the waves of the sea. Her hand clamped to her mouth just in case.

It was then she noticed that the source of the Beethoven was Hannah. And, not surprisingly, there was the mother, Gladys, at her side, coaching.

A dining room steward brought a basket of freshly baked bread and placed it in front of her. Not waiting on anyone she immediately tore off a piece and placed it in her mouth. It was fresh and warm and its heavy texture felt soothing as she swallowed. She chewed another piece cautiously as she watched Hannah play. The girl's face was intense with concentration but lacked joy. Sydney felt sorry for her. When the piece came to its conclusion the room erupted into applause. Gladys coaxed her daughter to stand and take a bow. Hannah seemed to enjoy this part of the performance and smiled and waved to the audience, a charming gesture that increased the applause and her smile.

The stewards had begun to serve dinner and her attention turned from the little girl to the food. She and the other passengers would be feasting on roast pork. Sydney was surprised when Hannah and Gladys joined her table.

"Sydney." Gladys nodded in her direction. Sydney smiled back.

"That was lovely, Hannah," Sydney said.

"It wasn't her best," Gladys responded. "But she has to get used to the ship's motion."

Hannah sat picking at her food, ignoring her mother's negative comment.

"Are you heading to England for school?" a man at the table asked.

"We have other plans," Gladys said. "Hannah is going to be on the stage."

Sydney noticed that Hannah was eating her roast pork very slowly.

"The West End?" asked a woman, who was dressed in a severe black skirt and matching jacket. "What show?"

Gladys beamed with pride. "We're considering all options."

The woman who had asked the question smirked. Sydney shared the woman's doubt that little Hannah was cast in any show. But she was too polite to display her skepticism.

"I heard Charles Frohman is on board," the elderly man said.

Sydney watched Gladys; from her expression Frohman's presence was not news.

"You don't say?" she said, pretending it was.

"He is. First class, though," the man continued, unaware that he wasn't telling the mother anything she didn't already know. "You should find a way to have him hear your daughter play."

"That is an idea," Gladys said casually. "But I wouldn't dream of trying to get the attention of such a man."

Wouldn't you, Sydney thought.

"You might need to have her play something more modern than that old stuff," said a younger man at the table. He couldn't be older than twenty-five and spoke with an Irish lilt.

"Don't worry, Hannah can play anything," Gladys said.

"What do you like to play, Hannah?" Sydney asked the little girl directly.

"Tell the nice lady, dear," Gladys urged.

Hannah looked up as though aware for the first time that she was the subject of the conversation. "I like 'The Entertainer,'" she said.

The young man grinned. "That will do! Can you play it for us after dinner?"

For the first time Hannah smiled and nodded. But Gladys wasn't as willing. "She has to get her rest. Maybe tomorrow." Hannah's eyes returned to her dinner.

"Do you know Mr. Frohman?" the old man continued.

"I've not had the pleasure," Gladys said.

"He's a very approachable man," Sydney said, then immediately regretted it.

"You've met him?" Gladys asked, beaming a very artificial smile.

"Or so I've heard," Sydney corrected. "He's supposedly very friendly."

Gladys sighed, as though she had always doubted that Sydney would know a man like Frohman, and with a smile laced with condescension she said, "That's nice, dear. I'm sure he will be if he ever hears my Hannah play."

The dining hall had grown even louder as passengers began to relax and get to know one another. There was little formality amongst them. Children who had had their fill of supper were running up and down the aisles between tables, the stewards doing their best to avoid collisions while carrying trays stacked high with dirty dishes. The bread and the rest of the meal had done the trick. Her seasickness had abated. She stood up from the table and walked toward the door to the deck. Fresh air would solidify the cure. She opened the door and paused to check her hairpins before stepping out into the night air.

Edward

The orchestra was playing *The Blue Danube*. The after-dinner gathering in the lounge was to capacity. Ladies sat on the sofas in dresses chosen to make a striking first impression. Gentlemen, those who had not already retreated into the smoking room, listened patiently to their wives discuss the other passengers or wonder why Captain Turner had not presided over his table on the first night of the voyage.

Edward stood behind his fiancée, his hands resting on the back of the rose velvet sofa as they listened to the music. Brooke was seated placidly beside a well-dressed matronly woman who was sailing with her daughter, a spindly thing of twenty-eight whose bare ring finger announced her spinsterhood. He observed with bemusement Brooke toying frequently with her pearl-and-diamond pendant earrings that nearly dusted her shoulders. Each time she did, the square-cut Colombian emerald-

and-diamond engagement ring she had insisted on sparkled in the light of the chandelier like a beacon. He thought back to the demure diamond-and-sapphire ring that remained at Rathfon Hall unworn—while pretty it would not have garnered a reaction such as this. For despite Brooke's subtle show, her performance wasn't lost on the matron or her daughter, nor was it missed by a smattering of other ladies who sat nearby and were trying their best not to fixate on the enormous ring. He brought his eyes back to the nimble talents of the five-piece band and closed his eyes. But his attempt at serenity was abruptly ended by a loud outburst from a man near the lounge entrance who appeared to be arguing with a ship's officer—Staff Captain Anderson, second-in-command of the ship. Edward moved away from the music to see what the matter was.

Edward had never set eyes on the man before. He was middle-aged with finely trimmed moustaches carefully shaped into thick handlebars the colour of steel. His agitated eyes bore right through Anderson, who managed a polite smile in return but his body language spoke volumes of impolite thoughts. Edward had met Anderson on his voyage to New York. He had often taken Turner's place at the captain's table and had infinitely more patience for the needs and grumblings of passengers. This passenger's anger could stem from some silly oversight in his stateroom. Vanderbilt and Frohman had also heard the ruckus and come forward, and watched with Edward at a respectful distance.

"I assure you there is nothing to fear," Staff Captain Anderson told the irate man.

"I demand to speak to the captain!"

"Captain Turner will only repeat what I've just told you," Anderson explained politely but the man was having none of it.

"I heard your men discovered German spies on board! Stowaways!" he shouted. "What I want to know is what, if anything, is being done about it?"

Anderson glanced around the first class lounge. The man's booming voice had carried above the band's exquisite notes and more than a few of the passengers had turned their attention if not their heads to listen.

"We have arrested three men," Anderson explained calmly and

quietly. "And they are locked up in one of the cabins below decks until we determine who they are."

It surprised Edward to hear such an admission. Stowaways on the *Lusitania*! He looked back to Brooke who was still fanning her engagement ring like it was a feather. The majority of the guests seemed in blissful ignorance for now. But the three men exchanged concerned looks.

"Have they been interrogated yet?" the man persisted, wiping at his brow with a handkerchief.

"The ship has a detective inspector on board, as well as a German interpreter," he said. "They know the job that's to be done."

"What did they find out?" the man snapped.

Edward watched Vanderbilt step forward to interject. He admired the millionaire's easy manner and confidence, even boldness. But backbone was not the sole province of the American male and Edward followed, Frohman nipping at his heels. The man narrowed his eyes at them as though they too were spies.

"They could be analyzing the ship," Vanderbilt suggested. "Before the war the Germans came on board and spied on the *Lusitania* to learn how she was built. They were none too pleased she took the Blue Riband from them."

The man kept swiping his forehead like a pane of glass. Anderson gave a slight bow to Vanderbilt.

"Good evening, Mr. Vanderbilt," Anderson said, then greeted the others. "Mr. Thorpe-Tracey, Mr. Frohman, good evening." He turned back to Vanderbilt. "And you are correct, sir. The men we discovered this afternoon had photographic equipment with them, to your point."

This wasn't enough to satisfy the man who violently tossed his handkerchief to the floor.

"Then they have an added interest in destroying her!" the man continued.

Anderson glanced about the room. As though reading his mind, a steward dashed over and retrieved the handkerchief from the carpet and held it out to the man who snatched it back rudely. Edward did not wish to side with someone as unreasonably behaved as the mustachioed man but, like him, he wanted to know what was really going on.

"Staff Captain Anderson," Edward said gently. "You must understand that the presence of three German stowaways is going to alarm the women." He looked at the irate man. "And some of the men as well." The man scowled at him. "What is being done? Have your men searched the ship to ensure nothing is amiss?"

"We have, sir," Anderson said with authority. "The ship is as right as rain."

Edward clenched his jaw. That was the official line and would not be deviated from. The crew was duty bound not to reveal details. The *Lusitania* had been under direct control of the Admiralty ever since the start of the war and the German prisoners would be handed over to the navy as soon as they reached Liverpool. There seemed little else to say and Anderson bowed to the group.

"Now if you'll excuse me, gentlemen, have a pleasant evening." He smiled and walked away.

"Have yourselves a nice time. It might be a very short trip!" the mustachioed man said, and stormed out of the lounge just as the orchestra started up another waltz.

"I think the captain and his men know a lot more than they're telling us," Frohman said. "I don't like it."

"Are you afraid, sir?" Edward asked.

Frohman considered a moment. "No. I think we could use a bit of mystery and excitement. Eight days on a boat isn't exactly a romp."

"Even if the ship is speeding toward a war zone?"

"I don't know if you've noticed but I'm not so sure we're speeding," Frohman said.

"What do you mean?" Edward responded. "The *Lusitania* is the fastest ship in the world."

"So she is," Frohman said. "But this doesn't feel like full speed to me."

"A question for Captain Turner," Vanderbilt said dryly.

"He's not much for socializing with passengers," Edward said. "He hosted only one captain's table when I sailed on her two weeks ago."

"Now that's a scandal an English gent can really get his ascot in a knot over," Frohman said wryly.

Edward glared at the theatre impresario. The man smiled back.

"I assume you're on your way to London to take in some shows?" Edward asked Frohman to ease the tension.

"I am," he said. He fished around in his trousers pocket and produced a sweet wrapped in wax paper. Edward bristled at the casual manner with which Frohman unwrapped the candy and popped it in his mouth as though he were a boy of ten. "I go twice a year."

"And you weren't nervous taking a British ship?" Vanderbilt asked.

Frohman sucked on the candy, relishing the rapt attention of the men who surrounded him. Then with a mighty crunch his teeth cracked the sweet in half. Edward raised an eyebrow at the sound. He wondered if he should excuse himself and return to Brooke but he saw with alarm that she had abandoned the matron and her daughter and was now chatting with that group of theatricals who were sailing with Frohman. There was no escape.

Frohman swallowed the candy as he rocked back and forth on his feet, using his cane for balance. "Put it this way, I had plenty of friends and business associates beg me to take an American ship. But I've always liked the *Lusy*. Though as a precaution I did dictate my program for the next season and left it with my secretary." Frohman smiled. "Have a good evening, gentlemen."

The little group dispersed but Edward caught Vanderbilt's attention. "Mr. Vanderbilt," Edward began. "I shouldn't be too alarmed by the German spies."

"You know something the rest of us don't?" he asked.

Edward shook his head. "Afraid not. But I do know some very good men in the Admiralty and they assured me the *Lusitania*'s safety is a top priority," he said confidently.

Vanderbilt extended his hand and the men shook on it as though a wager had been placed. "Then we have nothing to worry about," he said, and walked away.

MAY 2

Sydney

The low deep moans had continued throughout the night. The sound was eerie, as though a great beast was emitting a long sorrowful wail. The first time Sydney heard it she had sat up in bed, the covers clutched to her for safety. Such a ghostly groan. It sounded like something was beneath her, haunting the sea, shadowing the *Lusitania*. She feared it was a submarine but one got such crazy notions in the middle of the night. Eventually she calmed down and remembered: Mr. Garrett had explained to her how the ship's hull was designed so that it moved subtly against the tide otherwise the pressure would crush her. It was no different from how a skyscraper was designed to sway in high winds, he had told her. Only people standing on the fiftieth floor didn't hear the motion, she planned on telling him when she got home. It didn't lessen her anxiety that she was alone for the first time in her life. Her father or Brooke had always been near her as she slept. But her snap decision at the pier had forcibly removed such comfort. *I bet the moans are barely discernible in the Regal Suite.*

She looked out the porthole. It was morning yet she couldn't see the sun. The sky was a dark heaving mass of grey clouds and rain was pelting down on the ocean.

She was thankful that yesterday's *mal de mer* had vanished and as she dressed all she could think of was breakfast. Well, that and whether she shouldn't give in and join her sister and Edward. The food in first class would be gorgeous. Yet for all of Sydney's good-naturedness and passion to do good she was also extremely stubborn—a trait that was a Sinclair gene—and there would be no admitting defeat, not *yet*. She would wait for Brooke to meet her halfway and accept who she was. She would work on Edward too.

She was surprised by the quality of her breakfast. She'd gone to the early seating and while the food was a simple plate of eggs and rashers of bacon with toast and marmalade, it was fresh and prepared perfectly. What more could a person want?

She had brought her overcoat and a hat, determined to stroll outside on the deck despite the weather. As soon as she opened the door she regretted it. The sea was the colour of slate; a dark grey-blue mass that rolled with a life of its own, folding in on itself, white foam cresting and roiling over and over. Sydney could feel its power tugging at the ship as she stood at the rail. The water appeared cold and unwelcoming, very unlike the summer beachfronts of Nantucket that had been such a wondrous part of her growing up. This Atlantic was bewitching but also something to be feared. She shuddered at the thought of the many lives it had swallowed whole over the course of mankind's desire to triumph over her.

To her surprise a seagull soared in front of her, keeping pace alongside the ship, floating with ease on the wind. How was it able to survive out here? There was no land in sight. Did it fly for hours, then rest on the surface of the ocean? The bird was so graceful and peaceful. It swooped down and Sydney leaned over the wet railing to watch where it was going.

"Be careful, Miss," a voice called to her. She turned to see a junior officer approach. He wasn't especially tall and had dark hair and equally dark eyes. His full lips parted to allow a polite smile but Sydney knew he wasn't looking to pass the time.

"You'd be more comfortable inside," he said firmly but kindly. "The weather isn't going to clear all day and we're entering rough seas. It's for your safety."

"What is your name, officer?"

"Bestic, ma'am. I'm the junior third officer, at your service."

"Can't I have a few moments more?" she asked. "The fresh air helps with seasickness."

Bestic began to look nervous. "I can't allow that. Sorry, ma'am."

"It's Sydney," she said. "What is your Christian name?"

Bestic hesitated a moment. "Albert."

"Just ten minutes, Albert, then I'll go inside."

But Bestic stood his ground and she knew she was beaten. "Very well," she said glumly, and walked away from the railing. He escorted her toward the door. "What is it you do on the ship, Albert?" she asked. The question seemed to make the young officer uneasy for he began to cast glances about as though the question had been a trap.

"I have many duties, ma'am," he said. "I have watches on the bridge, make entries in the logbook, perform midnight inspections of the ship and ensure the baggage is safe and secure."

Sydney grinned. "Have you always wanted to sail?" She could see that he didn't want to be talking further but he was too inexperienced to know how to extricate himself from the questions of a female passenger and that amused her. Besides, she hadn't spoken two words to anyone since last night's dinner and she liked the company.

"I'm from Ireland," he admitted, his eyes still darting around in case a superior caught him extending his conversation.

"How lovely!" she exclaimed. "You do have a wonderful accent."

At this Bestic blushed. "Thank you, ma'am. When I was about eighteen I saw the *Lusitania* on the River Clyde when my family was holidaying in Scotland. I said to myself that if ever I could work on a ship like the *Lusy* then I'd go to sea."

"And here you are," she said. "I'm envious of you."

"You wanted to be a sailor?" he asked incredulously. Sydney smiled and shook her head.

"It isn't as easy for a woman to follow her dreams," she explained. "But I'm happy yours came true."

Their conversation was interrupted by the sound of men above banging and shouting. "Good Lord, what is that commotion?" Sydney asked, and looked to Bestic for reassurance.

The young man smiled. "That's the crew doing their lifeboat drill. We do it each morning," he explained. "There are two boats that are kept swung out over the side in case of emergencies . . ."

She arched her brows. "Emergencies?" When he hesitated she understood. "You mean in case someone falls overboard?"

"Exactly," he acknowledged.

"Good heavens, does that happen often?" she asked, thinking how far she had leaned to watch the seagull.

"Almost never," he said.

Another man's voice shouted from above, "Man the boats!" The call was followed by a series of footsteps and the clattering of men slipping inside the lifeboats.

"Drill's almost done," he said to Sydney.

"Officer Bestic!" came another shout only this time from behind them. They turned and saw another ship's officer hastening toward them.

Sydney guessed that this was Bestic's superior, unhappy that he had spent so long chatting with her. "I'm so sorry. I've kept Mr. Bestic longer than I should," she explained. "And you are?"

"First Officer Jones," he answered.

"Well, First Officer Jones, this is my first voyage and he was answering questions I had."

Jones gave Bestic a disapproving glance before pasting a smile on his face to appease Sydney. "If you have any questions, ma'am, I'm sure I can answer them for you."

Sydney didn't like Jones's condescending manner, like he was dismissing her concerns as childish.

"Very well. I want to know about the lifeboats," she said sternly, even though the thought had only occurred to her this instant when she'd heard the drill.

"What about them would you like to know?" Jones answered impatiently.

"Are there enough of them? We all know what happened on the *Titanic*," she said sharply.

Jones's smile was unchanged though his tone grew even more patronizing. "In the three years since that awful tragedy, Cunard has seen to outfit the *Lusitania*, and all her fleet, with enough lifeboats to ensure, in the case of an emergency, everyone can be saved."

Sydney kept staring at him. "And how many would that be?"

It was clear from his sour expression that Jones wasn't enjoying this one bit. But Bestic piped up. "She has twenty-two standard lifeboats and twenty-six collapsibles. When we enter the war zone the captain will order the davits be swung out on all of them as a precaution."

"Bestic," Jones warned. Bestic stood at attention in silence.

"Don't snap at him, Officer Jones, he was merely answering a concerned passenger's question when you didn't."

She could see Jones steaming now. But she wanted him calm so he didn't take his anger out on poor Bestic. "I heard the drill just now. When will there be one for the passengers?" she asked. She had read about such practices in a magazine before they sailed. It seemed like a wise idea yet there had been no announcements of such a thing.

"The captain feels it is unnecessary and may alarm passengers," Jones explained.

"But clearly you do drills each morning with the crew. Not giving us the same skills seems rather reckless, wouldn't you agree?" she asked. Neither man would look at her now. "Well? Will neither of you answer me?"

Jones looked at her again. "I think there is nothing to worry about. This is the *Lusitania*'s two hundred and second crossing and she's never given cause for alarm."

"Yes, but that German warning," Sydney said. "Surely we need to take extra steps to ensure safety."

"You can trust Captain Turner," Jones insisted. "He's in constant communication with the Admiralty. Should there be any need for concern he knows how to handle it."

"The *Lusitania* is also faster than any submarine, ma'am," Bestic spoke up again. "They can't do faster than nine or twelve knots. We can go as fast as twenty-four."

Sydney took this fact in and it mollified her. "And are we going that fast?" she asked simply.

"Not as yet," Jones said. "We're conserving her for when we enter the war zone."

This would have made her feel more confident if she hadn't caught a brief glance between the officers that said differently.

"Please tell Captain Turner that the passengers would like a lifeboat drill," she said. Sydney hadn't brought it up to anyone, nor had she heard mention of such a drill but for some reason once it was in her head it became very urgent.

"We will pass along your concerns. But I would like to add, if it's of comfort to you, that should a rare incident occur that requires passengers to abandon ship the *Lusitania* would remain afloat for at least a few hours so we could calmly load everyone on board into the lifeboats."

"Very well then." She spoke just as the ship crashed through a large wave and she teetered against the rail. Her eyes cast down into the heaving slate sea. Bestic pulled her away from the rail.

"You're okay," he said soothingly. "You weren't even close to falling overboard."

"You're right," she said, somewhat embarrassed by her decided lack of sea legs. "It's just that I don't know how to swim."

Jones and Bestic exchanged looks, as though this was the reason behind her nagging questions.

"You won't need to know," Jones said, more kindly. "You'll arrive safe and sound on dry land soon enough. Enjoy your day, ma'am."

The two officers marched away and up the steel staircase to the bridge. Sydney continued her walk along the deck, hugging the wall as she went, avoiding the railing at all costs. She was headed to her berth. But a few strides later her foot stepped onto a wet patch of deck and she slid and slipped toward the railing and nearly fell to her knees. She crouched there a moment, afraid to move, wondering how close she might have come to falling overboard, when an unfamiliar Englishman's voice spoke.

"Are you quite all right?"

The man held his hand out to her. She took it and rose to her feet, flushed with embarrassment. "Thank—thank you," she stammered. "I slipped."

He grinned. "You weren't anywhere near close enough to going over. I would have caught you before you had anyway."

Sydney peered cautiously over the railing. He was right. She was being ridiculous. She studied her rescuer. He wasn't a tall man, and was of slight build, but there was something pleasing in his manner. He was handsome and had a boyish glint in his eye that intrigued her.

"Thank you for helping me," she said. "Mr.—?"

"Dawson," he said, and stuck his hand out. "But call me Walter."

"Sydney Sinclair," she said as they shook hands. Her eyes glanced about the deck. They were the only two people braving the weather. "Are you sailing alone?"

"Yes," he explained. "I have a family. A wife and daughter, they sailed ahead and are waiting for me in Yorkshire. And yourself?"

Sydney wasn't sure how to answer. This man was a complete stranger. "Yes," she said simply, preferring to keep the truth to herself. "Have you sailed often, Walter?"

"Not really. I'm only a tradesman," he explained. "Paint and wallpaper. I make rich people's houses pretty."

He walked toward the Bostwick gate that separated third from first, the very same one she had discovered yesterday, and gestured for Sydney to follow him. She did. He put his hands on the gate like it was bars on a jail cell and shook.

"You shouldn't do that!" she gasped. "What if you're caught trying to get in?"

"You mean what if we're caught?" he teased, and gave the gate another shake but it wouldn't yield.

Sydney was truly alarmed; she couldn't risk being caught breaking through gates. "You keep doing that if you want but I'm leaving."

"That's the first class dining saloon just over there," Walter said. Sydney peered through the gate. She imagined that Brooke and Edward were sitting down to a handsome breakfast.

"I'd love to take a gander inside and see how the other half lives. People like us don't often get to see how they behave amongst themselves. It's like watching a play," he said, then added, "or maybe it's more like a zoo." He continued to stare through the gate with the curiosity of an anthropologist. Sydney tugged at his sleeve. He stepped back. "Have you read about the ceiling in there?" he asked. Sydney hadn't. "First of all the dining saloon is three decks high and capped off with a domed canopy. I'm dying to see the painted panels, I hear there's one for each month of the year."

"You don't say?" Sydney asked. She wanted to be interested but all she could think about was getting as far away from this famous room as possible before someone recognized her. But Walter wouldn't be deterred.

"The chairs swivel and are covered in velvet. The whole place is in colours of ivory and gold." He shook his head in amazement. "I got to get inside the first class areas. Just to see."

She smiled. He was passionate about décor, that was certain. It would be easy to take him where he wanted to go; all she had to do was present her first class ticket.

"The upper level seats 321 passengers, the lower 143," he continued.

"I'm sure if you ask they will let you have a look," she suggested.

Walter made a face. "Unlikely. But maybe once we're in Liverpool and the swells have disembarked."

She laughed. "And you do this decorating work in England?"

He shook his head. "In Lowell. It's outside Boston," he continued. "But I'm going home to join up."

"That's brave of you," she said, sensing his thoughts had drifted away from the inner lives of the wealthy to more meaningful matters. "When you could have waited out the war in America."

They walked through the door into the third class entrance and she shivered at the sudden warmth.

"My family has fought in every war as far back as anyone can remember," Walter explained. "My older brothers, Herbert and Francis, are already on the front. I had a letter from Herbert before I sailed. It's my duty as an Englishman and as a Dawson."

When they reached the staircase Sydney held out her hand again. "Nice to meet you, Walter. Have a lovely voyage."

"The *Lusitania* isn't that big." He grinned, the glint having returned. "I'm sure we'll be seeing each other again."

She took the steps nearly two at a time. She wanted to change her clothes and get a hot bath to take the chill off. But mostly she wanted to put some distance between herself and her sister. Walter wanted to get an inside look at rich folk, her rich folk. Yet those people didn't seem any more like her than Walter did. Maybe she didn't belong anywhere.

Isabel

There was a newsstand down the street from the boarding house. The newsagent was an old man who was nearly deaf, so that when he shouted the headlines loud enough that he could hear himself it would often cause passersby to jump out of their skins, a fact that he learned to enjoy, particularly at the expense of young ladies. But when he spotted Isabel moving toward him, her shoulders slightly slumped, with a stern expression, he kept quiet. When she arrived to buy a paper he smiled; his mouth was missing several teeth and the few that remained were stained a nutty brown from tobacco.

"Miss Isabel!" he shouted. "Lovely to have a weekend off. You enjoying it so far?"

Isabel couldn't manage a smile. "Not exactly."

The man was undeterred. "On your way to meet your beau? 'Tis Sunday afternoon—romantic, ain't it?"

"I don't have a beau."

He seemed disappointed to learn this. "N'ver mind. You'll meet the right chap soon enough."

Isabel was content to let him think her sour mood was due to a lack of romance. She paid him for the *Times*. She didn't want to return to the boarding house. The other girls would be lolling about on their day off and would be chattering about boys and other nonsense. None of them knew what sort of job she had but they were accustomed to her not joining in on their conversations. How different from her time with Mr. Chamberses' when she would delight in lengthy discourse.

It was an evening at the end of last August when Isabel carried a silver tray with a crystal whisky decanter and three glasses into the Chamberses' parlour. The third glass struck her as odd since there were only two gentlemen to serve. It was a room that Mrs. Chambers had spent an extraordinary sum decorating. Velvet brocade and satin stripe, maroon and gold, cherry and mahogany, altogether the parlour was warm and welcoming if not altogether too much. There was even a palm tree in one corner to evoke the tropics. Isabel always thought it an odd touch in a room that otherwise brought to mind a brothel. Not that she'd ever seen one with her own eyes. But she'd read novels and seen enough illustrations in magazines to guess that if Mrs. Chambers ever wanted a career as a madam she had the knack for ensuring the right atmosphere.

"Thank you, Isabel." Mr. Chambers smiled at her. She smiled back. He was a very attractive man. All the servant girls thought so. He did seem to like her particularly, showing deference to her by giving her the newspaper to read when he was finished, asking about her family and education. She placed the tray on the table.

"Shall I pour, sir?"

"Indeed." It was the other gentleman who spoke, a Mr. Leslie Lambert, who was a writer. He and Mr. Chambers were friends and shared the unusual hobby of intercepting wireless transmissions from their home stations. Isabel poured the drink. "I've got another story for you to read, Isabel."

"I very much enjoyed the last three, Mr. Lambert." She wasn't just being kind; the stories that he wrote were full of intrigue and suspense. Far from the Jane Austen novels she loved, his were tales of crime and ghosts. Her mother wouldn't have approved, but Isabel omitted such things from her letters home.

"I'm going to teach Isabel Morse code," Mr. Chambers announced. "I've enrolled her in a night course on typing and shorthand too. With this war we'll need all the able bodies we can get. Especially with so many men signing up."

She stood blinking. This was news to her. Mr. Lambert laughed good-naturedly. "Don't look so frightened, Isabel. It's not a punishment."

"I'd be honoured to learn," Isabel said as she looked at Mr. Chambers. "I want to be useful."

"Then you shall," he said. "My wife will be away next month for an entire fortnight. That will be our chance."

Lambert put his tumbler down empty. Isabel leaped to refill it. "Only finish pouring my drink if you give yourself one too," he said, and looked to Chambers for affirmation.

Isabel froze. "Go on, Isabel, that third glass is for you. You're done for the day. Mrs. Chambers is in London until tomorrow. Have a seat and join us. I know how interested you are in hearing about what's going on with the war."

Isabel didn't need convincing. She poured the whisky and sat across the room, so as not to appear forward, and sipped the drink. She'd never had whisky before. It was a man's drink. But it didn't take more than a few sips before she realized she'd been missing it her whole life. The men went on to discuss the war, going into details that she didn't understand. She asked the occasional question and they took patience explaining it to her. Then their conversation diverted back to their wireless work. They spoke about secret codes and systems of encryption. It was like they were speaking a foreign language. To Isabel it was the start of her education though she didn't know it at the time.

Mr. Chambers had honoured his promises from that night. He took time to teach Isabel rudimentary Morse code, emphasizing that she

memorize the sounds rather than the dots and dashes. She loved learning. It made her feel like she was one of the Oxford students getting private tutorials. At night she would lie in bed and imagine one day reading
engineering at the university—a girl among men, their equal in intellect
if not opportunity.

But there was more to their time together and thinking of it now
pained Isabel. The first time Mr. Chambers, George, kissed her had been
after one of their study sessions. His wife was away again visiting a friend
in Bristol, which had allowed him and Isabel an especially late evening.
It was nearly midnight when he offered her a drink.

"I shouldn't," she told him. "I must be up early to start my chores."

The way he looked at her made her self-conscious and she stood up from
the desk to leave him alone in his study. She was nearly at the door when he
grabbed her and spun her around, holding her tightly in his arms.

"Isabel, you must know how I feel about you by now?" he had said, and
stroked her face. His touch was so gentle and soft. "You're as beautiful as
you are intelligent."

Never before had anyone, not even her mother, told her such things. A
man of his stature fussing over the likes of her? It was thrilling. *He* was
thrilling. "You flatter me, Mr. Chamber—" she began but he cut her off.

"Call me George," he said, and without another word kissed her on the
lips. The kiss was only the beginning . . . *If I had been as intelligent as he
said then I would have resisted.*

Isabel had decided that night that she was in love with George
Chambers and he did nothing to discourage her. They became lovers and
spent many a night tucked away in the spare bedroom. It was a small bed
made of dark polished wood; its covering wasn't glamorous, as one might
expect for an illicit tryst, but of white cotton patterned with yellow roses
and a lace frill around its edges. But it was a room that Mrs. Chambers
never bothered with because it was on the topmost floor, across from
George's office, and the narrow staircase made her nervous for there was
no handrail and she was a large woman. After their lovemaking Isabel
would lie in George's arms and they would discuss her studies, the war

and his promise to one day leave his wife and marry her. *I was a fool to believe him.*

Their time in Oxford seemed long ago as Isabel sat on a bench in a park to read the paper. The sun was warm and the air fragrant with spring blossoms and wet grass. It was a happy day for most and she watched young children playing on the lawns, their mothers minding them nearby. A few couples strolled hand in hand. She envied them a little.

The paper was full of coverage of the war. More details were emerging on the mustard gas used by the Germans. She read about the Battle of St. Julien where Canadian troops had held off the enemy until reinforcements arrived, battling through despite machine-gun fire and the poisoned air, vomiting from it and using muddied handkerchiefs to breathe through it, their guns jamming at nearly every turn. It was terrible. In the end the Canadians won but paid the price; more than two thousand of them had perished.

Isabel sometimes had to force herself to read these stories. But it was necessary fuel to keep her and the others motivated to work day and night. She turned the page. It was full of advertisements for ladies' fashions, but at the bottom corner was a notice. Normally she didn't pay attention to advertisements but this one screamed for attention despite its small size. It announced that yesterday, May 1, 1915, the RMS *Lusitania* had sailed from New York, headed to Liverpool, scheduled to arrive on May 8. This wasn't news to Isabel. But it was an alarming reminder. Rotter had told her that the right people would be told about the position of U-20. *The men know what to do better than me.* She repeated these words over and over in her mind but it was no use. She folded up the paper and threw it away.

Sydney

She passed the entire afternoon reading over the women's movement literature she'd brought with her—pamphlets printed by several of the groups she had joined as well as articles torn from magazines and newspapers. She had also packed a couple of samples of newly designed prophylactics—risky contraband to be sure—to deliver to Margaret Sanger's group when she went to London after the wedding. It was comforting to immerse herself in this work. *This is my life, my new life.* Then it occurred to her. Why wait to return to New York to spread the word of Margaret Sanger? There was something she could do about her work right now on this ship.

The third class ladies' lounge was nearly filled to capacity with women old and young seeking a refuge from the rain and wind. Sydney's entrance drew only cursory glances. But it was as good a start as any.

"Dear ladies," she began, but when no one noticed her standing by the door she repeated her words more loudly. "Dear ladies! May I have your attention?"

It worked. The women were staring at her with a mixture of annoyance and alarm. Sydney swallowed. "I wanted to see if anyone here was interested in learning about the work of Margaret Sanger?"

She waited for a show of hands, an affirming nod, anything but the bemused silent audience before her. Undeterred, Sydney continued without the encouragement of her fellow passengers. "Margaret Sanger, as some of you may know, is an advocate of birth control. And as we are sequestered here in a so-called room for ladies, I feel we can take advantage of our joint seclusion from men and discuss the future of our sex."

They started leaving one by one. Filing past Sydney and out the door with dirty glances and derisive clucking beneath their breath. One woman firmly gripping the hand of her young daughter "accidentally" kicked Sydney's shin as she passed by. For her part Sydney was unmoved by their protests and focused on the handful of women who remained.

"There's a movement in America and in England that seeks to educate women on sex and birth control and I have literature here for any of you who wish to know more. And I can tell you what I've seen at abortion clinics in New York and it's not the conditions we'd wish on our daughters."

That seemed the last straw for within moments she stood alone in the ladies' lounge, the fistful of pamphlets at her side.

"Excuse me, Miss?"

She turned around and saw a stern-looking steward standing in the doorway. *Oh bother.*

"Yes?" she asked calmly.

"We've had complaints from some of the other passengers that you have been"—the steward hesitated as though his next words might pain him—"you have been talking about inappropriate things."

"Filth! That's what she's been spreading!" The voice came from the passageway. Sydney looked over the steward's shoulder and found a small woman about the same age as herself standing there, arms folded. "Filth and lies. She's a bad influence."

"I did not lie," Sydney argued.

"I suggest we leave the ladies' lounge now," the steward suggested. "Let me escort you to your berth."

The woman looked pleased with herself. Sydney set her jaw and didn't budge. "I'm no liar and I'm not spreading filth. You, sir, may also wish to learn about contraception to prevent unwanted babies."

"That's it, Miss," the steward said, and grabbed her arm, sending the pamphlets scattering to the floor.

"Unhand me," she snapped, and freed herself to pick them up. "I'll leave but I don't need an escort."

Sydney gathered her papers and walked out the door. The woman sneered at her as she passed by. "Just because we're booked in third don't mean we have to put up with the likes of her. We're people too!"

The steward kept pace behind her as she moved along the deck. His presence irritated her. She wasn't accustomed to being asked to leave *anywhere* and the experience was humiliating but at the same time it strengthened her resolve. These women needed to learn the truth about their bodies.

She walked by the locked Bostwick gate, just behind the second funnel and forward of the first class entrance where she and Walter had been only a few hours earlier. All she had to do was present her first class ticket and she'd be admitted. She wondered what her sister would think if she presented her pamphlets to the first class ladies. She stopped and looked through the metal gate.

"Move along, Miss," the steward said in an official and annoyed tone.

It was then that she saw Alfred Vanderbilt walking down the steps on the other side. She considered running away but it was too late. He'd seen her.

"Good heavens, Sydney!" Alfred shouted, and ran to the gate, trying to open it. He shouted at the astonished steward, "Unlock this at once. This is Sydney Sinclair. She and her sister are sailing in the Regal Suite."

The steward panicked and began to fumble for the keys.

"No, don't bother," she said, and smiled at Alfred. "Didn't Brooke tell you? I bought a third class ticket."

Alfred was taken aback. "You did what?"

She laughed. "You heard me correctly. I thought it would be fun," she said. "Instead I managed to empty the ladies' lounge and get escorted here by this charming steward."

Alfred looked past her and glared at the man who withered under the scrutiny.

"What happened?"

"Oh you know me. I was trying to educate women," she answered.

"Let me guess." He grinned. "Your political views upset the ladies?"

She showed him the pamphlets. He glanced at them only briefly.

"Ah, Sydney. At least you didn't get arrested this time," he said warmly.

"You heard about that?" she asked. Of course he had.

"Are you sure you won't join me for dinner this evening?" he asked, politely dropping the matter.

She shook her head. "Thank you, Alfred. But I prefer to stay here."

"As you wish," he said. "Although I wager you will be the one who receives an education."

He walked away and she turned and smiled at the steward.

"I'm sure you—you can find your own way from here," he stammered.

"Yes, thank you," she said.

Edward

L unch in the first class saloon was a lively affair. The air was buzzing with the latest chatter, which of course was dominated by the war and submarines. The threat had become somewhat of a hobby to pass the time. The tables for the first seating were nearly full when Edward saw Alfred Vanderbilt arrive, search the room and make a beeline for him and Brooke. Edward rose to greet him.

"Brooke," Alfred said with a grin, after a nod for Edward.

She was elated that he had selected them as luncheon companions. "So lovely to see you, Alfred. Have you enjoyed the voyage so far?"

Edward shook hands with Alfred just as the soup course—tomato bisque—was being served from a large white porcelain tureen. He sat down and was content to eat his soup and quietly observe Alfred as he chatted to Brooke.

He was a formidable man. He ran huge companies and made a fortune with shrewd real estate deals. He also had a fine eye for horses and had purchased several of England's best Thoroughbreds for breeding. Alfred was what Englishmen of Edward's ancestry distrusted most: a refined American. Nothing of the crude or crass was present in Vanderbilt's appearance or manner even though the whole world knew of the scandal that had rocked his first marriage. Yet here he was, unashamed, as though what had happened was as insignificant as the colour of socks he wore. Edward peered down. They were deep burgundy. His own were a more practical, albeit typical, dark grey. *If I had a fraction of his wealth I would wear socks the colour of daffodils.* And the worse part of all was, try as he might, he could not help liking the man.

"I wanted to ask after your sister, Sydney," Alfred began.

Edward balked slightly at the sound of her name. Brooke put her spoon down as though her appetite had vanished. "Yes, Alfred. What about her?"

"I spoke with her this afternoon," he said. "She's quite a girl, sailing in steerage."

The spoon Edward was holding slipped from his fingers and fell with a splash into the bowl of soup. His shirt and jacket got the worst of it and were splattered with the thick red liquid.

"Edward! Your clothes!" Brooke gasped.

To his credit Vanderbilt didn't even smile; he looked on with as much concern as a stained shirt could arouse. "If you need help my valet, Ronald, is very good with stains," he offered kindly.

Edward bristled. "My own valet will suffice, but thank you," he said, and began to dab his shirt with a napkin. He knew that the stain would set if he didn't immediately get it to Maxwell and a bottle of soda but he wasn't about to leave now.

"Edward isn't usually so clumsy," Brooke said, excusing her fiancé. Then she turned to Alfred. "Yes, well, you know Sydney," she said politely, and waved to a waiter. The waiter came at once. "Can you bring some soda water?"

The waiter looked on the spilled soup and sodden shirt with alarm. "Yes, Miss." When he dashed away she turned to Alfred and laughed. "She always has been independent."

Alfred agreed. "That she is. She got into trouble earlier by spreading the gospel about birth control to unappreciative ladies in the third class lounge."

Edward wasn't sure he'd heard correctly. "She did what?" he asked.

"Sydney's a suffragette, with a keen interest in reproductive rights," Alfred explained carefully. "But of course you know all about it, I'm sure."

"Of course," Edward lied. His mind raced back to the engagement dinner and his brief exchange with Sydney about Margaret Sanger. He stared at Brooke but she wouldn't look at him. "Is that the real reason she didn't join us for dinner or breakfast or lunch? She prefers the company of third class to ours?"

Alfred appeared uncomfortable. "I seem to have opened up a can of worms."

"Don't fret, Alfred," Brooke said, and turned to Edward. "Yes, I should have told you. I didn't think you'd be interested in my sister's odd pursuits. Sydney likes to experience life from all angles. She was curious, that's all. This women's voting and birth control, it's all a phase." Brooke laughed half-heartedly. "I'm sure she'll be in the Regal Suite by breakfast tomorrow."

Edward contained his irritation. He was furious that his fiancée and her sister had concealed Sydney's travel arrangements. It was as though his opinion didn't matter. Like he was a child being left out of adult conversation and shooed away.

"What difference does it make?" Alfred said cheerfully. "Let her have an adventure. Her fellow passengers are probably a lot more fun than we are. And as you say, she is independent. It's why so many young men in New York are terrified of her."

Edward was taken aback by such a description. "Is that so?" he asked.

Alfred grinned. "Positively terrified. She's beautiful, rich and full of strong opinions, what's more terrifying than that?"

Edward grimaced as the waiter returned and helped to dab his shirt with the soda. "Indeed I can think of nothing more off-putting in a female," Edward responded, hating the image he was projecting. Brooke forced a smile, which he took for approval.

"It's not very English, I'll give you that," Alfred said. His voice jolted Edward from his thoughts, which was a relief. "There are a lot of changes happening. The war with Germany is only the beginning. The twentieth century is going to rock the establishment in ways we can't even imagine as we sit here enjoying a seven-course lunch brought to us on silver trays by waiters wearing white gloves. But mark my word, the world as we know it, that's you and me, Edward, will be unrecognizable and sooner than we'll likely be comfortable with."

Another waiter brought out lamb with mint sauce. Edward picked up his knife and fork and stabbed the pink meat with all his might. Change wasn't a topic he wanted to discuss. Over the past year he'd heard enough about what the future held or didn't hold, but he didn't want to think of it now.

"My, you men are all the same," said Brooke, injecting her words with a teasing tone. "You worry so much about what hasn't happened that you neglect what is in front of you."

Edward finished a mouthful of lamb and sipped wine to wash it down. "Perhaps you're right. And in that regard, try and have Sydney move back up here with us for the remainder of the voyage," he said flatly. "In fact why don't I speak to her and set her straight?"

Alfred and Brooke exchanged looks. "I think it's best if I do," Brooke said, and squeezed Edward's hand. "Sisterly advice."

"I insist," Edward said firmly. "I saw her only yesterday on the bow and we got on very well."

Brooke's hand froze. "You never told me," she said, a hint of accusation in her tone.

"It would seem neither of us tell each other everything," Edward said, and sipped wine. "It's like we're married already."

Sydney

Two men were playing a game of shuffleboard as Sydney approached along the starboard side. In good weather the shuffleboard courts would be in constant demand but on a day like this? Those men must be very bored. As she drew closer she saw that one of them was Walter. He had seen her too.

"Looking to spy on the saloon class again?" he called out jokingly.

The other man stared at him aghast. But Sydney smiled and came toward them.

"Hello, Walter."

"It's not exactly a fine day for a stroll," he said.

"You're here," she pointed out. "Besides, I like this weather. Makes me feel alive."

"Makes me sneeze," the other man said, and coughed to get her attention.

"Forgive me, Sydney," Walter said, and tossed his mate a look of disapproval. "This is my friend Frederick Isherwood."

"Nice to meet you," she said. He was another Englishman. "You look like you're about to start a game of shuffleboard."

"Pass the time well enough, I reckon," Frederick said, and tossed a cigarette overboard.

"You want to play?" Walter asked.

"I would love to," she said, finding it ironic that moments before the women who she was trying to help had summarily rejected her, and now she was being taken in by a group of hard-working men. "Can the three of us play?"

"It's either for two or four," Walter explained as he smiled at his friend. "Fred here can keep score."

Frederick looked none too pleased being relegated to scorekeeper but he kept his mouth shut and held out the cue for Sydney.

"Come stand here with me behind the line," Walter explained, and Sydney did as she was told.

When she took the cue her topcoat opened revealing a navy dress with a dropped waist. Her gloves matched the dress. She wasn't bothered by the dampness and cold. She could feel the men watching her. A man like Walter who appreciated design and knew fabrics could probably tell her clothing was made to measure and from fine cloth. "So how does the game work?" she asked.

"The goal is to use the cue to slide the weights, which are called biscuits, across the court," he explained. "The aim is to put your own biscuit into the scoring area for points while pushing your opponent's biscuits off the court or into the minus zone at the back of the grid."

She listened intently to him and when he had finished she sized up the court as though there was some secret not yet revealed.

"Want me to take the first shot so you can see how it's done?" Walter offered.

"Ladies first," Frederick said. Walter glared at him, causing a sly smile to form across his lips.

Sydney aimed her cue at the red biscuit and with her eyes fixed firmly on the other end of the court she shoved the cue and sent the biscuit sliding down. The biscuit moved at a fair speed and settled within the lines of the bottom end of the triangle. Frederick's eyes popped. Walter clapped.

"That's seven points!" he said.

"Beginner's luck," she said appreciatively. "Now it's your turn."

Frederick had finished smoking his fifth cigarette by the time the game was over and Sydney had been declared the winner. He tossed the butt overboard and clapped his hands as much to keep warm as to applaud.

"You have a knack for sport," Frederick said, obviously bored out of his skull. "Let me guess, you probably ride to hounds in the spring, skate in the winter and dance all night in the summer?"

Sydney's expression hardened, which made him cough again. "You seem a bit critical of a woman's athletic abilities," she said, and fixed her eyes on him.

"He's feeling sorry for himself because he didn't play," Walter explained.

"I didn't mean anything by it," Frederick answered.

"Well, you're partially right about me," Sydney said firmly. "I do ride and I ride as well as any man on the hunt. I've never ice-skated, but I can ski. I've even raced a few times when I was younger. Beat most of the boys in the club too. And as for dancing—"

"You prefer to lead?" Frederick asked sarcastically.

Sydney blinked a few times and the three of them were silent.

"My wife likes to ice-skate," Walter said, breaking the silence.

"You never did explain why your family sailed ahead." Sydney said. Walter's face fell.

"Because of the Germans," Walter said. "Alice and my daughter, Muriel, she's two, will be safely at home in Elland by now."

"That seems very extreme," she said.

"Not really," Frederick said. "Fritz plans to blow up the ship." Sydney looked at him, then back to Walter.

"Frederick's right. The *Lusitania* is carrying contraband, ammunition for the war effort, and I'm afraid the Germans will target her just like that warning in the paper says."

Sydney was stunned. "That's a rumour."

Walter shook his head. "About a month back, after I'd bought passage on the *Lusy*, I saw it with my own eyes."

She did her best not to look worried. "Tell me everything."

Walter explained that he had gone to New York to pick up a shipment of supplies for his foreman. He despised this part of his job, and the wharfs. The shipyard docks were a haven for the disenchanted. Men who had been shipped to America in search of a new life now found they could never leave. The work was hard but it paid enough to feed their families and keep a roof over their heads, even if the roof was shared with other families from the same county or town they hailed from. But there was never enough work to go around to keep up with the flood of immigrants with little skills and even less hope.

Walter disliked the mess of the place. The stench of rotting fish and other food that had spoiled on its journey. The roughness of the men. More than once he'd observed fights break out between immigrant factions over who would get a job that morning.

"You need to sign for it here, Dawson," the duty officer had said, and handed Walter a clipboard with a clearance form to sign.

Walter scribbled his name. "Are you sure that's everything?" The shipment was smaller than usual and he didn't want to return to Lowell and hear about it. "Can I double-check?"

The duty officer looked over Walter's shoulder to the long line of men waiting for him. He scratched his chin. Walter saw that his nails were dirty and yellowed from smoke.

"Be quick," the man said, and hurried on to the man behind him. Walter took the list and walked back to where the shipment was sitting. He had only just begun his task when a firm grip on his shoulder told him it was about to be a very long day.

"Dawson!"

Walter turned to face Patrick O'Brien, a boy of nineteen he had met on the voyage over two years earlier. He had come to America trying for a boxing career. Patrick's nose had been broken three times and by the looks of it he had given up trying to have it mended. His coveralls were smeared with what looked like flour and blood, as though he had been baking a pie made with freshly killed meat.

"Hello, Patrick."

The young man helped Walter check off everything and to his relief it was all in order. There was a wagon waiting to cart the supplies to the train station and between the two of them it was loaded and on its way so quickly that Walter, checking his watch, saw he had another hour before the train left.

Patrick removed his hat and ran his fingers through greasy hair that had already begun to recede. "The *Lusitania* is in port. You want to have a look?"

Walter wasn't sure he wanted more time with Patrick but seeing the famous ship was irresistible. They passed through the remainder of the cargo docks, leaving behind a steady stream of goods waiting to enter New York. Everywhere men were shouting and cursing to duty officers and foremen about late or missing shipments as a few policemen stood streetside surveying the mayhem with bored expressions.

There was no mistaking her. The four black funnels rising above the pier shed caught Walter's eye first. He quickened his pace. When they got to her starboard side Walter drew his breath at the sight of her.

"She's magnificent," he exclaimed.

"That she is," Patrick agreed. "Now let's get closer." The young Irishman gestured to Walter to follow him and the two men walked nonchalantly through the Cunard gate like they belonged. Down on the dock Walter could see supplies being loaded onto the *Lusitania* for her next voyage. Patrick waved to one of the Cunard men who seemed to know him and came over. Walter was introduced to Dermot Eaves. He was much smaller than O'Brien and Walter was glad to be able to look him in the eye.

Patrick wasted no time telling Dermot that Walter was sailing on the ship in May. Dermot seemed unimpressed.

"I'm quitting once we get to Liverpool," Dermot said.

"Why is that?" Walter asked.

"Don't much like the captain," he said bluntly. "Morale isn't good either. Sailing through a war zone when half the men aren't skilled seamen hasn't helped. Many of the real sailors have gone off to fight on battle cruisers so that leaves Cunard picking up riff-raff for a ship like her. I'm not interested."

Walter was surprised to hear this yet it made perfect sense. He was off to fight, so too were thousands of others, all leaving their regular jobs to join the war.

"Then there are the rumours," Dermot continued. "Word is that the Jerrys plan to torpedo the ship."

"They'd never have the guts," Walter objected. His outburst drew a smile across Dermot's face.

"Every man on the docks has heard that since the blockade begun. Why else did Cunard lower ticket prices? Why else did the old captain fly an American flag when she entered the war zone? The docks are crawling with German spies too."

Walter was speechless. He scanned the dockyard. The many men darting about seemed like him; working class, trying to make a life, not wanting trouble.

"There are German workers all over the docks," Patrick agreed.

"But what are they looking for?" Walter demanded.

Dermot ran his tongue over his lips. "Can't tell you that or they'd hang me for treason," he said. Walter couldn't tell if he was teasing or not. "Let's just say that maybe those speculations of blockade-running are true. Or maybe they ain't."

B ut you didn't see the ammunition, did you?" Sydney said, relieved to point this out when Walter had finished his story.

"I didn't have to," Walter said. "The ship's manifests from previous voyages all have shrapnel and shell casings and rifles on them. It's not just this ship, Sydney, most of them do it. How else are we going to win the war? The Allies need ammunition."

"Then why did you sail on her?"

"I had no choice. I'd already bought passage for us on the *Lusitania*. I only had enough of our savings left to pay for Alice and Muriel's passage on the other ship."

The information was overwhelming. Sydney thought back to her discussion with Bestic about the lifeboats.

"Thank you for teaching me how to play, Walter," she said, and swallowed. "I think I will get some tea to warm up. Goodbye."

Sydney walked at a brisk pace, wanting to get some distance from Walter and Frederick and their tales of blockade-running. It was absurd. The British Admiralty would never endanger American lives.

Isabel

The night shift crew were known as the "watchmen." When Isabel had begun working in Room 40 she had assumed the name was a straight-up take on "keeping watch." She preferred to embellish its meaning with dark, even sinister undertones like in the spy stories she read. It was the romantic in her. It had proven disappointing when after several late nights she discovered that the watchmen did nothing more diabolical than play penny card games to pass the time awaiting the latest transmissions.

Such a game was in progress between Anstie, Norton and Henry when she entered after ten o'clock that night. "Who's winning?" she asked.

"We're all in debt to Anstie," said Norton.

She noticed that Henry had failed to acknowledge her. He must be angry at her after last night's spat with Mildred. Who knew what Mildred had told him? Isabel wanted to shake him until he came to his senses. Instead she ignored him. Two could play at that game.

"What are you doing here so late?" Anstie asked.

"I couldn't sleep, thought I'd come see what you lot were up to. Working hard, I see," she said, and lit a cigarette.

"It's been hellish this evening," Norton said. "We're glad for a respite."

"As bad as all that?" she asked.

Since Captain Hall's scheme to trick the Germans there had been a huge increase in wireless transmissions and the code breakers had been pulling double shifts. The Admiralty's goal had been that the Germans would divert forces away from France and head to the coast to await the British troops that would never arrive. The dispatched submarines, including U-20, had been part of the German strategy but from what Isabel could surmise neither this nor the fact that the Admiralstab was still broadcasting the *Lusitania*'s schedule seemed to be causing enough alarm for her liking. Though that was about to change . . .

"We got word over the wireless that the Germans ran an advert in the American papers warning passengers about their submarines," Norton told her.

Isabel felt the blood drain from her face. "They did what?"

"You heard right. Telling them that they would be in danger once they sailed into the war zone. But according to our sources the ship left New York with most of its passengers," he said. "I'm sure they thought it was just a scare tactic."

"Maybe that's all it is," Parish added.

"Did they alert the captain at last?" Isabel asked. "Surely Captain Hall and the Admiral would put two and two together?"

"And do what?" Norton scoffed. "You're forgetting one thing, Isabel." She was halfway through the cigarette. "What is that?"

Norton didn't look up from his cards. "The *Orion*."

The *Orion* was a battleship that had been docked at Devonport for some much-needed refitting. She was ready to rejoin the Grand Fleet, and the Admiral of the Fleet, John Rushworth Jellicoe, was desperate to have the ship back.

"What does the *Orion* have to do with the *Lusitania* sailing into a mass of submarines?" Isabel demanded. She stamped out her cigarette and stared at the pack in her hand. Another would be extreme. She reached for the bottle of whisky the men kept on hand and poured a shot, determined to make it last.

"I'll take one of those," Parish said.

She poured another and one for Rotter and put the glasses on the table in front of them. Henry was studying his cards like they held the key to the universe. She didn't bother to offer him a drink.

"The *Orion* is due to sail on May 4, day after tomorrow," Norton explained. "The Admiralty has ordered four destroyers as an escort. She's also being diverted away from the known submarine path based on our transcripts. That's the priority, dear Isabel. She's more valuable in wartime than a boatload of civilians."

Isabel drained the glass in one gulp. "Are you saying they are deliberately ignoring the *Lusitania*?"

Norton shook his head. "I'm saying they're distracted by the *Orion*."

Isabel didn't know what to do. So she went to her desk and found some leftover transmissions that needed typing. The deciphered codes were fairly routine broadcasts the Admiralstab sent to its navy about the weather patterns. But it gave her something to do. She couldn't go home. Not now.

Three cigarettes and half a glass of whisky later she was surprised when Henry skulked over and drew up a chair beside her. She refused to look at him and continued to type as though he wasn't there.

"Isabel," he said.

Type, type, type, she repeated the word to herself in rhythm. The Germans really were sticklers about temperature and barometric pressure.

"Isabel, I need to tell you something," he said. "It's important."

She inhaled sharply and her fingers fell to her lap. "What is it?" Before Henry could begin she started at him. "You've got a bloody nerve sitting next to me like we're still mates. You've hardly spoken to me outside of work since you began walking out with Mildred. Why should I listen to you now?"

She watched his Adam's apple move up and down as he swallowed. He was holding his hat, like he was preparing to leave for the night. It was too late for meeting his girl; he must be going home. Briefly Isabel considered taking the bus with him rather than travelling alone after midnight. But she quickly came to her senses. She'd leave shortly but not with Henry.

He picked up her glass and drank the remaining whisky. Isabel raised an eyebrow. "It's Mildred . . ." he began.

She rolled her eyes at the girl's name. "I don't give a fig about Mildred. Deal with your romance on your own, Henry. I've got work to do." She turned back to the transmits and started typing again.

"I shouldn't have said anything," he muttered. "I'm sorry. That's all."

He got up and left for the night. Isabel struggled to focus. She did give a fig about Mildred. The girl knew everything and couldn't be trusted.

The memory flooded through her. She had been wearing the red shoes. George had attended a lecture in London and had seen them at Selfridges and bought them for her. They had a small heel, the sort showgirls wore in revues. They were scandalous, especially given their colour—and were satin with straps that had rhinestone buckles. Evening shoes they were called. He'd bought a red lipstick for her on the trip before. She was also wearing another gift, a red negligee—yes, George had a thing for red. She'd never been given such gifts in her life. They made her feel beautiful and when she wore them she rather liked seeing the impact they had on George. He was an altered man. For once she was the one with power, at least over him.

That night they were in bed. They were kissing. They hadn't been alone together in a couple of weeks and couldn't get enough; there was no other way to account for the fact they didn't hear the footsteps on the stairs. Isabel saw her first. Mildred standing on the threshold, a look of disgust mixed with envy on her porcelain face. George threatened to sack her but it was no use. She was determined to "do the right thing." Mrs. Chambers came home to a whole pack of drama. Isabel was dismissed. But George wrote to Mr. Lambert and together they found her a position at the Admiralty. So much for love. Shortly thereafter Mildred was let go on George's insistence. And now she was here too, poised to destroy Isabel's life once again.

MAY 3

Sydney

I hear you and Edward had a fine time together after we sailed," Brooke said stonily. "Don't look surprised. We're engaged. We tell each other everything."

The sisters had found a small alcove near the third class entrance to meet. A determined yet shaky Sarah had summoned Sydney after breakfast and she had relented. She couldn't avoid her sister for the entire voyage; eventually they'd have to talk things through. She hadn't anticipated this particular line of conversation; if she didn't know better she'd say Brooke was jealous.

"I would expect you do," Sydney replied, equally stony. "So what about it? I didn't tell him anything if that's what you're worried about."

"Unfortunately that was part of the problem," Brooke said.

"I beg your pardon?"

"Alfred told him you're sailing in steerage and about your attempt to convert passengers to feminism. And now Edward thinks I lied to him." She paused, as though realizing this latter part were true. "Which I suppose I did but it was for his own good. And he feels you concealed it from him too."

Sydney rolled her eyes. "Because you asked me to. Ever since you returned from England you've done nothing but beg me to hide who I am from your precious Lord Muck."

"How dare you," Brooke said. "I would never beg."

"Whatever you want to call it," Sydney continued. "He's an English snob. Who cares what he thinks?"

"You may despise Edward but I do not," Brooke said.

"You don't despise him but you don't love him," Sydney responded. "I'm relieved he knows the truth. There are no secrets and clearly he hasn't called off the engagement. So the matter is closed."

She attempted to march away but Brooke grabbed a handful of her hair and yanked. Sydney gasped in pain and slapped her sister's hand away. "What on earth? We're not ten!"

"You don't understand, Sydney. We are landing in Liverpool on Saturday. That's still five days for Edward to stew over your—your—attitudes. He's not modern like Alfred and some of the others back home. He's traditional. Once we're in England and he's surrounded by his own kind he may change his mind about me and call off the wedding."

"What do you want me to do?" Sydney asked, rubbing her head.

Brooke smiled and gently held Sydney's chin in her hand. "Edward is determined to convince you to move back into the Regal Suite with me. He'll probably want to talk you out of your politics too. Just go along for now. Please," she said, her voice calm but steely.

Sydney pulled her face away. What was the point in continuing their fight? "Fine. I'll meet him and he can talk my ear off. But I'm not promising to move to first class or change my politics."

Brooke's face fell. "Just hear him out. He wants to meet you after lunch. I'll have him send a steward to fetch you."

It was like she'd given an order, for she didn't wait for Sydney to respond before she disappeared into the ship's interior. Sydney considered a walk around the deck to clear her head. But the gloominess of yesterday and of all the talk about blockade-running and contraband hadn't lifted and now with the added pressure of Edward looming before her, she wondered if it ever would.

A ren't you going to deny it?"

Isabel sat stiff-backed, knees touching, hands folded delicately in her lap and stared at Mrs. Burns.

"Is there any point in my denying it?" Isabel asked, her eyes never wavering, which seemed to unnerve Mrs. Burns for she began to pace.

"It's like you're daring me," the older woman said, walking back and forth. "You must have some evidence to refute the claim?"

Mrs. Burns stopped her pacing and stood in front of Isabel, imploring her to co-operate. Isabel wanted desperately to cross her legs. It was more comfortable than this formal posture but it was that type of thinking and carelessness that had landed her in this mess. What she wasn't, however, was a liar.

"I have none," Isabel said plainly. "I won't deny it because I cannot. It's done. It was part of my past—"

"Your recent past," Mrs. Burns interjected.

Isabel inhaled deeply, impatiently, as a mother would before explaining to a three-year-old why he cannot have chocolate for breakfast. "If you prefer, my *recent* past," she continued. "But I do a good job here and that should be all that matters."

Mrs. Burns swooped down toward Isabel so that she was leaning over her eye to eye. Isabel recoiled slightly but not from fear. The older woman's breath reeked of stale coffee.

"Aye, but it's not all that matters," she snapped. "I hire respectable young women here."

Isabel cowered at the words. Mrs. Burns stood up again as though sensing Isabel's discomfort, taking it for feminine weakness. She was wrong.

"I should be getting back to work," Isabel said impatiently, and stood up. She took a step toward Mrs. Burns's outraged face. "I'm needed."

"You are needed when and where I say you are," Mrs. Burns stated, and paused. Her hesitation seemed to fuel her anger. "You are suspended until further notice, Miss Nelson. And without pay."

Isabel's jaw went slack. "Suspended? Can you do that? What about the men?"

"Exactly, Miss Nelson. It is the men I'm thinking of. If what I'm told is true then I'm not sure you will return to work with the men at all."

Isabel's heart sank. "What am I to do?"

"That is for you to think on as I decide if I'm to terminate your employment altogether," Mrs. Burns said. Isabel was suddenly light-headed as though her knees might buckle and she would be sick. Mrs. Burns shook her head at the unfortunate girl. "I can't risk a girl like you, with your reputation, one you won't deny, and all those men who can't have distractions. We're fighting a war. There is no room here for loose women."

"I'm not a distraction," she said as she caught her reflection in an oval mirror hanging on the wall. The severe bun held against its will with too many bobby pins. Her face, bare and pale like a nun's. Her uniform of a plain grey skirt and a long-sleeved blouse that was at least one size too big. A less stylish ensemble would be difficult to imagine. No, Isabel considered, there was nothing to distract a man here.

The tears managed to elicit some sympathy for Mrs. Burns put her arm around Isabel as she led her to the door. She opened it and gently pushed her out. "You'll hear my decision soon. I have to think about it. Now go home and rest. It's a lovely day for a stroll."

It was true that the weather was fine, but the last thing Isabel wanted was a day off. Not when everyone else was hard at work without her. The thought of being unable to keep an eye on the Irish Sea and the *Lusitania* was unfathomable. There was only one person to blame.

"This is all because of Miss Fox," Isabel said. Mrs. Burns appeared shocked.

"Don't be accusing people, Miss Nelson."

"I don't have to because I know it's true. She warned me and I was too naïve to believe she'd do it. No one else but her could have said anything."

Isabel was angry now but she could see by Mrs. Burns's face that any sympathy she'd had for her was gone.

"Goodbye, Isabel," she said firmly. "I'll send for you when I've made my mind up."

The door closed on Isabel and she was alone in the hallway. She walked outside into the warm spring air and stood staring up at the place that had been more of a home to her these past few months than had anywhere in her life. The tears were back only this time she removed a handkerchief from her purse and dabbed at her eyes. The tears continued until her vision blurred and the building took on a fuzzy, dreamlike appearance. Then she remembered Henry's odd apology last night. He knew this was going to happen. He was trying to warn her. Good God. If Henry knew her secret perhaps all of Room 40 did. Isabel could hardly bear it.

Sydney

The hours passed slowly as though it was time itself that rolled beneath the hull, bow to stern. The foam streamers left in its wake were all that remained, bubbling over like freshly poured champagne before disintegrating into eternity. Sydney stood at the stern watching each minute dissolve on the ocean's surface.

"They call the wake the Cunard highway," Edward said. "Thank you for meeting me."

"My pleasure, Edward," she responded as she took in his grave expression. He was taking this talk too seriously as far as she was concerned. What did it matter where she laid her head as long as once they landed in England she stepped into the maid-of-honour role with the right amount of decorum. "You wanted to talk to me, so here I am." She had no time for silly patter. She wanted him to get to the point. Edward put his hands on the rail and stared out to sea.

"Do go on, Edward," she said. His continued silence was as pompous as his windowpane suit. "You look too serious for words."

He didn't answer. But his fingers were grasped tightly around the railing like he was holding on for dear life. The confidence she had found appealing in him in New York and even on the bow yesterday was nowhere to be found. She'd not seen a man this uncomfortable since she'd turned down a marriage proposal from an Astor—it wasn't her fault he'd asked for her hand in front of a dozen or so childhood friends at a picnic in Central Park. She thought it best to spare Edward further discomfort.

"I hear you found out that I'm the black sheep," she said playfully. "Baaaaa."

She expected him to recoil but to her amazement he laughed and teased her, "You call that a sheep? Maybe an American goat. This is a sheep." And he proceeded to emit an elaborate bleat the like of which she'd never heard. "Baaaaaa, meeehhh." He stopped, a sly grin on his face. "That's a sheep."

She couldn't stop from grinning back. "You shock me, Edward. What does my sister think of your barnyard impressions?"

"She has yet to hear my sheep but she was quite amazed by my bullfrog."

"You must be joking?" she asked, not picturing Brooke finding any of this amusing.

"You act like you expect me to be humourless," he said with mock gravity. "You do know that we English are known for our wit."

"Is that so? Then go on, witify me."

"Witify? Is that an American word?"

"I made it up," she confessed. "It's good, isn't it?"

Edward rubbed his chin as though the answer required serious analysis. "It might be at that. But before we descend into further madcap discussions I must tell you how worried Brooke is about you," he said, the gravity seeping back into his voice. "We both are."

Sydney pulled her shawl around her shoulders; the lightness of the moment had passed and they had returned to solemnity. "She's worried about you, not me," she replied. "She's convinced that now you know about my politics you'll call off the wedding. Though we both know you would never do that. You can't afford to."

"My goodness, you are blunt," he said.

"I like to think I'm honest," she said. "Why should we have secrets?"

She was playing with fire and had said more than she ought to have. He was staring at her now, possibly in disbelief, she couldn't be sure. She smiled despite herself.

A few feet away a little boy was dangling his yo-yo over the railing as another boy begged him not to throw it overboard.

"You don't want to lose the one bit of entertainment you have," Edward advised. The boys appeared stunned to have a strange man address them.

"We's just playing, sir," the boy with the yo-yo answered. "I'm not tossing it."

"It ain't yours to toss, Mickey," the other boy yelped. "That's my yo-yo, and you know it."

"It's not yours. It's Molly's," Mickey said.

Edward grinned. "Then I suggest you find Molly and return her yo-yo."

The boys grinned back sheepishly, then tore off down the deck. Edward's easy bearing with the children touched Sydney. She had thought him too uptight to have fun with children and toys. Then again any man who could make animal sounds couldn't be as stuffy as all that. Perhaps Edward was going to be a pleasure after all. There was only one way to find out . . .

"Edward, I can stand the suspense no longer," she said impatiently. "I know you don't approve of me and the things I believe in but it's my life. And quite frankly I love third class." This wasn't entirely true but surely deceiving oneself wasn't the same as lying to another?

She expected him to react, even overreact to her defiance. She assumed his view of the world would echo her sister's. She was wrong.

"I know you are well versed in the work of Margaret Sanger. I feel foolish for not guessing you were a suffragette when we spoke in New York," he answered calmly. "After what you said about my sister I should have known."

Sydney bit her lip. "I feel badly about what I said," she admitted. "I suppose I can't help myself. There is no reason why Lady Georgina can't go to college and make something of her life. A woman's role doesn't have to only be marriage and babies. She can be useful in so many ways. Contribute to society." She stopped talking when she noticed that Edward's gaze had returned to the ocean. For a brief moment she had hoped he would see her side. She waited and listened to the sound of the ship as it cut through the waves.

"I love my sister," he said after a few minutes. "I never imagined her living anywhere but Rathfon Hall, spending her days in that damn chair, reading, sewing, playing the piano . . . My home has never been a prison to me but after what you said at the Plaza, I wonder if perhaps Georgina feels caged. You've given me much to think about."

He smiled at her and she smiled back despite wanting to drive home that she hoped to give Georgina much to think about. But seeing that he was willing to listen and not stomp away gave her patience. England was still five days away and she could be very persuasive.

"I envy you and Georgina. Your closeness," she said sincerely. "Brooke and I have never been close, which I'm sure comes as no surprise." His expression said it wasn't. "Growing up without a mother should have made us thick as thieves."

"That is unfortunate," he said.

The breeze picked up again and a fine mist sprayed across the stern. Sydney decided that since he was determined to marry into her family then he should know everything. "The truth is, I'm staying in third class because Brooke and I quarrelled the morning we sailed and I—"

"Wanted to teach her a lesson?" he asked.

She stared at him. He knew how to read women better than she expected. "Yes, I suppose I did," she admitted.

"So you never had a headache or seasickness or malaria or whatever illness you both concocted?" He teased and waited for her answer.

She felt dreadful. Lying had seemed the right thing to do at the time. But the dishonesty made her and Brooke look, well, dishonest. "I tend not to get ill, except for a little bit of seasickness," she confessed. "We were wrong to lie. Brooke didn't want to upset you. It was a spat between sisters and unfortunately you got in the way."

She felt silly admitting to their ruse. Here she was trying to come off as a sophisticated and worldly young woman with a serious cause to champion and instead she was confessing to what amounted to telling fibs with her sister to avoid a spanking. Edward suddenly seemed parental to her. She didn't like the way the power had shifted between them.

"Shall we walk?" he asked, and held his arm out for her. She took it and they walked along the deck.

"Tell me one thing," he said. "Why are you pursuing a life that will only result in scandal, ridicule and spinsterhood?"

She glared at him. The parental figure was now replaced by a titled and entitled boob, wit or not. Her power flooded through her once again just as the wind picked up and the seas turned rough. Overhead the clouds blew about like ashen cotton. If the weather hadn't turned for the worse she would have yanked her arm free of the man. Instead she had little choice but to cling to him as crewmen scurried about securing deck chairs and suggesting politely that they and other passengers nearby retreat inside. Men and women alike grasped their hats and pulled their coats tight as they scrambled for the doors.

"I know a quiet place for us to continue talking," Edward suggested.

Sydney could think of few things she wanted to do less. He led her up a flight of steps into the Observation Room, a narrow companionway lined with portholes that overlooked the ship's forecastle. It was as he'd said it would be, quiet and solitary. The only sound was the wind whistling overhead. Sydney had not seen this part of the ship and forgetting for a moment how annoyed she was, she darted toward a porthole to watch as the keen-edged bow cut through the waves like a swordsman on the battlefield. And a female swordsman at that.

"The *Lusitania*'s a powerful girl," Sydney said, watching the sea lift the ship, clutching her in its grip as though it would strangle the life from her. Then, as swiftly, it dropped her down, plunging her bow beneath its frothing surface. And again the sea raised her, but the *Lusitania* would not relent. "She's like a mermaid. A beautiful, glistening sister of the sea," Sydney said, her voice tinged with emotion. "It's as though she is playing a game with the ocean."

From so high a vantage point Sydney felt the immense sway of the *Lusitania* beneath her. As though channelling the strength of the ship she cast her eyes at Edward. "The *Lusitania* is such a valuable and treasured ship in England, to the Royal Navy, even the Germans haven't underestimated her."

Edward cleared his throat and ran his hand through his hair. "I suppose that's true."

"It gives me hope," she said.

"What does?"

"Ships are considered female, aren't they? To my mind that means men are capable of valuing women as equals or on certain occasions as superiors."

Edward pursed his lips. "I don't think it's a reasonable comparison."

She returned to the porthole. There were clearer skies ahead. "I feel it is my duty to help women lead healthier and more independent lives." She paused. "I think you would want the same for your sister." Edward bristled at the mention of Georgina but remained silent. "I think it's a human right to control access to our bodies, to control how we use our bodies. It should not be up to a man or men to tell a woman how she should feel, or what she should do. In fact when I return to New York I am enrolling at Bryn Mawr to earn my doctorate in social work."

He began to pace back and forth. She concealed her pleasure at having got to him with her words. *Scandal. Ridicule. Spinster. You asked me to explain myself . . .*

"Sydney, you're missing my point. What I'm after is, why do you care about this? Help me understand," Edward interrupted. "Surely with your family name and wealth you never have to worry about being told what to do with your body or anything else for that matter."

He stopped pacing and waited. Sydney took a deep breath. If this man truly wanted to know then she would tell him. "You know our mother died when we were very young, I was only five," she said. He nodded. "Do you know the circumstances of her death?" His face told her he did not. "Brooke doesn't like to talk about it, nor do I really. She died in childbirth." She paused; the years had done little to dull the pain. "After I was born she wasn't supposed to get pregnant again. The doctors told my parents that another baby would most likely result in heartbreak. But she found herself with child anyway and with few options open to a woman in her position. I remember my father being very upset when she told him we were to have another sibling. I lay on her lap crying and shaking but no one explained to me why everyone was so distraught.

"Then the birth came. It wasn't a long labour. And as the doctor had warned, my mother perished, as did the son she had given her life for. You should have seen my father. The guilt. He disappeared into his study. Weeks turned into months as he tried to drink himself to death. To this day I can barely stand the smell of liquor. 'I am to blame. I should have left her alone,' he said over and over. He spent the rest of his life trying to make it up to us. Of course you can't make up for a mother's absence.

"As I grew older and read about other women who found themselves pregnant, some against their will, and how few options were available to them I knew I'd found what it was I was meant to do. Contraception is a viable option to all women, yet too many people, men and women, find it disgusting and insist it should be banned. Of course most of these people are upper middle class. They haven't seen what I've seen." She stopped, thinking she'd gone far enough.

"But your parents must have wanted to take that risk? Surely you can't compare a poverty-stricken woman with nine children at her feet or a young girl taken advantage of with your own good mother?" he asked.

"You're right. They aren't the same. But the issue of a woman's choice is a personal one. I don't want another child to lose its mother for a reason that could easily have been prevented. In any event, Edward, I believe you have your answer." She smoothed her skirt, waiting for an argument.

Instead Edward stepped closer to her, his hand reaching to her cheek. She froze, unsure what he was about to do.

"A loose pin," he said, holding the offending item between his fingers. "You really do need to consider a hat when outdoors, especially on such a breezy day as this."

She took the pin from him and unceremoniously shoved it back in her hair. She felt flushed.

"I'm sorry about how you lost your mother," he answered, and without warning reached out and took her hand. "You are a brave woman."

She swallowed. Her hand was wrapped up in his. She could feel the warmth, the firmness of him. Why hadn't she worn gloves? Hat and gloves, were there no simpler parts of a woman's wardrobe? They gazed into each other's eyes for a moment longer than was respectable. He smiled again. "And I must say that I envy you."

His words caught her off guard. "Envy me?"

"Very much," he explained. "Not only have you found your passion, however sad its origin, you are dedicating your life to it. I do not have such luxury."

Sydney understood him to be talking about his marriage to Brooke and she gently removed her hand from his, a gesture not lost on him.

"You must find it difficult to respect me," he continued. "I'm not sure I respect myself."

He had gone too far and this time Sydney grabbed his hand and held it. "Please do not imagine what I feel or think."

Edward stared down at his hand held firmly between hers and smiled. "Come, can you honestly say my marrying Brooke and taking her share of the family fortune sat well with you? If nothing else you must have thought me less than masculine."

Sydney pondered this. She had bared her soul to him moments before and not been ridiculed. He deserved the same. "You are doing what you have to in order to help your family. And you are off to fight in a war in which you might die. In my opinion both are sacrifices that only a true man could choose to make."

Edward bowed his head and presented his elbow. "Shall we continue our walk? Or would you prefer tea?" he asked.

They made their way out of the Observation Room in silence. Dusk was settling in as the sea roiled like a grey blanket billowing up and down on a clothesline. All along the deck, crewmen lit the gas lamps and from somewhere in the ship the band had started to play.

"Tell me, Edward, what is your passion?" she asked him. "I really want to know."

She watched his face. He was looking up at the sky. She followed his gaze to the darkening clouds overhead.

"Flying," he said. "I would love to fly an aeroplane. The Royal Flying Corps has a small squadron that is being used for aerial reconnaissance. I have friends in the military who contend that before long there will be battles fought in the sky. I'd like to be part of it."

Sydney was impressed. There was much more to Edward Thorpe-Tracey than a fancy title and ancestral land. "You are a patriot then? Or an adventurer?"

"Can't I be both?" He smiled.

They reached the stairway entrance that led to her berth.

"So have I convinced you to return to the Regal Suite?" he implored her.

Sydney smiled. She didn't want their time together to end. "I'm afraid not, but I enjoyed our conversation very much. Good day, Edward." Then instinctively she placed her hand over his once more and squeezed gently.

"I'd like to see you again," he said.

Sydney sensed a note of urgency in his voice and wanted to tamp it down. "You mean with Brooke?"

"Of course, with Brooke," he agreed. "I would like to know more about your work and tell you more about flying machines." He was grinning now. His face was brighter and happier than she'd seen it before and he was far more attractive because of it.

"I'm sure Brooke would love to hear about it—" she began.

"No she would not," he interrupted.

Sydney was feeling uncomfortable with the turn their conversation had taken. She would not be drawn into a negative discussion about her sister. "Maybe not, but once you are wed she will likely buy you an aeroplane if you ask nicely."

Edward recoiled, hurt. Sydney regretted her harshness at once. "I didn't mean that the way it sounded," she said but the damage was done. Edward backed away and bowed once more.

"Have a lovely evening, Sydney." He turned and walked away from her. She watched his tall, lean figure march away until he disappeared into the dim light.

Isabel

The other girls in the boarding house had clattered down the stairs and off to their jobs hours ago. When she had returned home early she had feigned a migraine to Mrs. Ogilvie and said she was taking the day off from work.

Up in her room she undid her hair, letting it fall in loose waves below her shoulders. She even traded in her studious grey skirt for a pretty summer dress—the only one she'd kept and one she would never dare slip on for work. She placed the day's papers she'd bought to occupy her mind on the bed. The newsagent had shouted at her as usual when he thought she wasn't looking. She was accustomed to reading the dailies during her breaks in Room 40, happy to be able to discuss the stories with the men as an equal just as Mr. Chambers had treated her, and not shy and retiring like so-called respectable girls. All this trouble that Mildred had created made her think of Mrs. Chambers. If Mrs. Chambers saw her amongst the men chatting about submarines and destroyers she would have a fit. Isabel smiled at the thought.

She went to her vanity and picked up a lipstick. Staring intently at her reflection she swiped the colour across her lips. It was a deep red. The bright colour gave her complexion new life. Isabel studied her face. Then she got onto her knees and pulled a box from under the bed. Inside was the pair of red shoes George had given her. She sat on the bed and slipped one onto her right foot with all the care of Cinderella. Making circles in the air with her foot her initial reaction was joy at the memory, but with each spin of her ankle joy turned to wistfulness and then to sadness before stopping at anger. She ripped the shoe off. Shoved it back in the box with its mate and wiped the lipstick off with a handkerchief. *I've no time for foolishness.*

She unfolded the *Times* and perused the endless coverage of the endless war. Battles and casualties on the Western Front, reports from the Eastern Front and the Russian armies, anti-German sentiments, tips for homemakers in England to help with the war effort, all stuff that had become routine. Then she saw it: an article about the German warning given to merchant ships and ocean liners crossing the Atlantic and entering the war zone, just as Norton had told her. The *Times* had reprinted the warning that was in the New York papers on Saturday. The reporter had connected the warning to the RMS *Lusitania*.

According to eyewitnesses several of the ship's prominent passengers, including millionaire Alfred G. Vanderbilt, received anonymous telegrams warning them not to sail on the Lusitania because "she was doomed," the implication being the great ship was going to be torpedoed. Of course this could all be rumour and fear mongering. Everyone, including those in the highest ranks of the Port of New York Authority, is aware that the wharves are crawling with German spies. According to Cunard the German warning did not lead any of the passengers to cancel. Cunard's New York manager, Charles Sumner, was quoted in the New York Times saying there was no need for passengers to be overly concerned about the war zone as "There is a general system of convoying British ships. The British navy is responsible for all British ships, and especially for Cunarders . . .

Taking a deep breath, she quickly checked the other papers. They all carried similar accounts of the warning and the *Lusitania*. It was too much to imagine. She cursed Mrs. Burns then and there. Isabel wanted desperately to be at Room 40, to be part of the solution in any way she could. Then the sound of the doorbell drifted up to her room.

"Isabel! There's someone here for you!" It was the landlady.

"Coming, Mrs. Ogilvie!" she called down.

"I'm sure your visitor can't wait all day!" Mrs. Ogilvie shouted again.

She looked at her wristwatch. It was after three o'clock. Isabel descended the stairs slowly so as not to appear as if she was fit as a fiddle. Mrs. Ogilvie was waiting at the bottom, eyeing her in her usual disapproving way.

"Who is it?" Isabel asked meekly.

"I put her in the sitting room," the older woman barked.

So it was a woman who called on her. It must be Mildred. Come to gloat. She walked to the sitting room. Mrs. Ogilvie sniffed loudly. "Don't be long, Isabel. I want to listen to the wireless when I do my knitting." Mrs. Ogilvie stomped upstairs to her own room. "There's nothing sickly about *that* girl," she muttered.

Isabel smoothed her hair, took a deep breath and entered the living room. She gasped with a mix of surprise and relief at the sight of Dorothy.

"Isabel, so good to see you." Dorothy leapt to her feet and hugged her. "I didn't mean to give you a fright."

Isabel regained her composure. "Why aren't you at work?"

"I took the afternoon off. Was up all night working and needed to get home. Give it a rest for a bit. Shall we sit?"

Dorothy moved to the sofa and Isabel sat beside her. She never used the sitting room and had not noticed before how pleasant it was. The sofa was a soft velvet damask in faded gold. The curtains matched and were drawn wide, letting in a wash of spring sunshine. The tables were a dark walnut. The bookcases that were built into one side of the wall were filled with books that appeared well-read and well-loved. It was a comfortable room. Who knew Mrs. Ogilvie cared for such an atmosphere? Sitting on the mantel were two large photographs: one of her husband who had died five years ago and another of her only child, a son, Gerald, who was somewhere on the Western Front and, hopefully, very much alive.

"You know, I've never seen your hair like this," Dorothy said. Her words jolted Isabel who grabbed a big strand and twirled it nervously between her fingers. Her loose hair made her feel naked. "It's lovely. You should do it that way more often. And that dress. I almost didn't recognize you." Isabel felt her face flush with embarrassment. "Oh don't be self-conscious. You're a pretty girl. Who knows why you hide it so much?"

"Thank you, Dorothy. It's a nice surprise seeing you."

"I thought I'd check in. I'd heard you were taken ill. We all did," she said. So her suspension hadn't made its way round the Old Admiralty Building after all. Then there was hope that Mrs. Burns was considering letting her remain on staff.

"Yes. A migraine," Isabel said softly. She hated lying to Dorothy. But there were more important things on her mind, more vital than her own troubles. "What's happening at work? Did they alert the ship?"

Dorothy looked confused. "What are you going on about, darling?"

"The *Lusitania*. Did we tell the captain about U-20?" Her voice rose in irritation. "The submarine that was headed toward Ireland."

The severity of Dorothy's glare made Isabel stop talking. She was being stupid. The sitting room in Mrs. Ogilvie's rooming house was not secure and they could both be sacked or worse for discussing their top secret work here. "It's my headache . . ." she said, to make an excuse. "I've been reading the papers and was asleep when you came. I must be confused."

"So when are you coming back?" Dorothy asked. "We are feeling rather short-staffed without you."

Isabel smiled, flattered and relieved that she was missed, but there was no answer she could possibly give.

Sydney

The evening air was warm enough that a woman didn't need more than a shawl to be comfortable on deck. Sydney wore an aubergine wool wrap that matched closely the deep purple dress she had chosen. Her pre-dinner strolls had become a habit. She liked to walk at least ten times around the deck each day, saving two turns for the dinner hour. She had completed the ninth when she reached the locked Bostwick gate and paused. She hadn't been able to get the conversation with Edward out of her mind. He had surprised her. She had pre-judged him before ever meeting him, and upon meeting him had judged him further. It wasn't until this morning that she'd had an inkling of the real man that lay beneath the stiff upper lip and fine tailoring. He had listened to the story of her mother's passing and how it had motivated her to help other women escape the same fate and he had shown warmth and sympathy. He understood her and what her work meant to her more than Brooke or Mr. Garrett ever had. But their parting was regretful. She had pushed him away in order to defend her sister. Was that really it? Or had she pushed him away for another reason she couldn't bear admitting?

Sydney stood just behind the Bostwick so those in first class passing by on the other side couldn't see her. It was a good vantage point to observe the saloon passengers undetected. As expected at this hour, the main entrance was packed with elegantly dressed couples and families heading into the dining saloon for yet another multiple-course dinner. The men strutted in black and white as the women paraded their style in a wave of feathers and sparkling jewels, velvets and silks, reds and greens and every imaginable shade. The gossip flew as swiftly as a seagull diving for scraps.

"Did you see what she's wearing this evening? It's the same gown as the first night."

"At least she had the good taste to leave the ruby necklace in her stateroom."

"I hear her husband has been spending a good deal of the voyage in second class with a woman who is not known to any one of us."

"No!"

The ladies' voices were drowned out by a group of gentlemen who had entered the space.

"Why don't we play in the ship's pool? I'm going to wager we will sail six hundred and fifty miles today."

"That seems unlikely. Yesterday we only travelled about five hundred. Seems slow for twenty-five knots."

"We certainly haven't made top speed so far. I dare say we're going as slow as twenty knots."

"I don't mind an innocent wager but I'll be damned if I'm getting tricked by some seafaring gambler. These ocean liners are beacons for card sharks that take advantage of passengers' boredom to earn a tidy sum. Have you read all the cautions in the Cunard's handbook for passengers?"

Sydney listened to these tidbits of conversations with amusement. The fascination with each other's secrets and with the ship's speed was no different in steerage. She was about to move off when she heard the unmistakable flutey sound of her sister's voice. Sydney froze.

"She's been a great deal of trouble to me ever since Father died," Brooke said with a touch of self-pity.

Sydney felt a flutter in her chest and leaned closer to the gate for a look. Sure enough, there were Brooke and Edward standing at the entrance with people she didn't know. There was an older man and a woman of about thirty, who could be his daughter. Then there was a very well-dressed couple; the husband held his chin up like he was sniffing the air while the wife wore a diamond necklace the size of an anchor. Sydney had never seen any of them before.

"Grief does terrible things," the diamond lady said.

"I wish it were that simple," Brooke retorted. "But my sister has caused me embarrassment quite a few times."

Sydney's eyes widened. She leaned back against the wall out of sight. How could her sister say such a thing, and to strangers?

"Perhaps, my dear, 'embarrassment' is too strong a word," Edward said solemnly.

Sydney risked discovery to peer around the corner and through the gap in the gate to see Edward standing beside Brooke, his posture rigid but his expression carefully bland. She watched Brooke's face harden.

"What word would you choose, darling?" asked Brooke, her jaw set.

"I think you are new to marital peace, sir," the husband of the diamond lady said to Edward. "You will quickly learn that a husband must never defend nor criticize his wife's relations."

Brooke laughed stiffly at the man's attempt at humour. "What Edward doesn't yet comprehend is how difficult it is to be Sydney's sister. Her actions bring great shame to our family name."

It was like being stabbed through the heart: the pain, the shock and anger. It took all Sydney's resolve not to rattle the gate and scream.

"I take offence at such an opinion of Sydney," Edward responded. Sydney pressed her nose to the gate so that it touched the cold metal. "In fact I would say quite the opposite," he continued. "She's to be admired for living her life as she is, true to her desires and beliefs."

Brooke's mouth pursed tightly. Sydney recognized the expression. Her sister was furious and would erupt any moment. But it was the diamond lady who struck first.

"I'm afraid I agree with your fiancée, Edward. To hear her tell it, her sister's behaviour is shameful. Marching in protests and talking about things such as . . . I can't even say the words, they are too crude. Then to speechify down in third class, why those poor souls have a dreary enough life without being lectured to."

Brooke demonstrated a remarkable restraint, happy to let the other woman speak for her. Edward was beaten. It was then that the other woman, the daughter of the older man, spoke; she had a Welsh accent. "Then you must think me shameful and embarrassing as well. For I was a fervent member of the Women's Social and Political Union even when it became a radical group. I didn't really think their arson campaign was the right way to approach getting women the vote but I did manage to be involved in blowing up a postbox," the woman said to the utter dismay of her companions, except for her father, who looked proud, and Edward, whose smile had returned. "I went to prison, of course. But they released me when I went on a hunger strike. They didn't want a woman from my class to die in their atrocious jail."

It was Sydney's turn to smile. Brooke would be regretting this woman as a dining companion.

"Lady Mackworth, you too are to be admired," Edward said. He turned to the woman's father. "Mr. Thomas, I'd say you have a very clever daughter."

"Indeed I do," Mr. Thomas agreed.

"But Edward," Brooke insisted. "What you don't seem to understand is how spoiled Sydney is. Our father saw to that. He indulged her. The only reason she behaves as she does is because she wants attention. It's foolishness and all it's doing is ruining her reputation, and mine too if she isn't careful. She's really a mess of a girl."

Sydney had never heard Brooke speak about her like this. It was as though she was in the audience of a Broadway play and what she was hearing was playacting about some other family. Edward stepped away from the group in protest.

"I won't hear another word against Sydney. She's a bright and strong woman who knows her own mind and her heart," he said sternly. "You would do well, Brooke, to emulate your sister's example more often. Now let's go in to dinner."

He strode away, leaving Brooke seething; anyone could see that. The diamond lady placed a silk-gloved hand on her arm. "There, there," she said soothingly. "Men can't think straight with the war going on."

The group slowly made their way into the saloon. Sydney was dumbstruck. She was touched by his defence of her. Perhaps she was forgiven for her hurtful words on the deck. But she also felt bad for Brooke. Edward didn't understand the complex emotions between sisters. Brooke was only lashing out to protect what was hers as was her habit. The simple fact was that the two girls didn't want the same things. They didn't see eye to eye. They fought. They stung each other with words. But they were still the Sinclair sisters and would always look out for each other. That didn't mean Sydney forgave Brooke for her insults, only that it had always been this way between them and always would be. Sydney wrapped the shawl around her shoulders and headed to the third class dining room.

It was after dinner as Sydney sat with Walter and Frederick. The other passengers at their table, an English couple, Albert and Agnes Veals and her brother, Fred Bailey, had gone to find a game of cards. She had sought their company for the meal; they were amusing and full of stories. She learned that before the war started Walter had big plans to better his circumstances in America. Painting and wallpapering were only the beginning, and his own home was the starting line. He had scooped up leftover materials from the grand houses—including William Morris & Co. Leicester print wallpaper—to renovate his modest home. He explained to her that Lowell was a manufacturing town and it was bustling with people wanting to move in to take up one of the many jobs on offer. Eventually those workers would want to own their home and when they were able to afford it, he'd sell his at a tidy profit. Buy a house in a better class of neighbourhood. More fresh paint and paper and anything else that needed bettering and then on to the next. Boston wasn't so far away. By the time his daughter, Muriel, was of age she would be attending a school in the city. She could study dance if she liked. Or piano. There would be decent young men for her to meet and one day marry. And there would be other children besides Muriel to benefit from his plan.

Sydney enjoyed hearing Walter speak so excitedly of his baby girl, who would be turning two on May 11. He was going to stop in Liverpool for a present. He also spoke of his wife, Alice, who worked as a buyer for ladies' fashion at a department store in England before their move to Massachusetts. "She turned down an offer from Selfridges after I proposed," he boasted. Walter had commented on Sydney's fine clothing and how Alice would be able to tell where it came from. Sydney sensed that Walter knew her dresses were expensive, more than the average steerage passenger could afford but he never addressed it directly.

As she listened to Walter she noticed several disapproving glances from the women who had been in the ladies' lounge yesterday when she'd attempted to sway their opinion. It was this type of reaction that embarrassed Brooke. *Should I be embarrassed?* Sydney watched how the women were gossiping feverishly about her, even pointing and sneering. They were not a pretty sight. *No, I am not embarrassed.*

Walter and Frederick's conversation drifted to the voyage and the war. Sydney, though interested, found her thoughts straying to Brooke's insults (she could handle those), but Edward's praise? She replayed his words over and over and each time her smile grew wide until this too troubled her. *It's wrong of me to enjoy how he spoke about me.* She realized that if she felt odd about his misplaced gallantry she knew that Brooke would be outraged by it. Then again maybe he was only being a well-bred gentleman, wasn't that what her sister coveted so badly? But it was more than that. She and Edward had made a connection. He was accepting of her world view and she understood and accepted his. She shuddered once more, recalling the aeroplane insult she had left him with. She would have to make amends on that front.

"Say, Sydney, you think we'll get to Liverpool on time?" Walter asked, drawing her back into the conversation.

Sydney welcomed the distraction. "I expected us to move faster. Then again I'm not sure what fast feels like. This is my first voyage."

"And you still don't. She ain't moving at full speed," Frederick said.

"Shut your gob," Walter said.

"What do you mean, Frederick?" she asked.

"One of the seamen was smoking a cig with us up on deck. He told us they only got three boiler rooms in service. Doubt she can go more than twenty-one knots."

She was taken aback. "I understood there were four boilers. Is the captain saving it up for when we're in the war zone so it will be full steam ahead?"

Walter bit his lower lip. "According to the crewman the *Lusitania* has been down to three boilers for several crossings. Conserving coal for the war," he said. "Orders of the Admiralty. The ship is technically under Admiralty command, so Cunard has to do what it's ordered to do."

All thoughts of Brooke and Edward had vanished. "Why hasn't the captain or one of the officers told us about the low speed?" she asked. "And what else do these orders include?"

Frederick shrugged. "You know those types. They keep themselves to themselves and things close to their chests. They don't care much for the likes of us."

Walter and Frederick exchanged looks. Sydney narrowed her eyes. "What?"

Walter leaned across the table and spoke in a hushed tone. "Freddie and I are thinking of investigating a little. See if we can't get below decks and sneak into the cargo hold, see if there is any truth to the rumours about carrying ammunition," he said.

Sydney was stunned. "That seems dangerous. What if you're caught?"

Frederick shrugged. "We play dumb."

"Look at his face, Sydney," Walter said. "That won't be tough to believe."

Frederick elbowed Walter and they all laughed. "Don't worry about us, Sydney. It's not a matter for a lady. We shouldn't have said anything about it."

She stopped smiling. "Why should the fact I'm a woman stop me from caring about the contents of the cargo hold?" The men looked surprised. Their reaction amused her. "I'm up for a bit of an adventure if nothing else. If you two are going to explore the ship, then I'm coming with you."

Walter and Frederick stared at each other a moment, then as Walter opened his mouth to respond Hannah's mother flew to their table, her face streaked with excitement.

"I know who you are!" Gladys boomed.

In the background Hannah sat down at the piano and began to play ragtime. But her mother was too focused on Sydney to object to her daughter's musical choice. She had the page of an old magazine open and was shoving it under their noses.

"You're Sydney Sinclair," she gushed.

"I told you I was," Sydney answered grimly. The magazine was *Vanity Fair* and inside was a photo of her and Brooke at the opening of the opera season. The caption clearly identified them as society girls and heiresses to a vast fortune. She wanted to disappear.

"But you didn't say you were *that* Sydney Sinclair." Gladys continued to wave the photo around. "Someone left this magazine in the ladies' lounge and I happened to pick it up."

Walter grabbed it and he and Frederick stared back and forth between Sydney and the photo until she blushed. "Is this really you?" Walter asked, holding on to a sliver of doubt.

"Guilty," she said.

Gladys clapped her hands. "Then you must know Charles Frohman," she said, getting to her point as quickly as possible.

"I've met him once or twice," Sydney admitted, knowing where the conversation was heading. She looked at Hannah who was playing her favourite music with verve. She couldn't disappoint her. "Perhaps I could ask him to listen to Hannah play."

Walter handed the magazine back to Gladys. Frederick tried to grab it but the older woman snatched it out of reach.

"Did you hear that, child?" Gladys called out to Hannah. "Mommy told you that I'd get you an audition with Mr. Frohman."

Walter and Sydney exchanged looks and smiled. "Perhaps the ship's concert on Thursday night would do," Sydney suggested.

Gladys clasped the magazine to her chest. "I don't know what to say."

She strutted away, no doubt bound for the ladies' lounge to regale anyone who would listen about her daughter's future.

"How about 'thank you,'" Walter said.

"If you're a rich girl then why are you down here with us?" Frederick asked.

Walter elbowed him.

"I wanted to spend time with different types of people," she explained, not wanting to get into her family woes.

"Well, we're glad you did," Walter said warmly.

Sydney got up from the table and went to the piano and sat beside Hannah. The girl finished her song and looked at Sydney.

"Mommy said you're very rich," Hannah said.

"I'm afraid so." Sydney smiled.

Hannah contemplated this. "Do you live in a castle?"

Sydney laughed. "Not a castle. But it is a very nice house. Now, Hannah, what is it you want to play for Mr. Frohman?"

The girl bit her lip, thinking on the matter. "Mother wants me to play Mozart or Beethoven. But I want to sing and dance too."

"I think that's a fine idea," Sydney said. Gladys might have wanted a concerto but she knew that a Broadway producer would want something more accessible. And besides, Hannah needed someone in her corner. "I'll tell you what, why don't I play piano for you and you can sing and dance. I'm not as good as you but I'll do. We should rehearse between now and Thursday if we want to impress him. I'll invite my friends Walter and Frederick to be the audience."

Hannah leapt off the piano bench and stood at the ready as Sydney took her place. "Ready, Hannah?" she asked.

The girl stood poised, her brow furrowed in concentration, and nodded. Sydney took a deep breath and brought her fingers down onto the keys.

MAY 4

Isabel

The newsagent had shown better judgment that morning and had not teased Isabel about beaux or any frivolous matter. Her stern expression must have thwarted the old man's usual cheeriness. She paid him for the papers and made her way home, dreading another day unfolding as slowly as yesterday. She was only a few feet from the boarding house when she saw Mildred waiting for her outside the gate to the front walk. Isabel stiffened and attempted to march past her, but it was no use. Mildred leapt in front of her and blocked the path.

"We need to talk," Mildred said.

Isabel glared at her. "I have nothing to say to you," she answered, and placed her hand on the gate.

"You'll want to hear what I have to say," Mildred insisted. "If you value your job as much as you say you do." Something about how Mildred looked at her gave Isabel pause and she let go of the latch.

"But not here. Let's go for a walk," Mildred said. "Is there a park nearby?"

They found an isolated bench beneath a willow tree and sat down. Isabel didn't know what to make of it. They hadn't uttered a word on their way there and now Mildred sat silent.

"What is it you want? To gloat?" Isabel asked.

Mildred smiled. "I want you to help me," she said.

Isabel flinched. "Me help you? Are you daft?"

Mildred lifted her chin. "I'm nothing of the sort. Would a daft girl have manipulated things as good as I have?"

Isabel breathed deeply, trying to calm herself. "So you admit you are trying to ruin my life? Again?"

"I didn't ruin your life in Oxford. You did that. All I did was be honest. And I've been honest with Mrs. Burns," Mildred said. "I've never lied, Isabel."

She had no response. In this regard Mildred had a point. "But you didn't have to tell Mrs. Chambers or Mrs. Burns. You could have minded your own business."

"I was sick of you getting special treatment," Mildred snapped. "That's what you want to hear, isn't it?" It was. But hearing her admission wasn't as satisfying as Isabel had once thought it would be. "Mr. Chambers treating you like a pet. What about me? I am every bit as pretty as you and yet . . ."

Her voice trailed off into silence. Isabel watched the spindly bows of the willow bend in the breeze above them. "And yet he chose me."

"You might have asked me if I wanted to learn to type and do secretarial things," Mildred said. "But once you were with him you didn't even hardly speak to me."

Isabel was affronted. "That isn't true. We were never friends, Mildred. We worked together, that is all." Mildred stood up and paced back and forth in front of the bench. "If that's all you have to say then I'm done listening," Isabel said, losing patience.

The dark-haired girl stopped pacing and sat down again. She smiled at Isabel. "I want a job in Room 40. Like you and the other girls have."

"What?" Isabel gasped. "After what you did? Having me suspended? You expect me to put in a word for you?"

"You will, Isabel," Mildred insisted. The smile was gone from her face. "If you get me a job as a clerk then I will go to Mrs. Burns and say that I was mistaken in my accusations. She will restore your position."

"How dare you!" Isabel said.

"I know how much the job means to you," Mildred continued,

completely ignoring Isabel's horrified reaction. "I also know that having the respect of those men means even more. Right now only Mrs. Burns and Henry know about your affair with a married man. But if you won't get me a job then I will tell all of the men in your precious Room 40 about your past." Isabel stood this time. But she didn't pace. She was as rigid as the statue of Nelson in Trafalgar Square. "I'll tell them that all your plainness is an act. You're really a tart on the hunt for another man."

Isabel stared down at Mildred, whose smile had returned. "What makes you think I can get you a job?"

"Those men respect you, for now," she said. "Especially that Mr. Denniston. And Room 40 needs more help. Henry said they were looking to hire more girls."

"So why don't you ask him then?" Isabel asked. Mildred cast her gaze to the ground.

"Henry didn't think it was wise to have us work together," she admitted sourly. "Besides, you're more motivated to help me."

At this Isabel couldn't help herself and she laughed. "Motivation? Is that what you call this? Blackmail is more like it."

Mildred stood up to face Isabel. She was a few inches shorter and had to lift her chin up to meet Isabel's eyes. "I don't care what you want to call it. But you must do it or else."

Isabel didn't answer. Mildred seemed to take her silence as acquiescence. "The men will be at the pub tonight. It's your chance to speak to Mr. Denniston and tell him what an excellent addition I will be. Then tomorrow I will go to Mrs. Burns on your behalf. See, we both win."

She smiled at Isabel again and, not waiting for a response, strolled away. Isabel sat back down on the bench. There was much to think about.

Edward

love my sister and want her to be happy." Brooke was seated across from Edward. He had come to apologize for his behaviour last night. He expressed to Brooke his regrets at making a public display and causing her embarrassment; however, the sentiments he had spoken to their companions, he meant. She was not happy and had not accepted his apology. "You gave those people the wrong impression, that you prefer Sydney to me."

Edward chose this moment to stare at his oxfords. Maxwell had done his usual exceptional job brushing them to a shine. Without looking up he said, "What she said about Georgina made sense."

This seemed to soften Brooke. She was smiling at him now. "Sydney assumes all women are miserable and need to be emancipated," she explained. "And once she educates them they will rise up together. But it's just not the case with all women. Your sister will be happy with us at Rathfon. It's her home."

Edward was confused. Sydney had made sense. But so did Brooke. He would have her speak to Georgina. Let his sister decide. "Am I forgiven?"

Brooke stood and crossed the few steps to him and held out her hand. He took it and she squeezed his. He felt no rush of relief, no sway of emotion at her touch.

She dropped his hand and moved to a mirror hanging on the wall and examined her reflection, smoothing her hair with her fingers and turning her face left and right, studying herself, smiling faintly as she did so, pleased with her own beauty. Her behaviour was odd to Edward. Such prolonged preening was considered unbecoming. It brought to mind an article Georgina had read to him from a ladies' magazine about something called gargoyling. He remembered one particular line: *Fascination springs from the hidden depths of character. It will never be gained by face-posturing before the looking-glass.* At the time he and Georgina had had quite a laugh; now it seemed prescient. Brooke was a gargoyle and such fixation on her looks was in stark contrast to her sister. Standing with him on the bow that first day of the voyage Sydney hadn't given a damn how she looked, her hair a mess of waves and loose strands. Edward had drunk in the sight then and the image excited him still. Even when she had cut off their talk with a sharp reminder of his upcoming marriage he hadn't stopped thinking her one of the most beautiful women he'd ever seen. He started at the sound of Brooke's voice.

"Before we sailed I instructed Mr. Garrett to buy stock in Bethlehem Steel. It's a Pennsylvania company that manufactures armour plate and large-calibre guns for the British navy," she said, turning back to him. "I thought you should know since you're to be involved in running things once we're married. It seemed smart business."

"You can't mean to profit from the war?" He was aghast. He couldn't tell her that he knew from his military connections that the *Lusitania* carried in her cargo hold approximately twelve hundred cases of shrapnel from the very company she named, as well as aluminum powder and ammunition. Though, given her view of things, perhaps the thought of reams of explosives deep within the ship wouldn't alarm her.

She sat back down and sighed impatiently, looking at him as if he was an upset toddler who needed soothing. "Darling, it's part ownership in a steel company that produces ammunition that will be used *against* the enemy. Loads of Americans are making money this way. It's not our war, remember? Besides, Rathfon Hall needs the money."

"Surely there's another way?" The idea of her wealth, and his once they were married, growing larger from the deaths of thousands sickened him.

"Think of it this way, Edward. I'm helping England win the war," she said sharply.

"To make money from the war is unethical," he said.

"My dear, this is something you will have to learn when you're helping manage the finances," she said. "Ethics and business don't mix."

Edward couldn't respond because Brooke was right in one vital way. His marrying for money was no different than profiting from bullets. The truth rattled him. He was caught between ideology and tradition, needs and wants, morality and duty. His honesty, however, was not for sale.

"Do you think we are making the right decision?" he asked after a long pause.

"About what?" she asked, though from her face she seemed to know.

"Our marriage."

Brooke's flared nostrils were the only discernible reaction. The rest of her expression remained soft and pretty. "Did Sydney tell you to ask me that?"

"What on earth makes you say such a thing?" Edward said as blandly as he could. "The answer is no."

Brooke smiled. "I was teasing you, Edward. I'm going to send her a note. We've been invited to dine at the captain's table tomorrow night and I want her with us."

"Do you think she cares about such things?" he asked, doubting an honour even such as dinner with the elusive Captain Turner would hold much sway with Sydney.

"I'll tell her Lady Mackworth will be there. She'll come if she thinks she has a like mind in her camp." Brooke stood and walked to a small writing desk. She sat down.

Edward thought more about his time with Sydney. How easy it was for him to tell her about his dreams. It was worth a try. "Brooke," he said. "I'm thinking of learning to fly. Perhaps for the war effort. What do you think?"

She looked at him as though surprised he was still in the room. "I think you should focus on the field commission, Edward. Flying doesn't suit you. That sort of thing is for harder men." Brooke picked up pen and paper and began to write to her sister, no longer interested in Edward and their conversation.

Sydney

The innards of the ship seemed designed to discourage land-loving passengers. Tight corridors, minimal lighting and loud echoing chambers were built for efficiency and speed and were part of the *Lusitania*'s engineering marvel, but for a person not familiar with each cavernous turn or staircase she was a labyrinth. Sydney, Walter and Frederick walked as stealthily as possible but Sydney's small heels clanked loudly on the metal steps and she had resorted to walking on her toes. They hadn't gone far when they heard something fall to the ground ahead. Whatever it was clanged and crashed down the metal steps until it landed far beneath with a dull thud.

"What the devil?" The shocked voice belonged to a crewman working below. "What are you doing here, lass?" He spoke gently.

Curious to learn who else had snuck into this part of the ship, the three of them poked their heads over the stairway railing to find a little girl cowering on the steps below.

"Hannah," Sydney whispered. Walter placed his index finger over his lips to silence her.

"Let's see what the bloke does," Walter said quietly. "It's a nice distraction for us."

"I lost my shoe," Hannah said matter-of-factly to the crewman.

"Aye," the crewman said. "Nearly brained me with it too."

Hannah stood up, her left foot bare. "My mom will be angry."

The crewman pondered this a moment. "We can fix it so she won't. Let's say we go down and get the shoe for you? But then you must promise to never come down here again," he said sternly.

Hannah nodded. The crewman took the girl's hand and they walked down the steps. "The shoe is just outside the cargo hold," he explained. "Just a few steps down and we can get it back on yer foot."

Sydney perked up at the mention of the cargo hold. "This is our chance, Walter," she murmured. This was even more fun than the women's rally. Perhaps she'd be arrested again. She smiled at the idea.

"A wise man would quit now," Frederick whispered. "Before being detected, and go back to where he belonged."

Sydney and Walter glared at him. "There's little to be gained in being a coward," Walter said. "We can use Hannah to get access."

"How?" Frederick asked, skeptical.

"Watch me," Walter said, then called out, "Hannah?"

The crewman looked up and saw the three of them. "Oi! What are you lot doing in here? This area is forbidden for passengers," he snapped.

"I was looking for the kiddie," Walter explained. "Her mum is awfully worried."

The crewman looked to Hannah. "Are these people your family?"

Hannah shook her head. "They're my friends."

Sydney guessed what Walter was up to and was the first to run down the steps to Hannah. "What are you doing down here, Hannah?"

The girl made a face. "My mom wanted me to practise Mozart so I'm perfect for Mr. Frohman. But I didn't want to so I hid," she said reasonably.

"She prefers to sing and tap dance than play the piano," Sydney said, as though that clarified the matter.

The crewman scowled. Walter glanced down the remaining flight of stairs and saw the tap shoe resting upside down against a heavy metal door. He nudged Sydney.

"Say, where's that door go to?" Walter asked innocently enough.

The crewman followed his gaze. "That's the baggage room. Also off limits. If you need something of yours tell a steward but I can't let you three scamper about in there."

"Can you give us a tour?" Sydney asked the stunned crewman. "Your yelling frightened Hannah, and seeing other parts of the ship might get her mind off being lost and then scolded for it."

The crewman looked guilt-ridden. "I didn't mean to frighten the wee thing."

Walter winked at Sydney. Impressed with her tactic. But the crewman seemed to come to his senses regarding the rules and shook his head. "That would be impossible, Miss."

Any further argument was prevented by the sudden arrival of a ship's officer and a man of about fifty. It was only two more people but in such a cramped space they made Sydney claustrophobic; she felt a pang of *mal de mer.*

"What goes on here, crewman?" the officer asked. Before the terrified crewman could respond, Sydney stepped forward.

"And you are?" Sydney returned confidently.

"I'm Officer Sloane, the junior assistant purser," he said, sounding indignant. "And who might you be?"

The gentleman beside him grinned knowingly. "That, Mr. Sloane, is Sydney Sinclair, one of New York's wealthiest young ladies."

Mr. Sloane and the crewman appeared chagrined. Sydney held out her hand. "We've not had the pleasure, Mr.—?"

"Mr. Charles Cheever Hardwick," the man said. "Also from New York. I'm in importing and manufacturing. Assistant Purser Sloane here is giving me a tour of the ship."

"*Junior* Assistant Purser, Mr. Hardwick," the officer corrected politely. Hardwick's grin widened.

"What a coincidence. That's what we were trying to do," Sydney said. "I'm delighted we ran into you, Mr. Hardwick. May my friends and I join you?"

Sydney quickly introduced Walter, Frederick and little Hannah. Hardwick was a jovial and gregarious sort and didn't seem to mind the added companions. "Well, Mr. Sloane, have at it."

Sloane and the crewman exchanged looks before the latter left them to return to his duties. Sydney could see they weren't impressed with the extra company, and that the assistant purser wasn't keen on being seen with steerage passengers. But he recovered quickly.

"Very well, next we have the baggage room," he explained, and opened the door that was directly beside them. They all stepped through.

Sydney, Walter, holding Hannah's hand, and Frederick stood on a metal platform overlooking the baggage room. It was immense as were its contents. Rows of meticulously stacked suitcases and enormous steamer trunks lined the walls in every direction. Each piece of luggage was tagged and coded to coincide with the cabin number of each passenger.

"Blimey, people don't pack light," Frederick scoffed.

"A lot of people are moving their entire lives," Walter said, his own life neatly boxed up and lying in wait to return to England. "It's not a weekend in the country."

"Weekend in the country? You live like that, do you? Country homes and fox hunts?" Frederick teased.

"Not in my time." Walter laughed. "Sydney here does."

"I can't lie," she said, and smiled.

Hardwick and Sloane had already descended the stairs. Hardwick waited at the bottom for Sydney to climb down and held her hand when she reached the last step.

"Have you seen anything interesting on your tour so far?" she asked him as Walter and the others followed.

"I was looking for bombs to be honest," he said bluntly.

Sydney gasped. "Why would there be a bomb?"

"You haven't heard about the German spies they caught on the first day?" he said, grinning once more.

Walter and Frederick seemed as perplexed as Sydney. Hardwick appeared to enjoy being in the know. "They found three of them hiding in a pantry and arrested them."

"What happened to them?" Walter asked.

"Tossed overboard likely," Frederick said.

They were all looking at poor Sloane now. He fidgeted. "I'm not at liberty to say. You only need to know that they are being held prisoner and are no threat to anyone," he said. "There is nothing to fear. A complete search of the ship was done thoroughly as soon as the stowaways were caught. Nothing is amiss. Now let's have a quick look here, shall we?"

They wove their way through the baggage room. Each following the other carefully to avoid banging into one of the dozens of stacked piles of luggage. Sydney stopped at a large metal hatch in the floor.

"Excuse me, what is this?"

"Cargo hatch," Sloane announced.

Sydney and Walter looked at each other. This was it.

Frederick screwed up his face. "We got one in the third class section. Looks the same to me."

"It is," the junior officer admitted. "There's a few throughout the ship."

Walter nonchalantly bent down and grasped the handle and turned it. There was a click and he smiled up at them. Both hands firmly on the turned handle, he lifted. And lifted. But the lifting was all on his part, as the hatch didn't budge an inch.

Hardwick laughed. "It's locked. They all are. Guess you can't take us into the hold?"

"I'm afraid that won't be possible, Mr. Hardwick," Sloane said.

"Come on, man," Hardwick insisted. "You hiding something? Is that it?"

"Mr. Hardwick, Cunard does not allow passengers into the hold. It has nothing to do with hiding, it has everything to do with obeying the rules."

Hardwick winked at Sydney. "That's the English for you, all rules and no fun."

She couldn't help but giggle. He had a point. She could only imagine the scandalized expression on Edward's face if he saw her here.

"The spies are being kept in a cabin, probably on F Deck," Hardwick said to her. Sydney started at the mention of F Deck. The idea that German spies were near where she slept frightened her. "But there's a detective on the Cunard payroll. I'm sure he's got them locked up tight. It's lucky for us we're far above them in first class."

"Isn't it though?" Sydney agreed.

The group made their way back to the corridor where Sloan announced the tour had come to an end. "Would you like me to escort you to the saloon for luncheon, Mr. Hardwick, Miss Sinclair?" he asked, and tossed the others a look of disdain.

"I'm starving," Hardwick said, and waited for Sydney's response.

"I've got plans with my friends here," she answered. "I'm sure we'll meet again, Mr. Hardwick." They shook hands and parted company. Sydney, still holding on to Hannah, and Walter and Frederick behind them, made their way onto the deck where the brilliant sun blinded them.

"Well, that *was* an adventure, gentlemen. I thank you for that," Sydney said.

"Not the friendliest blokes on the high seas, are they?" Walter said. "Thank goodness that man was American and knew who you were. If it weren't for that we'd have been tossed in with the Jerry spies."

Hannah tilted her head at Walter. "Are you a pirate?" she asked.

Walter laughed. "Do I look like a pirate?"

"Not really. But you do act like you're up to no good."

"That, my dear, is Walter's charm," Sydney said. "Now I'm going to rest and get changed because in a couple of hours we're meeting in the saloon to practise for the concert. I expect you there, Walter. You too, Frederick."

"We will be there with bells on," Walter said, and performed an awkward jig. Hannah giggled, tapping a toe here and a heel there, in time.

Sydney looked across the deck to the ocean. The weather had cleared at last and the day was beautiful. The Promenade was clogged with passengers because of it. She almost preferred the grey and the rain for the privacy it afforded. The voyage seemed endless and she had enjoyed the rush of excitement when searching the ship. That they'd come up empty-handed with no proof of illicit cargo was beside the point. She wouldn't worry about the contents of the hold or the German prisoners. Cunard, the captain, the Royal Navy, they knew what they were doing.

Isabel

Isabel had spent the rest of the day pondering Mildred's blackmail. She kept imagining her secrets written on a piece of paper and stuffed into one of the pneumatic tubes and sucked up into the vacuum. Then she pictured the tube landing with a crash in Room 40 before being read by one of the code breakers. It would be so humiliating.

She wondered if getting Mildred a job to prevent the men finding out the truth was really such a bad idea. Dorothy had said that they were short-staffed. The men were familiar with Mildred. It wasn't inconceivable that a tea girl would move up to clerk. Yet the idea rankled Isabel. It was a dirty trick that Mildred was pulling—acting the outraged moralist to Mrs. Burns, all the while blackmailing Isabel.

It was nearly six o'clock when the doorbell rang. Whoever it was at the door didn't linger as within minutes Mrs. Ogilvie appeared outside Isabel's bedroom. "You're a popular one, Miss Nelson. It's a message for you." Isabel took the envelope. "I hope it's good news." The older woman hovered as though waiting to learn its contents.

Isabel thanked her, then shut the door. It was a letter from Mrs. Burns. She ripped open the envelope.

Dear Miss Nelson,

I'm requesting your presence at my office at the Admiralty tomorrow morning, 9 o'clock, 5 May, to discuss your situation further.

Regards,

Mrs. D. Burns

Isabel wanted to be optimistic. The woman could have sacked her in the letter but she hadn't. Yet the words left no clue whatsoever. Mildred had said she would speak to Mrs. Burns tomorrow morning. Had she anticipated Isabel's co-operation and set up such a meeting? The thought of Mildred sharing a desk inside Room 40 gave Isabel a chill. The girl had caused trouble twice now; there was no way she could be trusted. There would be future requests, insinuations and threats. She had to be stopped and there was only one way to do it and get what Isabel needed—which was to be back inside Room 40 to know what was evolving in the Irish Sea . . . she had to be with *her* men.

It was time the true Isabel Nelson emerged from hiding. Her colleagues needed to see her as she really was and accept her. Only then would she belong in Room 40 without question. And if they did receive her, she would never have to fear the likes of Mildred ever again.

Isabel stood at the mirror fixing her hair. Only this time she didn't draw it back off her face. Instead she allowed the soft waves to dominate and even cascade down one cheek. She reached for a pot of rouge and the lipstick. The lipstick slid across her mouth leaving its deep red tint. She rubbed the rouge on the apples of her cheeks and stroked a whisper of it across her eyelids. Her features didn't seem so plain anymore. She knelt down and grabbed the box from under the bed. Isabel kicked off her sensible brogues and slipped on the red shoes. She turned around in the mirror and examined her reflection. The dress wasn't her smartest but it would have to do. She looked like someone else. Someone she hadn't seen in a long time.

Edward

B ut sir, are you sure about this?" Maxwell asked. He had finished brushing Edward's navy twill jacket and held it for him to slide his arms through.

"Yes, Maxwell," Edward said. "My mind is made up."

His discussion with Brooke had ended with them being no closer, and no fonder of each other. Instead all his thoughts were consumed with Sydney. It was wrong. He had to set his mind straight and rid himself of silly romantic ideas. At least he was determined to try, and to his mind the only way to fix this was to meet Sydney and ask her to join them for dinner in the hope that the two sisters could work out their differences. Then once they were getting along, they could all carry on as before and he would see Sydney as a sister and only a sister.

"That will do, Maxwell," Edward said when he'd taken a final glance in the mirror.

Maxwell sniffed his disapproval and opened the Parlour Suite door. "I will accompany you, sir."

"No need," Edward said gamely, and walked along the passageway to the staircase. Maxwell was equally determined and nipped at Edward's heels the whole way down. When they reached the entrance to third class both men hesitated as though grave danger lay ahead.

"We can return if you wish," Maxwell suggested hopefully.

"Certainly not," Edward said, and began the descent down the third class staircase. He was determined to retrieve Sydney at once. Though he expected her to put up a fight, he would be disappointed if she didn't.

The two men disregarded the strange glances they received from the other passengers and politely declined to be redirected to first class by more than one dutiful steward. A cursory glance into the third class ladies' lounge as well as a hurried stroll along the Promenade had so far yielded no sign of Sydney. They were nearing the staircase that led down to the Saloon Deck, where the third class dining saloon lay, when the sound of music and singing drifted up to them.

"It seems early for tea," Maxwell said.

"Perhaps some of the band members are rehearsing," Edward said. "Let's have a look, shall we."

The performance was in full swing when Edward and Maxwell entered the saloon. The spectacle before them was surprising enough, but once they recognized the pianist it was beyond shocking. It was Sydney playing her heart out as a girl of about ten was singing with a voice that sounded like a person twice her age. Two men Edward didn't recognize were dancing a jig as stewardesses stood watching enthusiastically. Then one of the men grabbed one of the stewardesses and swung her around the floor, a gesture that made everyone laugh.

"It's Miss Sinclair," Maxwell said with solemn alarm. "And she's playing 'Alexander's Ragtime Band.'"

Edward looked at his valet. "I'm surprised at you, Maxwell. You never struck me as a fan of show tunes."

"Irving Berlin is a genius, sir."

Edward was grinning. Such a display of uncensored liveliness was not the sort of thing one expected from an heiress of Sydney's repute. He strolled toward the piano for a closer view as Hannah sang.

"Come on along, come on along
Let me take you by the hand
To the man, to meet the man
Who's the leader of the band."

To his surprise Edward began to nod and clap in time.

*"Come on and hear, come on and hear
Alexander's Ragtime Band
Come on and hear, come on and hear
The best band in the land."*

Sydney

The newly added percussion made Sydney look up from her piano keys and directly into Edward's eyes. The sight of him made her forget where she was in the song. Her timing, now fully disrupted, forced Hannah to quit singing and Walter to stop dancing and release the stewardess from his arms. For a moment everyone stood motionless, unsure what to do. All eyes were bearing down on Edward who appeared more uncomfortable by the moment.

"I didn't mean to disturb you," he said anxiously. "I came to find Sydney. The music drew us here."

Sydney suppressed an urge to thank him for sticking up for her last night. But he could never learn that she overheard. "Is Brooke unwell?" she asked. His presence made her uneasy twice over; firstly, because he should not be paying her such special attention, and secondly, because the sight of him thrilled her.

"She is quite well," he said. "I need to speak to you a moment."

"We need to rehearse," Hannah interjected, rescuing them all from further awkwardness. "You can listen to us make music. But you have to be quiet."

Sydney smiled. "I'm forgetting my manners." She proceeded to introduce Edward to Walter, Frederick and Hannah. Edward was gracious and brought Maxwell forward to make their acquaintance. "You know, Hannah, Edward does wonderful animal sounds. You should hear his sheep." She watched as the others looked at Edward in disbelief. He didn't bat an eye but the same sly grin came across his face.

"You don't frighten me," he teased.

"I would never want to," Sydney answered. "Perhaps he can accompany us, Hannah. What is a good percussive sound? A moo or a heehaw?"

The girl looked thoughtful for a moment. "I think Mr. Frohman only wants to hear me," she said wisely.

"Hannah, you demonstrate exquisite taste," Edward said approvingly. "Please continue."

"From the top, Sydney," Hannah ordered.

"Yes, Miss," Sydney said happily, and began the song again, occasionally peeking at Edward as she played.

Walter walked over to stand with Edward. "She's very talented," he said.

Edward didn't take his eyes from Sydney when he answered. "She is."

Walter smirked. "I was talking about Hannah."

"Yes, of course," Edward answered, completely flustered. "That's who I meant."

Walter patted him on the back, much to Maxwell's consternation. "I bet you did." With that he grabbed the stewardess's hand and once again twirled her around to the music. Edward began to tap his feet until he noticed Maxwell, stiff and stately, a few feet from him.

"Maxwell, you really should loosen up," he teased the older man.

The valet further straightened his posture. "I'm as loose as I can be, sir."

Seeing Edward moving to the music Hannah danced over to him and grabbed his hands. "Can you foxtrot?" she asked.

His horrified look was the only answer she needed. "Don't worry. I can teach you."

Hannah took the lead. Sydney tried hard not to laugh. Edward was stiff all right, but his young partner knew her way around footwork and soon enough even he was able to swing a little.

"You're doing wonderfully," Hannah said encouragingly.

Edward glanced at Sydney imploringly. "I'm trying."

"That's all you have to do," Hannah said, then let go of him and continued to sing and tap dance.

The impromptu concert continued with the music drifting out of the saloon and into the passageway where it reached the ears of Sarah, clutching the note Brooke had written to Sydney. An ardent fan of ragtime, the maid followed the music and found herself in the saloon doorway hoping for a brief respite from her duties. She wasn't prepared for the sight of not only seeing her mistress playing a bawdy tune for a kiddie, but also finding Edward nodding and tapping his foot. He was gazing at Sydney. Only a fool wouldn't notice how he looked at her. Sarah raced back in the direction she'd come from.

"What's next, Hannah?" Walter asked when the song was over. "Do you know that bumblebee song?"

"Yes!" she shouted, and turned excitedly to Sydney.

"You bet I do," Sydney said.

Her fingers were poised above the keys and she was about to begin when without warning Edward sat beside her on the piano bench. Even Hannah was caught off guard and looked to Walter for an explanation. All he could do was shrug.

"I'm better at watching than dancing," Edward whispered to Sydney. "I hope you don't object."

She looked around at the others who averted their eyes politely. "Why should I?" She spoke loudly so there was no doubt everyone could hear. "We're going to be brother and sister in another week."

From his expression she might as well have stabbed him with a steak knife. "Yes. Indeed. We're practically family," he agreed politely.

He edged closer to her, so close that their thighs nearly touched. She chose to ignore him and forced a smile that was intended to be neutral, as though she were smiling at Mr. Garrett, even though her breath seemed to catch at his nearness. Her fingers nimbly beat out the opening bars of the song and once more Hannah sang like a seasoned vaudeville performer.

Walter gestured to Maxwell. "Why don't you dance a few steps? Makes you feel alive," he said. The valet merely sighed. Walter laughed. "I thought as much."

Sydney used every ounce of discipline she possessed to focus on playing the piano. She could feel Edward watching her intently as he leaned his elbow on the edge of the instrument and rested his head on his hand. They could easily be in one of the music clubs in the Village.

Everyone was so consumed by the song that no one noticed when Brooke and Sarah entered the room.

"I told you, Miss," Sarah hissed. "It's dreadful."

Brooke marched toward the piano. Hannah was the first to see her and smiled: the larger the audience the better. But her glee was short-lived when it became apparent that the woman bearing down on her was as enraged as a charging bull. She stopped singing abruptly and gulped. Sydney also halted her playing and turned around to see what was the matter. There stood her sister, eyes narrowed, hands on hips. The image would have been humorous if she hadn't been the cause of it.

"Brooke—" Sydney began but her sister cut her short.

"Well, what have we here?" Brooke said, wrestling a note of cheerfulness into her tone.

But Sydney knew better. She saw her sister look at Edward, who slowly rose to his feet. "We were practising for the ship's concert," Sydney explained.

"How lovely," she answered. "Edward, I'm surprised to find you *here* of all places."

He looked annoyed. "I came to speak to Sydney about returning to the Regal Suite. It is what you wanted."

"You knew I had written to Sydney about that very thing," Brooke said. She smiled through gritted teeth. "How forgetful you are. And have you convinced her, darling?"

"We got consumed with the music," Edward said. "But now that I've succeeded in bringing you two together I shall let you discuss it. Good day, Sydney." He bowed slightly in Walter and Frederick's direction then without another word departed the saloon—Maxwell not three feet behind him.

His actions seemed to further humiliate Brooke. As though sensing this, Sarah dashed over from the doorway and shoved the envelope into Sydney's hands. "For you, Miss Sydney," she sputtered.

Sydney and Brooke regarded each other warily. "Brooke, I didn't mean—"

"Come now, Sydney, ever since you were a child you've gotten your way," she said. "And now you've managed to bring Edward down to your level."

Walter coughed loudly in protest, but Brooke took no notice.

Sydney was about to respond but Brooke raised a hand to silence her and followed Edward out the door. Sarah hesitated.

"I think you should go with her," Sydney instructed the maid. The girl took off at a run. Everyone was still silent as mice. She took a breath. "Now, Hannah, from the beginning—"

When the rehearsal was over Sydney went and stood out on deck to get some sun and air. Walter found her there. He lit a cigarette and they basked in the warmth for a moment.

"Hannah has a gift, don't you think?" she asked him.

"She does," he agreed. He took a drag from the cigarette and blew the smoke over the railing, watching it disperse on the air. "I hope you know what you're doing."

Sydney was taken aback. "With Hannah or my piano playing?"

Walter tossed his cigarette overboard. "With your sister's fiancé."

She flinched. "Edward and I have become friends."

"He's falling head over heels with you," Walter told her. "And you don't seem to object, if you don't mind my saying so."

Sydney felt embarrassed, annoyed and defensive all at once. "That's absurd, Walter. Edward is engaged to Brooke."

"That may be, but there are feelings between you two," he warned. "Be careful. You're a good girl from what I see."

She continued to gaze out at the ocean. "I would never let anything happen with Edward," she said firmly. "I wouldn't hurt my sister."

Isabel

The Coach & Horses was a short walk from the Old Admiralty Building. It had rained earlier but by the time Isabel stepped off the bus the sky had cleared. She stepped lively along the sidewalk that was packed with people heading home or out for a pint.

She was a few feet from the pub's front door when she caught sight of Henry and Mildred huddled closely. Isabel's eyes narrowed into tiny slits. She could feel the muscles between her brows squeeze into tight folds. She thought of her mother. Remembering her instructions to never frown or scowl (it caused wrinkles), Isabel smoothed her face and walked directly to them. Henry and Mildred didn't notice her at first, too busy whispering to each other to hear her footsteps.

"You should come with me. It will be a lark . . ." Henry said.

Mildred blushed (a little too much, Isabel thought) and giggled. Isabel slid up beside them and they practically leapt apart at the sight of her.

"Isabel!" Henry exclaimed.

"Good evening, Henry," she said.

Mildred forced a tight smile but her eyes took in every inch of Isabel in her dress, shoes and makeup. "I'm so glad you decided to come tonight."

"I thought I'd get a pint with my colleagues," she explained sweetly.

"I'm sure you have loads to say to the men, especially Mr. Denniston. He's already here," Mildred said coolly.

"What have you to say, Isabel?" Henry joked, oblivious to the tension. "We were told you were sick as a dog. Here you are all dressed up."

"This old frock?"

"You look like a screen star," Henry said. "What gives?"

"I'm sure Isabel has her reasons," Mildred offered.

"Nothing at all, Henry," she answered.

Isabel stepped into the pub. As always the room was dark and it took a moment for her eyes to adjust. She walked through the main room, past the bar and into the backroom where the code breakers could usually be found. Sure enough, seated at a corner table, half-finished pints in front of them, were Curtis, Rotter, Norton, Anstie and, sitting facing her, Denniston. He saw her first.

"Well, look who's decided to show up," he said, and sprang to his feet. "Gentlemen, stand up for the lady."

They obeyed and greeted her warmly, genuinely happy to see her. But it was the looks of astonishment on their faces that was the most remarkable. It was as though they were seeing her as a woman for the first time. She couldn't blame them. Inside she was flattered.

"Come have a seat," Rotter said, and he grabbed a chair from another table and situated it between himself and Anstie.

"Thank you," she said. As she removed her light jacket she could feel the men still studying her. She hid her pleasure as best she could by removing her gloves slowly, deliberately, aware that she had a captive audience.

"Say," Norton said, "you don't usually wear colour on your face."

"Don't I?" she asked innocently.

Curtis kicked Norton under the table. "You don't comment on a girl's face, you idiot."

Everyone laughed. "Your hair does suit you like that," Anstie added, then stared at his beer.

"Thank you, Anstie," she said.

"Let me get you a draught," Rotter said, and got up.

"Whisky, please, Mr. Rotter."

He grinned and nodded. As the men's behaviour returned to normal, which is to say they relaxed around her again, like she was their old colleague and not some pretty girl they wanted to dance with, she noticed that Denniston was still staring. His expression was unreadable. Was he disapproving of the change in her appearance? Was he suspicious of her absence?

"Where have you been hiding?" Denniston asked as if on cue, peering at her over the rim of his beer glass.

"Didn't Mrs. Burns tell you?" she asked, her voice louder than usual to ensure it didn't waver.

He seemed surprised by the question. "Tell me what?"

Rotter appeared with her whisky and she cupped the glass in her hands but didn't drink. It was time to come clean. These men were accustomed to filtering out the facts and deciphering secrets yet they had clearly missed hers. There would be no holding back. They needed her and by God she needed them.

"I'm on suspension," she said, and lifted the glass to her lips. She took a long drink of the whisky as silence followed her words. The men exchanged looks with each other. Not Denniston. He continued to stare at her.

"I wasn't informed," he said. "Perhaps Hall or Hope knew of it."

"Perhaps," she said.

"Why would they suspend you?" Curtis asked. "You caught stealing a biscuit?" He laughed but ceased immediately when he saw no one else was.

"Can you tell us?" Rotter asked. "I mean . . . it's not top secret or anything?"

"That's why she's here," Denniston said firmly. "Isn't it, Isabel?"

Isabel forced herself to stare back at Denniston. "Yes it is, Mr. Denniston."

He opened his mouth to speak but the sudden arrival of Henry made him shut it again. Henry was alone. The timing could not have been more perfect. "What's going on? You all look so serious," he said, and sat down.

"Where's Mildred?" Isabel asked.

"She got a sudden headache," he explained, an earnest note of concern in his voice. He was an innocent sort. He could detect no amount of feminine wiles.

"How awful for her," Isabel lied.

Anstie jumped in. "Isabel was telling us she's been suspended."

Henry looked at her. It didn't seem such a shock to him. "How dreadful," he said quietly.

Isabel forced a pleasant expression and turned back to Denniston. "It is true," Isabel said. "I'm afraid there's a fallen woman in our midst." They all sat up straight. "I don't mean to shock you. It's nothing to do with the war or Germany."

The men relaxed again but were all trained on Isabel, waiting. She took her time. Her wording had to be exact, or did it? *To hell with it. I did what I did and it's time to own up to it.*

"As some of you know, when I was in Oxford," she began, "I worked for a man named Mr. Chambers. He was a professor of engineering science. I started there as a housemaid for him and his wife. But he soon saw that I had more to offer. He thought I was clever. And as many of you can attest, I've always been curious." She paused as though waiting for one of the men to disagree; when they didn't, she continued. "He had an interesting hobby—"

"He has a radio interceptor," Henry piped in. "Chambers is a friend of Leslie Lambert."

Isabel glared at Henry. She had told him about it in one of their many bus rides home. Of course he never got the full story. "Yes, they are very good friends. Mr. Lambert came to the house several times. And on more than one occasion I was allowed to discuss their hobby."

"That seems unusual," Rotter said, not unkindly. "I mean for a maid to be invited to chat with guests. Mr. Chambers is a very forward-thinking man?"

It was the opening Isabel needed. "He is when his wife is away."

Curtis knocked over his beer, causing Norton to leap up to avoid being drenched.

"Go on," Denniston said. Of all the men only his expression remained fixed.

"Let me begin by saying that I'm ashamed of my role in my own story. What happened in Oxford is the biggest regret of my life . . . but the truth is that Mr. Chambers and I were lovers," she said, taking note of the slack jaws and wide-eyed looks that followed her words. "He said he loved me and that he would divorce his wife. She wasn't the warmest of women. I didn't think she cared, to be honest. And even if she had, I'm not sure I did. I was in love with him too, you see. Mr. Chambers believed in me. He took an interest. He thought I was smart. No one had ever taken an interest or thought me clever before but here was this great man, an Oxford professor no less, teaching me Morse code, allowing me to listen to the wireless interceptor and letting me read his books. Then he paid for my typing and shorthand lessons so I might one day better my position. It was glorious."

Her throat was parched. She sipped the whisky, thankful that so far none of the men had stormed out. Only Henry seemed uncomfortable. His discomfort was about to get a whole lot worse.

"Then Mrs. Chambers found out," she said, and paused. It was like a performance and she held her audience captivated. "Mildred saw George, Mr. Chambers and me together and she told his wife. I was dismissed but Mr. Chambers helped me find this new position. You see, I felt a fool for falling in love with a married man," Isabel said stoically. "I had learned so much and wanted to contribute to the war effort and it was going well until someone I knew in Oxford came to London and told Mrs. Burns. She suspended me until further notice."

The group fell silent. The sounds of the pub's other customers drifted over to them. A game of darts was in play as was a debate over the cost of beer, which the publican was sure to win. Curtis shifted his chair and the legs squealed against the floor.

"Why would someone tell Mrs. Burns any of this?" he asked.

Henry shifted uncomfortably, scrunching his hat in his hands. "It was Mildred."

"She told on Isabel twice?" Norton asked, astonished. "Why on earth?"

"She felt it was her moral duty," Henry said.

A collective grunt rose up from the men at the table. "What a load of rot! We're in a bloody war. You can't get more immoral than killing, can you?"

"That's why she did it," Henry said defensively, refusing to look at Isabel. "Mildred, I mean Miss Fox, felt it was her duty to ensure the Admiralty retained the highest of standards for employees." He looked at Isabel at last. Isabel pressed her red lips together and inhaled. There was no way she was going to tell the men about the blackmail. It wasn't up to her to explain Mildred's actions, nor to get her a job with these men. Isabel had to restore her position on her own terms.

"Just what we bloody well need at Room 40," Norton scoffed. "Jealous women out to stab each other in the back."

"Mildred isn't part of Room 40," Parish reminded him. "Isabel is."

"So what's to happen?" Anstie asked Isabel. "When can you come back?"

"I'm not sure I can come back," she said. "Mrs. Burns said she is thinking it over. I'm to meet her tomorrow morning. There's a chance she'll keep me on—"

The men's posture slackened a little with relief. "Thank goodness!"

She shook her head. "In the kitchen."

Denniston had emptied his glass and lit a cigarette. She watched him. He was so composed, so cold. She had underestimated him. Or perhaps overestimated her own value to the team.

"That's why I'm here tonight. I decided to let you all see the real me. The tarnished Isabel Nelson," she said, and smiled. "I wanted to tell you the truth and ask for your help. I want my job back."

The silence returned as the men exchanged looks with one another. Except for Henry who once again was fixated on his footwear, and Denniston who was playing with a pack of matches.

"I'm not sure what we could do," Rotter said at last.

"I'm hoping one of you will speak to Mrs. Burns on my behalf." She directed her words at Denniston. "Mr. Norton was right when he said Room 40 doesn't need jealous and spiteful women doing battle. There are too many real battles to be won. I can put what happened behind me and I hope you gentlemen can as well. I work hard and will continue to. I stand here humbled by my own regrettable actions. I want only the opportunity to redeem myself. I'm to meet Mrs. Burns tomorrow morning at nine a.m. to hear her decision."

Denniston stubbed out his cigarette even though it was only half done. "Gentlemen, it's time we got back to our job," he said, and stood up. He was always the de facto leader of Room 40 and the men followed his lead. Isabel sat still.

"Good evening, Isabel," Rotter said quietly as he passed her. The other men echoed his words as they each walked by. She hadn't expected a uniform cheer of rah-rah-rah, but she had hoped for a more concrete sign of approval and acceptance. Isabel reminded herself that these men were following Denniston's orders to get back to work. They wouldn't show emotion, but that didn't mean they didn't feel it.

When it was Henry's turn he paused as if he wanted to say something, but deciding against it he simply nodded at her, then followed the others. Denniston waited until it was only the two of them and paused in front of her. She couldn't bring herself to look at him.

"Don't give up, Isabel," he said. She met his gaze and a thin smile unfurled across her mouth. He smiled back, the faintest of smiles. "I always find right wins out in the end."

Then he was gone and she was left with only the sounds of the dart game.

MAY 5

Isabel

She hardly slept all night. But a lack of sleep wasn't going to affect her course of action. Isabel took only a cursory glance at the lipstick on her dressing table before picking it up. Her finger expertly glided the colour across her mouth. She rubbed her lips together. Perfect. She put her hair up but not in the severe bun. Instead a chignon with soft wisps would do nicely. If Mrs. Burns wanted to paint her as a scarlet woman then she'd better dress the part.

She clattered down the steps of the boarding house and out the door. The skies were overcast again but there was a hint of blue peering through the murk and it was warm enough to make do with a cardigan. The bus ride seemed longer than usual. She was anxious to get this over with. She could scarcely tolerate Mrs. Burns's fierce eyes and witchy demeanour. Who was she really? Why was she or Mildred Fox any better than her?

The bus left Isabel in Trafalgar Square, which was packed with people on their way to work or the galleries. A group of schoolchildren were climbing up the stone lions as their schoolmistress was trying in vain to chase them down. Isabel touched the statue of Lord Nelson for luck, then walked down Whitehall, passing several navy and army personnel. Then she was standing once again in front of the Old Admiralty Building. Isabel paused briefly to work up the courage and then stepped inside.

The door to Mrs. Burns's office was closed. Isabel knocked.

"Come in."

Isabel took a deep breath and opened the door. She found Mrs. Burns, not bothering to glance up at her, writing in a ledger. Isabel waited. Eventually the older woman closed the ledger, removed her spectacles and, with a stern face, looked at Isabel. Seeing the lipstick and loose chignon, she scowled, creating a deep V between her brows.

"Please be seated, Isabel," she said, and waved to the chair directly across from her. Isabel said not a word as she sat down, folded her hands in her lap and without hesitation crossed her legs, which didn't go unnoticed by Mrs. Burns.

"I've given the matter a great deal of thought," the older woman said. Isabel stared blankly, determined not to show emotion. Her composure made Mrs. Burns uncomfortable and she shifted in her chair. "And while I appreciate your dedication to Room 40, I fear you will be too much of a distraction should your past become known. There are too many single men working there and, well, they cannot be blamed for following urges should the truth get out. But you'll be pleased to know that I have a heart and I've decided to find you a place as a charwoman."

Mrs. Burns smiled as though that settled the matter. Isabel's face remained blank.

"Have you nothing to say, Miss Nelson?"

"No," Isabel answered. In truth she was deciding exactly what to say, how much to say and at what volume.

Her response flustered Mrs. Burns, who began to fiddle with the pencils on her desk and some loose ledger sheets. "Then you may report to the kitchen immediately. And wipe off that lipstick. They will provide a hairnet. That is all."

Then the door opened abruptly. Isabel turned in her chair to find Mr. Denniston standing in the door frame. Mrs. Burns stood up deferentially, but Isabel stayed put. She looked at Denniston but it was almost as though he didn't see her there for he walked inside and stood beside her without even a glance in her direction.

"What can I do for you, Mr. Denniston?" Mrs. Burns asked politely. "Isabel, you are dismissed."

Was he ignoring her out of embarrassment? Had he forgotten that she'd be there? She stood to leave, her eyes averted from Denniston. She could take offending Mrs. Burns, but disappointing him was too much.

"Stay, Isabel," he said, and touched her arm. She followed his hand up to his face and he smiled. She sat back down. He turned to Mrs. Burns.

"I dare say you've been steered off course where Miss Nelson is concerned," he said. Mrs. Burns had to take her seat. "She is an exemplary member of the Room 40 team and we can't do without her. We've spent countless hours giving her specialized training and she has been cleared for top secret information. You can't expect us to take time from our work to find another girl and train her, can you? There is a *war* going on, Mrs. Burns."

He stared at the older woman. She glared at Isabel for a few minutes before shifting back to him. "I think I know how to manage my staff, Mr. Denniston."

"Indeed you do," he said, then produced a paper from inside his jacket. He unfolded it and placed it on her desk. "But Miss Nelson is no longer under your command. As you will see from the letter, Commander Hope has requisitioned her for Room 40. Miss Nelson is no longer under your charge. And as I am sure you are aware his authority supersedes yours."

Isabel would have enjoyed the look of astonishment on Mrs. Burns's face but she was too occupied looking at Denniston. Then there were the tears that needing fighting back. He had listened. She was valued.

Mrs. Burns exhaled loudly and slapped both hands on her desk in protest. But when she spoke it was calmly and graciously. "Very well, Miss Nelson. You heard the man."

Isabel leapt to her feet. She wanted to throw her arms around Denniston but knew better.

"Thank you, Mrs. Burns. Mr. Denniston, shall I come with you now?"

"Of course," he said.

With that they both headed for the door. But Mrs. Burns wasn't done yet. "Miss Nelson."

Isabel turned back and the two women stared at each other.

"I hope you know what to do with this."

"With what, Mrs. Burns?" Isabel asked, and smiled, happy she had worn the lipstick.

Mrs. Burns's own lips were pursed. "This second chance. Few women get one, you know. Don't waste it."

"I can assure you I won't," Isabel said. "We have a war to win."

Sydney

The note was lying on the unmade bed. Sydney had read it many times since Sarah had shoved it into her hands yesterday. Brooke had written it before finding her playing piano with Edward at her side, which made her wonder if Brooke would stand by what she'd written or if her conciliatory offer would be rescinded.

Dear Sydney,

Edward tells me you and he had a delightful conversation. I'm so happy you two are getting along. Now that the truth is out we can all relax and enjoy the voyage. I know you'll need time to pack and say farewell to your new friends (in steerage, egads!), so why don't we plan on your moving up tomorrow? We have been invited to dine at the captain's table, you know what an honour that is—even more so considering how rare Captain Turner's appearances have been all this time. We can have a lovely dinner and maybe some dancing. Alfred has asked about you each time we see him. See you in the Regal Suite.

Yours, Brooke

Sydney doubted she was still welcome in the Regal Suite. Her sister was so angry. Her fiancé had publicly criticized her and now she'd found him sitting beside her like a lovesick fool. How had it happened? She had never meant to hurt Brooke. She vowed to go to dinner in the first class dining room and perform the part of the ideal sister. The formality of the captain's table was perfect. There could be no opportunity for emotions to get the better of anyone. After all nothing untoward had happened. It was all a misunderstanding. Even on her part. It could be said that Edward was being attentive because he was a gentleman, all politeness and chivalry. He had no notions about her that Brooke need worry about or that she need reject. Edward had shown an interest in her life and that was immensely flattering, but no more. It didn't mean she was *attracted* to him. Her mind was made up. She would send a reply to her sister and agree to dinner. Sydney scribbled the note and headed out her door to find a steward to deliver it. She felt better already. *I will fix this.*

B
ut why do you want to have dinner upstairs?" Hannah asked.
  Sydney was in her corset and underpinnings holding up a navy gown in front of her. Hannah sat perched on the bed as they both looked in the mirror. "My sister and I have been invited by the captain. I have to go. Besides, my sister really wants me there," she said. "We fought yesterday and it's time to make up."

"My mother said that because you are rich you are supposed to be up there all the time," Hannah continued. "And that the reason you aren't is a secret."

Sydney looked at Hannah aghast.

"What secret?" she asked.

"I don't know. Isn't that why it's a secret?" Hannah answered.

Sydney laughed nervously and returned to her reflection in the mirror. Hannah wasn't finished though. "That man Edward?"

"What about him?"

"I think he likes you better than your sister," Hannah said.

"I don't think so," Sydney lied. Goodness, was it so obvious that a child could see? "So is this the dress for tonight? Navy is flattering on me."

Hannah scrunched up her face and shook her head. "You have yellow hair. Do you have a yellow dress?"

It was Sydney's turn to scrunch up her face. Then she remembered. She went over to her trunk and found the amber dress that Sarah had brought her on the first day. It was a little creased but otherwise glorious. She rushed back to the mirror and held it up. Hannah beamed.

"That's beautiful!" she exclaimed. "Look at the pink flowers on it. You will be the prettiest lady upstairs."

Sydney smiled. Wearing the gown that Brooke had bought would be a gesture of solidarity, an olive branch.

"Wear it," Hannah said excitedly. "You have to."

"You don't think it's too much?" she asked, then felt a fool putting such a style responsibility on a young girl. "I mean, do you think other ladies will not like me if I wear this?"

Hannah twisted her mouth in concentration. "I would want you to be my friend. Don't ladies want their friends to look nice?"

"Not always," Sydney said, and smiled at Hannah. "You'll understand more when you're older." She continued to study her reflection and swung her hips a little so that the dress swayed to the motion. It was beautiful.

For the first time since the ship had left New York harbour, Sydney chose to ride the elevator up the levels to the Shelter Deck where she was to meet Brooke and Edward. She had the lift to herself and nervously kept securing the pins in her hair as the wrought-iron cage rose through the ship.

Isabel

When she returned to Room 40 with Denniston, Isabel fought hard to contain her excitement. She had won. Her colleagues took her as she was and she no longer had to fear the likes of Mildred. Dorothy rushed over and hugged her as Joan and Violet waved from the typewriters.

"You can have your machine back. It's missed you." Violet laughed and practically leapt away from the typewriter.

"And I, it," Isabel exclaimed.

The men on her normal shift—Rotter, Anstie, Norton, Curtis and Henry—were all there. They gave her a restrained but welcoming acknowledgement, except for Henry, who continued his eye-contact boycott. *He's such a child.* Commander Hope swept into the room. Seeing him made her smile like he was a long-lost friend.

"Right, I see our team is back on track," he said without addressing her directly.

Everyone was occupied with his or her duties. Isabel had been gone only a couple of days but felt very out of the loop. But she had no time to catch up because Curtis leapt up, waving a telegram that had just come through the pneumatic tube and made a beeline for Commander Hope.

"Sir, we just got this in," he said.

"Go on, what is it?" Commander Hope ordered.

The room went quiet as Curtis read the telegram. *"This morning at approximately 2 a.m., the schooner* Earl of Lathom *was sunk off Kinsale Head. The submarine captain spared the crew before firing guns on her."*

The Old Head of Kinsale was a headland on the southwest coast near County Cork, Ireland. There was only one submarine in that area.

"It's the U-20," Isabel spoke up.

Commander Hope stared. "How do you know that, Miss Nelson?" he asked.

"I've been helping track her since she left port, sir," Isabel said. She felt a wave of self-consciousness. "I meant, I was tracking her before my absence."

"She's correct, sir," Denniston confirmed. "I wager Schwieger is still out there searching for trophies. Our last confirmed reports on U-20 are from May 1." Denniston handed a sheet to Hope who studied it a moment.

"Nothing further?" he asked. The men shook their heads.

"Not until today," Denniston said.

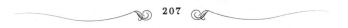

Isabel was relieved that no lives had been lost. It seemed almost silly to target and sink a schooner. "Was the *Earl of Lathom* armed?" she asked.

"Yes," Curtis said. "If you count a cargo of bacon and potatoes as armaments."

The men laughed but Isabel didn't find it amusing. Sinking an unarmed schooner with a small civilian crew was so unnecessary. The Germans would have wanted to prevent the English getting the food supplies and she supposed on that level it was an enemy victory. It reminded her yet again that this war was about nothing but waste, waste of resources and waste of lives. Couldn't the men in charge see that and come to a better understanding? *That's why they don't let women into politics.* She watched Denniston move a pin representing U-20 to Kinsale Head on the map of the British Isles that hung on the wall. It was probably still lurking there, searching for another strike.

"What about the *Lusitania*?" she asked the men. Her words were greeted by silence. She saw Henry out of the corner of her eye, keeping busy with whatever task he was performing. Commander Hope sighed impatiently.

"It's not up to us," he said. "As you well know, Miss Nelson."

Isabel pressed her lips together. There were too many lives at stake to not push ahead. "We know the Admiralstab has been broadcasting the *Lusitania*'s schedule for days, telling its submarines when she's expected in Liverpool," she said firmly.

"I have a meeting with the First Sea Lord now," Commander Hope said, ignoring her. "I will inform him of the intelligence. Anstie, did you finish that report I asked for?"

Anstie held out a file folder. "Yes, sir. It's all here."

Commander Hope took the folder and left them. As soon as the door was closed the men continued their work. Isabel followed Denniston who made his way to the latest batch of intercepts.

"Would you like me to begin with those?" she asked, and indicated the pile of paper in his hand.

Without studying them he took the top half-dozen from the pile and handed them to her. "Over to you," he said. She waited for a smile or any sign of warmth, any indication that they were more intimately connected since he had come to her defence, but he was his usual cool, detached self. He continued to rifle through the pages and she knew their conversation had come to an end. Not that it mattered, she told herself. She had work to do, that was why she was here, the reason he'd come and gotten her. All these thoughts should have been enough to console her and get her on her way but Isabel couldn't let it go. "Did I do wrong to speak up?" she asked Denniston.

He continued sorting the paper. She regretted asking.

"It was unusual that you did," he said, at last looking at her directly. To her relief he smiled. "The *Lusitania* has safely completed the transatlantic crossing many times since the war started. Why should this week be any different? Now get to work, Isabel."

Anything more than an affirming nod would be an error in judgment so she took the pages of transcript and sat down at the typewriter. Dorothy stopped her work and grinned. "Look at you, speaking up about U-boats and targets," she said, and paused. Isabel stiffened, expecting to be reproached. "I'm proud of you."

Isabel grinned, threaded a fresh sheet of paper into the typewriter and began the fast rhythm she was known for. Dorothy laughed and tried to keep up. For a few moments they were in a race, their fingers flying, but before long she gave in and allowed Isabel to pull ahead.

After the excitement of the *Earl of Lathom* the rest of the day passed without incident. Isabel found her routine once again and was feeling nothing but contentment. It was the dinner hour and her shift was over. She had remained on to catch up on her work. Dorothy and the other girls had gone home. Only the men were left; few of them had made any move toward leaving, including Henry. Their work was addictive, something Isabel understood. Despite the stress of her ordeal she couldn't bring herself to go home. Not yet.

She looked up when the door opened. It was Mildred. She held a tray of sandwiches and cake. The two women stared at each other. Mildred must be furious, thought Isabel, seeing her back in Room 40 no worse for the wear and the men happy to have her there despite her past. The slightest smile formed on Isabel's lips and her eyebrows arched. This girl was no match for her.

"What wonderful timing. I'm positively famished," Isabel said. "Please do bring your tray here."

Reluctantly, yet knowing all eyes were on her, Mildred marched over to Isabel's desk and held the tray out for her. Isabel picked up a sandwich and took a bite.

"Thank you, Miss Fox," she said, and returned to her typing.

Mildred stood fast as though she might speak. Isabel looked up from her work.

"Don't you think you should take that tray around to the others?" Isabel said. "The men work long hours, you know. I'm sure they're all as starving as I am."

Mildred didn't answer. She picked up the tray and walked off but it was clear she was flustered by their encounter. Isabel watched as she took the food around to the men, silent as the grave.

Henry was the last on her rounds. "Thank you, Mildred. Very kind," he said as he took a sandwich. "You best be going," Henry suggested. "We've got a lot to do."

It wasn't what Mildred wanted to hear from her beau. In retaliation she shoved the last sandwich onto Henry's desk and squished it with her palm. An ooze of egg mayonnaise squirted across his papers.

"Oh I'm so sorry, sir," Mildred said sarcastically. She turned on her heel and marched out of the room, pausing only to give Isabel a scathing look.

Isabel couldn't help herself and laughed. She caught Rotter's eye and he joined in. Soon the whole of Room 40 was in hysterics. Except for Henry.

"Guess your girl is trying to tell you to lay an egg, Henry," Rotter teased.

Isabel was vindicated but her satisfaction vanished at the sight of Henry skulking out the door after Mildred. She tore into her sandwich like it was the meat off a bone.

Edward

He stood with Brooke across from the lifts. She was wearing a claret evening dress and a sour expression. Even the multiple strands of garnets around her neck couldn't brighten her countenance.

"Really, Edward, I don't see why we don't go to the table and let Sydney arrive on her own," she said. "Captain Turner is waiting."

"Let him wait," Edward said coolly.

Brooke was about to respond when Lady Mackworth and her father, Mr. Thomas, arrived.

"Good gracious, are you two practising the receiving line for your wedding?" she teased.

Brooke smiled thinly. "We are waiting for my sister."

Lady Mackworth's face lit up. "How marvellous," she said brightly. "I can't wait to meet her after everything I've heard."

"She sounds like quite the young lady," her father added as they made their way toward the dining saloon.

The lift doors opened to reveal Sydney. Edward had never seen anyone more beautiful. Her dress was the colour of honey, which perfectly suited her golden hair. The soft pink roses that adorned it were strategically placed across the bias, which accentuated her curves. And around her long neck was a double string of gold pearls that fell below her breasts. Her gloves were a delicate pink satin that matched the roses. But of all the things remarkable about Sydney it was her large hazel eyes that took Edward's breath away.

"Sydney," he said politely, almost indifferently, as he stepped forward and offered his arm. "What a flattering colour your dress is. It nearly matches your eyes."

"Oh good heavens, Edward," Brooke said. "Her eyes are brown."

Edward held his tongue as he led Sydney toward her. The sisters kissed each other on the cheek, as Brooke's own eyes glared as though Sydney, not genetics, was to blame for her hazel eyes.

"I'm so happy to finally join you for dinner," Sydney said.

Brooke was smiling but it was clear she was still very angry with her. "Nothing pleases me more than your happiness."

They strolled to the captain's table, a sister on either side of Edward, a gloved hand each holding on to an arm. The other passengers tried not to stare at the beautiful new arrival. There were murmurs and whispers as they passed several tables. Even some of the stewards took notice of Sydney. Brooke sighed heavily at the attention her sister was receiving.

"I see you decided to wear the dress I bought you," she said coolly.

"You were right about it," she answered. "It does suit me. I never thanked you properly for it."

Edward knew he was at least partially to blame for the tension between the sisters. Maxwell had been right. He should not have pursued Sydney into third class and hovered over her like an aspiring Byron. Brooke had hardly spoken to him all last evening. The sympathy he'd received after his apology for his previous transgression was gone and replaced with an icy politeness. Edward knew he was fooling no one, least of all himself. He was drawn to Sydney, more than he'd ever been to Brooke. And what was worse, perhaps, he feared it would always be so. Rather than deal with the matter he had spent much of his time today in the gentlemen's lounge playing cards and avoiding being taken advantage of by several superior players.

Then by mid-afternoon his fiancée had informed him that Sydney would be joining them for dinner. He thought the matter resolved. Yet she was giving her such a chilly reception. Was there no pleasing the woman?

They arrived at the table where Lady Mackworth and her father were seated alongside several other passengers. Captain Turner stood as Edward made the requisite introductions.

"Welcome," Captain Turner said. He was solemn, yet at the same time appeared slightly bored, as though he wished to be called away on urgent ship business. The rest of the dinner party included Mr. Michael Papadapoulos, a Greek carpet magnate and his Italian wife, Angela; Mr. and Mrs. Harry Keser—Mr. Keser was the president of the Philadelphia

National Bank; and Mrs. Jessie Taft Smith, an American who was travelling to England to join her husband, John. He had designed aeroplane engines for the French that were being used in the war effort and was currently working out plans to do the same with the British. Mrs. Taft Smith let it be known she was carrying the blueprints for the famous Smith engine in her stateroom. Edward would have been enthralled with conversation about aircraft but he had more pressing matters to deal with.

"My, my, Edward, how did you ever choose between two such handsome women?" Mr. Thomas teased. Edward swallowed uneasily as the other guests looked from Brooke to Sydney as though to compare. The sisters smiled demurely at the compliment.

"Indeed. Sydney looks like a film star," Lady Mackworth gushed. "Beauty and brains are a deadly combination."

With an unsubtle roll of her eyes Brooke picked up the menu. "It's always so complicated," she complained. "So many dishes to choose from."

"The chef has printed a sample menu with suggestions as to what goes best with what," Captain Turner pointed out.

"That is very helpful, Captain," Brooke said sweetly. "You must be thrilled to be in charge of such a ship." He grimaced and turned to Mr. Keser. Brooke shrugged. "Edward, be a dear and order for me." She then gave her attention to Angela Papadapoulos and began to discuss the ship's speed for the day's betting pool.

Edward pretended to study the menu and as he did so he glanced at Sydney, hoping to catch her eye. But she seemed determined not to meet his gaze. He felt a hand on his arm and saw that Lady Mackworth was leaning in closely like she was about to divulge a secret.

"I'd say there's a sibling rivalry brewing," Lady Mackworth whispered. "Be careful not to get in the middle of it."

Edward had no appropriate response and he could hardly own up to the truth, which was he was already very much in the middle.

The arrival of Alfred Vanderbilt at the table provided a much-needed injection of levity. Captain Turner sprang to life and was almost jovial as Sydney and Brooke embraced Alfred like a brother. He fawned over

Sydney and lightheartedly chastised her about her third class folly, which she defended eagerly. He sat down beside her and they immediately launched into an intimate chat. The sound of their gaiety made Edward squirm. How he envied their ease with each other. Then Alfred grasped her hand and held it for a moment and she smiled. Edward was jealous. There was no other word for the rotten sensation in his stomach.

"Edward, darling." Brooke's voice shot right through him. "Order the wine. I'm dying of thirst."

He forced himself to look away from the joyfulness that was occurring across the table and turned to the wine list. But another outburst of laughter made concentration impossible.

"Alfred!" Edward shouted at the millionaire, who finally turned his attention away from Sydney.

"Yes, Edward?"

Edward saw with some alarm that everyone was looking at him. Captain Turner's eyes were slits. He hadn't meant to shout. "Alfred, I'd like your opinion with the wine. Would you mind studying the menu and giving me your suggestion?"

Alfred grinned. "I'd say it's up to Captain Turner to choose," he said. "Our wish is yours to command, sir." The other guests chuckled. Even Turner smiled and called a steward over so he could order the wine. Edward continued to watch Sydney until, after an eternity, she looked at him. He smiled and waited for a sign of the shared intimacy that had passed between them during their conversation days before. But she had already turned her attention to Mrs. Taft Smith.

Dinner had been unbearable. Edward was largely ignored. He had sat through the meal listening to Sydney discuss horses with Alfred, that is, when she wasn't engaged with Lady Mackworth on women's politics. The two suffragettes had spent a great deal of time comparing notes on how their two countries addressed the women's movement. Particularly how England's Mrs. Pankhurst and her militant tactics worked and didn't work. Her group, the Women's Social and Political Union, which Lady Mackworth belonged to, had halted all activities when the war began in order to support the British government's fight against the Germans, and had encouraged her followers to do their part. On the opposite side of the table Brooke continued to punish Edward by being entirely captivated by Mr. and Mrs. Papadapoulos.

So Edward was immensely relieved when their party eventually made its way into the lounge. The orchestra was already playing a waltz when they arrived. The ladies caught sight of Charles Frohman and hurried over to him.

"Why Sydney Sinclair," he gushed, and shook her hand. "I was beginning to doubt your existence."

"I've been keeping to myself. Seasickness," she explained.

"I told you she's a sensitive creative," Brooke added.

"I have a favour to ask, Charles," Sydney said. "I'm wondering if you wouldn't mind listening to a young girl perform at tomorrow night's concert."

"Is she talented?" he said, and smiled. He was always on the lookout for the next big thing.

"Very," Sydney said. "She sings and dances. You won't be disappointed."

Edward watched Brooke. She wasn't amused by Sydney's line of conversation. Perhaps it reminded her of this afternoon's rehearsal.

"The child is from steerage," Brooke said.

Everyone looked at Brooke, who smiled sweetly. Frohman chuckled. "If she's got talent I don't care if she's from Queens." They all laughed at his joke, even Edward who had no idea why it was funny.

Frohman excused himself and the ladies took up residence on one of the sofas to listen to the orchestra. A steward was passing around glasses of port and Edward took one from the tray. Alfred joined him on the periphery of the dance floor as passengers swirled around them. He shouldn't resent Alfred's relationship with Sydney. The man was *married* and was a lifelong friend of the Sinclairs. No, it wasn't Alfred he despised but his own cowardice. Duty to family was paramount. But how could he not admit his true feelings before his marriage took place? The Sydney he had spoken with so openly days before would want him to, wouldn't she? The ship was on international waters; surely that neutralized his Englishman's sense of propriety.

"I could use something stronger," Alfred said as he sipped the port. "A brandy would do the trick."

"Make it a double and I'm in," Edward said.

Alfred chuckled. "Let me see what I can do."

Alfred stepped away. Edward continued his thoughts of betrayal. Brooke was his fiancée. He had proposed to her at Rathfon Hall, its walls were sacred to him and he was a man of his word, or so he had always believed. His feelings, this conflict, were ludicrous. He hadn't even met Sydney until a week ago. Yet how could he deny what this past week had meant to him?

Alfred returned with two snifters of brandy.

"Thank you, Alfred," he said, and took a large swig from his. The warmth soothed him as it passed down his throat.

"You're welcome, old chap," Alfred said with a smile. "Sydney looks lovely tonight."

Edward bristled. "Does she?"

The orchestra began to play *The Blue Danube*. Edward polished off the brandy in one gulp and, to Alfred's shock, handed him the empty snifter. "You ride to hounds, Alfred. Do you know what we English call a shot of brandy before the hunt?" Edward asked. His eyes locked onto Sydney who was sitting beside Brooke.

"A cup of courage," Alfred said.

"That's it," Edward said, and marched toward the ladies. Brooke forced a smile as he approached. Sydney continued to chat with Lady Mackworth, completely ignoring him. His hand came up before his words could and he stood before them like a ballroom beggar, waiting for a handout. Sydney stared at his outstretched arm, a look of embarrassment on her face. Alfred walked up behind Edward and also offered his hand. "Sydney, would you care to dance?" he said. "Edward wants to waltz with your sister but I didn't want you left on the sidelines."

The men exchanged looks. "That's very thoughtful, Alfred," Edward said, and adjusted his position so that there would be no doubt his intended partner was Brooke. "My dear."

Grim-faced, Brooke allowed herself to be led onto the dance floor. Sydney followed with Alfred and the two couples began to waltz gracefully to the orchestra's playing. Edward silently twirled Brooke around the floor, but it wasn't long before Alfred and Sydney interrupted them.

"Shall we switch partners?" Alfred suggested with a knowing look at Edward.

Edward was stunned. He needed to give the man more credit.

"Only if my fiancée will release me. Brooke?" Edward said, careful not to display any emotion.

"I'd love to dance with Alfred," Brooke answered. But as they switched partners Edward was struck by how much Brooke resembled a gorgon when she was annoyed. He didn't let her stony face bother him too long once he had glided Sydney off in the opposite direction. But he noticed at once that her usually lovely face was troubled.

"I'm not that bad a dancer, surely," he teased. "I can prove it." Taking a firmer hold of Sydney's waist, he swept her across the floor in the long, flowing steps of the foxtrot that Hannah had taught him. It was similar enough to the waltz that he could guide her around without crashing into other dancers. Although everyone on the floor appeared alarmed, including Sydney.

"Edward," she said, looking around the room at everyone staring at them. "Waltz properly."

Obediently, he slowed their steps down to the three-quarter time signature required by *The Blue Danube*. "Aren't you tired of not having any fun? You've been hiding away all week," he said. "This is the *Lusitania*, the grandest ocean liner in the world, and you should be enjoying yourself." Her face said she didn't agree but he wasn't going to give up. "Where's my black sheep? If you don't smile soon I will bleat until you do."

"Don't make jokes, Edward," she said. "What are you trying to do? You're engaged to my sister yet you act like a bachelor at a speakeasy."

"A what?" Edward said, astonished by such a comparison.

"You heard me," she answered harshly.

He didn't know how to respond but he didn't care because she was finally looking at him. "It's only a dance, it's not like I kissed you," he said cheekily. "Or is that why you're upset? You want me to kiss you."

No amount of willpower could prevent her smiling. "Just shut up and waltz," she said.

They continued to dance in silence. She was right to chastise him. But it didn't seem to matter that he'd met Brooke months before and Sydney only days ago. He had tried with Brooke in England, New York and on the *Lusitania*, yet despite his best efforts he felt nothing for his fiancée. It was this creature in his arms who was tugging at every emotion and it was time to tell her, no matter the consequences. "May I be honest with you, Sydney," he said, the teasing tone gone from his voice.

He saw a flicker of unease cross her lovely face.

"Of course, Edward."

"I will be going to France next month and I may die."

"Don't say such things," Sydney said.

"I must say it because of you," he said. His words had the intended effect for she was gazing into his eyes now. "If death comes to me in the next few months I want to know I've lived every moment."

The music rose to a crescendo and he swept her up in his arms before she could respond. They circled and twirled amongst the other dancers until the music steadied and he brought them to a slow swirl so they were barely moving. "If I am killed, I want to die knowing the woman I *love* is my wife."

Her eyes widened. "What are you saying, Edward?"

"You know I don't love your sister. Nor does she love me."

"Please don't say that. Even if you mean it." She looked around, searching for her sister. Edward followed her gaze and he too saw Brooke, with Alfred, still dancing, oblivious to the conspiracy he was launching against her.

"But I do, Sydney," he continued.

"But you wanted the arrangement. Both of you did. You can't pretend otherwise."

"I hadn't met you," he explained earnestly. "You weren't the American who came looking for an aristocrat with a title."

"You make it sound vulgar," she gasped.

He was pushing her toward a truth neither wanted to face but to his delight she wasn't running away. She remained firmly in his hands and he would keep her there as long as it took him to confess it all.

"It is," he responded with a light laugh. "And I was willing to go along with it for my family, my home, all of it. I thought it was noble to sacrifice love for those things."

"Well, maybe it is," she said. She was shaking. He knew he didn't have long before she would turn and run back to the comfort of political talks with Lady Mackworth and then his chance would be over forever.

"It's not noble. It's idiotic," he said, his smile gone. "I want to break it off with Brooke," he added bluntly, his hand clasping hers tighter and tighter. "I want to be with you."

Sydney concentrated on the dancing and would not look at him. "Edward, you must stop this," she hissed.

"Am I wrong to think you feel the same about me?"

Her hand went limp in his, her back stiffened in his arms.

"If I've given you the wrong impression you must forgive me," she sputtered. "I think we must stop dancing. I'm feeling flushed."

"Do you feel nothing for me?" he pleaded. It was the last thing he had in his arsenal. It was everything.

She looked at him closely, longingly. It gave him hope. "How can you ask me that?" she responded quietly, and walked away. He had no choice but to follow. They headed back to the sofa where Brooke and Alfred had also returned and were watching them.

"You two looked like you could dance all night," Brooke said with a tight smile.

"It's a fine band," Alfred said, trying to keep the peace. "Sydney, would you care to get back out there with me? Let the betrothed couple have a turn about the dance floor?"

But Alfred was looking at Edward as he spoke.

"I can't—" Sydney shook her head. "I'm not feeling well. I must go. Good night." Sydney then turned and fled the room. Edward was going to go after her but someone had grabbed his coat sleeve. It was Alfred. The men stared at each other a moment and Edward knew he was right to stand him down. Edward gave a subtle nod and Alfred let go of his sleeve.

"Goodness, I hope she's not going to be seasick," Lady Mackworth offered.

"There's no need to worry about Sydney," Brooke purred. "She's had too much dancing for one night. More than is good for her." She turned to Edward. "Come, darling, my turn."

MAY 6

Sydney

It was six a.m. when Sydney stepped onto the Promenade Deck and was greeted by raised voices and the banging and clanging of metal. She had barely slept and for a moment doubted her own ears. But as she reached the port side and looked up she saw the source of the noise. Crewmen were in the process of swinging out the lifeboats, *all of them*. It appeared to be a tough and frustrating exercise. She watched as teams of six or more wrestled with the davits and the heavy ropes, the men heaving and pulling and swearing as they worked until the boats hung suspended over the sea. Sticking out from the sides of the ship the lifeboats seemed precarious and fragile, like eggs perched on the edge of a nest, not vessels of safety. The noise had been loud enough and went on long enough that several of the first class passengers had come outside to see what was going on. Like Sydney, they watched in fascination but at the same time it was a solemn event. The reality of the waters the ship had entered made this activity a necessary precaution. But instead of being reassuring, it instilled a sense of anxiety.

"The captain must be worried about submarines to order this," a woman whispered to her husband.

The man put his arm around his wife protectively. "It's just a show," he explained. "Better to be safe than sorry." Her fearful expression said she didn't share his view.

Sydney didn't want to watch any longer. It was too unnerving to think of any event that would cause them to need lifeboats. She walked sombrely along the deck dressed in her black wool crepe. It was a mourning dress, the only one she hadn't packed away since her father's death. After such a fitful night she had naturally gravitated to it at dawn.

"Good morning, Miss."

The voice startled her. She jerked her head up and saw Junior Third Officer Bestic striding along, a forced smile on his lips. "Good morning, Officer Bestic," she returned. "I see the captain has ordered all of the lifeboats to be swung out. It's unsettling but I suppose it has to be done."

Bestic glanced out to sea. "There is no reason to be afraid," he insisted in a tone that belied his own nerves. "All precautions are being taken."

Sydney smiled. "Have we officially entered the war zone now?" she asked.

He nodded. "Yes, Miss. We sailed into the war zone early this morning."

"When is the Royal Naval escort arriving?" she asked. "I keep expecting to see a cruiser on the horizon any moment."

"I can't comment on that," he answered flatly. "But as I said, there is nothing to be worried about. Captain Turner has the ship under the strictest naval orders and we will be in Liverpool on schedule."

"Are we sailing at top speed now?" she asked. "It doesn't feel very fast." She almost questioned him about the fourth boiler but didn't want to admit she'd been listening to rumours.

"The captain is the judge of when to increase her speed," he answered. "Have a good day, Miss. I'm needed on the bridge." He marched away from her.

She continued her walk, wishing she had spoken to the captain in more depth at dinner last night. There was much she wanted to know. She found a few people on the starboard side watching a school of dolphins cavort in the ship's wake. The mammals leapt out of the water and wiggled with joy before disappearing below the surface. Again and again they played, much to the delight of the human audience high above. Sydney envied their ease and grace.

A gull appeared and glided above the dolphins, soaring upward until it was eye level with Sydney. It looked like the same gull that had been flying alongside the ship for the entire voyage. She doubted that it was the same bird but still, the fantasy of that possibility made her smile for the first time that morning. Perhaps it was watching over her and the other passengers. Children's stories and fairy tales were full of guardian angels and fairy godmothers, why not a guardian gull? But mostly what Sydney saw as she gazed at the dolphins and the gull was freedom. Survival was their only concern in life. Not family strife, not politics and war and certainly not inappropriate feelings for a sister's fiancé.

She headed toward her cabin. It was convenient that everyone was preoccupied with the war zone. It gave her behaviour a passable explanation. No one would question why she was anxious. If anyone noted her paleness or questioned her grave expression she could simply say it was the war zone. Then whomever she was speaking with would reassure her that all was well, as Bestic had done, or would agree that the world was terrifying, and commiserate. Yes, it was frightening to imagine submarines lurking below the surface, lying in wait. The German warning was imprinted on everyone's mind and had been the talk at every meal, at every tea and conversation. But the source of her misery and anxiety was not the war zone. And as she padded her way toward breakfast she knew that later this morning she would enter the Regal Suite where Brooke would be waiting for her. She had done nothing wrong, at least nothing tangible. Her thoughts and emotions were her own private nightmare.

The Regal Suite was in a state of disarray. Gowns and dresses were strewn across divans, chairs, the bed and even the floor. Shoes, hats and various feminine accessories were scattered amongst the clothes. Sydney stood against the door and watched Sarah frantically pick up piece after piece as Brooke continued to aggressively scour her wardrobe for some unnamed jewel or other precious item.

"I can come back," offered Sydney. She took the chaos as an indication of her sister's state of mind.

Brooke wouldn't look at her. Instead she buried her face in lavender silk; it was her favourite gown and had been selected for the wedding breakfast. "Sarah, would you leave us alone?"

Sarah dropped the armful of clothes where she stood and scurried away, past Sydney and out the door. Brooke ignored the mess and walked over to the divan that was covered in garments and with one sweep of her arm the whole mass landed on the floor with the others. She sat down and waited. Sydney reclined in one of the petal-pink Queen Anne chairs opposite. They faced each other like two opponents about to duel only instead of twenty paces in a fog-draped field it was twenty feet of silk and lace that stood between them.

"Did you find whatever it was you were looking for?" Sydney asked. She noticed a hand-knit scarf lying at her feet. She picked it up. It had been decorated with needlepoint at the ends in a sort of crest pattern. "Is this yours?"

Brooke raised an eyebrow. "That atrocity was made especially for me by Georgina. Hideous."

Sydney smiled. "The needlepoint detail must have taken her weeks. I think it's pretty."

"You want that too?" Brooke spoke bluntly and stared at her. It was a tactic that Brooke had employed many times when she was growing up. She would stare wide-eyed at people—the nanny, her father, a child—until they gave in and asked her what was the matter, how could they help or apologize for some perceived slight. But Sydney wasn't about to give in and so the stare down continued.

"I'm sure Georgina is expecting you to wear it," she said, and placed the scarf in her lap.

"Did you enjoy the dancing last night?" Brooke asked in an accusatory tone.

Sydney stroked the scarf. "I did."

"I'm so glad to hear it," Brooke said, her tone stating otherwise. "Edward seems to like you."

"Isn't that what you wanted?" Sydney asked, wishing this confrontation to be over quickly, like the blow from an executioner's axe. "You were worried I'd ruin your wedding."

"I was worried your political views would ruin my wedding," she said. "I had no idea that I had to worry about you stealing my fiancé."

There. The words had been spoken. All that had to be done was to deny it and move on. "I have no interest in stealing Edward," Sydney answered. "It's not my fault he pays so much attention to me."

"No? You looked very fine in that gown."

"In the gown you chose for me."

"So it's my fault Edward has a sudden appreciation of ladies' fashion. As if," scoffed Brooke.

"You wouldn't know what he appreciates. You don't even know him, not the real him," Sydney said, and regretted it immediately when she saw Brooke's accusing face.

"And you do? All the time you've spent with him talking his ear off has made you an expert on Edward Thorpe-Tracey?" she taunted.

"You see him as the means to an end. A title and an English estate," Sydney continued. "He's a man with a passion for the world, with an understanding of its people, wars and politics. He wants to fly . . ." The wide-eyed stare returned to Brooke's face. Sydney chose not to play her game. "And he can dance the foxtrot and bleat like a sheep."

Brooke flinched. "I see. Then his talent knows no bounds. Neither does your capacity for being ridiculous. Bleat like a sheep?"

"Because I'm the black sheep. It was a joke."

"You've shared jokes, have you? How nice for you," Brooke said.

Sydney took a deep breath. What was she doing defending Edward this way? He wasn't hers to defend. And Brooke wasn't the enemy. "Let's not do this," she said.

"Do what?"

"Argue over a man," Sydney snapped. "Especially one you don't even love."

Brooke threw her head back and laughed. It was a bellowing raucous laugh.

"Do you really think that love has anything to do with this?" Brooke asked. "You're right. I don't love Edward. But this isn't about love or romance, it's about business. You're not the only modern woman in the family." Sydney recoiled slightly. Brooke saw and smiled. "Our father taught us to value honesty, honour and the art of a good business deal. He also gave us ambition. You have your women's issues. I have society. I'm getting a title, Sydney, just like our mother and I always dreamed of. I will live on a great estate and raise children who will inherit that estate and who will practically be royalty."

"Those were books she read to you so you'd sleep. You can't assume Mother expected you to live like a princess," Sydney said.

"She would have been as thrilled as I am. I will be staking a claim in the old world and be someone and something more than just a rich girl from the colonies. I want authority and respect and being a member of the English aristocracy will give me that in spades," Brooke said quickly and passionately. "That's the only romance I'm after and I've found it and I'm not letting you ruin it because you have a crush on Edward or he has a crush on you. Or you have crushes on each other. I don't care and it doesn't matter."

Sydney was silent. Brooke had never quite put it that way before. Marrying Edward was her strategy for gaining power. She wondered what their mother would make of them fighting over such matters as power and influence.

"If our mother had lived do you think we'd have turned out softer, more feminine?" Sydney asked.

Brooke's face calmed. Her eyes were glistening and she wiped them with the back of her hand. "You mean kinder and gentler? Perhaps. But then you wouldn't be a suffragette," she said with a faint smile. "Our determination and practicality we owe to our father. He's made us men in some ways."

Sydney took this in. Her father had raised them like they were sons. They weren't coddled and protected from the world the way their friends were. At the dinner table Augustus did not shelter them from his business dealings and financial concerns; instead he discussed these matters with them. *You will inherit my fortune one day*, he would say. *You need to know how to manage it.* Of course, Mr. Garrett had been hired to oversee the details but in reality both girls knew how to balance a ledger, read the stock exchange reports and recognize when to buy and sell stock. It was ingrained in them.

"But why marry a man you don't love?" she asked. "I'm not being flippant. I really want to know."

Brooke paused a moment, then smiled. "You don't seem to get that love doesn't matter to me. I've got the perfect husband. Edward and all the trappings, that's what I want. Have no fear, I will be a good wife and mother."

"I'm sure you will," Sydney answered. She felt Edward fading away from her with each word her sister uttered.

Brooke looked at Sydney, the flash of warmth gone. "You need to remember one thing in all of this, Sydney," she said. "If Edward has professed his love for you—"

"I never said—"

Brooke cut her off with a wave of her arm. "Whatever he may tell you, keep one thing in mind—switching his affections to you doesn't change a thing for him."

Sydney bristled. "What do you mean?"

"Isn't it obvious?" Brooke laughed. "Even if he were passionately in love with you, rest assured he is fully aware that no matter which Sinclair he marries the money remains the same. He gets to keep Rathfon Hall."

This was a blow to Sydney and Brooke seemed to relish it. She stood and gently took the scarf off Sydney's lap and wrapped it around her own neck. Then, with a look of disgust, she tore it off and threw it back at Sydney. "It scratches my skin. I won't be encouraging Georgina to make any more of those awful things."

Sydney clutched the scarf and ignored her sister. She was too deep in thought. She had allowed herself to be swept up by Edward's charm, his intelligence, how he listened to her go on about her causes, her mother, all of it. Her sister was right. There was no risk in his jilting Brooke and marrying her. He left England to fetch a rich American bride and he would land in England with one. What would it matter to any of his family which sister he wed? It made his attentions less flattering, less sincere. How stupid she felt.

"I have to go to my room," Sydney announced, and stood up.

"Of course, dear," Brooke cooed. "Go pack your things and come back here so we can finish the voyage together." She put her arm around Sydney and walked her to the door, then kissed her cheek. "I will send Sarah down to help you."

Sydney was downcast. Their fight was over and Brooke had won. "I can find a steward," she said flatly, and walked out the door.

Isabel

"Another telegram just came in from Queenstown Naval Centre, Commander Hope, sir," Anstie said.

"Well, what does it say?" Hope asked. He was going over the transcripts from the night shift with Denniston. Isabel was seated beside them taking shorthand for the daily report. There hadn't been word on Schwieger's U-20 since yesterday.

"It's a report of a submarine sighting off Daunt Rock off the south Irish coast," Anstie said. "It submerged a few moments later."

Isabel listened intently. Daunt Rock was close to Kinsale and Fastnet, both points along the southwest coast of Ireland.

"Schwieger hasn't left the area then," Denniston said. "Must be getting low on fuel by now."

"Perhaps," Hope said. "But if the captain keeps her at a slow pace or rests on the sea floor she can conserve fuel. Isabel, make a copy and take it at once to Lord Fisher."

She took the telegram and sat at her typewriter and banged out the copy as fast as she could.

Lord Fisher's secretary was a grim-looking woman in her fifties who wore wire-rim specs and always had the same diamond brooch in the shape of a beetle on her jacket. Isabel often wondered if the diamonds were real.

"This is for Lord Fisher," Isabel said. "We received it a few moments ago. It's of vital importance."

The secretary looked bored, as though the war was a chore, like dusting, that had to be done but wasn't worth getting excited over. "Very well. Give it to me and I'll be sure he gets it."

Isabel handed over the telegram. The secretary dropped it on top of a paper tray and did nothing more. Isabel was dumbfounded. Had the woman not heard her?

"I'm sorry, but I'm afraid it's rather urgent," she said.

The woman stole another glance at her. "And I'll be sure to give it to him when the time comes. Now if you'll excuse me, I have a lot of work to do."

The fog that had cloaked London earlier in the morning had lifted and the sun shone brilliantly. Isabel took her lunch and sat on a bench in Trafalgar Square. She took a bite of her sandwich. It was sardines again.

"May I join you?"

She watched Henry approach, his own bagged lunch in hand. She didn't want company, least of all his. They had barely spoken since her return. It made Isabel sad to think that when she had started at the Admiralty, Henry was her friend. Now she looked at him as an enemy. *He might as well be a Jerry.*

"Needs must," she answered without looking at him. He sat down and unwrapped his sandwich.

"Last night's pork," he said, and bit into it.

Isabel's sardine sandwich lacked more appeal than it had when she first sat down. Of course he had real meat. Mildred probably stole it from the Admiralty's kitchen. She bit the head off a sardine.

"I'm glad I finally found you alone," Henry said when he'd finished swallowing. "I've wanted to apologize." She chewed in silence and stared up at Horatio Nelson. "Mildred was wrong to have told Mrs. Burns about what ..." He hesitated but seeing Isabel was still looking up to the sky he continued. "You know, what happened in Oxford. She knows it too. She feels terribly."

Isabel popped the last corner of sandwich in her mouth and crumpled the wrapper into a ball. The last thing she needed on her lunch break was to listen to this sort of drivel. She started to rise but Henry grabbed her. Isabel glared at him so fiercely he not only let go of her but dropped his sandwich. The slice of pork jumped out of the bread and landed with a dull plop at his feet. She didn't even attempt to conceal her laughter.

"I'm sure Miss Fox can steal another slice of pork for you," she said, and stood up. "I can't forgive you, Henry. You were my friend and yet you took her side."

He picked up the meat and tossed it into the paper bag. He stared down at the empty slices of bread for a moment, then he threw them in too. "We are friends," he said fiercely. "I shouldn't have listened to her without speaking to you. I wanted to warn you but I couldn't bring myself to say it."

"You should have tried harder," Isabel said wearily.

Henry was looking at her with a mixture of guilt and anger. "I didn't betray you, you know. Not even after you read Churchill's letter."

Isabel froze. The air was so still, not even a spring breeze to mask the exasperation in Henry's tone.

"You didn't tell Mildred about the letter, did you?"

"Don't be daft!" Henry said. "You can trust me, Isabel. I swear it."

Isabel breathed a sigh of relief. She was safe once again from losing the only thing that mattered: her work.

Edward

The bow was empty but for one man leaning on the railing smoking a cigarette. Edward's heart sank. He had sent a note to Sydney asking her to meet him here. She had run off last night because he had spoken the truth. Now he needed to know what she felt for him, if anything. As Edward drew closer to the man, he recognized him as Sydney's friend Walter. Perhaps he would know her whereabouts.

"Good day, Walter," Edward said. Walter nodded and took a drag from his cigarette, continuing to stare at the ocean. Edward settled in beside him. He wondered what Walter knew about his pining for Sydney. He doubted she would have confessed anything to another man. Then again, with Sydney you could never be too sure.

"I keep looking across the surface, studying it," Walter said at last. "It's like a plate of glass today."

"It is," Edward agreed. "You looking for anything in particular?"

Walter grunted. "Submarines. We sailed into the war zone early this morning."

Edward followed Walter's gaze across the endless water to the horizon. He'd noticed the effect of the war zone had been to rouse patriotic fervour from passengers and crew alike. The thought brought Edward back to reality. The rush of romance was momentarily cast aside for the grimness of the enemy.

"I wonder how many are lurking out there. Waiting for us," Walter continued.

"German U-boats are ugly machines," Edward said. "They do ugly work."

"You're right about that. Their telescopes are like the eye of a sea monster," Walter said.

"I'm always amazed how invincible our countrymen seemed to think we are," Edward said. "Listening to them go on about a swift end to the conflict like it were a football match and not a bloody battlefield."

"Bloody it is. I've read enough of my brothers' letters to know that. Got two of them already over in France, Herbert and Francis. The trenches and fields are clotted with death. As is the sea the *Lusitania* is pushing through. Submarines and battleships are no less deadly than infantry and cannon fire," Walter said. "Even the skies are part of it and if what the newspapers are reporting is true, soon enough there will be combat in the air above us all."

Edward thought back to Mrs. Taft Smith and her engine blueprints. He would seek her out later to learn more. "Aircraft are being designed with machine guns already," Edward said. "And when that is perfected there will be no part of the world free from bloodshed." His words didn't alter his desire to join the Royal Flying Corps.

Walter offered Edward a cigarette. He declined. "I'll soon be part of it. My younger brother, Gerry, is going to join up with me and together we'll find our brothers and fight," Walter said, and grinned slyly. "A family reunion on the battlefield. Surely Britain's got to triumph."

Edward imagined that fighting alongside one's family would be a comfort. But not so for Walter's parents should the worst happen. "I'm to take up a commission in June," Edward said.

If Walter was impressed he didn't show it. He took a final drag of the cigarette, then tossed it overboard. "What rank?"

"Lieutenant."

"Perhaps you'll command my unit," he said, and continued his vigil at the rail. "Fritz is out there somewhere. I aim to spot him if I can."

"They have a lookout for that," Edward pointed out.

Walter smiled. "I trust my own eyes."

Edward looked up at the Navigation Deck and saw the figures of Staff Captain Anderson and Captain Turner emerge from the bridge and make their way down to the Boat Deck. He had tried in vain to send a message to his parents to warn them that the wedding might not take place. But the purser, a man named McCubbin, had thwarted his plan. The *Lusitania* was banned from transmitting messages when she entered the war zone and was only able to receive them. No amount of his insisting had made the purser budge. The Marconi operators were up there on the bridge too. Would it really be such a travesty for him to plead with the young men who were in charge of the transmitter? He doubted Captain Turner would be any help. He and Anderson seemed to be inspecting the lifeboats that had been swung out earlier.

"You haven't seen Sydney today?" Edward said, turning back to Walter.

"She was at breakfast."

"How did she seem?"

Walter glanced at Edward, judging him. "You're engaged to her sister, aren't you?"

"Yes," Edward said. "Brooke."

Walter tilted his head, his eyes narrowed. "Then why are you always looking for Sydney?"

.

Sydney

She had avoided Edward all day. The note he sent was waiting for her after she'd left Brooke in the morning. He wanted to meet on the bow in the same spot they'd accidentally met on the first day of the voyage. Let him and his financial agenda wait. But the *Lusitania*, for all her immense size, wasn't large enough to prevent Edward finding her in the end. She had kept inside much of the day but the need for fresh sea air had tempted her onto the third class Promenade Deck. She didn't think he'd come there.

"Sydney!" he called out when he saw her. She stood her ground as he approached.

"Edward," she said flatly, and turned away.

He noticed the scarf immediately. "Why do you have the scarf Georgina made?" he asked. "Did Brooke give it to you?"

Sydney removed the scarf from her shoulders and held it out to him. He took it, puzzled.

"I forgot I'd taken it," she said. "You may give it back to her."

She avoided looking at him because she might burst into tears or, worse, pound her fists into his chest for playing her for a fool.

"What's wrong? Did something happen?" he asked her urgently. She shook her head but she felt tears filling her eyes. Why did she always cry when she was angry? Couldn't tears wait until she was alone in her cabin? "Tell me, darling," he pleaded.

"Don't call me darling," she snapped, and forced herself to look at him. "I had a talk with my sister this morning."

"I see," he answered.

"She knows," Sydney said simply.

"What does she know?"

"Oh Edward, don't be a simpleton! She knows you don't want to marry her. She suspects you have feelings for me—"

"I am in love with you," he said, cutting her off.

Sydney's face was stone. "Are you, Edward? That is convenient. Brooke made another point. That it doesn't matter which one of us you marry. We're interchangeable to you. I'm as wealthy as she is. Perhaps you're playing the both of us." She attempted to walk away but he grabbed her arm and held her. Alarmed, she yanked herself free.

"I'm sorry," Edward said, distressed by his action. "But what she says isn't true. I don't want to be with you because you're wealthy. This whole exercise has been a disaster. You've proven to me that a person can live the life they want without fearing what society thinks. I want that too. I want to be with you. I want to marry you."

"Maybe you do, Edward. But marrying me means you don't have to choose. Well, I'm deciding for you. You can marry Brooke if saving Rathfon Hall means that much to you. And you can leave me alone," she said, glowering at him.

"I would be with you if you had no fortune," he said firmly. "That you do have one is a nice addition, I won't deny it. I won't deny it because that would be dishonest. I'm no liar, Sydney."

"If you say so," she answered. "I must go and pack my things. I'm moving to the Regal Suite to be with my sister. Now if you'll excuse me."

"Before you go, tell me one thing," he said. She stopped and waited, her eyes focused on the scarf in his hands. He took a step toward her. "Did Brooke tell you she loves me?"

Sydney didn't want to answer. She went and stood by the railing and watched the sea. Her gull was back, soaring peacefully alongside the ship. They weren't particularly handsome birds but there was something regal about a creature that could fly above it all. Edward followed and was hovering beside her.

"Tell me, Sydney," he insisted. "I'd like to know."

Sydney's gaze moved from the seagull to the water below. It made her dizzy staring down like that. The surface so far beneath, the water churning with the power of the *Lusitania*'s engines—it was transfixing but also terrifying.

"Tell me," Edward said, his voice rising.

"No!" Sydney shouted, and whirled around to face him. "She doesn't love you. There, are you happy?"

"But that's good news, isn't it? Brooke doesn't love me and I don't love her." He grasped Sydney's hand in his. "Surely that must make it right. We won't be breaking her heart."

She took her hand away and turned back to the railing. The gull had disappeared.

"You should know one more thing," he continued. "Even if you reject me I will not be marrying your sister. I'm calling off the engagement. It is over."

Sydney let his words sink in. "You would end things with Brooke and risk losing Rathfon Hall? That would create a bit of a scandal."

"I am not afraid," Edward said, and smiled. "*We* love each other, Sydney. We should be together."

"I never said I loved you," she whispered.

"But you do, don't you?" he asked her, his voice unsteady. "If you don't, then tell me and I will leave you alone."

Her eyes drifted out to sea once again. The water was a very dark slate. The tinge of blue that the sun produced had faded with the arrival of the clouds. The voyage would soon be over and normal life would resume. A transatlantic crossing was akin to running away and joining the circus. Men and women were thrown together in close quarters for days. Of course emotions would fly, out of boredom if nothing else. This was a shipboard romance, just like in a novel. She tried to convince herself that was the reason for her predicament, for behaving so unlike herself. Except the truth struck her with the weight of the *Lusitania* itself: she did love him.

"Yes," she murmured.

His reaction was as if she'd shouted it from the bridge. He took her in his arms and kissed her. The pressure of his mouth against hers was more than she could take and she kissed him back. His arms were strong and held her protectively. Then came a wash of shame.

"Please stop," Sydney said. He released her. "Whatever is between us it is too complicated to ever result in our happiness. I am a woman of principle, Edward. You must know that about me by now. And I will be damned if I will intentionally hurt my only family." They stood in silence a moment, each waiting for the other to speak. Sydney was reeling inside. She had never felt such a rush of emotions for a man and to have it be tainted by guilt was overwhelming. As she looked at him, part of her was desperate to be held and kissed, part of her wanted to slap his face. She compromised and said simply, "I've never been in love before, Edward."

Her words proved to be more encouraging than she had intended. "As it turns out, nor have I," he said, his voice edged with excitement. "This isn't your fault." She gazed at him, hopeful. "And it isn't mine either. We didn't plan this, Sydney. It happened."

That much was true. She also knew that what would happen next was her decision. Her choice. She could turn and walk away or she could run into his arms again. It was up to her. "Then let us part as friends," she said, and held out her hand.

Edward took her hand and wouldn't let go. "Come with me . . ."

"No," she said, and shook her head.

"I cannot let you go so easily," he insisted. "I want to kiss you goodbye and hold you one last time."

She felt herself give in to her feelings—what was one last kiss—and allowed him to lead her into the ship and along the passageway and down the many steps to her berth. He didn't seem to care whom they passed or who saw them. They reached her cabin and entered. The bed was freshly made and the porthole was open, letting in the ocean breeze.

"We shouldn't be here," she said faintly, not really wanting to resist.

"Just for a moment. I want to kiss you again and not worry about—"

"Anyone seeing us?" she said. "That's my point. We can't be together without hiding."

He put his fingers on her lips to silence her. She kissed his fingers softly and this time it was she who leaned in. They kissed passionately and she couldn't stop despite the voice inside her head telling her that she was throwing her principles overboard. That her sister would be devastated. That her behaviour went completely against everything she believed in. Yet the feel of him against her, touching her, was more than she could take. And within moments all thoughts of guilt and betrayal were washed away. Their bodies became intertwined as they moved toward the bed. Gently Edward lifted her into his arms and placed her on the bed. He removed his topcoat and loosened his shirt. Sydney looked up at him. He was ending the engagement no matter what. She could trust him. He didn't love Brooke. Her sister didn't love him. She had never loved him. She never would love him. *I love him*. Sydney's emotions were no longer under her control.

He lay beside her and cradled her in his arms. She stroked his chest with her hand. His muscles were hard, taut. She kissed his chest and neck until he couldn't take it and pushed her away lightly. "Sydney, I'm a gentleman but I am also a man," he teased. "We mustn't go further."

"Love me, Edward," she said. "I want you."

He stared into her eyes. She knew it wasn't what a girl with her upbringing should do. But neither was marching in protests or punching a policeman. She was a modern girl; she knew a woman could enjoy a man. And she knew about precautions. The contraceptive samples she'd brought with her were within arm's reach.

"Are you sure?" he asked.

"Yes," she told him, and kissed him again. This time their lips parted and she felt his tongue enter her mouth. In that moment and for the next several moments there was no fear of being found out or of worrying about weddings and angry relatives, there was just the two of them alone, their bodies melting into each other's and the sensual feel of him. She cried out when he first entered her but then it was all pleasure. He kissed her hungrily and his movements were more frantic, more intense than anything she'd imagined. This Edward was not so proper. She couldn't imagine this man sitting at the head of a table of posh Englishmen and women. She found herself smiling as he kissed her and then suddenly those particular thoughts vanished and more instinctive feelings arose from deep inside her body.

When it was over she lay naked in his arms. She had never envisioned how sex could change how you felt about someone, how it deepened feelings that were already there and stirred new ones. But it also made Sydney ashamed of what she'd done.

He studied at her. "You look upset," he said tenderly.

She forced a smile. "I was thinking we shouldn't have done what we did."

"Your sister—"

"Please, don't speak about her. Not while we are lying here like this," she said, and sat up. "You should leave."

He lifted her hand in his and kissed it. "Do not regret what happened."

She watched their entwined hands. "I can't promise that," she confessed. "I heard you the other night. When Brooke said I brought shame to my family name. You stood up for me, in front of her and those other people."

It was his turn to look serious. "I didn't know you were there."

"I was hiding, I've found a spot near the Bostwick gate where I can look into the main entrance," she explained, tears welling up. "But maybe she is right. Look at me now. I am capable of bringing shame to the Sinclairs."

Edward held her tightly as she cried. "Falling in love is nothing to be ashamed of," he said.

She could see from his face that he was suffering as well. "What are we to do, Edward?"

"I will speak to Brooke when we arrive in Liverpool," he said, and kissed her bare shoulder. "I will make her understand."

Sydney was skeptical. "You think she will?"

"I think by now even she will have to admit we are ill-matched," he said, and smiled at her. "We will all find happiness when this is over."

Isabel

ours had passed since she'd given the telegram to Lord Fisher's secretary. She was desperate to know what was being done to warn the ships in the area. Her opportunity came with the arrival of Rotter and Denniston who had been in a hush-hush meeting the past two hours with Captain Hall and Commander Hope. Their expressions gave her no indication of what had happened and there was no legitimate reason for her to ask.

"Smile at Alastair, Dorothy," Isabel instructed.

"Whatever for?" Dorothy asked, looking up from her pile of paperwork. "Not that I mind."

"I need you to get his attention please," she said.

Dorothy winked at her. "Mr. Denniston, may I have a word?" She smiled conspiratorially. Her charms worked and within seconds Denniston was at the typing pool.

"Yes?" he asked.

Dorothy opened her mouth but her jaw went slack. She had nothing to say. Denniston tilted his head.

"Mr. Denniston, do you know from your meeting if the Admiralty is sending a warning to the ships in the area, such as the *Lusitania*?" Isabel blurted out. Dorothy shut her mouth so hard her teeth clicked. He rubbed his chin a moment.

"You will be relieved to know that the Admiralty is sending out messages *en clair* and encoded messages to all British ships in the area," he explained confidently. "And that includes the *Lusitania*. All will be warned that there are submarines active off Fastnet."

"Thank you, Mr. Denniston" Isabel said. She was relieved. But he wasn't finished.

"We're also reminding all ships to steer a mid-channel course, pass harbours at high speed and zigzag to avoid giving the U-boats a clear target," he said. "These captains know what they're doing."

Dinner had been bland. Or perhaps it was flavourful but Sydney couldn't tell. She was too consumed with what had happened with Edward. What she had allowed to happen. She stepped out onto the deck for some air. In another hour she would be making her way up to first class for the concert and Hannah's debut. She found Walter alone, smoking at the railing. He smiled when he saw her.

"You were quiet at dinner," he said, and waited patiently.

Sydney wasn't about to confess the details of her afternoon but she needed to unburden some of it. "What you said about Edward," she began. "You were right. Things have become complicated."

"You love him?"

She nodded once and looked away, expecting hard recriminations but Walter took his time, blowing a ring of smoke from his lips and watching the blue edge drift into nothingness. "That's quite the mess, isn't it, then?" he said, and smiled. "What does Brooke say?"

Sydney's eyes widened. "She suspects, Walter. But I didn't admit it, not really. Edward is ending the engagement when we reach Liverpool." Walter nodded. Sydney exhaled, relieved to be speaking about the matter with a neutral party. "I shouldn't have let it happen. But when I'm with him, it's like a fog comes across my eyes and I can only see Edward and how much I want to be with him. All sense is gone."

"And loyalty too?" Walter asked.

Sydney bowed her head. "It's torture, Walter. I love my sister."

Walter patted her arm. "Love is a strange animal, Sydney. You never know where it will land you. But I will tell you this, as complicated as it may get, if you truly love Edward then hang on to him. We never know how long we are for this world and we don't all get to love the right person. Embrace it. But make things right with Brooke as well. If you can."

Sydney hugged him. "Thank you, Walter. You're so kind. And I intend on fixing things with my sister if it's the last thing I do."

Edward

The ship's concert given on the second-to-last night of the voyage—the final night was left open for packing—was a command performance for passengers. In each class there was entertainment: beyond the ship's band, talented crew and guests (and those who thought themselves talented) could sing, play an instrument or do whatever they felt would enthrall an audience. But for first class passengers this rose to a level of amusement beyond amateur showmanship. For it was the last occasion for ladies to be seen in their best fashion and most glittering jewels and the final time to survey their fellow travellers and decide if new friendships formed on the ship would transfer to land. For others, shipboard romances, dalliances and flirtations would be given a last-ditch effort at something more permanent.

Edward found himself, with only Brooke for company as they made their way into the lounge after dinner. Sydney was not at the meal. They had agreed that she would appear for the concert, bringing young Hannah with her. He hoped she wasn't having second thoughts about taking him as a lover. Reluctantly he had agreed not to spend time alone with her until they reached Liverpool and he could end the engagement. But suffering through another tense five-course meal with Brooke was nearly unbearable. He was racked with guilt. She was cool. She couldn't possibly know about his tryst with Sydney. But there was something in her air, her tone of voice and the way she looked at him that made him squirm.

Edward found seats and was saved from making painful conversations with Brooke by listening to the ramped-up fears of the passengers about the war zone and submarines. He listened to the bits of chatter that floated through the air.

"Where is the naval escort?"

"Why haven't we reached top speed?"

"The boats are swung out and the windows are blacked out. It's a precaution but it's making me more afraid."

"Oh I really wish these people would quit all the doom-and-gloom nonsense." Brooke sighed. "It's going to ruin the fun."

"That's not what's ruining the fun," Edward muttered.

"What?" she asked.

He was rescued by the appearance of Alfred, Frohman and Rita. Edward imagined that Frohman was coming over to find Sydney.

"My, what a dour crowd," Rita exclaimed. "I've never seen so many serious faces at a concert."

"Isn't that the truth?" Brooke agreed. "I was just telling Edward they're going to wreck everything with their war talk. It will be real enough when we land in England."

"It's normally quite the party," Frohman said. "But entering the war zone has thrown a damper over things."

Brooke lit up. "Party. Say, that's a wonderful idea. After the concert, why don't a slew of us head to my suite and continue the champagne."

The idea seemed to please everyone within earshot except Edward who had hoped for an early evening.

"That's a great idea," Frohman said.

"Adore it," Rita exclaimed.

Brooke took no notice of her fiancé's lack of enthusiasm. "Then it's settled. I'll get a steward to bring up the champagne and some canapés," she said, then nudged Edward. "Won't it be delightful, Edward?"

He gave a tight smile but the entrance of Sydney in her amber gown prevented his response. Edward waited for her to look at him. She did not.

"Sorry if I'm late," Sydney said.

Edward felt shaky. Why wouldn't she look at him? Even a slight glance would suffice. "You're not late. We just arrived," he said. That did the trick. Her eyes lifted to his and she smiled. But it was a reserved smile, as though he really was nothing more than her future brother-in-law.

"I certainly am intrigued to hear Hannah perform," Frohman explained and fished in his pockets for a candy, which he unwrapped and popped in his mouth. "Though to be honest, Sydney, you might have warned me about the mother. She's written me three times since I agreed to this."

"I didn't want to scare you off."

"How old is the child?" Alfred asked.

"Twelve, but she looks younger," Sydney said. "She's wonderful."

Frohman waved a finger at her playfully. "I'll be the judge of that."

"How about right now?" Sydney asked and gestured ahead of her. "There they are."

Heads turned to where Hannah and Gladys stood accompanied by a steward. Sydney waved them over. Hannah followed her mother as she swanned across the room toward Frohman.

"Mr. Frohman, we are dee-ligh-ted," Gladys said. "Hannah is ready to play her heart out."

Hannah curtsied politely.

"I'm not the king of England," Frohman joked, and pulled another candy from his pocket. Only this time he held it out to Hannah. But the girl didn't take it. Instead she looked at her mother for guidance. Gladys took the candy from Frohman and placed it inside her bag. "I will give this to Hannah after she plays," she said. "We can't have sticky fingers during your performance. Go on, Hannah, take your place."

Frohman grimaced at Gladys, then moved to the front of the audience. The men and women stopped their chatting and gave him their full attention.

"Ladies and gentlemen, I am Charles Frohman—" he began.

"Oh darling, everyone knows who *you* are," gushed a female passenger wearing an elaborate peacock-feathered fascinator. A ripple of laughter went through the audience and Frohman bowed graciously.

"I've invited this young lady into the lounge this evening to hear her perform. And if she is as good as I've been told she is then when I'm done launching her career everyone will know her too," he said with a wave toward her. "Hannah MacGregor."

Gladys applauded madly but ceased once she realized she was the only one. Sydney felt embarrassed for her. But more unsettling was Hannah.

Her small hands smoothed the piano keys in anticipation but her face was stony, almost as though she was lost in another world. Her mother gave the cue and Hannah began to play. Only it wasn't the popular songs of the stage that Sydney and Hannah had rehearsed for hours and what Sydney had promised Frohman he would hear, it was Beethoven. Her playing was competent and precise but wholly uninspired. The audience, who didn't know they weren't supposed to hear the classical composition, listened politely. No doubt the girl's expertise was impressive enough for most, but when Sydney saw the look of boredom on Frohman's face, she knew it wasn't enough for him. Frohman leaned in to her and whispered, "I thought you said the girl could play contemporary numbers?"

She bit her lip. "Let's hear this first to make her mother happy. Then you'll hear what she can really do," Sydney said.

When the sonata was complete Gladys gestured wildly to her daughter to stand and take a bow, which she did. When the audience had finished their polite applause Frohman stood up.

"What else can you play?" Frohman asked.

"She can play a nocturne," Gladys said proudly.

Hannah looked to Sydney for help. Sydney went and sat down at the piano. "I know what would be fun," Sydney said to the room. "I can play 'Alexander's Ragtime Band' and you can sing and dance, Hannah."

"Yes I can!" Hannah squealed. The audience laughed at her childish enthusiasm.

"Oh but Mr. Frohman doesn't want to hear a child sing like that," Gladys said as though Sydney's suggestion was utterly ridiculous.

"Hannah, do you want to give it a try?" he asked the girl, ignoring her mother. Hannah nodded. Gladys grinned at him politely.

"Would you gentlemen accompany us?" Sydney asked the band.

"We'd be delighted," said the bandleader.

"One, two and three," Sydney counted, then she and the band began to play the song. Hannah was beaming and swaying in time to the music, her face happy and alive. Then, just as they had rehearsed in the third class dining saloon, she began to sing, a little too softly at first.

"Come on and hear, come on and hear
Alexander's Ragtime Band
Come on and hear, come on and hear
The best band in the land."

When she saw the smiling faces watching her, many of the people tapping their feet to the tune, her confidence grew and she began to sing more fully and the very adult voice that had captivated Sydney was freed. Rita joined in on the chorus and then hummed along when Hannah began her tap solo.

"She sounds like a girl twice her age," Edward whispered to Brooke, who sighed with boredom.

Frohman overheard but was too enchanted to look away so he shouted for all to hear, "She has a hell of a voice!"

The audience agreed and was equally captivated by Hannah. As the song played on Edward felt comfortable enough to let his eyes fall on Sydney. But his attentions didn't go unnoticed. Brooke tracked her fiancé's enthralled gaze to her sister and in response shifted slightly away from him in silent protest, and her foot wound up stepping onto Alfred who was standing at the edge of the sofa. The millionaire smiled politely and stepped aside.

When the song finished the audience erupted in applause as Sydney and Rita took the girl by the hands and bowed.

"Hannah!" Frohman bellowed. The girl tore off to where he stood with her mother. "That is exactly the sort of performance I wanted to see." Frohman looked at Gladys. "Mrs. MacGregor, you have a talented daughter but from now on I decide what she plays and sings, understood?"

Hannah looked ecstatic. Gladys seemed caught off guard but she recovered and smiled. "You're the Broadway producer, not I."

"Exactly," Frohman said. "Now where's that candy for Hannah?"

Edward crossed the floor to the piano where Sydney remained standing. He placed his hand on her arm.

"Edward, no," she said softly.

He removed his hand. "My apologies."

Sydney was about to step away from him when Brooke appeared. "That was charming, Sydney," she purred. "Edward, you certainly seemed to enjoy yourself."

"I did, Brooke. The child has an incomparable voice," he said. Sydney looked around the room and found Hannah and Gladys still chatting with Rita and Frohman.

"I'm going to congratulate Hannah. You have a lovely evening," she said to them and had taken a few steps when . . .

"Won't you join us for the party in our suite?" Brooke asked sharply. "You must come. I insist."

Sydney stopped and rubbed her lips together. "Of course I'll be there."

"I'm so glad," Brooke said.

"Ah, Captain Turner has arrived," said Edward. The ladies turned around and watched the captain walk into the centre of the room. Turner's face was drawn and tired, as though he hadn't slept in days.

"Ladies and gentlemen," Turner announced. "I don't mean to interfere with the concert. But I wanted to update you on our situation. As you know, early this morning we entered the war zone. We have received warnings of submarines being active in the waters ahead of us. I can assure you we will take every precaution and move full speed through the Irish Channel. There is nothing whatsoever to be concerned about and we will be in the care of the Royal Navy. Enjoy the remainder of your evening."

He was gone as swiftly as he'd arrived despite the rush of concern that erupted from the crowd. The momentary distractions of music and Hannah's performance were forgotten and once again the war and submarines dominated. Edward wanted to take Sydney in his arms and reassure her.

"All the more reason to retreat to the Regal Suite after the concert," Brooke insisted. "Get our minds off everything."

Edward wasn't sure if he caught a note of suspicion in her voice for she was looking at him when she spoke. It was Sydney who responded, warmly and enthused.

"You're right. I can't wait. Now if you'll excuse me, I must speak to Hannah."

Edward watched after her longingly. "Let's get a seat, Edward," Brooke said, her hand on his arm. Her touch jolted him back to earth. "The concert is about to resume."

Sydney

The party was in full swing when she arrived. The Regal Suite had been transformed. Just that morning it had looked like it had been through a hurricane. Now it was spotless. Sydney assessed the crowd; she recognized many of them from the dinner at the captain's table including the Kesers and the Papadapouloses. Of course there were Frohman and Alfred, and even Captain Turner, Staff Captain Anderson and a couple of other officers in attendance. There was never a question of Brooke's influence in society or of her uncanny ability to create an invitation list at the last minute. Sydney found her sister holding court on the divan with a glass of champagne in her hand. Perhaps a title was necessary to fulfill her potential. Then from out of another part of the suite Edward emerged. He too held a glass of champagne in his hand as he made his way toward Brooke. Sydney continued to stand near the door, letting the revellers conceal her as she watched.

Edward took a bottle out of an ice bucket and poured Brooke more champagne. Her sister didn't acknowledge him; she was too busy flirting with one of the young officers as several female passengers looked on admiringly.

"Hiding from anyone in particular?" It was Alfred. He had crept up beside her, two glasses of champagne in his hand. She took one and smiled.

"Whatever do you mean, Alfred?" Sydney asked, knowing very well what he meant.

"Nothing really," he said. "I have noticed that you and Edward seem close friends."

Sydney felt the redness come into her cheeks. "Is that so," she said.

"Your sister has noticed too," he said. Sydney stiffened. Alfred smiled warmly. "Don't fret, Sydney. I doubt your dalliance with Edward has caused any real damage. She'll still marry him. And he'll marry her."

"Dalliance?" Sydney asked. Her voice rose with each syllable as she tried to conceal her unease.

"There are always several flirtations on every voyage," he said. Alfred took another sip of champagne. "The *Lusitania*'s popularity depends on it."

She understood what he was implying, that what was between her and Edward was a flirtation and nothing more. He was wrong.

"Sydney!" Brooke had spotted her. A wave of her hand commanded Sydney to her side.

"Excuse me, Alfred." As she crossed the room she felt Edward's eyes on her. The distance from the door to the divan seemed to stretch for miles under his stare. Alfred's choice of words—*flirtation*, *dalliance*—had hit their mark. When she reached Brooke and Edward she could not bring herself to look at him.

"Here's to the voyage nearly being over," Brooke said. She clinked her glass against Sydney's. "Have you enjoyed it?"

This was so typical of Brooke. Despite the tension between them she would put on a pleasant public face. "Very much," Sydney said. There was no point in acting any other way. She still hadn't moved her things into the suite but Brooke hadn't mentioned it either. Maybe the reason she hadn't was because she sensed what had happened between her and Edward. If Alfred was aware of their *dalliance*, then surely her own flesh and blood could tell something was different about her.

"Now where did my fiancé get to? He was just here," Brooke said. Sydney searched the room. Edward had been there a moment before. "Be a dear and find him for me, I want you both here for this," Brooke ordered. Sydney gaped at her. Was this a ploy of some kind? *Don't be ridiculous. She can't know.*

"Shouldn't you find him?" she suggested.

"Do as I ask," Brooke persisted. "I'm the hostess. I can't go in search of a man. Even one I'm engaged to."

Sydney moved through the parlour and into the dining room, both of which were packed with people enjoying the party and the free champagne. There was no sign of him. She entered Brooke's bedroom. He wasn't there either. She walked to the second bedroom, what would have been her bedroom. The door was closed. She placed her hand on the door handle and opened it.

Edward sat on the bed, the champagne in one hand and the scarf Georgina had made in the other. He didn't even lift his head when she opened the door.

"Edward?" she said, and closed the door behind her.

He smiled faintly. "I can't help but wonder what Georgina will think of me when I break the news to her."

Sydney swallowed. "Is she close to Brooke?"

Edward chuckled. "No, not especially. It's just that I'm her older brother and she thinks I'm perfect. Not a Lothario that travels the world falling in love with women he hardly knows and breaking off engagements. It's not very English."

"Have you changed your mind?" The question had sprung from her lips against her will.

He didn't answer straightaway. His silence was like a knife through her chest. Maybe he was a Lothario. He had taken advantage of her and was going marry her sister anyway. It was like Alfred said, she was a mere dalliance. The joke would be on her because she could never tell a soul. My God, Edward was a cad and a villain.

"Never," he said. He stood and went to her, lifting her hands in his. "Never will I change my mind. But I never thought I was capable of betrayal. I suppose I didn't know my true character until now. And I'm not sure I like the discovery." Sydney studied him. He was saying the right words and she should be relieved. But she sensed remorse. Sensed it and echoed it. Could anything good come of their union? Edward smiled reassuringly. "If I can't live up to my little sister's image of me then so be it." He draped the scarf around Sydney's shoulders. "Take it."

She took it off. "I can't. Georgina made it for Brooke."

He shook his head. "Brooke despises it. And don't try to tell me otherwise. It's not her style."

Sydney gripped the scarf tightly. "We should return to the party. I think Brooke wants to make some sort of announcement," she explained. She opened the door and walked out still holding the scarf in her hands.

When they returned to the parlour she found Brooke standing off to one side with Alfred. The sight of them huddled so closely made Sydney nervous that they were talking about her. When Brooke saw her, her eyes popped. Sydney remembered Georgina's scarf; she had forgotten to leave it in the bedroom. But Brooke didn't come near her. Instead she climbed on top of the coffee table and clinked her glass with a spoon several times. The guests looked on, startled by the sight of a refined lady standing above them like a high priestess addressing her subjects. A few laughed awkwardly. Sydney knew Brooke's extreme behaviour was for her benefit, a way of showing her who was in charge. "Attention! Attention please!" she shouted, and the room hushed. "I think we've all had enough talk about the war and submarines."

A collective "Hear! Hear!" erupted.

"What we need is to bring a bit of excitement and joy back to this voyage. And to do that I've decided to invite each and every one of you to attend my wedding tomorrow, on board the *Lusitania* at sunset."

Edward froze. The guests applauded madly, which made Brooke beam. Her eyes locked with Sydney's and her smile grew wider.

"Captain Turner will officiate," Brooke continued, encouraged by the reaction. "I haven't asked him yet, but trust me when I tell you nobody says no to me." Again she stared at Sydney. Everyone turned to Captain Turner, who couldn't help himself and grinned.

"I'll take that as a yes." Brooke smiled. "Now, where is my fiancé? Come here, darling."

Sydney had no choice but to watch Edward inch his way toward her sister. Brooke grabbed his hand and held it tight. Sydney clutched the scarf just as tightly, as though it was the only thing that held them together.

"We were to marry at Edward's estate in a couple of weeks but you know how it is when you're in love." Brooke stole a moment to take pleasure in Edward's stony face as the irony of her words sank in. "Two weeks can feel an eternity. And I think a wedding celebration will cheer everyone up immensely."

"Hear! Hear!" The shouts rose once again from the crowd.

The guests rushed to the couple, excited about the wedding. Sydney glanced around the room and her eyes landed on Alfred. He shrugged and went to congratulate them. There was little else for her to do but to give them her own good wishes.

Edward

You might have discussed this with me," Edward whispered in Brooke's ear.

"Oh darling, don't be a bore," she answered, a wide smile planted firmly on her face. "You must marry me despite how you feel about my sister." Edward recoiled. "And don't try denying it. You act like a man in love. I know the look. I've seen it many times, usually pointed in my direction."

"I wasn't going to deny it," he said plainly.

"That is a relief," she said. "Does she love you?"

He hesitated. It was all Brooke needed. "Then I have my answer."

"You can't force me to marry you," he said.

"Don't be absurd," she said. "Of course I can. You must realize that if you leave me for Sydney you'd ruin all your plans."

Edward was seething but he listened. "How do you mean?"

"Sydney is only twenty-one. She won't inherit any of our father's money until she is twenty-five, which means she can't help you in time to save that precious pile of stone you're so mad about. But I can."

Without a word Edward stormed away, brushing past Alfred who stood behind them, his hand outstretched to congratulate the happy couple.

MAY 7

Sydney

The lights of the ship were extinguished and the windows blacked out, turning the *Lusitania* into a ghostly mirage. The crew manoeuvred around the decks like nocturnal predators. Darting here, marching there, performing tasks expertly as though illumination was an unnecessary invention. It wasn't the same for the passengers who were navigating the ship like the newly blind. The men and women cast nervous glances over the railing at the dark sea, or up at the night sky, hoping that the answer lay with the stars. Some paced back and forth anxiously, as though news would arrive at any second, while others seemed to float along the deck like spirits, whispering to one another, to calm themselves, that this was routine.

Fear has a way of provoking the unthinkable. Many passengers remained dressed in their day clothes, bundled up in topcoats and hats and scarves. Some walked the decks until they could hardly keep their eyes open and exhaustion forced them to return to their berths. Others made the decision to eschew a warm bed entirely and instead took up residence on deck chairs, determined to spend the night outside and ready for anything that might happen.

The threat of torpedoes wasn't what kept Sydney awake as she walked in solemn step behind the others like a funeral procession. Brooke had played her hand and won the tournament. *And rightfully so.* She deserved punishment for falling in love with Edward. What sort of sister was she to let that happen? *But I love him.* Brooke was there first, she was his fiancée, shouldn't she get what she wanted? *But I love him.*

She walked on, Georgina's scarf wrapped around her shoulders as an extra layer of warmth. A crewman stepped out of the ship's interior right in front of her and she jumped.

"Apologies, ma'am."

"That's all right," she said, taking a deep breath to calm down. "Can you tell me the time?"

"It's quarter after midnight," the answer came as the crewman brushed past.

"It's too late for you to be out walking the decks like an elegant spectre." The voice belonged to Alfred, who quietly fell into step beside her.

"Good evening, Alfred. Or should I say good night?" She wished he hadn't found her. She wanted to be left alone in her misery.

"I'm sorry about what happened tonight," he said sympathetically.

"I had it coming."

"Had you?" he asked.

She hesitated, unsure how much she should divulge when none of it mattered any longer. "My *dalliance*, as you called it, is the reason behind Brooke's sudden inspiration to marry at sea."

"So you're in love with Edward and he's in love with you and she knows all about it," Alfred said matter-of-factly. "But Brooke isn't so fond of the idea and is determined to marry him anyway. I think I said as much to you earlier."

"I guess I am transparent," she said dejectedly.

"Like freshly blown crystal," he said.

"And you don't hate me? Or Edward?"

"Sydney, I'm hardly someone to judge a man's romantic entanglements," he said. "But unlike me, Edward's not in a financial position to do what he wants."

"That's not true at all. If he married me he would still have the money to save Rathfon Hall. I'm as rich as Brooke."

"Is that so?" Alfred asked.

"You know that, Alfred. Why do you sound doubtful?" she asked. His tone was so strange. He'd known her and Brooke since they were children. He had done business with Augustus. The Sinclair fortune was hardly a secret to anyone in New York society and to an insider like Alfred it was known on practically intimate terms.

"But isn't your money tied up in a trust until you turn twenty-five?" he asked. The air had taken a sudden turn and was crisp and cold and the wind had picked up.

"What gave you that idea?" she asked.

"Brooke."

"I don't understand. Why would Brooke tell you such a thing?"

"Not me," he clarified. "Edward." When he saw Sydney's alarmed face he continued. "She told him loud and clear that your share of the fortune wouldn't be yours until you reached twenty-five."

The cold wind did nothing to cool the rush of heat that shot through her. Her heart was pounding. She felt sick as though the *mal de mer* had returned for a final farewell.

"I need to sit," she gasped. They had come to a pair of vacant deck chairs and sat down. Alfred's hands atop his walking stick, hers hidden beneath the many layers of wool and the scarf—the beautiful scarf handmade by a girl who might have been her sister. "Why would she tell him that?"

"You're a smart woman, Sydney. Why do you think?"

Her eyes had adjusted to the darkness and she could make out his features now. His expression was sympathetic. There was only one reason Brooke would say such a thing. It was her final card. She knew Edward needed money for Rathfon Hall or else it would be lost. He couldn't afford to wait until she was twenty-five. It would have been sold by then. And despite Edward saying it didn't matter and that he loved her more than his ancestral home, Sydney knew that her sister was banking on his promises to his family and to her. She felt her body tremble against the cold.

"It isn't true," she said. "I received my inheritance last fall on my twenty-first birthday."

Isabel

It was half past midnight. Isabel had spent the evening typing up transcripts between the Admiralstab and the Ottoman Empire. The Gallipoli Campaign had begun and Room 40 was overrun with intercepts about the battles. The Allied offensive was failing to open up the strait into the Black Sea. After the naval campaign had failed in March, the Allies sent in ground troops from Britain, Australia, New Zealand and Newfoundland; the troops had trekked down from Egypt. Casualties were heavy and the information flowing through Room 40 indicated that despite Turkish ammunition shortages they were holding off the Allies.

Isabel wasn't the only one who had stayed late. Most of the men had stayed on and joined the night shift to keep up with the extra work. It had so far proved a quiet and long evening. Isabel considered going home until Norton dashed across the room to Commander Hope. She saw that he held a fresh wireless transmission in his hand. "Sir! This just arrived from Queenstown."

Everyone stopped their work and watched anxiously. Few things got Norton excited. Whatever he had in his hand it was incendiary. Commander Hope took the telegram. It was from Vice Admiral Sir Charles Coke, the man in charge at Queenstown, a small port village on the south coast of Ireland. The vice admiral regularly sent transmissions to the Admiralty in London but rarely did such communications raise an alarm. She watched the commander closely. Too closely apparently. Dorothy, who had also volunteered to stay late, gently kicked her foot under the table.

"It's okay to listen but at least pretend to be doing your job," she whispered to her.

Her eyes studied the deciphered code in front of her but her ears were trained in the direction of Commander Hope.

"Denniston, come read this. You too, Rotter, Curtis."

The men formed a close circle and the message was passed along.

"At least we can confirm its location," Curtis offered grimly.

"We should get this to Fisher immediately," Denniston stated.

"What should I tell Queenstown?" Norton asked, his voice sharp.

Isabel could hardly stand it. Why were they being so furtive? Everyone in Room 40 knew what was happening in the war. Surely they didn't need to keep the contents of a wireless message from the rest.

"Isabel!" Commander Hope called out to her. His voice seemed to echo in the hushed room.

Isabel shot to her feet, sending her chair crashing to the floor. This created a chain reaction whereby Dorothy jumped out of her skin, scattering the pile of transcripts that had been stacked neatly in front her. "Yes, sir!" Isabel answered, her voice on the brink of shouting.

"Type two copies and see if Lord Fisher is still in his office," he ordered, and held out the message. "If not then we shall telephone him at home."

Isabel ran over and he handed the paper to her. The men dispersed and returned to their duties. She picked up her chair and sat down. Dorothy leaned over. "What's it say?"

Isabel placed the telegram on the edge of her desk so they both could read it.

The steamer SS Candidate *shelled by submarine this morning off the coast of County Wexford, Ireland. Crew abandoned ship. The* Candidate *lost.*

"Another one?" Dorothy whispered. "Isn't that close to where the schooner was sunk on Wednesday?"

"Too close," Isabel confirmed. "According to the date on the telegram, 'this morning' was actually yesterday. But we're only receiving the news now."

County Wexford was on the south coast of Ireland. She was glad that the crew wasn't lost with the steamer but it was disturbing that a second ship had been sunk by a submarine in as many days. Again her mind flooded with images of the *Lusitania*. "It's Schwieger again."

"Is that what Commander Hope said?" Dorothy asked.

"I'm saying it," Isabel retorted. "It's him."

Isabel marched toward the First Sea Lord's office, the copy of the message in hand. She passed the hallway that led to the Lord of the Admiralty's grand office and thought briefly of taking it directly to Mr. Churchill. But his office showed no sign of life. He lived at Admiralty House, which was steps away but she dared not set foot near there. She continued on her way to Fisher's office, but it was Churchill's letter that rolled over in her mind. *It is most important to attract neutral shipping to our shores in the hope especially of embroiling the United States with Germany . . . For our part we want the traffic—the more the better; and if some of it gets into trouble, better still.*

Why had she read it? The *Lusitania* was a passenger ship, surely even a German submarine captain, even one as ruthless as Schwieger, was more man than monster. He had allowed the crews to abandon ship, hadn't he? She hesitated and stared at the message. *You've only just got your job back. Don't be a fool. Do as you're told.*

The grim-faced secretary was long gone for the day but to Isabel's surprise there was a light coming from beneath Fisher's door. She knocked.

"Come in!" Fisher shouted.

Isabel opened the door and wasted no time with small talk. "This just arrived, sir."

He took the telegram from her. She remained there as he read it. His face scrunched up in concentration. Try as she might Isabel couldn't discern from his expression what his next move would be.

"Can I relay a message back to Commander Hope, sir?" she offered.

He ignored her and rubbed his chin, his eyes never leaving the telegram. It felt like an eternity to Isabel. The *Lusitania* was well inside the war zone now; time was not on their side.

"Follow me," Fisher said, and stood up and marched out of his office.

Isabel had to practically jog to keep pace. Fisher was a small man but he could move like a hare. "Where are we going, sir?" she asked.

"We're going to send a message to Queenstown and to every merchant vessel in the area," he said firmly.

Sydney

Someone was touching her but she couldn't see who it was. The hand felt like a paw. It was powerful and she could swear whoever or whatever it was had claws that were digging into her flesh. The longer it grasped her the more she wanted to scream. She tried but no sound came. There was only a muffled gurgle where her call for help should have been. Then suddenly she was awake.

"I've been looking for you all night." It was Edward. His eyes were raw as he smiled at her. She was so bundled up she couldn't move and had to be content to remain prostrate on the deck chair.

"What time is it?" she whispered, her voice raspy from a night outside in the damp.

"It's nearly six thirty," he said. "Your face was covered up. I didn't realize it was you until the sun began to rise and I recognized the shawl."

"There's so much fog," she said. The air was choked with the stuff.

"It's thick all right," he answered, and cast his eyes around them. "We should sail out of it soon."

Before she could respond the *Lusitania*'s foghorn blasted from above.

"What's he doing?" Sydney asked, alarmed by the deep-throated growl. "The captain must stop it." Another blast blew into the air. This time it made a slightly different but equally terrifying sound. "The Germans will know where we are!"

She wasn't the only one who was concerned. Other passengers had begun to emerge from their cabins to investigate the blaring foghorn that was preventing them from sleep.

Edward continued to kneel beside Sydney as if he was going to propose.

"The captain knows what he's doing," he said reassuringly.

She thought he looked ridiculous on his knees. "It's not great weather for your wedding day," Sydney said.

Edward sat beside her on an empty deck chair. "I wasn't able to speak to her last night," he explained dourly. "The party lasted until after two.

Then she insisted I go to my cabin and let her sleep. Sarah wouldn't leave us alone. I had no choice."

"Of course," she said. In truth she wasn't sure what to believe. He needed money and now that he thought she couldn't help him . . . There was only one way to find out. "Why the urgent need to talk to her? Isn't everything settled?"

"To call off the wedding, of course," he said. "Brooke had her moment last night. I shouldn't have indulged her but I didn't know what to say with everyone there discussing the wedding on board the ship."

"Let's hope the fog clears then," she said blandly.

Edward leaned toward her. "Nothing has changed. I'm in love with you and want you to be my wife when we reach England," he said to reassure her. "I've been up all night looking for you to tell you it doesn't matter. I will end things with her this morning and a simple note to the captain will make it right."

One part of her wanted to throw her arms around him and shout that she loved him too but the other part, the practical-Sinclair-business-tycoon part, won out. "What else did she tell you last night?"

Edward recoiled. "I'm not sure what you're asking."

This was too much. Tired of feeling trapped in layers of clothing, she began to unwrap the scarf from her head and neck. She did this slowly, like someone who enjoys preserving the giftwrap on Christmas morning. Free of the scarf she removed the heavy wrap that was over her shoulders. It was only her topcoat left. Finally able to move she tilted her head side to side and stretched her arms up to the sky with the casual grace of someone waking from a summer-afternoon nap. When she had finished stretching she swung her legs over the side of the deck chair to face him. Her bravado faded at the look of hurt on his face. There was only one way forward as far as she was concerned. "I know my sister told you that I don't have access to my inheritance until I turn twenty-five," she said bluntly.

Edward grunted softly. "Alfred?" She nodded. "I should have guessed he would have sought you out. I'm sure he disapproves of me."

She laughed. "He doesn't really," she said. "He just cares what happens to me."

"He doesn't matter. None of it matters," he said, and placed his hand on her knee. She stared down at it. It was large as a bear's yet so gentle. Their secret afternoon seemed like a dream. "I want you. Not your money."

She fought back the tears. Brooke had referred to her engagement and impending marriage as a business arrangement. Maybe she had a point, in which case now was not the time for emotion. She had to understand Edward's mindset, just as her father had taught her to learn how your competitors think. To that end she needed the full measure of Edward. "You would give up Rathfon Hall for me?" she asked unconvincingly. "It's your home. What will your family do?"

"I'm sure we can sell off parcels of land to stave off debtors," he said solemnly. "The estate has been in our family for generations. We won't lose it without a fight. But if we do, then we will deal with it then. And with you as my wife we shall survive no matter what."

He means it. I can tell he means it. Sydney thought she might burst from happiness. He wasn't going to throw her over for money. Brooke's ploy had failed. He closed his eyes and pressed his lips onto her hand and kissed it softly. Sydney wanted to be happy but it wasn't so easy. *I must tell him the truth about the money.* "I can't believe you'd risk everything for me."

"For us," he said, stroking her hand. "I know you don't want me to say it but I must. I'm going to fight in this war and I may die. And even if I do survive the world will never be the same again. Not for English landowners like me," he said, and forced a smile. "Not even for American heiresses like you."

"We're not even in the war," she said, his words shaking her to the marrow.

"Not yet, my dear," he said. "But soon. The way things are going on the front we shall need our Allies to put boots on the ground, not just ammunition in our guns."

"Edward, you're frightening me," she said.

"I don't mean to," he said soothingly. "I only want you to enter into our marriage with your eyes open. We may not be together very long, you need to think about that."

It was all she could take and she flung her arms around his neck. He lifted her to her feet.

"I don't need to think about it," she gushed. "I want to marry you. Even if it's for one day I want to be your wife."

He kissed her. She melted into his arms at the feel of him against her. They could be together, they would be. Then like a bucket of ice water had been dumped on her head she remembered Brooke, no doubt awake and preparing for a wedding ceremony that would never take place. The thought tore her up. She hated to be the cause of her sister's pain. *But she doesn't love him.*

As though reading her mind Edward straightened himself and smiled. "As much as I want to spend all morning kissing you, I have to talk to Brooke." His tone was firm, determined.

If Sydney was going to tell him the truth about her financial situation it had to be now. She hesitated. She would wait. *I need to be sure it's me he wants.*

"I wish it didn't have to be now," she said. "It would have been easier on us all if we'd landed in Liverpool and were able to take separate cars and hotels. Why did she want to marry today? If she hadn't announced it so publicly some of the humiliation would have been avoided."

"You know why," he said. "She knows I love you. It's her last stand." He kissed her hand. "I will speak to her as soon as I can and send a note to you when I'm finished."

"I'll be in my cabin."

"Very well, then," he said, and kissed her cheek once more.

She watched him walk away, he made a very solemn figure as he disappeared into the fog. She questioned her decision not to tell him the truth about her inheritance. *I did the right thing. Let him see Brooke again and speak to her one more time. It will be his final chance to decide. Then I will know for sure that he loves me.*

Isabel

I t was nearly seven o'clock in the morning when Isabel stirred. She had put her head down on the desk for a moment and now the sun was crawling up the sky. Her mouth was parched. She blinked several times until the room came into focus. She lifted her head up, still blinking. A cup of coffee was placed in front of her.

"Morning sleepyhead," Dorothy said with a smile.

"Am I the only one who fell asleep?" she muttered, and grabbed the cup. The steaming coffee was black, no sugar, and so strong it made her sit upright.

"Hardly," Dorothy answered.

"Any news?" she asked, trying to sound alert. The last thing she remembered was a third message being sent to Queenstown as per the strict rules. Room 40 relayed the information on the submarine's whereabouts to the Admiralty in Queenstown, who then relayed it on to the *Lusitania*. The ship couldn't respond so there was no way to confirm she had received them.

"No news is good news," Curtis answered as he passed by. His shirt was rumpled and the top two buttons were undone, revealing the top of his undershirt.

She walked over to where Denniston and several others were eating breakfast and reading over transcripts that had arrived during the night.

"I'm told we sent the *Lusitania* three messages," she said.

"We sent six," Denniston said coolly. In a room packed with tired and overworked men only he remained as he had been all day yesterday and every day before: crisp shirt, jacket done up, each hair on his head perfectly placed. "I'm sure Captain Turner has been notified by Queenstown and is taking evasive action."

Edward

B rooke had pushed him off all morning, refusing to see him on the grounds that it was bad luck for the groom to see the bride the day of the wedding. It was eleven o'clock before his persistence had won out. And now here they were face to face. But Brooke looked like a wounded animal. A gazelle perhaps, or something more feline, a lioness, yes, it was a lioness. The way she stood, backed into the corner, her fingers clawing at her throat, her chest rising and falling as she panted like a predator who had miscalculated its prey, expecting a weakened animal only to be met by a strength and valour that she couldn't match. Yet despite all this her eyes remained large and cunning. Edward had never seen her like this before, vulnerable yet vicious.

"You won't make a fool out of me," she snapped. The force of her words made him take a step backward.

"I'll tell everyone you ended it," Edward said calmly, trying to keep emotion out of his voice. "You won't be subject to public scorn this way. Your friends, my family, everyone will think you tired of me or decided you could never love me. Whatever story you wish to tell I will agree to wholeheartedly. No one need ever learn the truth."

Brooke laughed at him. The sound was worse than her silence had been when he first arrived to tell her he was breaking off their engagement.

"Shall I assume your laughter to mean you aren't taking me seriously?"

Her laughter ended. She padded across the room until she was inches from him. The blood had drained from her face.

"You're the one who can't be serious, darling." She was purring now. "You heard me last night. But just in case, let me repeat it: Sydney won't inherit for another four years. Where will you and your precious Rathfon Hall be then?"

She lifted her hand and stroked his cheek. He recoiled, which only made her smile and continue to caress him, like a cat playing with a

mouse before breaking its neck. "There, there," she murmured soothingly. "It's all right, darling. Shipboard romances are all the rage and why
not? You're entitled to have a final fling before our wedding. But my sister? Tsk tsk." Brooke stopped talking and, with her hand still touching
his cheek, she rose onto her tiptoes and kissed him.

Sydney

It was shortly after one o'clock, lunch was being served and the fog had
lifted. The sun was shining brilliantly in a clear sky. The coast of Ireland
was visible and it was reassuring to the passengers to see land again.
Sydney had left her berth and returned to her favourite position on the
bow. She had waited for hours without a word from Edward. Tired of
waiting, tired and afraid of what might have happened, she needed fresh
air. There was an obvious answer to why Edward was silent. An answer
she couldn't face—that he had chosen Brooke. Pragmatism and family
loyalty had won out over love and he had chosen the money. Surely it was
better that she knew his true colours now? She couldn't help but imagine
the shock on his face when he learned the truth about her own money
after he'd said his vows and placed the band on Brooke's finger.

"Ma'am?" Sydney turned to find a first class steward standing behind
her, envelope in hand. "Are you Miss Sinclair?" She nodded and he
handed her the envelope. "A note for you."

The handwriting on the envelope belonged to Brooke. She opened it
and unfolded the vanilla paper.

Sydney,
Come to the Regal Suite as soon as you get this.

B.

Short and simple were not words often associated with Brooke. If her
sister was summoning her to gloat so be it. As Sydney walked along the

deck toward the Regal Suite she devised a plan. When the ship docked in Liverpool she would congratulate the happy couple, then make her way to the train station and London. There would be no need for a tour of Rathfon Hall now. She couldn't take it.

As she reached the door her hands started to tremble. Would they both be waiting for her? Her sister would insist that she keep up appearances and attend the wedding dressed in full maid-of-honour glory. She pictured Edward and Brooke in their finery, the aloof Captain Turner before them in his white uniform and peaked cap as his officers of varying ranks fanned out behind him in honour-guard fashion. Then the guests . . . Would Alfred be the best man? Perhaps Mr. Frohman would convince his players to perform. The sun would be low in the sky at that hour, casting a tangerine glow on their faces so that the couple would appear lit from within with happiness. Sydney wanted to jump overboard. Her only consolation was that she would return to live in New York and only rarely have to endure seeing Edward. Letters home from Brooke would be superficial, that she could count on, as would be her replies. She would learn to accept and even love the inevitable nieces and nephews.

She paused, her hand on the door knob. *To hell with them.* She opened the door and stepped inside. Her breath caught at the sight of her sister standing before the mirror in her wedding gown. The dress Brooke had chosen befitted a princess. Flounces and ruffles overflowed, cascading down her slim figure; handmade lace and carefully sewn pearls adorned the skirt and bodice. Sydney found Sarah on her knees fussing with the train.

"You like it?" Brooke asked, and dotted her cheek with a handkerchief, also made of lace and silk with a single pearl weighing it down in one corner.

Sydney nodded. "It's beautiful. I was there when you chose it. Remember?"

"I remember," Brooke answered. "I wonder though if the pixie corners on the waistline aren't too much?"

Sydney stepped toward her sister and gently lifted one of the many layers of lace. The points faced the floor, which drew the eyes down and made the bride appear taller and slimmer. But on the wrong figure it could appear Harlequinesque and court jester was not a Sinclair role.

"I think they're perfect," Sydney said. So this was how she was to learn the answer. Edward was a coward and had made himself scarce rather than face her with the obvious fact that the wedding was going to happen. And here was her sister making her usual grand statement with pomp and circumstance. *Brooke is getting even and I deserve it. So stand here and take it like a woman should.*

"You know the kitchen staff on this ship are quite excellent," Brooke said gamely. "You should see the elaborate feast they planned for the reception. I do hope the Americans like Cornish hens as much as the English."

"I'm sure the hens will be delicious," Sydney answered.

"There is loads of champagne left too! It's as though Cunard knew this voyage would be special and stocked extra just for me." Brooke stepped closer to the mirror and fixed her hair. "And don't get me started on the weather. It's perfect."

Sydney wanted to scream. She looked at the clock on the wall—one thirty p.m. Sunset was hours away. *I only need to get through today, and tomorrow we dock in England and I will go to London and forget I ever met Edward.* "You're dressed so early," Sydney said. "What time do you want me here?"

Brooke turned to her; she had a queer look on her face. "Want *you*? *Here*?" Brooke laughed. "Why on earth would *I* want *you*?"

Sydney was taken aback. She knew Brooke would be angry but she'd gotten her way and that normally mollified her. "I take it you've changed your mind about me being your maid-of-honour?" It was a huge relief. She would remain down in the bowels of the ship, as far from the wedding on the bow as was physically possible.

Brooke took a couple of steps toward her until they were only a few inches apart. The queer look had returned but she said nothing, just continued to stare. Sydney stood tall, not wanting to cower from her sister's angry countenance. She had spent her life not cowering from her, unlike every other person who knew her.

"He doesn't want *me*," Brooke snapped. "He is in love with *you*."

"I don't understand," Sydney said, unable to comprehend the words. "That dress, I thought—"

Brooke picked up her skirt and returned to the mirror. "Sarah!" she commanded. The maid scurried over.

"Yes, Miss," she said.

Brooke wouldn't look at Sydney. "Help me take off this monstrosity." Sarah began to carefully unfasten the dozens of silk-covered buttons that ran the length of the gown from nape to hem.

"I told him I wanted to speak to you first," Brooke said, her tears held at bay by an unwavering pride. "He gave me that dignity at least. It appears he doesn't mind a suffragette for a wife. Who would have guessed a stuffy Englishman could be so progressive."

So Edward had broken it off. The news split Sydney in two—part of her wanted to cry with joy that the man she loved and had given herself to hadn't let her down; the other part was overcome with guilt for destroying Brooke's fantasy, knowing this would tear them apart. "I am sorry, Brooke," she began gently. "Can you ever forgive me?"

Brooke began to unpin her hair; dark chocolate waves fell in tendrils about her shoulders as she stepped out of the dress wearing only her corset. "Sarah, go fetch me some tea."

Sarah, arms full of silk and lace, hesitated as though not wanting to miss this final showdown. "Now!" Brooke shouted. Sarah jumped and dropped the gown onto the floor, hopping over it and out the door. When the door shut Brooke slipped a yellow satin robe on.

"Why should I forgive you?" she asked, and sat down on her bed. "You've ruined everything. And for what? A too-thin Englishman who will probably be killed in another month."

Sydney recoiled. "I love him," she said. It sounded feeble now.

Brooke rolled her eyes. "And here I thought all this time that you had more important things to do with your life than fall in love," she said sarcastically. "What about all the women you are so desperate to help? Who will save them now?"

"Don't, Brooke—" Sydney began but her sister cut her off.

"I have a right to say whatever I want," Brooke interjected. "I never imagined that you of all people would be my undoing. My own sister!"

Sydney rushed to embrace her but Brooke thrust her hand in the air to stop her. "We didn't mean for this to happen," Sydney said.

"*We.*" Brooke sniffed. "Sydney and Edward sitting in a tree. How sweet."

Sydney had never seen her sister so angry with her before. "You must believe me."

"Why should I?"

"Because I've never acted foolishly over men, you know that," Sydney said. "And if I'm behaving the fool now it's because I am in love. I'm sorry I've ruined things. I feel like a terrible person."

"You are a terrible person," Brooke said, her voice quieter now.

"What do you want me to do?" Sydney asked helplessly.

"Well, I'd say give him up but unfortunately he won't agree to marry me so that's not useful," Brooke said sharply.

"You don't love each other," Sydney said, trying to get her sister to see sense. "It's better this way."

"Better for you, maybe. You're such a selfish girl."

Brooke sat rigidly on the bed like she was poised to pounce. It was then that Sydney noticed that her sister still wore the enormous diamond-and-emerald engagement ring; she had been so proud of it when she had first shown it to her. Brooke caught her gaze and clutched her hand to her chest.

"You want my ring too?" she asked icily. "Well, you can't have it." Brooke wrenched the thing off her finger and tossed it on the bed where it lay like a severed limb. "I'm going to have the gold melted down and the stones made into a pendant and I will wear it around my neck every time I visit with you and Edward as a reminder of what you did."

Sydney had never felt as horrible at any previous time in her life as she did in that moment. Yet she knew her sister better than anyone.

"Edward means nothing to you other than a title," Sydney said as gently as she could. "You've said so many times."

"And what does he mean to you?" Brooke asked, her voice harsh.

Sydney felt faint. Her nerves were getting the better of her. "I love him, Brooke. It's not a fling."

"Don't lie to me," she said.

"I'm not lying," Sydney said, her voice rising like her anger. "You're the one who lied, Brooke."

"I beg your pardon!"

"You lied to Edward about my inheritance," Sydney accused her. "Alfred told me."

"It wasn't a lie," Brooke snapped. "It was a test."

Sydney was dumbstruck. She paused, taking in the words. "What sort of test?"

"Dearest, if Edward wasn't going to marry me for my money, then I wanted to be certain he'd only leave me for love," she explained. Her eyes were moist and she dabbed them with her hand. "So I told him you had no money to see if it made a difference. It didn't. Turns out my fiancé, whoops, my former fiancé, believes in true love."

Sydney didn't know what to say. She was stunned. "You were trying to protect me?"

"Is that so surprising?" Brooke asked. "Using money for marriage is my specialty, not yours. I couldn't stand the idea of your thinking you were marrying for love only to discover it was your oil stocks that netted a husband. You really are quite naïve when it comes to men, darling. Someone had to look out for you."

Sydney was on the verge of tears. She had underestimated Brooke. There was so little she could think of to say. Brooke looked away from her and ran her fingers through her hair. "I am your older sister, aren't I? I'm not happy with what you've done and I will probably hate you for as long as I think it's necessary," she admitted bitterly.

Sydney flinched at the idea that Brooke would *hate* her—even temporarily—but what did she expect, a congratulatory telegram? Brooke seemed to notice her expression for she smiled suddenly. It wasn't exactly warm, but it gave Sydney hope.

"Take heart, dear Sydney, you're my only family. Blood does mean more than a husband. Besides I can always find another dirt-poor aristocrat. England is teeming with them," Brooke said with a hint of her usual high spirit seeping into her voice. "And eventually I may forgive you. Once you've grown fat with child and I've married a baronet. As long as you are absolutely convinced Edward will make you happy then I suppose I can live with it."

"He will make me happy," Sydney said. And he would. She was certain. Her sister didn't love him, which meant she would be free to find a man she did love. They would all be happy one day.

Brooke sat up and clapped her hands together. "See! That's what I was banking on," she said. "Banking on? That's funny."

For the first time in days the sisters exchanged knowing smiles and after a moment, some laughter. It was a small step toward reconciliation and it gave Sydney the strength she needed. She didn't want to leave her sister just now, but she was desperate to find Edward and tell him what had happened. "I want you to fall in love with a man who truly loves you too," she said softly.

"Oh don't worry, I will," Brooke said, sounding overly confident. "That's just the sort of romantic I am."

Isabel

The morning had unfolded routinely. The team deciphered wireless transcripts at a steady rate. There were coordinates for the German fleet near Belgium. There were intercepts about the ongoing battle in Gallipoli. And then later in the morning came a telegram that raised the alarm of the night before all over again. Commander Hope didn't hold back this time and read it aloud for the entire staff.

"*Submarine has torpedoed SS* Centurion *off the coast of County Wexford.*

We believe same U-boat that sank the Candidate *is responsible. Crew safe.*"
Commander Hope paused. "She was sunk yesterday afternoon at approximately one p.m."

Isabel and Dorothy exchanged looks. The *Lusitania* had only one more day at sea. She would dock in Liverpool in the morning; surely nothing would happen so close to home port. Isabel looked anxiously at Commander Hope for an order or any type of action that she could heed.

"That's only a few hours after the *Candidate*," Denniston remarked. "Schwieger is determined to go home a hero."

"Let's see if we can make sure that doesn't happen," Commander Hope said, and glanced at Isabel.

"Isabel, copy it at once and bring it to Lord Fisher," he said.

She took the message from his hand and paused, wondering if she should mind her place. Everything and everyone was so tense, many of them had hardly slept these past few nights.

"Perhaps she's run out of torpedoes?" Isabel suggested hopefully, and waited but thankfully no one berated her.

"They carry six," Denniston explained. "She's used only three." The gravity of the situation played on his features and he looked into her eyes and squinted. "Isabel, you had better get going."

She returned to her desk to type the copies. When she left the room she broke into a run and without missing a beat turned down the hallway toward the office of Winston Churchill. He wanted a reason for the United States to enter the war. He had practically said he desired a neutral ship with Americans on board to be sunk to get that reason. But surely he wouldn't knowingly let it happen.

The sound of her heels striking the marble floor made an alarming echo and people scattered to let her pass, scowling after her when they realized the terrible clatter was merely a pair of shoes. She nearly slid to her knees trying to stop outside his office door. She caught her breath and patted her hair down. She opened the door and went into the reception where Churchill's secretary sat. The woman seemed startled to see her.

"Miss Nelson, what in the devil—" She paused.

Isabel held out the telegram. "Mr. Churchill needs to see this straight-away," she said. "It's urgent."

The woman frowned. "That won't be possible, my dear."

Isabel frowned in return. "But you don't understand—"

"It is you who doesn't understand, Miss Nelson. Mr. Churchill is out of the country. He left two days ago for Paris."

Isabel felt the floor swim beneath her. "I didn't realize," she said glumly.

"I'm surprised Commander Hope sent you." She tsk-tsked. "He should have remembered."

Isabel nodded and backed away. "I'll take it to Lord Fisher."

"Very well. Good day, Miss Nelson."

"Good day," she answered, and shut the door behind her.

She marched to Lord Fisher's office and delivered the telegram. The secretary held out her hand to receive it without even looking at her.

Even though some time had passed since Isabel was back at Room 40, she jumped each time a pneumatic tube crashed into the metal tray. Each time she watched as one of the men opened the tube and unrolled the paper inside. Each time she waited for any mention of the ocean liner in the chatter that came from the wireless stations. But there was none. It was as though for a brief moment the *Lusitania* didn't exist. Then Lord Fisher arrived.

"We're advising Vice Admiral Coke to send another warning message to the *Lusitania* at once," he announced, and Denniston rushed over to jot it down. "The message is '*Submarines active off south coast of Ireland.*' Full stop."

Denniston stuffed it into a tube to be sent to the basement where the wireless operators would send it onward. Isabel breathed a sigh of relief. It would be all right now. The *Lusitania*'s captain would heed the warning and go full speed until she safely docked in Liverpool.

"Very good," Fisher said. "I'll be in my office with Captain Hall.

Commander Hope, I expect you to apprise us of any developments immediately."

"Yes, sir," Hope answered.

Around eleven thirty Lord Fisher was back, a slip of paper in his hand, and he was agitated. "Commander Hope, I've decided to send another warning to the *Lusitania*. It will give the ship's captain more details." Fisher held up the telegram. "Read it to your staff so they are all aware of what is transpiring."

Isabel pricked up her ears. Commander Hope seemed to cover the length of the room in two strides as he took the telegram from Fisher and read it out loud. "*Submarines active in southern part of Irish Channel. Last heard of 20 miles south of Coningbeg Light Vessel.* Make sure the *Lusitania* gets this." He looked at Fisher. "Should we tell Captain Turner about the *Candidate* and the *Centurion*?"

Fisher shook his head. "We feel that is too much information to broadcast."

"Yes, sir," Commander Hope answered.

Isabel sensed he didn't completely agree with Fisher. Neither did she. Something must have occured to make Fisher think this new message was needed. Exactly what that was he wasn't going to tell them. Dorothy stood at the cabinet filing the past week's worth of decoded messages. Isabel quietly went and stood opposite her. The room was unnaturally quiet and she didn't want to risk a reprimand.

"Do you think the danger for the *Lusitania* will be over now?" Isabel asked her.

Dorothy glanced at her but went back to filing. "I wager that Captain Turner will heed all the directives that the Admiralty gave him and sail through into Liverpool without incident," she said, not looking up. "After all, there's not a submarine built that could catch her."

"That isn't true," Isabel said. "Just last month I heard Captain Hall and Lord Fisher say that the Admiralty had the ship's fourth boiler put out of use to conserve coal. She can't go more than twenty or twenty-one knots. Hasn't been able to since the winter."

"That's still faster than a U-boat," Dorothy offered.

Isabel wasn't satisfied. "Why isn't Fisher ordering a naval escort for her? Surely there are several cruisers docked in Liverpool or Southampton that can reach her. What's the use of all our Intelligence if we don't use it?"

Dorothy pressed her finger to her lips to silence her. "Don't you get it, Isabel?"

Isabel's face showed she did not. Dorothy whispered, "The Admiralty won't send its cruisers to an area they know is rife with submarine activity. The *Candidate* and the other boats mean nothing to them. But they won't risk a battleship for anything."

Sydney

Sydney walked along the starboard side searching for Edward. He wasn't in his cabin when she'd knocked. Where could he be? So far her walk had been fruitless. Then she saw a familar face: Walter. He stood midship with several other passengers. She recognized Albert and Agnes Veals and Agnes's brother, Fred Bailey, from their meals together in the third class dining saloon. With them were two young ladies she'd not met before. Everyone seemed fixated on the water.

"Almost there," he said when she joined them. He glanced at her quickly. "Then I get to see my Alice and Muriel. It will be a happy day."

"That will be lovely for you, Walter." Sydney looked out at the water. "Have you seen Edward?"

"No I haven't," Walter answered.

Sydney checked her wristwatch; it was ten minutes past two o'clock. The only place she hadn't checked now seemed the most obvious. He must be waiting at her cabin. She was about to walk away but the intensity of Walter's face made her stop. "What are you looking at?" she asked.

"Porpoises," Agnes answered. "There was a whole school of them this morning."

Sydney was relieved to hear their focus was as innocent as that.

"Look, there's a porpoise!" Mr. Veals shouted, and he pointed out a white streak coming across the water toward the ship. Sydney followed the direction the streak had taken and saw what looked like the periscope of a submarine in the distance.

"That's not a porpoise!" Walter yelled. His words were immediately followed by a shout from the lookout.

"Torpedo! Starboard side!" came the cry from the crow's nest.

Sydney and Walter stared in horror as the torpedo struck the ship forward of where their little group stood. The explosion shook the *Lusitania* and threw up a huge volume of sea water, drenching them. The ladies screamed in terror as debris from the explosion rained down on them. Elsewhere frightened voices tried to explain the crash.

"I bet we hit a mine!" someone said.

"Don't be stupid! It's the Germans!"

"Get your lifebelts and head to the lifeboats," Walter instructed them all.

Sydney spotted Frederick Isherwood inching toward them along the railing just as a second explosion more powerful than the first rocked the ship, sending another cloud of debris and dust from the hull to the bridge. Sydney grasped the railing in terror.

"What in God's name?" Isherwood asked when he reached Walter and Sydney. He was visibly shaken.

"A second torpedo?" Agnes asked.

There was no time to answer. The deck beneath them began to tilt to starboard. They slid and teetered, desperately trying to remain on two feet. The sensation was sickening and Sydney saw the terror on the faces of her companions. The deck had become crowded as passengers ran outside. People were asking what had happened and what to do next. But one thing was certain: the *Lusitania* was maimed.

"I must find Edward and Brooke!" Sydney yelled, and moved away.

"Don't go back inside the ship!" Walter shouted. But she kept going.

She began to run down the staircase passing men and women climbing up. Many seemed as confused and panicked as she was while there were others who seemed nonchalant and calm. She wasn't sure which was right for the situation. She reached the Grand Entrance on C Deck and kept going, so convinced was she that Edward was at her cabin waiting for her. Once she found him, they would go get Brooke together. Down she went past D, then E, each step and turn she was thrust against a crash of people trying to climb up. The passengers—men leading wives, mothers clasping children and crewmen attempting to create order out of chaos—were a frightened horde that saw no need to let Sydney pass with ease. If panic had an odour it was the smell of sweat. She had to fight her way through them and down the final flight of stairs until at last she reached F Deck, when the lights went out, plummeting the entire ship into darkness. Then came the screams.

She clung to the railing and pulled her way along, counting cabin doors until she was sure it was her berth. But there was no Edward waiting impatiently for her. There was no one. Only blackness and a sickening motion beneath her feet that she couldn't quite place. She fumbled in her purse for the key and, finding it, managed to unlock the door. It flew open, startling her. She stepped inside and bumped into the dresser, which was on its side, all of her things spilled onto the floor. It puzzled her until she felt herself stagger to regain balance. Then she knew. The ship was listing. And that meant one thing: the *Lusitania* was taking on water and rapidly. She felt around under the bed until her fingers closed on the lifebelt. She couldn't be sure she was fastening it correctly. It was too dark to know. She tied it quickly, then looked around her berth. The amber dress lay on the floor in a tangle of silk. For a second she wanted to grab it but sense took hold. Instead she grabbed Georgina's scarf and left the berth not bothering to close the door.

Back in the passageway she took a few clumsy steps before realizing that the uneven floor was not the floor at all. Her right foot was walking on the wall.

"Help me find my baby!" a voice called out in the dark.

"Where did you leave it?" Sydney called back.

"Help me find it!" the woman shrieked, and shoved past Sydney.

"Don't go down there," Sydney warned. "You must get up to the Boat Deck."

The woman ignored her and continued down the passageway yelling for her baby but no one answered her calls. Sydney managed to find the staircase and started up but the going was tough and she had to pull herself along. The past seven days of climbing the four flights between F and B Decks had strengthened her legs and arms and for that she was thankful. With each step the rising volume of human fear swelled in her ears. There were screams of terror, cries for help and calls for loved ones. There were also shrill shouts from Cunard crewmen but Sydney couldn't discern what the instructions were. She just knew she had to climb back up the stairs. Surely Edward and her sister would be at the Boat Deck by now. Then she remembered Brooke's fearlessness when it came to intense situations. *She's probably already in a lifeboat.* She had no fear of her sister being left behind. She managed to get to D Deck when the staircase became clogged with people trying to make it to the lifeboats three flights up.

Panic-stricken, the men and women began to jostle and fights broke out. Sydney was shoved back down several steps before resorting to shoving and pushing herself. She had fought her way through the protest in Washington Square and she could fight her way through this lot. With elbows held up she carved a path until she at last reached the landing of D Deck. But unlike the other third class passengers who continued to crowd the staircase she took off down the passageway toward the first class dining saloon. The main staircase was steps away when she heard a ghastly sound. It seemed to be coming from below. The elevators! Men and women were trapped between floors without electricity to move the iron cages up or down. She watched horrified as they attempted to claw their way out of what were certain to be their tombs.

"Help us! Pray God help us!" one woman shrieked.

Sydney closed her eyes. There was nothing she could do. She

continued upward. The main staircase was less crowded and she ascended with dozens of passengers all of whom had to climb with the pitiful cries of the trapped lives growing dimmer beneath them.

At last she arrived at B Deck and, gasping, she raced for the doors to the Promenade. All she wanted was to breathe fresh air after suffocating amongst the pushing and shoving limbs. But what she saw when she stepped onto the portside deck horrified her.

The peaceful Promenade where she had spent countless hours walking in the sunshine and fog, played shuffleboard with Walter and Fred and, most of all, where she had fallen in love with Edward was no longer recognizable. The deck she stood on was covered in ash, black soot and debris. Passengers were covered in the stuff and struggled to stand against the list that had to be nearly fifteen degrees by now, either too stunned to move or patiently awaiting orders like they were students on a school trip. She walked over to a seaman who addressed her before she could utter a word.

"Get up to the Boat Deck, Miss," he said urgently. "In case we need to launch the lifeboats."

"In case?" she asked, stupefied. "I can't think there's a doubt?"

She looked out across the ocean; its surface was littered with flotsam, torn-up wood and other unidentifiable items. The placid sea had become a battlefield.

In the midst of the chaos she recognized Staff Captain Anderson from Brooke's party in the Regal Suite. He was ordering people out of the boats so that they could be safely lowered into the water first. But that proved impossible and Sydney stood by as two of the portside boats crashed into the sea empty. The sight of such catastrophic failure sent a roar of fear into the air. Panic had set in amongst the passengers.

"What good is 'lifeboats enough for all' if you can't work them?" someone shouted.

"Your men are incompetent!" screamed another.

Staff Captain Anderson maintained calm throughout the ordeal but it was obvious that he had no solution to the crisis.

One of the crewmen struggling with the ropes spotted a few passengers who seemed paralyzed. "You best find a lifebelt!" he shouted to them.

"Land's just there." A passenger pointed to the green hills incredulously.

"The captain tried to make land but he's lost control of the ship," the crewman explained in hushed tones. "All the systems are dead. We got no rudder and no electricity."

His words numbed Sydney. How was that possible? How was any of this possible?

"Will she really sink?" someone asked, echoing her thoughts.

"We don't have the men to launch all these boats in time. A lot of them were trapped below in the baggage room when the torpedo hit. Save yourselves."

She couldn't move. She stood in a daze until someone grabbed her arm. It was Walter. "Thank God, you're all right." Sydney couldn't answer him. "Frederick's gone looking for lifebelts but I told him we had to stay on deck," he continued just as the ship seemed to right itself momentarily. For the first time since the torpedo had struck they stood evenly on both feet. This caused more confusion amongst the passengers. The crew seemed unsure too and for a brief time the previous chaos quieted with the righting of the ship. Captain Turner appeared on the bridge and shouted to his men.

"Don't lower any more boats! Get those people out of them now!"

Was the danger really over? The answer came as the ship abruptly keeled over once again to her starboard side and in the same instant began to go down by the nose. This was it. There was no more time to think. "Walter, what do I do?" she asked, finding her voice.

"Go up to the Boat Deck and find a lifeboat," he said.

"What about you?"

"I'll be fine," he said, and she watched as he ran down the port side toward the stern crashing into people and debris along the way. He wasn't the only one with the same idea, as dozens of others knocked into him struggling to reach the highest point of the ship as her forecastle broke the surface.

"Sydney!" A voice called her name, jostling her. "Here!" She looked up and saw Brooke on the Boat Deck with Sarah. Her sister was wearing the bright daffodil-yellow dress she had worn when they had sailed from New York. There would be no difficulty spotting her. Both were wearing their life jackets. She sobbed with relief. She'd never been so happy to see her sister. But where was Edward? She feared the worst—that in all the chaos he had gone below deck searching for *her*. What if he were trapped below like those poor people in the elevators?

"Hurry!" Brooke yelled at her.

"I'm coming!" she shouted, and with renewed energy darted and pushed through the mass of people and up the final flight of stairs to the Boat Deck. As she ran she was knocked off her feet time and again by the steepening list. Everywhere women were screaming for help and babies wailed in terror. But Sydney kept getting to her feet and scrambling for balance until she saw a familiar face in the crowd—Alfred Vanderbilt. He was wearing a lifebelt and was standing beside his valet, Ronald; both men were calmly instructing women passengers on how to fasten the lifebelts. The women were mostly hysterical but no matter how they flailed and cried, Alfred's voice soothed them into submission.

"Don't cry. It's quite all right," he told a woman who was clutching her infant to her chest. Seeing that she had no lifebelt he quickly removed his and tied her inside it. "Carry the baby in your arms. Now go to the starboard side. I doubt they'll get many boats launched here." The woman was silent but she nodded like she understood and left.

It was then that Alfred saw Sydney. He smiled. His composure and warmth made her cry and she stumbled toward him, a beacon of hope in a world gone mad.

"Sydney," he said urgently. "Your lifebelt is upside down."

She looked down. He was right. "Oh heavens, Alfred," she said, and began to unfasten it but found her fingers were tied up in worse knots than the strips of cloth that held the lifebelt to her waist.

"Allow me," Alfred said, and expertly untied the lifebelt and lifted it off her shoulders, turning it around and gently placing it back over her head in the correct way. "If you were to have entered the water like that you'd have drowned instantly. The damn thing would have turned you on your head."

She grinned stupidly. "I can't swim, Alfred."

"Neither can I," he said, but as he answered his smile vanished for a moment. "There. You're good. Now I suggest you get to the starboard side of the ship."

"I heard the captain order people out of the boats," she said.

"I think he's changed his mind," Alfred said. "The *Lusitania* is sinking and fast."

Her face went white. "How fast? Surely it can't go down faster than the *Titanic*. They had a couple of hours."

"We don't," he said grimly.

She shook her head, disbelieving. "There's land just there," she said hopelessly, her eyes darting to the Irish coast that seemed so close she could touch it. "We can see it."

"Be a good girl and come with me. We need to get the hell out of here."

He grabbed her arm to steady her and led her down the deck.

"But Brooke!" Sydney shouted.

"She's straight ahead," Alfred explained. She looked up and saw the unmistakable silhouette of her sister and the little maid floundering along.

"We won't lose sight of them," Alfred said. She was carried along far more easily with his strength. But she couldn't help wishing that it were Edward's strong shoulders and arms that bore her along.

"What about you?" she asked. "You gave your lifebelt away."

"I will be fine. Ronald and I will help ensure the women and children are in boats, then we will find one."

She was touched by the man's bravery. If he was terrified he showed no sign of it. As they picked their way along her eyes darted around. But she saw only strange and terrified faces. "Alfred? Have you seen Edward?" she asked. "I'm afraid he went searching for me. And now he's trapped below and it's my fault."

Alfred smiled. "My dear," he began, "never underestimate the quiet heroism of an English gentleman." He pointed. "He's right there."

She looked up and saw him at last. He and Maxwell were by a lifeboat filled with passengers, mostly women and children, and they were helping the crew to free it from the davits. She watched him utterly captivated.

"Go to him now," Alfred said. "Godspeed."

She turned to her friend. A haunting feeling swept over her as she looked into his eyes. "Good luck, Alfred," she said, and kissed his cheek. She watched him stagger forward along the deck, not fully able to comprehend that it might be the last time she would see him. She turned back to the lifeboat and Edward. The crew seemed to be having difficulty with the launch. The lifeboat kept swaying back toward the ship instead of out to sea, its occupants yelling at the men to do it right.

"Edward!" she shouted above the din. "Edward! I'm here!"

He turned and ran toward her but to her surprise he grabbed her shoulders and shook her.

"You have to get to the starboard side of the ship. They can't launch the boats on this side. The list is too great," he said urgently.

As if on cue the lifeboat was released from the davit and the men attempted to lower it but the list was too steep and instead of lowering downward the boat swung back in with such force that it smashed backward across the deck, just missing Sydney and Edward. It landed with a thunderous crash, crushing dozens of people who had been standing against the ship's wall and spilling its occupants along the deck and into the sea.

Everywhere people ran screaming. At least those who could still run. Those who were crushed lay dead or injured beneath the remains of the lifeboat while the agonizing cries of the people in the water, bobbing and waving to stay afloat, carried up and over the port side. Sydney felt herself being lifted to her feet by Edward. She covered her face with her hands and he held her.

"Don't look, darling," he said. "Whatever you do, don't look." He turned her away from the horror of broken and dismembered bodies, of people crying in agony to be saved. Placing his hands on her shoulders he forced her to look at him. "I'm going to get you on a lifeboat," he said, and led her back the way she'd come. It was a longer route to the starboard side but now that the deck was under siege from mangled bodies and the wreck from the lifeboat they had no choice.

They didn't speak as they moved in silent terror through the panicked throngs. They pushed their way through the first class entrance to get to the other side. Sydney's eyes darted around her, noting the furniture askew and palm trees knocked to the floor as other passengers rushed up the ornate staircase, while others stood awaiting orders. She wondered where Brooke was in this mess of humanity. When they at last reached the starboard side Sydney gasped. The list had lowered the side of the ship so far that she felt as though she might topple into the ocean. The smell of the sea was stronger than ever and it made her nauseated all over again, just like on the first day. Worse than the hideous angle and the proximity to the sea was the obvious fact that the ship had descended into utter bedlam. It was a mob scene. Edward dragged her along as she watched a young mother fling her child overboard into the arms of a man in a lifeboat. Then another and another. The poor wee things were tossed over like rubbish as their anguished mothers shouted to the people in the lifeboats below to save their babies.

It was then she caught sight of First Officer Jones shouting orders at lifeboat 17. She looked at the passengers and saw Brooke and Sarah on board. "There, Edward." Sydney pointed. "There's my sister."

Edward clasped her hand even tighter and they swayed and fumbled through the crowd until they reached it. First Officer Jones held his hand out to her.

"Come on board, Miss," he said firmly. "No time to waste."

She turned to Edward. "Come with us."

Edward cast his eyes about the ship. There were still several lifeboats to be filled and launched, women and children to be saved and with hundreds of crewmen already killed or trapped inside the ship there was a dire shortage of manpower to help.

"Not now, my darling," he said, and kissed her on the lips. "I must return to Maxwell and help all I can."

She was sobbing too much to feel fear or anything but anguish. How she longed to tell him how happy she was that they were free to be together, to marry and create a life. But there was no time. She felt his lips pull away and she opened her eyes.

"We will see each other soon. I promise," he said. "I love you, my darling Sydney."

"I love you, Edward," she said. But before she could hold him one last time she felt herself being hoisted into the air and placed on a makeshift gangway cobbled together by deck chairs. "The lifeboat is too far out to jump," Officer Jones explained calmly. "You'll be all right."

She crawled across the bridge of deck chairs and flopped into the life-boat at her sister's feet and immediately scrambled to stand. It was then she noticed the Papadapouloses from their dinner with the captain. The wife, Angela, nodded to her solemnly as her husband looked terrified. Sydney watched Edward help Officer Jones and other crewmen dislodge the lifeboat from the davits so it could safely be lowered into the water. *Why won't he look at me? I must see into his eyes one more time.*

"Sit down, Sydney," Brooke barked. "You want to flip us over?"

She felt her sister tug on her skirt, forcing her to sit. She kept her eyes on Edward. Maxwell had joined him too. Sydney realized she had never properly met the valet. She prayed there would be time enough for that once they survived this ordeal.

"We're going to be fine, Miss," offered Sarah feebly.

"What makes you so sure of that?" Brooke snapped in panic, and began to fiddle with her life jacket. "This confounded thing is on too tight."

"Leave it be," Sydney told her. "It's supposed to be tight."

"I can hardly breathe," Brooke argued.

"We're clear!" a man shouted from the ship.

"Begin to lower lifeboat 17, men," Officer Jones called out, the muscles in his neck and face straining as the weight of the boat pulled on the taut ropes. "Easy now," he continued.

Edward and the other men followed his instructions and foot by foot lifeboat 17 drew nearer to the sea. Sydney watched as Edward began to fade from view as the starboard side came into sharper focus. She could touch the steel hull if she reached for it. She had never doubted the enormity of the *Lusitania* but seeing her lying wounded like this made her seem mammoth, like a harpooned whale.

"Miss, you shouldn't do that." It was Sarah's voice. Sydney turned to see Brooke, her lifebelt completely undone.

"Just for a moment," Brooke said. "I need to catch my breath. Besides we've been saved now."

The sisters locked gazes for a moment. What came to Sydney was a memory from their childhood when they had both fallen off their ponies during a hunt. They had been racing but Brooke's pony bolted and was galloping out of control. They were heading for a ditch that was too big to clear and Brooke had begun to shriek. Sydney tore after her on her pony and somehow managed to steer him toward her sister and they galloped side by side until Sydney got hold of the reins of the other pony just as the ditch came upon them. "Grab my hand," she'd called out to Brooke who took it and held it with all her might. Sydney tried to stop the ponies but the running animals had seen what was ahead and knowing they couldn't jump the ditch they stopped abruptly and the girls were tossed over their heads and into the filthy watery hole. Yet somehow they were still holding hands. The girls had sat in shock, covered in mud, and stared at each other until they burst out laughing.

But no one was laughing now. The lifeboat was about twelve feet from the surface of the ocean. She knew that Brooke was frightened but didn't want to show it. Sydney held out her palm. "Grab my hand," she said. Brooke took it firmly and they continued to look into each other's eyes until Sydney smiled. Brooke raised an eyebrow; no doubt she recalled the pony incident too and smiled back.

"I will tie it up again," she said like a naughty child and began to do just that.

Sydney was about to offer to tie it for her when a sudden loud whooshing sound obliterated all others and the lifeboat plummeted through the air and flipped over.

Edward

There was no sign of Sydney or Brooke. They had vanished. The surface of the ocean was swarming with bodies struggling for survival amongst mangled corpses. Edward couldn't bear to see Sydney torn to pieces or drowning in the frigid water. He tried to jump in after her but someone had him by the arm. It was Maxwell.

"Don't do it, sir," he barked. "You can't help them."

"I can try!" Edward shouted, and broke away from him. He pulled himself along the railing searching the water. Almost in a trance he staggered and crawled toward the stern, which was lifting up to the heavens. It wouldn't be long before it was completely clear of the water. He looked back at the bow and saw it was submerged. The ship rocked in a sickening motion, listing ever farther starboard as she simultaneously dived nose first. Had Edward not been so filled with grief he would have been terrified. Every few feet he looked over the edge, always hoping for a sign of Sydney, but there was none.

Maxwell managed to keep up and together they reached the port side where they were greeted with mayhem but they shoved their way through. Everywhere passengers were fighting for room on the doomed lifeboats. Somewhere a pistol was fired. Shouts and cries of despair rippled along the deck. Somehow through the havoc he heard his name. Edward searched and found Charles Frohman standing with Rita Jolivet, George Vernon and a man he didn't recognize. Frohman was smoking a cigar but wasn't wearing a lifebelt.

"Edward," he repeated, and waved calmly like it was during intermission at the theatre.

Edward lurched forward gasping. "Sydney and Brooke . . . They are lost."

Rita shrieked. "How?"

"They were in a lifeboat on the starboard side. It was nearly in the water but it overturned," he said, and grasped the rail beside Frohman for balance.

"Were they wearing lifebelts?" Frohman asked.

Edward was struck by his calmness. "Yes," he answered, Maxwell at his side.

"Then perhaps they were saved," Rita said encouragingly.

"You're not wearing a lifebelt," Edward said to Frohman.

He smiled. "I gave it to a lady." Frohman puffed his cigar and watched the commotion before him. "I didn't think they would do it."

"Damn Germans," Vernon said.

Edward then saw the cane in Frohman's hand. He had great difficulty walking. Edward couldn't imagine how he would manage in the water on his own.

"Do you want me to find you another lifebelt?" Edward offered.

Frohman shook his head. "The four of us have agreed to hold hands and stay together."

"The lifeboats aren't safe, you said so yourself," Rita said. Then seeing Edward's crushed expression she added, "I'm sure they survived."

"There are hardly any lifeboats," Edward pointed out desperately. "I believe fewer than six were launched."

There was nothing left to say and they stood there, balancing like a high-wire act as moment by moment the *Lusitania* shuddered and dived farther beneath the ocean. Frohman exhaled a ring of cigar smoke and took in a final sweep of the hundreds of people surrounding him.

"'Why fear death? To die will be an awfully big adventure,'" Charles said wistfully.

Edward recognized Frohman's words from *Peter Pan*. Just then the ship lurched as though in agony and a collective shriek spread through the passengers struggling on deck. Edward looked up just in time to see a cliff of green water surge toward the little group and then there was darkness.

Sydney

She was pushed down farther and farther into the cold water. Sydney forced her eyes open and saw with a fright the upturned lifeboat above her and the bodies of several passengers dead from its impact. Not knowing how to swim she kicked back with her legs and reached toward the boat with all her might. She could see space between the boat and the water where air would be and she kept kicking and kicking but something clung to her ankle. Barely able to hold her breath for much longer she looked down through the dark green water and saw Sarah hanging on to her. She couldn't tell if the girl was alive or dead so she continued to kick and squirm until by some miracle she grasped the edge of the lifeboat and pulled herself underneath it where there was a few inches of air. She hung there gasping as the weight threatened to pull her down again. It was heavy, motionless, and that was when she knew that Sarah was dead. Horrified she tightened her grip on one of the lifeboat seats and managed to lift her arm over it. The boat began to sway and she prayed for it to settle. But loud banging echoed around her and she realized that some of the other passengers had survived the fall and were clinging to the outside of the lifeboat, unaware that she was beneath it.

With all her might she kicked her left leg and with her right foot tried to kick off poor Sarah. She couldn't fathom how the dead girl's grip could be so strong. She took a deep breath and shoved her head back under the water and saw that the girl's lifebelt was partially undone and its strap was twisted around her ankle. She came back up for air. Took three deep breaths, terrified to go back below the surface. She tightened her grip on the lifeboat seat with one arm, then with a final inhale dived below and fumbled with her hand, the sea water stinging her eyes, until at last she freed her ankle. She caught a last glimpse of Sarah. The girl's eyes were wide open in shock, her mouth agape in an eternal scream as her small body sank into blackness. Sydney had no time to think more of the girl for she felt legs kicking around the lifeboat as other passengers clung desperately and tried to right it. Staying beneath the lifeboat wasn't an option. There would be a tremendous undertow when the ship sank and she didn't want to be pulled down with it. She took another breath and dived beneath again, only this time she held on to the edge of the lifeboat and pulled herself to the outside. She came up for air and found herself in a sea of debris and bodies, some living, others drowning and even more already dead. The water had turned an awful colour. The cries were pitiful. It was as though the damned had gathered their voices into a single scream. The water was mercilessly cold and its colour had become tinged with red, the blood of the victims.

Sydney was elated to see Walter in the distance, struggling not to be sucked under with the ship. She called out to him but he couldn't hear her. All she could do was watch as he treaded water. There was a sudden thrashing near him. She looked on as he spun around to find a small child struggling in the water. It was a little boy, practically a toddler. Walter swam over and grabbed him. The child was weak and at first fought against him but seemed to calm down when he realized he could float by clinging to Walter.

"Help!" came another child's voice.

Sydney looked on in amazement as Walter headed toward a boy about seven years of age without a lifebelt trying to stay afloat. The toddler grasped Walter's back as he swam to the other boy and lifted his head above the water. The older boy was wide-eyed with terror and Sydney could tell even from a distance that the child was half-drowned already.

"Walter," she called again. This time he heard her.

"You hold on to that lifeboat," he instructed.

"Can you make it to me?" she asked him.

"We don't got room!" shouted one of the male passengers who clung to the lifeboat.

"Of course we do; they're children," Sydney snapped.

When she turned back she saw the older boy gasping and Walter lose his grip on him. The child disappeared below the surface. Walter desperately thrust his hands into the water searching. Then the boy's coat appeared on the surface and Walter grabbed at it and yanked him up again. But as he did the toddler fell off Walter's back and splashed into the sea.

"No!" Walter shouted and, hanging on to the older child, he took a deep breath and shoved his head below. He came back up but the toddler was gone. Sydney began to cry, for the children and for Walter's horror at losing them both. She wanted him to swim to her, to help her as he had tried to help the children but Walter was carried swiftly out of earshot by the power of the current.

She soon saw why. The bow of the ship—her bow—was entirely submerged and the stern was lifted out of the water, exposing its enormous propellers. The metal gleamed golden in the sunlight. It was beautiful yet sickening.

High up in the sky men and women were clinging to whatever parts of the ship they could grab while many were flung like rag dolls into the sea screaming and smashing into parts of the wreckage that was strewn across the water.

"There she goes. The final wave," a man said who was clinging for dear life to the same lifeboat as Sydney. "Those poor souls still on her. They'll be with God in a few minutes."

"Better swim out," said another man. "Else you'll be pulled under with the *Lusy*." He shoved off from the lifeboat and swam away just as the great ship took a final plunge beneath the surface. One lifeboat filled with survivors was still attached by ropes to the ship and as she slipped below the surface the small boat was dragged under. Then the *Lusitania* was gone but for her aerials that swung out in a final wave. Sydney saw the wires ensnare one of the lifeboats and threaten to pull it under but thankfully the wires snapped at the last second and the lifeboat was rowed away.

Then from deep below an underwater explosion erupted sending more debris and body parts flying up from the bottom of the ocean floor. Huge waves followed and scattered the debris field across the surface of the water. The power of the explosion tore Sydney away from the lifeboat and she smashed up against a deck chair. She grabbed on to it with all her strength. When she looked up she saw that the lifeboat she had been clinging to moments before was being dragged under, men and women tearing at the wood and clawing at the water to save themselves but it was futile.

The deck chair floated well enough but she didn't trust it to hold her weight so she let it bob along beside her while she tried to formulate a plan. It was difficult to think clearly when all around her were hundreds of people clinging to life and to thin scraps of refuse. Others floated by dead. What got her the most were the infants and children—too many to count—their angelic faces staring up at the blue sky. Sydney found it cruel that nature would provide such a glorious day for a tragedy. It should be raining with giant thunderclaps and lightning bolts. Not blue skies filled with sunlight. Perhaps worst of all was the sight of land so near to them. They were so close to Ireland. Surely someone on land had seen? The ship's Marconi officers must have sent an SOS? Where was the naval escort?

Sydney searched the water for Brooke but couldn't find her. "Have you seen my sister?" she asked several others who were in the water. They stared back at her with vacant eyes.

"No idea who your sister is," one woman groaned.

"Brooke Sinclair," Sydney said hopefully. Then realized that these people had no idea who she or her sister was.

A few feet from her two men were fighting over an oar to stay afloat. One of the men began to beat the other until a woman nearby chastised them.

"He's half-dead already," the man who was giving the beating said.

"We'll all be dead if we don't help each other," the woman snapped.

Sydney tried to heave herself onto the deck chair before someone else stole it from her. It was no use. Each attempt resulted in her falling off the other side. It was on closer examination that she saw the chair was broken in half. It would never hold the weight of an adult. She scanned the area and counted only six lifeboats on the water. Most of them weren't even full. A few of the collapsibles had drifted out to sea and people were fighting tooth and nail to get onto them.

"Won't they come rescue us?" Sydney asked.

"Who's going to do that, luv?" the woman said. "The Germans?"

"The Royal Navy of course," she answered. "They must know about the sinking by now."

"Aye," said a man. "Let's hope it's soon."

She was freezing. She knew she had to get out of the water to survive. A large flat piece of board, about six inches thick and around four-by-six feet in size floated by. It looked strong. She had to try. Had to take a chance. With her strength fading Sydney reached out but missed it. She would have to let go of the deck chair in order to grab the board. The thought terrified her. The lifebelt that Alfred had so expertly tied on would hold her up. That was its sole purpose. She had to believe. With a deep breath, summoning all her strength, she kicked away from the deck chair and just managed to grab hold of the wood. Her legs, submerged for so long now, were near frozen. It was all she could do to will them to work and swing herself on top of the board. Somehow she did it. She collapsed on top. She lay there panting from exhaustion but thankful to be out of the frigid sea. Where was her sister? Where was Edward? Alfred? Walter? She started sobbing pitifully but her cries were lost amongst the hundreds of others who were crying out in anguish.

Edward

There were no lifeboats within reach as Edward treaded water. The sea was thick with bodies, alive and dead. He had lost sight of Frohman and the others. Even Maxwell had vanished. The cold water was consuming the life from him but he was determined to swim his way through the debris field searching for Sydney and Brooke.

It was a German submarine that had sunk the *Lusitania* but Edward felt it was his fault. Wasn't he the reason the Sinclair sisters were on board to begin with? Didn't that make him to blame? He was responsible for their fate. He clung to the hope that they were in a lifeboat by now. But if they weren't, both had on lifebelts so they should be afloat and alive.

There were too many women amongst the bodies. He shoved his way through the mass of people struggling for breath. Too often he'd spot a shock of blond hair and swim over only to find the woman a stranger. Brooke was wearing yellow but she'd be soaked through and the colour wouldn't be as bright. Remarkably he couldn't recall Sydney's garments; he'd been too busy looking into her eyes to notice her dress.

The *Lusitania*'s distinctive four funnels were in the water and he watched as several people were sucked inside them. Edward imagined they were dead, smothered by the coal and steam but to his amazement seconds later the funnels spewed them back out again. One of them smashed into the water near him, covered entirely in black soot. The man began to swim for his life to get as far away from the ship as he could.

"You! Come here, man!"

Edward turned in the water and saw an older fellow, not wearing a lifebelt, one arm clasped to a piece of debris, waving at him. Did he know him? Edward swam over; each stroke took more effort than the last and his legs were becoming numb.

"Do you need help?" Edward asked. When he got closer he could see that the man's arm clinging to the debris was twisted at a horrible angle and bone jutted through the skin.

"I need you to keep me afloat!" The man flung himself on top of Edward. They struggled as the man, driven mad with fear, kept trying to use Edward as a human raft.

"I can't keep us above water," Edward gasped. The two men thrashed about violently. He felt the man's legs kicking at him beneath the water as he strained to pull himself atop Edward's shoulders in a piggyback. He was kneed in the stomach and kicked in the shins. He cried out in pain with each blow struck.

"I don't want to die!" the man screamed, and began to beat Edward with his good arm. The blows rained down on Edward's head over and over and, too weak to fend off his assailant, he lost consciousness.

Isabel

sabel picked at her sandwich. The girl who had brought tea was new and smelled of talc. *Like a baby.* While still employed at the Admiralty, Mildred had not set foot inside Room 40 since that day she'd slammed the tray down on Isabel's desk. Henry, however, did finally surface. Judging by his appearance he'd gone home to change and rest. He was bright-eyed and in clean clothes. Isabel sniffed her disapproval. She would take her cues only from Denniston. She'd leave when he did and not before.

"Get a load of him," she whispered to Dorothy. "It must be nice to not have a care in the world and go home for a bath."

"Oh stop," Dorothy chided her. "He's just a kid."

"Humph!" Isabel grunted. She was about to make a sarcastic remark when Captain Hall entered the room, Commander Hope on his heels.

Captain Hall came into Room 40 at least twice a day so his presence was not unusual. But his expression and stiff posture indicated this was not a routine visit.

"Gentlemen," he began, then seeing the women at their posts hastily added, "and ladies. We have received a telegram from the wireless station at Galley Head, at 2:20. It reads: Lusitania *S.E. 10 miles sinking bow first apparently attacked by submarine.*"

Isabel gasped. Schwieger had done it. He had his greatest triumph, his largest trophy. She felt a hand on her arm. She looked down expecting to see Dorothy's hand only to find Henry beside her. They looked into each other's eyes. He had to be thinking what she was. *The Admiralty had let this happen. The ship had been sacrificed for the war effort.* But she couldn't speak; she was in shock.

"How long does she have?" someone asked.

"*Titanic* stayed afloat a couple of hours," Curtis offered hopefully.

"There's a difference between hitting an iceberg and being torpedoed," Rotter countered.

Before anyone else could speak the door flew open and a young man rushed in and handed two more messages to Captain Hall. He read them at once then looked around at the men and women of Room 40 who had been tracking the U-boats and the ship traffic for months. It was because of them that the Admiralty knew so much about the enemy's movements. Everyone in the room was aware of the threat to the *Lusitania*. There would be hell to pay.

"At 2:25 the wireless station at Queenstown sent us the following: Lusitania *torpedoed reported sinking 10 miles s. of Kinsale. All available tugs and small craft being sent to her assistance. Aberdeen, Pembroke, Bungrana, Devonport, Liverpool informed*," Captain Hall said. Rotter attempted to speak but a lifting of Hall's hand stopped him. There was more. "At 2:26 the Marconi operators aboard the *Lusitania* sent out an SOS. *We think we are off Kinsale. Late position 10 miles off Kinsale come at once big list later please come with all haste.*"

The men and women looked at each other in disbelief. Isabel didn't know what to do. Violet began to cry and Dorothy put her arms around her to comfort her. Captain Hall continued to stare at the telegrams. Denniston's jaw jutted out sternly. Commander Hope leaned over the table laden with transcripts. It was odd to see even the most powerful men at a loss for words.

Then with a mighty swipe of his arm Commander Hope cleared the desk, sending the piles of paper flying to the floor. "Useless!" he shouted.

"Did they say if all the passengers got into lifeboats?" Henry asked nervously.

Captain Hall shook his head. "God bless their souls."

Sydney

I don't want to drown. Please, do not let me drown. Any death, any manner of dying would be preferable to this. Sydney continued her silent prayer over and over as a sort of talisman against fate. But it was of little comfort and, she felt sure, of no use. Death surrounded her. It floated by piece by piece atop the same anthracite water that chilled her to the marrow, threatening to swallow her whole. As much as she fought to stay conscious, to not slip beneath the surface, she knew death was coming as it had for the others, whose faces, frozen in terror and pain, taunted her to join them in the unforgiving sea.

Twilight came. Soon she wouldn't see the bodies. But she would still hear the low moans of the dying. A seagull flew overhead. She wondered if it was the same gull she had seen so often in the past few days. It looked so peaceful. Flying high above the carnage.

It was time to change hands. Sydney pleaded with the limb that was submerged to come out and let its mate take a turn. She'd quickly learned that if she kept one arm in the water it was enough to balance the flimsy yet buoyant piece of wood she lay precariously across. But her arm was uncooperative. She couldn't feel it, not even how cold it was. With her left hand Sydney grabbed her right arm and pulled it from the water as though it belonged to someone else. The wood began to teeter, left and right, back and forth. Sydney held her position as long as possible. Both arms cradling her for warmth. But what choice did she have? *Please, do not let me drown.*

It was time. She plunged her left arm up to its elbow into the water thick as pudding. The slat righted itself. Sydney closed her eyes. Relief was fleeting. Something struck the wood near her feet and lurched it forward for an instant before dragging a corner down. Farther into darkness. She gasped and turned to see an object caught on a piece of wood that jutted up from the edge of the makeshift raft. Heavy with drenched weight, it would sink the raft if she didn't act. She tried to kick it free with her foot but to no avail. It was snagged as securely as though it were bolted tight. She had no choice but to somehow manoeuvre around so that she could pry it off with her fingers.

Sydney summoned the memory of performing "around the world" on her pony when she was a child. She had mastered the balancing trick of swinging her right leg over her pony's neck so she sat sidesaddle, then her left leg over his hindquarters, leaving her facing backward. Then left leg sideways, then again until she was sitting in the saddle properly once more before repeating it in the reverse. The key to not falling off was concentration and careful, slow, gliding motions so that the pony didn't bolt or buck and she didn't lose balance and tumble to the ground. Was this slight piece of wood that much different? Yes, very, she admitted.

She dared not sit up like on a saddle, instead the scissor-like swing of her legs would be performed on her stomach. For this, both hands had to be free. Taking a deep breath she pulled her arm out of the water and with slight, nearly imperceptible movements she swivelled halfway "around the world," which was all she needed.

A sooty mist had joined her on the water and dulled the twilight. The object seemed made of fabric. Sydney reached out and touched it. Yes, it was wool. It was a coat, its collar caught on the wood. Sydney fumbled with her frozen fingers to loosen the collar. It was so heavy. She tried to lift the jacket out of the water to free it that way. But she wasn't strong enough.

It was then that a final puff of fading sun pushed through the mist and cast a circle of light onto the problem. The weight of the coat was the weight of a child's corpse. A little boy about two. Sydney gasped. The boy's head, its ginger hair matted, brushed her hand in the rhythm of the swaying sea as she gripped the collar. She lay there unable to move, the two of them trapped together as though she had chastised the child for stealing sweets and been cursed by a witch and frozen for eternity. She felt the warmth of tears stream down her cheeks and into her open mouth. They reminded her that she was still alive.

He is already dead. Let him go to his grave. If you don't, you will go with him. Devoured by darkness. *Please, do not let me drown.*

Sydney swallowed and with the final gasps of sunlight as her guide she pulled the boy closer to her, fighting the tide, until she could pluck the coat from the broken wood. It took three attempts; each time she lost her grip she felt the raft jerk and bob and the water soak her dress, her boots, her hair. Not that she could get any wetter, any colder. But on the third try—luck. She shook the coat hard enough that the wood itself broke off and the little boy drifted out, his tiny body floating on its back. Sydney watched him be carried away by the waves. He looked like a doll, staring up at the sky. She would never forget his face as long as she lived. But how long would that be?

Alone once more she prayed. And then, somewhere out on the ocean, a voice. It was a woman. What name was she was calling out? If a name at all. Sydney tried to respond, to be heard. But her throat was unable to utter anything more than a pathetic cry. She closed her eyes. It must be her sister, come to fetch her . . .

"Miss Sinclair!" a voice called out to her through the murk. "Miss Sinclair!" It was a male voice. Sydney lifted her head, squinting through eyelids swollen and heavy with impending death. She thought the man looked familiar. Was he from Cora Stratton's New Year's dance?

"Help me pull her in." The man gave the order as Sydney felt herself being lifted away from the wooden raft.

"She's almost dead," came another male voice. "Leave her and let's go find people we can save."

"Not bloody likely! She stays with us," the first man snapped. "She'll be all right once she's warmed up."

Sydney was cradled in the man's arms and someone threw a coat over her. She blinked a few times, willing her eyes to focus.

"Who—?" she murmured, her voice raspy.

"It's Bestic, Miss Sinclair," he said calmly. "Remember me?"

She tried to remember. This man Bestic was rubbing her hands. She felt the blood warming her fingertips.

"Where am I?" she asked him.

"We're in a collapsible boat, Miss," he explained. "The *Lusitania*'s gone."

Then she knew. Hearing the ship's name was like being slapped. She knew exactly where she was and what had happened.

"Bestic," she said. "It's all so awful."

"It's tragic," he said.

She looked out across the sea. The water had returned to the placid stillness of the morning, and worse, it was silent. The hundreds of souls who had been fighting for their lives had lost the battle and the hush that had descended over the scene was anything but tranquil; it was eerie, haunted.

"I need to find my sister," she said weakly. "And Edward." The feeling was returning to her limbs but all she wanted to do was sleep.

"We'll find them," Bestic reassured her. He picked up the oars and signalled to a few of the other men in the boat to continue their search for survivors. "And in God's name, shovel that water overboard." He smiled at her. "This collapsible is taking on water. The plug is missing. I stuffed the hole with whatever flotsam I could grab from the water but it's not good enough. We must keep emptying the water from the bottom."

Sydney watched some use their hands while one man had found a hat and was using it as a bucket.

Rowing through the water was slow going. The debris field was thick with items from the ship—china and pieces of furniture, and bodies. The cold had taken many. Sydney wondered if she had hypothermia. She asked Bestic and he told her the symptoms: the cold making your body shiver to keep it warm but as time passes it fails and your temperature falls further until you can't think straight and you're disoriented. Once the core body temperature reaches a certain point—below thirty degrees—death is near. She saw the evidence of it on every dead and nearly dead body the little boat passed but she had a chance at life.

Bestic and the others continued to pull survivors into the collapsible one by one. At least one woman they had rescued died in the collapsible and they dumped her back in the sea to make room for the living. Time passed slowly and few words were spoken.

"Why haven't we seen a navy ship?" a woman asked. "What happened to our escort?"

"There was never going to be an escort," said a man who was busy scooping water from the bottom of the collapsible with his hands.

Sydney managed to keep awake and watched the others, unable to do her part; she was simply too weak. But her eyes continued to roam the water for signs of her sister or Edward. When her boat drew near one of the other lifeboats she begged Bestic to ask after them. But none of the men and women had seen them. She refused to think either of them had perished. If she had survived the plunge into the sea surely Brooke had as well. And Edward must have stayed with Alfred. The two men would have stuck together when the ship went down and climbed onto another of the lifeboats or a piece of wreckage.

"Look! It's a ship!" one of the passengers shouted. "Two of them." The others began to wave and yell for help. Elsewhere on the water the cries of other survivors carried up into the sky becoming increasingly more frantic as the two steamers sailed away over the horizon and out of view.

"They mustn't know," a woman offered. "They couldn't know."

"Don't bloody count on it," the man who had spotted them said. "They're probably afraid the submarine will do to them what it did to the *Lusitania*."

"We need to head for Queenstown," Bestic said brusquely. "It's the nearest port."

"You're an Irishman, I take it?" the man asked.

"He is Irish," Sydney sputtered. "Be glad of it. You're in charge, Bestic." The man shot Sydney a look of contempt but otherwise was silent. She smiled weakly at Bestic, who nodded to her.

Hours later several fishing trawlers appeared and began to pick up survivors. The *Bluebell* came to the aid of the little collapsible and Sydney was once more picked up by Bestic and lifted into the arms of a sturdy fisherman who immediately wrapped her up in a warm blanket and gave her tea. There was much commotion on board the *Bluebell* and all around it as vessels arrived to begin the rescue operation. Of the many boats and trawlers that came to the aid of the survivors only one, the *Stormcock*, belonged to the British government. Sydney sipped her tea and repeatedly asked if anyone had seen Brooke and Edward. No one had.

She watched the fishermen pull a man from the water. He fell onto the deck, still alive. It wasn't until he sat up and coughed violently, gasping for breath, that she saw it was her friend.

"Walter," Sydney said softly. She was too weak to walk but managed to crawl over to him. Walter didn't seem to recognize her. He was delirious. "Walter. It's Sydney."

"He'll be fine. Make sure he takes the tea. Drinks what he can," the fisherman explained. "There's hundreds more like him."

Sydney held the cup of tea to Walter's mouth as the fisherman stood by. Walter shoved the cup away and used all his strength to speak. "The boy?" he managed to get out. The fisherman looked at him, waiting for him to finish. Sydney's eyes welled up. It was such an effort for Walter to talk, but he forced the words out. "There was a boy. I was holding on to him."

The fisherman shook his head. "There was no boy with ya when we found ya," he said, and looked at Walter with pity.

Sydney wanted to comfort Walter but she had no words. Then a rescued seaman from the *Lusitania* pointed into the water.

"Look! It's an officer's gold braid!" he yelled. "It's a ship's officer and he's alive!"

There was a scramble on board as the able-bodied men rushed to rescue the man. Sydney was astounded when the familiar stern face of Captain Turner, whose body was weakened from his hours in the water, tumbled onto the deck. The trademark gold braid on his coat had made him easy to spot. He sat still as blankets were brought to him but he shoved them away. He didn't look relieved to be rescued. *He must have wanted to perish with the Lusitania.* Sydney was sorry for him. But she was one of the few.

"My child's death is on you and you alone," scolded a woman Sydney didn't recognize. She was pumping her fist in the captain's face as she spoke. "He died because of your lack of organization and discipline amongst your sailors."

Captain Turner stood silent and motionless as the lady was quietly escorted away by the *Bluebell*'s own captain, telling him how she was ordered to place her son in one of the lifeboats but that it had capsized and her boy had drowned. Sydney understood the anger. She would be angry as well if she weren't so exhausted. Besides she still had hope that

Brooke and Edward were alive as she was, sitting on a deck somewhere on another trawler.

An hour later, as the *Bluebell* made its way toward Queenstown, Sydney and Walter were seated in the mess, trying to eat a simple meal of bread and soup. Captain Turner sat alone in a corner.

"Should we speak to him?" she asked Walter. He turned around and shook his head.

They watched as Bestic entered the mess. The third officer made his way over to the captain. "I'm very glad to see you alive, sir."

"Why should you be?" Turner asked. "You're not that fond of me."

"Fondness doesn't enter into it, sir. I'm glad to see you alive because I respect you as my captain and I admire you as a seaman."

Captain Turner had no response for Bestic. The third officer left the captain alone and departed the mess without further communication.

"It's tough to comfort a man when everyone will be asking why he survived when so many in his charge perished," Walter said. "That woman up on deck is only the first to cast blame."

"But it was the Germans," Sydney said. She couldn't believe people would hold Captain Turner responsible. It didn't make sense.

"It was," Walter agreed. "And I can't wait to get to the front and take my revenge on the bastards."

Isabel

It was after dark when someone, perhaps it was Curtis, suggested they needed a respite. More than half of the team had been working a twenty-four-hour shift with only short naps. And as they entered the Coach & Horses and settled into their usual section exhaustion seeped in. They sat drinking in silence, the shock still keenly felt. Rotter, Parish and Anstie chain-smoked. Henry ordered coffee. Norton shuffled a deck of cards. Violet stared at her pint of ale as Isabel nursed her whisky. Dorothy sat beside Denniston for comfort.

The silence irked Isabel. No doubt they were all thinking the same thing. But it seemed she would be the one to say it. "How could the Admiralty turn back their cruiser and let people drown?" she asked.

They had listened to the wireless traffic and read the telegrams, heard the phone calls between the Admiralty in London and Queenstown. When the *Lusitania* had sent out its SOS, Vice Admiral Coke had dispatched the *Juno*, a cruiser and the fastest ship available, only to recall it straightaway after receiving firm orders from London. Who exactly had made the decision couldn't be known—Churchill was still in Paris—but what was a certainty was that First Sea Lord Fisher and Captain Hall were involved.

"It's because of what happened last autumn," Denniston answered patiently. "Remember the *Aboukir*? The *Cressy* and the *Hogue* went to her aid and they were lost too, all their men gone to the bottom of the sea. The Admiralty has made it a rule since then that no cruiser shall attempt the rescue of a sinking ship."

"But that was different," Isabel persisted. "Those men were all Royal Navy. They were fighting in the war. The *Lusitania* was carrying civilians."

"I'm a navy man and I understand that we can't risk our battleships. We couldn't know where that submarine was. She could still be out there lurking, waiting to fire at the rescue vessels," Rotter said.

"But Isabel has a point. The *Juno* would have arrived at the site in about an hour," Parish said. "Those fishing trawlers and whatever else that went must have taken several. Hundreds of lives were lost because of the Admiralty's decision."

"The *Lusitania* was carrying weapons and ammunition," Norton said flatly. "Technically the Germans were in the right to have targeted her." He shrank from the blanket of stares that descended on him.

"It is a *war*," Curtis agreed grimly. "Thousands will be dead before it's over."

"Millions," Anstie added.

Isabel flinched. "I thought only soldiers would die."

"That's not what happens. Civilian casualties are an assumed cost of winning," Denniston said.

"Do they know how many survived the sinking?" Violet asked.

Denniston shook his head. "That will take several days. Some survivors may not last either. It's a tragedy to be sure." He raised his glass and the others followed. "To the *Lusitania* and her valiant crew and passengers. May God rest their souls."

"May God rest their souls," every one repeated, and drank.

"I think we should all go home," Denniston suggested.

"I second that," Curtis agreed.

It wasn't really an order but it would be taken as such. Isabel downed her whisky and followed her colleagues out the door. It had started to rain and she pulled her coat over her head.

"Good night, Isabel," Dorothy said as she and Violet headed off.

"Good night," she answered, and disappeared into the darkness.

MAY 8

Sydney

Sydney awoke in the middle of the night to the sound of weeping. She opened her eyes and found that she was in a large room lit by gas lamps. The space was vast but despite its size it was packed with people lying in stretchers and on cots; others were lying on blankets on the floor, as what appeared to be doctors and nurses and the like went from bed to bed. Sydney reckoned it was a makeshift hospital. She couldn't recall how she got here. She remembered falling asleep on the Blueball but that was all. Someone must have carried her here.

She sat up slowly. Someone had removed her clothes and dressed her in a muslin shift. She saw her dress and shoes in a pile on the floor. In the heap of clothes was the scarf. She picked it off the floor and hugged it even though it was still wet and smelled of salt water.

"Hey there, don't try to stand yet," a nurse called out, and dashed over, feeling her forehead for a temperature.

"Where am I?" she asked the nurse.

"You're in Queenstown, luv," the nurse responded. "In Ireland. Just lie back down."

"I'm fine," she said, her voice raspy. Her limbs felt weak but that couldn't stop her. "I need to find my sister and Edward." Sydney looked at the nurse imploringly. She couldn't know who Edward was.

"Looking for family, eh?" the nurse said, and gave Sydney a look of sympathy. "Who did you lose?"

"What makes you think I've lost anyone?" she asked anxiously. "What do you know?"

The nurse began to backtrack. "There, there, calm yourself," she murmured. "I only meant, who is missing?"

This new word mollified her. "Missing, yes. My sister and . . ." She hesitated. How should she describe Edward? "A man, her fiancé." The words hung on the air and she wished she could snatch them back. "Are all the survivors here?"

"No, dear," the nurse answered. "But have a look. The ones in better shape are in hotels, others in the hospital. They were bringing 'em in into the night. But mostly corpses now."

"Has anyone come looking for me? Sydney Sinclair?" she asked desperately.

"Hmmm, can't say they have," she said. Then, seeing the worry on the young woman's face, she added, "That don't mean a thing. Your sister and her fiancé could be in a hotel or too sick to move."

Sydney nodded. But if Brooke and Edward were in any shape to be in a hotel they would have come searching for her. Against the nurse's orders she stood up and got a head rush. She immediately sat back onto the cot and waited for the dizziness to pass. When the room had stopped spinning and her eyes were able to focus she pushed off the cot and stood again. Her legs trembled at first then steadied. It was as though she'd forgotten how to walk and had to concentrate in order to force one foot in front of the other.

"You might want to dress properly," the nurse suggested. "Several of the townswomen kindly brought over some things for you to wear." She pointed to a table that was stacked with simple cotton dresses. "You can change behind that curtain. But mind me when I say you should rest more."

Sydney must have cut a pathetic figure in her muslin shift as she inched along, for the same nurse came and took her by the elbow. At the table Sydney grabbed the first dress she found and headed behind the curtain. The dress was too big but it would do. Slipping the dress over her head she remembered the amber gown. The first night she wore it to meet Edward at the Grand Entrance. The beautiful gown was somewhere at the bottom of the ocean and she'd never see it shimmer in candlelight or feel its silky fabric again. Tears welled up and she wiped them away. How stupid to cry over a dress, she chastised herself. When she emerged from behind the curtain the nurse was waiting.

"Here's some boots," the nurse said, holding up a pair of battered lace-up boots that looked like they were from a farmer's daughter, caked in mud and manure. They fit perfectly. "I can stay with you if you like."

"I think I can manage now," Sydney told her, and smiled faintly for proof. The nurse smiled back and let her go.

"If you need anything let me know. And come back and rest when you've found your sister."

"I will," she said. "We will both need the rest."

Sydney began her painfully slow journey up and down each row of cots looking into the eyes of the living and barely living. Scared, haunted eyes stared back at her, set in faces that contorted in pain or heartbreak and attached to bodies that were mangled or whole. More than once survivors reached out with their hands and pleaded with her to locate their families. Sydney could do little but offer hope; it was all she had to give and all she had to sustain herself. But no matter where she searched none of the faces belonged to Brooke or Edward.

She reached the end of the last row. There would be the hospital and hotels to check. It would be like Brooke to check into a luxury hotel first thing. She'd probably already drawn a hot bath and was sleeping on a feather bed. The image gave Sydney an excuse to smile. She found a topcoat on the table of clothes and headed for the door. A man wearing a suit greeted her outside. He was carrying a gas lamp in one hand and several papers in the other.

"Good evening," he said solemnly. "I'm from Cunard." Sydney nodded and brushed past him but he caught up with her. "May I get your name, Miss? I need to update the survivor list." This stopped her in her tracks.

"You have the list? Can you check some names for me?" she asked, her heart pumping so hard that her head began to pound along with it. "Brooke Sinclair and Edward Thorpe-Tracey."

The man tried to scan the list but he was having difficulty so Sydney held the gas lamp for him. His finger traced the names up and down, page after page, until he reached the end. "Sorry." He could tell it wasn't what she wanted to hear.

"What about Hannah MacGregor? She's a little girl," Sydney explained, desperate for some good news.

Again he looked and shook his head. "Can I get your name?"

"Sydney Sinclair," she whispered. "Is that the whole list?"

"So far," he answered, and jotted down her name. "Where are you from?"

"New York," she said. "What do you mean 'so far'?"

"I haven't spoken to everyone inside, or at the hotels," he explained. "It's tough to find people."

She was immensely relieved. "That's the best news I've heard. Where is the hotel?" she asked.

"The Commodore is where most of them are. It's a bit of a walk," he said, his expression darkening. "You might want to check in there." He pointed to a large, imposing building a few yards away. Sydney didn't like the look of it. It was dark and foreboding.

"What is that place?" she asked.

"That's the Queenstown Town Hall . . . where they're putting some of the dead," he said gravely. "It's a sort of temporary morgue. It's closer than the hotel."

"I'm sure my people are in the hotel," she insisted, not taking her eyes off the brick building.

"I hope you're right, Miss. But the town hall is closer and you won't be waking anyone up in the middle of the night like you would at the hotel."

She became indignant. "Fine. I will go there. Just to prove you wrong." She wanted to storm away in a fit of temper but her weakened body would only allow a slow shuffle.

"Is that Sinclair with an *i* or a *y*?" he called out after her but when she didn't answer he crossed out the *y* and scribbled *i* in its place.

The gloom inside the town hall descended on her like a cloak. She felt
the weight of sorrow pressing down on her and the other survivors
who moved around slowly, searching out friends and family, practically
ghosts themselves. Several gas torches illuminated the floor where the
bodies lay. Volunteers were carrying in more bodies, drenched and swollen from their final death throes in the frigid water. Sydney knelt down
and peered under one blanket. It was a woman but not her sister. The
woman held a dead baby in her arms. At least they died together. She continued to crawl along the ground, checking body after body, lifting each
blanket in fear of discovering a familiar face.

Another body was brought in and placed close by. It was a man wearing
hip waders and a thick wool sweater.

"He was on the ship?" she asked. He didn't look like any of the passengers. Perhaps he had worked below deck as a stoker or fireman.

"He's a fisherman," the volunteer, a swarthy man, told her. "He
drowned pulling bodies out of the water."

Sydney could say nothing. The tragedy was determined to keep taking
long after the ship had made its final plunge. She crawled along until she
reached the end of the first row. It was especially dark at this end of the
hall because there were no gas lamps nearby. Once again fear gripped her
as she began to lift up the corner of the blanket, just as someone on the
opposite side of the body lifted the other corner. This annoyed her.
Searching through death was a private affair. She looked up at who was
doing this and gasped in shock. It was Edward. She stood up so fast she
nearly fainted again. Equally stunned, he stepped around the corpse and
grabbed on to her. She fell into his arms.

"Is it really you?" she breathed. "Speak to me! Edward? Please let it be
you."

"It's me," he said, his voice whisper-soft. "Oh Sydney. When I saw you
fall into the water I thought you were dead!"

"So did I," she said. He kissed her on the lips and held her tight to his chest so that she could scarcely breathe. She saw at once that his head was bandaged and his face was cut and bruised. She touched his cheek.

"It's nothing," he said. "But I had to escape a rather pushy doctor in order to come here."

"Have you found Brooke?" she asked, feeling a surge of hope that all would be well for her people. He shook his head. Sydney inhaled sharply. "Alfred?"

He shook his head again. "I was with Charles Frohman and his gang at the end. We were swept off the deck by a wall of water such as I'd never seen before. It was the thing of nightmares."

Sydney stared at him. He looked gaunt and tired. His clothes were torn and he wasn't wearing any shoes. "Our maid, Sarah," she said, shivering at the memory. "She's dead."

Edward pulled her back to him again. "Let's keep looking," he said.

They remained together, holding hands as much to steady each other as for intimacy, and checked body after body. The town hall was packed with corpses and with the living searching for loved ones. It was a quiet activity save for the shrieks of grief that broke out whenever a loved one was found. Consoling words between survivors were passed around like a church plate.

They had come to the end of yet another row, near the darkness of the dimly lit row where they'd discovered each other, and drew near a woman who was sobbing quietly. Her back was to them but Sydney thought she recognized her. When she got beside her she realized it was Rita Jolivet.

"Rita!" she called out. They hung on to each other for dear life. "My God! I'm so glad to see you."

Rita didn't respond. "I lost Charles," she said. "He helped save me. Told me what to do. But I can't find him."

"Of course he did," Sydney said to comfort her. "He may still be on a fishing boat on its way here. Like my sister could be."

Sydney looked away. She caught sight of a body. Or rather she saw the fabric of a dress. It was yellow silk—the same yellow that matched their car. Sydney cried out and yanked the sheet away. It was Brooke. The dress was ripped in places and she was barefoot. Her eyes were mercifully closed and she wore an almost angelic expression. Sydney had never seen Brooke look so at peace. But it was of small comfort as Sydney fell to her knees and wailed pitifully. Edward and Rita tried to soothe her but she was inconsolable.

"No," she kept repeating softly. "She can't be dead. She can't."

Rita looked at Edward. "Take her away from here. Get her to the Commodore Hotel. There are doctors there who can give her a sedative."

But Edward didn't move; he kept staring at Brooke. He reached out and brushed an errant strand of dark hair off her face. Sydney watched him do this. He did care for Brooke. She could see it in his eyes. He didn't love her and had broken off their engagement but he was grieving her too. It was a strange thing to unite them.

Eventually Edward stirred and lifted Sydney into his arms and carried her out. She continued to stare back at the torn yellow fabric laid out on the floor; its brightness seemed to challenge the darkness of death.

Isabel

The birds fluttered above her head as they flew from branch to branch. May was one of the loveliest months of the year in St. James's Park. The gardens were at their spring best, as though the flowers were marching in a parade. Isabel had walked the entire circumference of the park and with each step she had grown angrier. Her work had taken on the patina of death. Her Important employment was not supposed to include standing by while the British government used innocent lives as targets. *Maybe all the passengers were saved.* That was it, she told herself. *Perhaps few lives were lost.*

As she walked through the beauty of St. James's Park, she imagined that in Queenstown there were hundreds of rescued passengers. Children were reunited with their parents. Lovers found each other. It would be a grand adventure. Maybe the Americans would enter the war and Churchill would be seen to be a great leader. Then again, he wasn't even in England. He was nowhere near the Admiralty to direct the matter, a fact that made her conspiracy theory far less likely.

She had reached the Mall. She should return to Room 40 and see if there was more news. She sighed. For the first time since starting her job she wasn't in a hurry to get there. The air was warm and a light breeze lifted the hair off her neck. She stood still and lifted her chin and closed her eyes to feel the sun. It would turn out all right. The *Lusitania* might be lost, which in itself was tragic given her beauty. But the people would be saved.

"Careful, you may darken your skin."

Isabel didn't have to open her eyes to know who had spoken. "What do you want?" she asked, and opened her eyes to find herself face to face with Mildred Fox.

"I came for a walk. Just like you." Mildred stood with her hands on her hips. Her beauty was marred by a sneer that went from cheek to brow.

"You're nothing like me," Isabel said.

"That's true," Mildred said, and smirked. "I'm clean."

"What is that supposed to mean?"

"You know very well what it means, Isabel," she answered. "Look at you. Back wearing your hair like that and lipstick too! No more unattractive schoolmarm, eh?"

"I don't have time for this," Isabel said, and walked away. "I have important work to do."

"Oh yes. Your *work*. Everyone knows *how* you kept your job," Mildred called out after her. "All the girls are talking about it."

Isabel stopped dead. She closed her eyes and counted: One, two, three. Then turned and marched back to Mildred. "What did you say?"

Mildred laughed. "You heard me. After what happened with Mr. Chambers in Oxford? The only way you could have kept your job with those *men* in Room 40 is by bedding them, or at least one for certain." Isabel's chest tightened. Mildred was taking great pleasure in her words, and wore a big smile on her face, a great teeth-baring smile. "Denniston, isn't it? At least he's handsome, unlike—"

Her words were cut off by the force of Isabel's slap. Mildred's head snapped to the right. She drew her hand to her face; the big toothy smile had vanished and her left cheek burned red from the impact.

"If you ever speak one more lie about me and any of my colleagues, so help me God, I will find you and—" Isabel stopped speaking. She could see that Mildred was cowering in fright. She had said and done enough. Isabel straightened her hair; it had fallen across her eyes when she'd slapped Mildred. Satisfied, she walked away. She didn't want to be late.

"That's it?" Mildred cried after her. "That's all you have to say?"

Isabel turned around but continued to walk slowly backward, ensuring she was moving away from Mildred. "I don't have time for the likes of you, Miss Fox. I have important work to do. There's a war on, you know."

It was nearly seven thirty and as Isabel walked to the bus stop Kentish Town seemed a world away. She was so tired and hungry that even Mrs. Ogilvie would prove a welcome sight. The day had been long. The reports from Queenstown weren't good. Hundreds of people had perished. The final tally wasn't in yet but there were more dead than alive. Survivor reports indicated that there had been mass chaos on board and that the crew hadn't done their jobs. Rumours had already begun to circulate the Admiralty, saying that Captain Turner was to blame. He had miraculously survived the sinking and would be questioned immediately. The reports said he had not followed instructions and had kept too close to the coast and wasted precious time taking a bearing near Kinsale. Isabel found this ridiculous. Schwieger was to blame. So was the Admiralty for not warning Turner about the other sinkings and for not sending an escort.

"You mind if I ride with you?" It was Henry. He had caught up with her.

"No," Isabel answered. She didn't want to be alone with such thoughts.

"I saw Mildred," he said.

"And?" She was disappointed that he was bringing her up when there were far more interesting things to discuss.

"I saw Mildred after you slapped her," he said.

She lifted her chin proudly, challenging him to say anything further.

"Good for you." He smiled.

Isabel was stunned. "I thought you and she were—"

"Not anymore," he said. "She told me what she said to you. Bragged about it really."

Isabel shrugged. *Of course she did.* Henry was grinning now. "I told her if she wasn't a woman I'd have flattened her myself."

The bus arrived and they got on. It was nearly empty so they sat together at the back. "I suppose this means you want to be friends again?" she asked.

Henry inhaled deeply. "I'd like that. Can you forgive me?"

Isabel put her hand on his leg and squeezed gently. He smiled a moment, then stared down at her hand touching him. She wanted to laugh. It was more of her so-called improper behaviour but she didn't care. There were far more pressing issues to think about.

MAY 11

Sydney

Elland was an old mill town in West Yorkshire, just south of Halifax, by the River Calder. Sydney had travelled by train after resting in Queenstown. She, Edward and Walter had attended the funeral for victims of the sinking. Mass graves were dug and pine coffins lowered into the ground. There would be a memorial made. She had ensured her sister's body would be preserved to be shipped back to New York and buried alongside their parents. Rita Jolivet had made similar arrangements for Charles Frohman. His body was discovered the day after the sinking. Charles Klein and George Vernon had also perished.

Sydney was relieved when she learned that several of her new acquaintances had survived: Lady Mackworth had also been picked up by the *Bluebell*; her father, Mr. Thomas, made it as well, as did Charles Hardwick, Jessie Taft Smith and Angela Papadapoulos, although her husband and the Kesers had drowned. Edward's valet, Maxwell, had been plucked from the ocean by a trawler and was at his sister's home in Taunton convalescing. Frederick must have perished but his body wasn't found. The worst had been finding Hannah and her mother's name on the missing list. She hadn't seen the little girl at all that last day. She hoped that whatever had happened to her she hadn't suffered. Then there was Alfred. No one knew what happened to him or Ronald. Final sightings were as

Sydney had witnessed—Alfred without lifebelt, helping others. His body was never recovered.

Sydney wanted to call on Walter in Elland before heading to Rathfon Hall in Somerset. She needed some distance from Edward and his family. The sinking had left her in shock and the idea of being welcomed into the stately home like she was some sort of heroine for not drowning when so many had wasn't something she could tolerate. Neither was Edward tolerable. He had been loving and supportive but she had sent him on another train home. She couldn't bear seeing him break the news of Brooke's death to them. Nor was she sure she could marry Edward any longer. Brooke's death changed everything for her.

She arrived at the town house in Elland to find Walter's wife, Alice, and daughter, Muriel, waiting to greet her in the small foyer. She was a lovely woman, strong and sturdy with a no-nonsense manner. "To think that I argued with Walter about sending me and Muriel ahead on another ship," Alice told Sydney. "He was right to insist. Those rumours were all true."

His little girl, Muriel, was adorable and was singing a lullaby to her teddy bear—apparently Walter had bought the bear in Queenstown before returning home to Elland. She hadn't realized it was the child's birthday.

"Come along, Miss Sydney," Alice said. "Walter will be happy to see you."

Alice led Sydney to an upstairs room where Walter lay in bed. He had been in this bed in this house ever since he'd arrived from Queenstown. He was still very weak and had only been allowed downstairs for supper on two occasions. His doctor was amazed he had survived as many hours in the water as he had done. Walter claimed he didn't know how long it was in the end. Time lost all meaning after the ship sank. But his best guess was about eight hours. His face lit up at the sight of Sydney.

"You look better than I expected," she said, and sat down in a chair.

"You as well," Walter said. "This is a nice surprise."

"I wanted to see you, make sure you were okay," she said.

"I need to get well so I can get to the base for training camp," Walter said.

"Don't be in such a rush to get to the front," Sydney told him patiently. "You've seen enough of the war by now, surely."

He studied her a moment. "What about you then? You going to see that chap Edward?"

Sydney picked up a newspaper off the floor. On June 15 the Admiralty was launching a public inquiry into the sinking. Captain Turner would be testifying.

"Sydney?"

She placed the paper in her lap. "I don't know how I feel about him or his family now," she admitted.

"You still love him?" he asked.

She tilted her head. "I never told you that."

"Don't need to be told it. It was obvious. And he loves you. Now with your poor sister passed away I suppose you're free to marry him."

If only he knew that had been decided before the torpedo strike. "How can I, Walter? It seems wrong."

"Would it have been right had Brooke survived?" he asked.

"I don't know. I'll never know. At least I would have seen her happy with another husband. Now that she's gone . . . how can I be happy with Edward?"

Walter and Sydney sat in silence a moment. "You're overcome with grief. I see that. And Brooke is dead and that's a horrible thing. But you're alive and you must live your life," he told her. "If Edward can make you happy then you can't feel guilty about it. We all deserve love, Sydney. Even survivors of great tragedies."

Sydney wiped away tears and held his hand. Neither sure if what he said was true. Walter sat up in the bed.

"There's a local reporter coming to interview me for the paper. I'm something of a celebrity," he said with a slight grin to change the subject. "Alice told everyone about me surviving the sinking."

"How do you feel about giving an interview?" Sydney hated the press and had avoided it so far but she knew she would be swarmed in New York. From Walter's expression she gathered he felt the same.

"I don't want to talk about it," he said. "I prefer to lie in bed with Muriel beside me singing to that bear. She's a happy girl. Loves to sing."

"Like Hannah," Sydney said.

As if on cue little Muriel rushed into the room. She sprang onto the bed to cuddle with her father. He stroked Muriel's fine blond hair. Like Sydney she had large hazel eyes. "You want to be a singer when you grow up?" he asked her.

She nodded enthusiastically, which made him and Sydney laugh. "I knew a girl, a little older than you, who wanted to perform onstage," Sydney said. "Her name was Hannah. She was very good."

"Hannah," Muriel repeated gamely.

Walter and Sydney looked at each other.

"Walter!" Alice called up from downstairs. "Are you ready? The man from the paper is here."

Walter wiped his eyes with the back of his hand. "Yes, Alice. Show him up."

Sydney listened to the footfalls on the wooden steps. How different was the sound they made from the metal steps she had run up and down on the ship. A tall reedy man with a disturbingly lopsided moustache appeared in the doorway, pen and paper in hand, Alice behind him.

"I'm John Goodson," he said, and the men shook hands. "You've been through quite the ordeal."

Walter's smile was strained. Sydney could tell he really didn't want to talk about it.

"I mean it's bad enough being hit with one torpedo, but two," Goodson exclaimed.

Walter shook his head. "There was only one torpedo," he said.

The reporter seemed puzzled. "The official word is that the submarine fired twice," he said.

"I was there. I know what I saw." He was becoming agitated.

"He's right. There was only one torpedo," Sydney confirmed.

"There wasn't a second explosion?" Goodson asked.

"There was," Walter admitted. "Perhaps one of the boilers exploded, or . . ." His voice trailed off a moment. Sydney knew what he was thinking. The ammunition the ship was carrying had exploded. "I'm not a naval expert by any means. But it wasn't a torpedo. Whatever caused the second explosion came from within the *Lusitania* herself."

Muriel took this opportunity to burst into song and Walter was pulled from his misery. She could carry a tune and Sydney began to hum along quietly. But his wife had other ideas.

"Muriel, come with me. Your father has business to do with this man." Alice held her hand out and looked at Sydney. She could take a hint and stood to follow the little girl out of the room.

"Perhaps your mother has baked you a birthday cake," Sydney said. Muriel beamed.

"I want chocolate cake," she said.

Alice smiled and Sydney and nodded. It was chocolate.

"Save me a piece," Walter said. Sydney looked at him. They would probably never see each other again but they would never be strangers—they'd shared too much.

"Good luck to you, Walter," she said, and gently kissed him on the head. "I wish you a happy life."

"You as well, Sydney," he answered. "Remember what I said."

She nodded and with a slight wave left him behind. She headed to the train station and on to Rathfon Hall. Whether she could accept Edward's love or not, she could put off seeing him no longer.

MAY 12

Isabel

The world was still reeling from the loss of the *Lusitania*. The papers printed the shocking statistics: Of the ship's 1,959 passengers and crew only 764 survived, which brought the death toll to 1,195. Only 6 out of the 33 babies on board lived. And to fuel the international crisis there were 123 Americans counted amongst the dead. As expected the United States was in an uproar but so far President Woodrow Wilson had not been roused to declare war.

Despite the displeasure of the Admiralty, the local coroner in Kinsale, a man named John Hogan, conducted his own inquest. He felt justified because five of the dead had been found in his district. So on Saturday, May 8, Captain Turner was placed on the stand where he broke down in tears. The coroner's final verdict was that the submarine crew and indeed Kaiser Wilhelm of Germany had committed "willful and wholesale murder."

While the coroner in Ireland did not place blame on Turner, the Admiralty in London had other ideas and would pursue them at its own official Board of Trade investigation in June that was to be presided by a Lord Mersey. As Isabel had anticipated, the entire affair had become the talk, unofficially, of Room 40.

"He blatantly ignored the Admiralty's directions," Curtis insisted. A small group was huddled around the codebooks engaged in a heated debate. Isabel and Dorothy among them. "He was warned about the submarines in the area and told to steer a mid-channel course and at full speed. The bastard didn't even zigzag."

"Turner was overly confident, that was his undoing," Norton added. "He wouldn't trust the Admiralty to make decisions on how he should navigate his ship. The instructions were just a pile of paper to him."

"But the ship's fourth boiler wasn't even operational," Anstie pointed out. "And that was an Admiralty order to conserve fuel. She couldn't get to top speed."

"She was doing eighteen knots when she was struck. That's fast enough to outrun a submarine."

"Turner took a four-point bearing off the Old Head at Kinsale," Rotter pointed out. "He waited too long. They were lying in wait. Then he steered toward the bloody U-boat."

"He couldn't have known!"

"What's a four-point bearing?" Isabel asked.

"It's used in navigation to confirm the distance a ship is from an object . . ."

"But that second explosion . . ."

Isabel had heard enough. Everyone seemed to want to pin the tragedy on Captain Turner. Indeed the desire to place the blame went all the way to the top. She had managed to see notes Churchill and Fisher had exchanged; in one Churchill wrote, *We will pursue the captain without check.* She turned her back on the group and looked into the basket for new transcripts. She picked up a freshly arrived tube and opened it. "Gentlemen! We have new secrets to uncover."

She was trying to sound light but it wasn't working. Nerves were frayed. The group split up and Rotter retrieved the transcript from her. He sat down at the codebook and began to decipher. It didn't take him long but when he'd completed transcribing he dropped his pen.

"My God!" he exclaimed, which brought everyone to his desk.

"What does it say?" Anstie asked.

"It's from Captain Schwieger to his command," he said.

"He's back in range of his home port," Curtis said. "At least he's out of our waters."

"For now," Isabel added.

"The bastard confirmed he sank the *Lusitania* but that's not all," Rotter continued. "He said it was sunk by means of one torpedo."

"That's impossible. Every survivor spoke of a second explosion."

"But not every survivor said it was a second torpedo," Isabel pointed out.

"A few survivors swore they saw another," Dorothy added.

"There was a lot of confusion and debris flying around," Curtis said. "You can't necessarily trust their accuracy."

"What else could cause an explosion like that?" Anstie asked.

"I heard coal-dust fire," someone added. "Or a boiler explosion."

"Let's not forget the contraband ammunition she was carrying either."

"At the inquest Captain Turner thought it might have been the main steam line," Isabel declared. "I prefer to believe him, a lifelong seaman and an experienced captain."

"She's right," Rotter said. "If water flooded the first boiler room it would trigger the main steam line to rupture and that would cause a large explosion."

Isabel was pleased the naval officer had backed her up. "And now with this latest intelligence from Schwieger, we know the truth. It wasn't a second torpedo."

"I think Churchill needs to see this," Rotter said.

"I'll be glad to take it to him," Isabel said.

Churchill's secretary was out when she arrived. But his office door was open and he beckoned Isabel inside. He noticed the paper in her hand immediately.

"What have you got there?" he asked.

She gave him the transcript and waited. Churchill had returned from Paris after the sinking. She couldn't help but wonder if since his return he weren't locked into negotiations with the Americans to bring them into the conflict. He had studied the transcript for a long time when at last he asked, "Who has seen this?"

"The men in Room 40," she stated. It seemed an odd question. No one outside of the "great mystery" ever shared what they knew, and that was on Churchill's orders.

"Captain Hall?"

"Not yet. He and Commander Hope were meeting elsewhere."

Churchill smiled. "Very well. Thank you, Miss—?"

He never remembered her, which was annoying to Isabel. "Nelson, sir."

"Miss Nelson. That will be all."

Isabel knew she had to leave but she couldn't do it. *That letter.* And now that such a catastrophic event had occurred she needed to know. "Sir, I have a question . . ."

He looked at her quizzically. "And what might that be?"

She swallowed, working up the courage. "Did we allow the *Lusitania* to be sunk so the Americans would come into the war?"

There, she'd said her piece. But from the look on Churchill's face, he was not in impressed by her bravery. "What on earth is your meaning?"

"It's a rumour, sir. Something I've heard."

"Well, you heard wrong. We need the Americans to continue to do what they are doing—supplying us with ammunition and food. If they were to enter the war now we'd practically starve. The *Lusitania* was a tragedy but it was the fault of an irresponsible captain."

"Not of the submarine, sir?"

His eyes popped open wide. She could see his breathing had grown heavy. He was seething. "Are you looking to be sacked, Miss Nelson?"

"No, sir."

"You're lucky you are a woman and a civilian. If you were in the navy you'd be disciplined immediately."

"Sorry, it's just that I read the transcript. It clearly says it was one torpedo. At the Irish inquest many people, including some from the Admiralty, thought it was two. Now we know the truth."

"I don't care what a German submarine captain says. It was two."

Isabel scowled. "But sir—"

Churchill walked around his desk so that he was standing facing Isabel. To her surprise he smiled and when he did his entire face softened.

"My dear," he began. "I appreciate your concern and your diligence. But you must understand that as the First Lord of the Admiralty I know what I'm doing. Go back to your post."

She did as she was told. Once back inside the safety of Room 40 she asked to speak confidentially to Denniston. They found a corner in the far office and sat down. She had to share what had happened. Churchill had all but confirmed he was going to publicly claim there were two torpedoes when he knew it was false. She confided all of this to Denniston, including her insubordination with Churchill. When he had recovered from the shock of what she had dared to do he told her it shouldn't come as a surprise.

"You must understand, Isabel, that to use what we just found out, to make it public that we know for certain that Schwieger only fired one torpedo would be to tell the world—and most important, the Germans—that we are intercepting their communications. We can't even let them know we uncovered the name of the U-boat's commander, let alone which submarine did the job. It makes matters clearer if the world thinks the Germans fired two torpedoes."

"The holy of holies," Isabel whispered. She understood at last. Churchill had his reasons for concealing the facts.

"Exactly," he said. "The mystery would be revealed and then they'd change the key and the codebooks and we'd be back to square one. We're not winning, you know. It's going to be a long war."

She looked at her hands folded in her lap. Maybe she wasn't so clever after all. She should have known it. Even Churchill's letter was a sort of red herring.

"Churchill's no fool," Denniston added. "We can't let the enemy know we know."

"But doesn't the public have a right to know what really happened?" she insisted half-heartedly.

"History will decide that. But for now we must focus on defeating the enemy," Denniston answered. "Forget what you read."

Isabel returned to her typewriter. There were piles of decoded messages waiting for her. She threaded the paper into her machine dutifully and began to type. But with each keystroke her eyes began to fill with tears. Dorothy, seeing this, came to her side.

"Whatever is the matter?" she asked.

"I can't shake the thought of those people," she cried softly. "Struggling for their lives in the water. And we knew all along it might happen and we did so little . . ."

"Oh darling, you can't think like that," Dorothy said soothingly. "We did what was possible. The Germans are a horrid people. Sometimes these things happen no matter how much you try to stop them. Life is tragic at the best of times and with the war, it's tragic most of the time."

"I hate the war," Isabel exclaimed. She also hated secrets. Since starting her job she had come to terms with her own. Now she had to do the same with her country's.

"We all do."

Dorothy returned to her seat. The truth was that Isabel didn't hate the war, not entirely. She hated the cruelty and loss of life but the war had given her the opportunity to do a job she loved. As difficult as it was to reconcile those two things in her mind the truth was that the war had saved her from a hard and unfulfilling life.

She forced a smile at Dorothy. "Then we best get back to winning it."

MAY 14

Sydney

The scream shook Sydney awake. She sat bolt upright in bed. It was another of her nightmares. The dreams had plagued her since the sinking. Night after night she'd woken up terrified and in a cold sweat having relived those hours in the water. Sarah clinging to her ankle, the little boy and his tiny coat, the sounds of the dying, it all flooded through her subconscious until she couldn't take it anymore and she shook herself free of sleep. But then the scream shot through the darkness again. She recognized it this time. It was the blood-curdling screech of a barn owl. She closed her eyes in relief. Since arriving at Rathfon Hall she'd had to get accustomed to the sounds of the English countryside. The first time she'd heard an owl scream she'd rung the servant's bell. The poor lady's maid had dashed up to her room still wearing her nightshirt expecting Sydney had taken ill only to find her cowering beneath the covers.

"I heard a scream," she'd told the maid. "Like someone was being murdered."

The lady's maid had smiled kindly. She was a stout woman with blond ringlets streaked with grey and a patient manner to go along with her quiet, steady voice. "It's only an owl, Miss Sinclair. The estate is full of them."

"An owl?" Sydney had asked incredulously. "Making that hideous sound?"

The maid smiled at her. It took all her patience when foreigners questioned her knowledge of England. "Yes. It's a barn owl."

Sydney had slowly crept up from beneath the sheets. "Thank you. You may go."

The lady's maid nodded. "Good night, Miss Sinclair. I will see you in the morning."

Sydney had heard the owls many times since that first incident but it never ceased to terrify her. She stepped out of bed and went to the window and drew back the heavy damask curtains. The night sky was black as pitch. There was no sign of life in the skies or trees outside the window. The owl had apparently moved on. She went back to bed and tried in vain to return to sleep but it was no use. Every night was the same. She was afraid to sleep because then she might dream of Brooke and that horrible free fall before they landed in the sea. Her poor sister. Why had she perished? She must have been so frightened as she swirled violently in the water and was sucked down with the churning of the ship. Sydney made a fist. She would never have been strong enough to hold Brooke; even if her sister hadn't let go of her hand, they'd have been torn apart by the force of the sea. Though in truth they were torn apart before the torpedo strike, even if she hated to admit it. Edward had already torn them apart, no matter how unintentionally, no matter how many times she reminded herself that no one was to blame. Brooke had died knowing that her sister had betrayed her. She fought away the image of Brooke in her wedding gown that fateful afternoon. It was all Sydney could do not to hate herself for falling in love with Edward. She recalled Walter's words to her and tried to reconcile them to her feelings of guilt but it was no use. What was between her and Edward had been destroyed with the *Lusitania*. But there was one thing she could do for him and his family and when the sun rose this morning it would be done.

Edward

T he sunlight cast a speckled pattern across the library, giving the entire room the dapples of a dark bay stallion. The sun also dotted Edward's face as he peered out the window waiting to see Sydney ride into view, but he didn't need the aid of the sun to cast a shadow over him. He tried to banish the memory of the man who had attacked him in the water. Whoever he was, he knew the end was coming and was determined to stay alive. Edward wasn't even sure what had happened in the end. The last thing he recalled was being pummelled on the head and then the next thing he knew he was lifted into a lifeboat.

He would never forget the stunning image of a middle-aged woman at the oars, giving orders. Her name was Elizabeth Duckworth, a third class passenger and, according to a man on board, she had been on another lifeboat and had helped row away from the scene before being picked up by a fishing smack. Once on board that vessel, Duckworth asked the fishing boat captain to return to the site for survivors. But he had told her in no uncertain terms that he couldn't spare a soul. "You can spare me!" she had shouted, and leapt back into the lifeboat. Along with a couple of men she returned to the scene and picked up about forty survivors who otherwise would have drowned—Edward amongst them. He was eternally grateful. As he had looked at that stern but courageous woman, who had acted when none of the men would, his mind had immediately gone to Sydney. How these two would get along.

Mrs. Duckworth had continued to row all the way to the fishing smack, which Edward saw was called the *Peel 12*. As they were lifted aboard, a wave of cheers went up for Mrs. Duckworth. He was forced to lie down as another woman passenger helped bandage him up. Try as he might he couldn't recall what had transpired between the man's attack in the water and the arrival of Mrs. Duckworth's lifeboat. The truth was lost forever.

But as he stood safe and sound at Rathfon Hall the darkness that welled within him went beyond his personal story. The massive loss of life he had witnessed had deepened it. The faces of the dying haunted him: the anguish and horror, the shock and fear that passed across their faces with the realization that the end had come. Yet the human body, or perhaps the human soul, rarely gave up without a fight, its instinct for survival kicking in to thrash and gasp to the last breath, despite knowing it was no match for Mother Nature. This capacity for survival had impressed him. It seemed a trite point. But he could do something with it. He could carry it with him to the Western Front. The sinking was his first battle of the war and he felt prepared for what he would see in France. The glamour of war had been scraped off entirely. Since his return home, when what was left of his "gang" had come around, still bent on glory for all, he had listened politely. But he saw that Sydney couldn't handle their ideas and their foolish enthusiasm for killing and on one occasion it had forced her to retreat from the dinner table.

"She's been through a lot," Lady Northbrook had explained to the young men that night. The men had nodded in understanding, never thinking for a moment that Edward had also suffered.

"You must be devastated to lose your fiancée," Lord Stratham, a boyhood friend, had said consolingly. "But you'll get those Jerrys and avenge her."

"Hear! Hear!" went around the table.

They meant well. They couldn't know. No one could. And it seemed to Edward that no one would ever know the truth. It had died with Brooke. The truth and the dream had disappeared below the surface. Sydney had been kind but also cold to him and seemed to avoid being alone with him. She had taken care to spend time with Georgina but her zest for politics had ebbed somewhat. Still the two young women had enjoyed each other's company and it brought Edward joy to see the two women he cherished most getting along so well. If they were to marry he was convinced Sydney would guide Georgina into a life that was fully her own. But *if* was a large word. He stared down at the diamond-and-sapphire ring he had been fiddling with all morning. The real Thorpe-Tracey engagement ring that Brooke had decided wasn't grand enough. He hadn't yet shown it to Sydney. There never seemed to be a right time.

At last Sydney appeared. Each morning he'd made it his habit to watch her ride across the fields to the house from this very window. It was his only opportunity to see her, observe her, without an audience, without her knowing he was watching. She dismounted and handed the horse over to the stableboy. Her hair was askew beneath her hat. He smiled at the memory it brought to him. The pin he had removed from her hair, the back of her neck, bare and inviting. He daren't think of holding her or kissing her or making love to her. It was a sensation that was nearly as painful as the sinking.

Sydney

Despite the nightmares and the memories of her ordeal, she couldn't deny that Rathfon Hall was a glorious place in springtime. The gardens wore massive blooms and the trees and shrubs were varying shades of emerald and citrine. The grounds were kept immaculately as were the stables and Sydney had taken the opportunity to ride out every morning. Astride a horse was the only time she found peace and she was grateful when Edward had not pushed to join her and she was able to gallop across the fields unaccompanied.

His parents were very gracious to her. Sydney adored Georgina. She was a lovely girl who, regardless of her own tragic circumstances, was full of life. When Sydney had arrived after the tragedy she had shown Georgina the scarf.

"I'd borrowed it from my sister," she had fibbed. "She adored it as do I. It was by chance I was wearing it that afternoon."

Georgina had pressed the scarf into Sydney's hand. "Then you must keep it."

The family had welcomed her with sympathetic hearts, leaving her to grieve in private but inviting her to whatever social gatherings she was comfortable attending. The lady's maid had been sent to London and had brought home a dozen dresses from the shops, including some breathtaking gowns. Sydney liked the gauzy Lucile gowns the best and given that their designer, Lady Duff Gordon, was a *Titanic* survivor, it made sense to choose from her collection.

Sydney thought of her mourning clothes safely packed in a trunk in the attic of the Fifth Avenue brownstone. She had thought it silly to hang on to them at the time. *By the time a family member passes next they will be out of fashion.* Of course she never thought . . .

As she entered the home from the courtyard a footman greeted her bearing a telegram. It was exactly on time. She thanked him and rushed up the stairs to her room. It was from Mr. Garrett.

Dear Sydney,

I have done what you asked and the papers will arrive sometime today from a solicitor who is travelling up from London. But I must take this opportunity to object one final time. If you change your mind after the papers are signed it will be too late. My condolences once again and you must understand I'm also grieving Brooke's loss.

Yours faithfully,
E. Garrett

Sydney was relieved by the news. It wouldn't be long before she could tell Edward and his family her decision and then . . . she'd think of that later.

It was nearly four p.m. when she came into the drawing room for tea and found Edward waiting for her. The face she adored so was gaunt and pallid. It had only been a week since the tragedy and he hadn't recovered any more than she had.

"Darling," he said. "Before my parents and Georgina come in I want to know how you are, really. You have avoided being alone with me ever since you got here and I can't tolerate it any longer. We must talk."

Being alone with him again and talking was the last thing she wanted to do in this moment. "I'm managing, Edward. And I'm not avoiding you. Not really."

His expression turned grave. Her coldness had stung him. "That's all you can say? I love you, Sydney. We still have each other. We survived. You can't go on living with the dead."

"Don't say that," she said coolly. Hearing Edward say nearly the same words as Walter irritated her. Did no one besides her need to grieve? "My sister, Alfred, Hannah, all of them are gone and you ask me to behave like what? A girl in love on a Sunday picnic?"

He looked wounded. "I never said nor implied any such thing. But I miss you," he said. "You know I leave in a few days for the army." With no wedding to delay him the army had moved up the start date of Edward's commission.

"I know," she said quietly, and went to sit down on a pink chintz chair with too many cushions to be comfortable. She had tried to keep the thought of him going to war at bay. Even if it were wrong to love him and marry him, she would always care for him. "And I sail for New York with Brooke's body. She will be buried next to our parents."

"It will be a difficult journey for you," he said solemnly. "For many reasons."

"Yes, I have no desire to sail the North Atlantic so soon after what happened," she said. The idea was horrifying. What if there was another submarine attack? The world had protested the *Lusitania* attack vehemently and Germany, which had celebrated it at first as a victory, was making noises of regret. But if they had murdered so many civilians for their cause already why should they be trusted not to do so again? She was booked on an American steamer but there was no guarantee. The thought of New York and home was her only solace.

Edward knelt at her side imploring her to look at him, which she did against her better judgment. "Before you begin your journey we should tell my family that we plan to marry," he said eagerly. "I know it can't be arranged before I go to the front so we'll have to hope . . ." His voice trailed off into thoughts of battlefields and muddy trenches.

Sydney studied his face. How could she tell him now when he faced war as a soldier? But she was spared the decision by the entrance of the butler.

"There is a gentleman for Miss Sinclair," he said with the gravity of a bishop. "I've put him in the library."

"Thank you, Mr. Thompson," she said. "I will follow you there." She hardly looked at Edward.

"Who is it?" he asked suspiciously.

"I will let you know when my business with him is done," she answered with the tone of a banker, and followed Mr. Thompson out of the drawing room and down the gallery to the library. A footman swept open the door and Sydney entered to find a short and thin man of about forty waiting for her. His checkered suit was smart and he wore a flower in his lapel. It wasn't a carnation like poor Alfred had favoured, but a white rose.

"Miss Sinclair," he began, and extended his hand. "I want to begin by saying how sorry I am for your loss. But I think you'll find everything in order."

"Thank you. Please let's sit down," she said, and directed him to a writing table.

By the time Sydney returned to the drawing room Lord and Lady Northbrook and Georgina had joined Edward and were waiting for her. She hadn't wanted them to wait. The tea would be cold and then the servants would be made to scramble all over again to get it right.

"Oh Sydney! I have such a surprise," Georgina gushed.

Sydney couldn't help but smile at the girl's enthusiasm. "Then you must show me."

Georgina wheeled herself over to a large gramophone. "I want to play something for you."

Sydney smiled. "I can't wait to hear it," she said, and sat down opposite Edward. He was staring at her. It pained her to see him like this and know she was the reason.

Georgina put the record on the turntable and carefully placed the needle down. "I hope you love it as much as I do. It's all the way from America."

What followed were the unmistakable opening notes of "Alexander's Ragtime Band." Sydney held on to her composure for as long as she could but then the tears streamed down her face. Georgina saw her reaction and pulled the needle off the record so quickly it screeched.

"You don't like it?" Georgina asked, disappointed.

The tears blurred Sydney's vision and she wiped them away as fast as they came. "Just the opposite. I love it. It reminds me . . . I'm sorry, I just can't listen to that song again."

Georgina remained silent as she wheeled back to her mother.

"Let's serve tea, shall we?" Lady Northbrook suggested.

The family had danced around Sydney all week and yet another tearful breakdown had caused an awkward few moments of silence. She longed for her own space in New York.

"That's a splendid idea," Lord Northbrook added. And on cue the footmen began to pour tea and offer sandwiches to them.

"Are you all right?" Edward asked.

"Yes," Sydney answered. "Georgina, I'm sorry. It's just that the song reminds me of a friend, a girl about twelve, who drowned."

Lord and Lady Northbrook exchanged glances. Georgina looked like she might cry. "How awful. I didn't know."

"You couldn't have," Sydney said. "But please enjoy the record after I've gone home." She forced a smile and peered into her teacup. It was time to tell them. If only Edward wasn't staring at her the way he was. She would direct her eyesight to Lord Northbrook. After all this affected him most immediately.

"Since we're all here, I have something to say," she announced, hoping her voice would hold steady.

"Yes, my dear," Lord Northbrook said, and took a bite out of a sandwich.

"This afternoon I had a visitor. He is a solicitor from London sent by Mr. Garrett," she started.

"Your financial adviser?" Lord Northbrook asked, wanting confirmation.

"My guardian," she corrected. *Just say the words.* "I know how much

Rathfon Hall means to your family, Lord Northbrook, and I am going to help you keep it."

Lord and Lady Northbrook exchanged glances again but quickly returned to fixate on the American with the large purse. Edward clutched the corner of the sofa.

"And how do you propose to do that?" Lord Northbrook asked. "My understanding was that Edward would only be entitled to the Sinclair fortune after the marriage took place. Sadly, that was not to be."

This conversation was so difficult for Sydney on many levels. "That was true. But now with my sister gone I'm the sole heir to my family's fortune and I've decided to invest in Rathfon Hall."

"I beg your pardon?" Lord Northbrook said brusquely. His tone startled her; she wasn't expecting anyone to object let alone be offended.

"I would like to invest in the estate. Settle its debts and provide capital for renovations and upkeep and develop it so it can be self-sufficient," she explained calmly. Perhaps these Englishmen really had no head for business for the father seemed utterly perplexed. Edward on the other hand had at last ceased looking at her and was staring off into the distance.

"Renovate? Develop?" Lord Northbrook stammered. "We'd never sell Rathfon Hall to an American!"

Edward leapt to his feet and stood by the window. "She doesn't mean to buy it, Father," he said flatly. "She's giving us the money I would have had if Brooke had lived. But instead of a gift she's giving us the opportunity to pay it back like honest-to-goodness men." He turned and looked at Sydney. Her eyes burned and she swallowed to keep from crying. "Am I right?"

"Yes, but it never has to be repaid," she continued. "And there would be no change in title. I would only request annual reports to appease Mr. Garrett, and one further stipulation."

"This is absurd!" Lord Northbrook said.

"Is it, sir?" Sydney asked. She felt that she could take no more from him on the matter. She was being generous. "Is it any more absurd than selling your son into a marriage he didn't want to save your pile of bricks and mortar?" Lady Northbrook gasped. But Edward was smiling at her fondly. This was the girl he had fallen in love with and Sydney knew it. "At least this way you'll not have an *American* living under your roof."

When she was finished speaking she finally had the courage to look at him. Their eyes met but his smile was fading. He read between the lines and knew her true meaning: she would never marry him.

"But—" Lord Northbrook began to object until his wise wife waved him to silence.

"You are a dear and generous girl," she said, and smiled, but it was through gritted teeth. "I will leave the decision up to Lord Northbrook, of course, but you make sense. What is your final stipulation?"

"A portion of profits from the estate will be used to start a charity in my sister's name," Sydney said firmly. "It will be for young girls' education. Brooke was intelligent and well-educated and I'm certain had she lived and had girls of her own she'd have seen to it they were as well-schooled."

Sydney gazed around her. No one dared to object. Her eyes settled on Edward. "I sail for New York the day after tomorrow," she said. He bore the shock well; a slight twitch to his brow was all the reaction he gave. She forced herself to look at his parents. "You can take the papers to your own lawyer and give them a thorough going-over. We can sign them before I take the train to London."

Lord Northbrook began to fidget and bluster. The footmen arrived with more cakes and began to serve them. Sydney was grateful for the interruption. She grabbed a small slice of iced lemon cake.

"Can I visit you in New York?" Georgina asked.

"Of course you can," she answered. "Anytime you like."

Georgina seemed pleased with the situation but she was the only one. Edward began to pace. His parents watched him with puzzlement.

"But I thought you had planned to return to England after the funeral, to take up your work with Margaret Sanger?" he said quickly, and stopped his pacing.

"I will postpone my work for now," she explained, watching him stand like a statue, cold as marble. "As the women here have done. When I'm home I will see what I can do for the war effort."

"You hate the war," he practically shouted, much to the alarm of everyone present. His father glared at him.

"Calm yourself, Edward," he instructed.

"I hate the waste of war," Sydney said. "But after what happened to the *Lusitania* . . . that the Germans should target civilians . . . I will do what I can in *America*."

Edward continued to stare out the window. Lord Northbrook cleared his throat. "I wager your government will soon be in the thick of it," he said, sounding pleased. "Killing Americans won't sit well in Washington."

As if sensing the conversation was taking an ill turn, Lady Northbrook rang the bell. "I think we could all do with a brandy," she said.

Sydney smiled in agreement and met Edward's gaze. His look of adoration and love had been replaced by one of hurt and disappointment.

MAY 15

Isabel

Y ou mustn't let the *Lusitania* tragedy change your mind about the work you do, that we do," Denniston told her.

Isabel had barely slept since the sinking and had been obsessively poring over the news reports in the papers. She read every survivor account, every accusation lobbed at Captain Turner, every theory as to why the ship had sunk so quickly. She could talk of little else. Dorothy was worried about her and had voiced her concern to Denniston. Isabel tried not to be angry about it; her friend meant well.

"How can I not? All those babies," she said grimly.

"It's bloody awful to be sure," he answered solemnly. "But we did all we could."

"You mean we did all we were allowed to do," she said pointedly.

They were walking along Whitehall, the buildings of the British military surrounding them. So much power and might, yet so fragile it all seemed. Only a couple of hundred miles from where they stood were the front lines of the war. The stories coming from the trenches were every bit as horrible as what had happened off the coast of Kinsale.

"Yes, but that's what we are meant to do. Follow orders, Isabel. We may not be in the navy or the army in the truest sense, you and I, but we are soldiers in our own way. And we must trust that our superiors see the bigger picture."

What he said made sense. Yet she couldn't shake off the feeling that with all their Intelligence they could have stopped it, and that the only reason they didn't, was, well, too ugly to consider. But she had to consider it. She couldn't tell him about the letter from Churchill but she could hint at it. "Remember I told you about my discussion with Churchill?" she began. He raised his eyebrows. "Of course, how could you forget? I can't help but think that the sinking of the *Lusitania* was a conspiracy to raise international anger and support for the Allies. That it was all part of a master plan to drag the United States into the war."

He didn't answer straightaway and she chastised herself for speaking up. But if she didn't talk about it these thoughts would never leave her. Denniston put his hand in his pocket and retrieved a cigarette case. He offered her one. She declined. He lit a cigarette and took a long drag from it. Isabel watched the smoke float away.

"You have to stop trying to make sense of it, Isabel. There was no conspiracy, though I grant you that if there were, it would make the tragedy easier to explain." He spoke plainly but firmly. "But it wasn't a conspiracy. It was a ruthless act of terror. It won't ever make sense. War doesn't make sense."

He took another drag on the cigarette. Isabel bit her lip.

"I think I will have one, Alastair," she said. He took out another cigarette and lit it for her. She inhaled deeply; the rush of smoke filling her lungs made her cough a little.

"Then you trust them?" she asked, and continued to smoke. The nicotine was going to her head and she felt slightly dizzy. She trusted Denniston; if he believed in Churchill and Fisher then she could too. Or at least she'd try.

They walked a few more yards in silence before he answered. "I believe they are good men. Though even good men have egos and make mistakes," he explained thoughtfully. "But yes, I trust them."

It wasn't the most convincing argument to be sure. But it was enough for now. They passed a family walking along toward the Mall, a father and mother and three small children. Isabel couldn't keep her eyes off them; for some reason they made her sad.

"You know there was a time, before the war, when I thought I'd have everything I wanted. Of course I was still in Oxford and I was happy. I was in love with Mr. Chambers and I was learning so much. I fancied myself getting a degree and having a career. Engineering of some kind. But I also wanted a husband and children," she told him ruefully. "To be valued for my intelligence and be loved. That isn't possible for women, is it?" She stopped and looked up at Denniston. When he didn't respond she continued. "After what happened to me I suppose the choice was easy: my work."

They continued their walk in silence as though both needed to allow the words to settle.

"You will no doubt marry at some point," he told her at last, as though she was looking for reassurance.

"Come now. What would happen to my work if I were to marry?" she asked, and seeing his dumbfounded look, she laughed. "Dorothy loves her job as much as I do. Will you let her work when you marry?"

Denniston nearly stumbled on the sidewalk. "Good grief! Who said anything—?" Then seeing how Isabel was smiling at him he changed tack. "I would allow my wife a career if that was what she wanted."

"Ah." Isabel grinned. "You are a very unusual man, Mr. Denniston. Let me assure you that for the most part this world isn't designed for women. Maybe it will get better but not in time for me."

"I want you to think about after the war," Denniston said. She was startled by his words. In all their months working side by side he'd never broached the topic of peace. Did he know something she didn't?

"After the war?" she repeated. "Is it as near as all that?"

He laughed. "I have no Intelligence about it, so don't get hopeful. I only mention it because you've become such an integral part of the team and many of the men have jobs to go back to when the war is over. Lives to go back to . . ." She couldn't argue the implication: that she did not have a life to return to afterwards, even if she hated to admit it was true. "But we'll need good men, people, to stay on and continue the work. Explore new methods of decoding and monitoring other nations."

"Really? Do you think there will be a need after the war is over?" she asked, completely surprised.

"I'm afraid the world has changed forever. There may be a day and hopefully soon when the guns will fall silent and no more soldiers will perish. But believe me there will not be peace. The way we've treated each other, the new forms of savagery, the tools to outsmart one another. It won't stop simply because a few men devise a treaty. No, Isabel, we will continue to develop methods to spy on our enemies." Denniston paused. "And even our allies I should think. And you, Miss Nelson, have a knack for it. I'm going to have Rotter continue your cryptography training in earnest."

His words stunned her as much as they pleased her. "I would be honoured," she said, fighting the urge to hug him.

"The work requires patience," he continued. "And I've always been inclined to think women possess that particular quality in greater quantities than do men."

Isabel watched Denniston closely. He was always a serious chap but she'd never seen him be so foreboding, so pessimistic. Yes, the war had changed everything and it would seem everyone, including her. "You can count on me," she said stoically. "I never want to stop doing my job."

He continued to smile at her but his face was tinged with sadness and resignation. "Then you're in luck. With the way things are you shall be employed for as long as you wish."

Isabel tried to hide her enthusiasm. A career would sustain her very well. That and a good bottle of whisky.

MAY 16

Sydney

The train platform was overflowing with men in uniform and women crying after them. Mothers, sisters and wives and girlfriends had come to say goodbye to their men. Many of the soldiers were very young and this was their first trip away from the villages and towns they had been born and raised in. Caring mothers stuffed bagged lunches into the soldiers' hands as though their sons were being packed off for school and not a battlefield. Elsewhere kisses were given, and not the chaste peck of an aunt, but passionate kisses that were meant to last. Standing off to one side of the platform were Sydney and Edward. She was catching a train to Liverpool where a ship awaited to take her and Brooke's body to New York. He was to board a train a short time after on his way to officers' training. He wore his lieutenant's uniform proudly and cut a striking figure that didn't go unnoticed by several females within the vicinity.

Sydney was proud to be standing there with him. If things had been different she would be sending her *husband* off to fight. He looked so handsome. Her Edward. But things weren't different and here they were, gazing at each other, lost in the past and what might have been in the future.

"I can't stand losing you," Edward said.

"Edward, we can't change what has happened."

"We didn't kill her."

"Don't you think I know that?" she said, almost pleadingly. Then, seeing his pained expression, she softened. "It's better this way. We need to forget what happened and move on. We had seven wonderful days together, Edward. Let that be enough."

"It can never be enough," he answered. "A lifetime can never be enough. I love you. Don't you love me anymore?"

She wanted to say she didn't love him. She wanted to say it so badly she could scream. But what would be the point in that? It would be going too far, especially knowing that Edward was heading on a train to the army training camp and from there to France and the trenches full of mud and death. *Give him the truth*, she told herself. *If there can be no marriage between us, let there be no lies either.*

"I do love you," she said quietly.

His eyes filled up and he kissed her hands. Something told her this was his final gesture of romance. He was letting her go. She couldn't stand it.

"Wait for me," he said. "Wait for me until after the war and if you feel the same way then, I will respect your decision." She didn't know what to say. Then Edward pulled something out of his pocket and placed it into her hand. It was a small yet exquisite diamond-and-sapphire ring. It was so pretty and feminine, yet understated; it suited her taste perfectly. He smiled at her like he knew she approved of it. "Take the ring as a memento," he said. "You don't have to wear it, Sydney. Just keep it to remember me until I return from the front."

She smiled as she turned the ring over in her palm. "It's lovely. I will ensure it's safe."

"And you will wait for me?" he repeated.

The train whistle sounded. Their time was up and she had to board the train to Liverpool. His train would depart ten minutes later. Despite the swarms of people around them the platform felt so very lonely. Walter's words came back to her. *We all deserve love, Sydney. Even survivors of great tragedies.* She thought of Brooke, what she would do if things had been reversed. Brooke seized whatever moment was nearest and brightest. She never stopped herself from getting what she wanted—not because she didn't care about others but because she wanted to get everything out of life. Squeeze every second of time until it yielded. Sydney thought of her mother too, who also had died so young. Surely she would want her only remaining daughter to find happiness? And she thought of Edward and of the two of them naked in her cabin. She looked at him again. This might be the last time she ever saw him. The thought swallowed her whole. It was as though the sum of all their voices—Walter's, Brooke's, her mother's, Edward's and her own—added up to the only possible answer.

"Yes," she said. "I will wait. I promise I will wait."

"That's what I wanted to hear, my beautiful darling black sheep," he said to her.

A conductor blew his whistle a few feet away. "All aboard!" he shouted, staring straight at them. "If either of you is catching the train to Liverpool I'd be getting on now."

Then mercifully he turned away to give them a final moment of privacy. Sydney threw her arms around Edward and kissed him, allowing herself to love him again and the warmth gave her back some of the life she'd nearly lost.

"Be safe, Edward," she said, tears streaming down her cheeks. "Give the Germans hell and come back to me."

"I will, Sydney," he said. He gently took her by the elbow and led her to the train door. She climbed up the staircase, each clank on the metal step reminding her of the flights of stairs on the *Lusitania*. The four flights she knew so well from F Deck to the Regal Suite and every floor in between. The memories that raced through her mind were overwhelming, majestic and sorrowful. She stood in the train doorway facing Edward, not wanting to say goodbye.

"I'm closing the doors," the conductor said, and the choice was taken from her. He slammed the door shut and she was torn from Edward. She raced to a window as the train pulled away. He stood on the platform waving at her, an officer ready to face the enemy. She blew him a final kiss and as the train moved along the track he grew smaller in the distance until he vanished completely.

Sydney was alone in the first class compartment. She took her seat and let the tears continue to flow. She wept for Brooke, for Alfred, for Charles and for Fred, Sarah and Hannah and all the others. But she also wept for herself and Edward. They had escaped one doom and she had nearly condemned them to another. She examined the diamond-and-sapphire ring again. In the quiet of the cabin, she slid it onto her left ring finger and held her hand up to the light. She would not remove it until Edward was safely returned from France. The piece of jewellery was more than a memento. It was hope. Hope that once the war was over they could move past the tragedy together. Until then she would continue to march onward.

AUTHOR'S NOTE

Sydney, Brooke, Edward, Isabel and Henry are all fictional characters created from my imagination. However, many real people, who were either passengers on board the *Lusitania*, or worked in Room 40, inspired the characters in *Seven Days in May*. My great-grandfather was one: Walter Dawson, Sydney Sinclair's confidant. Walter did indeed place his wife and daughter, my great-grandmother and my grandmother, Alice and Muriel, on another ship after he heard rumours the *Lusitania* was a German target. He survived as is written in this novel and then went on to fight in World War I, where he was captured by the Germans. He escaped the Limburg prison camp with the help of the Dutch and survived the war. He never returned to Lowell, Massachusetts, and instead settled in Toronto, Canada.

Alfred Vanderbilt and Charles Frohman were perhaps two of the most famous passengers to perish during the sinking. I hope I did them honour.

Back on land the men of Room 40 were based on several written accounts including the official memoir of Alastair Denniston. The work of Room 40 continued after the war and evolved into Bletchley Park, which came to dominate espionage during World War II. At the end of World War I, Alastair Denniston went on to run Bletchley and did marry Dorothy, who worked alongside him.

Walter and Alice Dawson with two-year-old Muriel, circa 1915, before Walter set off to fight on the Western Front. Muriel's retelling of her father's story about the Lusitania inspired her granddaughter, the author.

Winston Churchill's failed campaigns in the Dardanelles and Gallipoli did irreparable damage to his reputation and he resigned from government in November 1915 to take up arms with a regiment in France. He would return to politics as the prime minister of Great Britain on May 10, 1940, and lead the Allies to victory against Nazi Germany.

My research extended beyond the selected bibliography printed here and included many British government and other history-based websites. I also sailed on a transatlantic voyage aboard the *Queen Mary 2* from New York to Southampton in the fall of 2013. I wanted to know first-hand what eight days on the North Atlantic felt like. Interestingly, the *Queen Mary 2* is owned by Cunard, the same shipping company that built the *Lusitania*.

The Runciman letter and all the telegrams and messages I included are accurate and taken from historical record.

As for the ship itself, Robert "Bob" Ballard, famous for discovering the wreck of the *Titanic*, made similar dives to the site of the *Lusitania* in 1993. Unfortunately the Royal Navy had set off depth charges several years after the sinking so Ballard was unable to do proper forensic analysis.

In this century the prevailing theory for the second explosion is as expressed by Captain Turner: that it was caused by the rupture of the main steam line.

While the conspiracy theory lives on and several official records remain sealed, the *Lusitania* remains an enduring mystery.

AFTERWORD

The morning of May 7, 2015, a group of friends set sail off the coast of Ireland. Their mission was to pay their respects to their relatives who had sailed on the *Lusitania*'s fatal voyage, one hundred years earlier. Later that day, thousands joined in to take part in memorials in Cobh, Liverpool and New York City. Like 9/11 and the destruction of the Twin Towers, the torpedoing of the luxury liner *Lusitania* was a terrorist act that altered the lives of many and changed history. One hundred years later, the families still grieve for the lost and celebrate the survival of others. One hundred years later, mysteries still surround the *Lusitania*'s final days and rapid sinking. To piece together such a large puzzle, we depend on the accounts of the survivors, which keep surfacing as researchers and relatives dig deeper like archaeologists. As in any event in history, there are false flags such as conspiracy theories, or some author inventions passed off as fact. We will most likely never know the whole story, but as long as relatives like Kim Izzo keep the memory alive, history will never forget the *Lusitania*.

—*Mike Poirier, co-author of* Into the Danger Zone: Sea Crossings of the First World War

ACKNOWLEDGEMENTS

In the writing of this novel I owe a great amount of debt to three men whose passion for the *Lusitania* provided me with a wonderful resource. Whether it was to double-check facts or toss around plausible fictional scenarios based on the layout of the ship, these gentlemen were gracious and obliging and each experts in the field. To them, a huge thank you. They are Eric Sauder, who has spent four decades researching ocean liners and was the historian for Dr. Robert Ballard's exploration of the wreckage of the *Lusitania* and dived in a submersible to the site; J. Kent Layton, who has spent twenty-plus years researching ocean liners, with a focus on the *Lusitania*; and last but not least, Mike Poirier, historian and author (and now friend) who was indispensable to me during the writing process, reading early drafts and correcting what I'd muddled up. Historical facts aside, Mike also demonstrated a keen eye for romantic fiction and there too his suggestions were welcome and inspired. He has devoted over twenty years to researching the "*Lusy*" and has become a go-to pundit for the media, particularly during the hundredth anniversary of the torpedo strike in May 2015. Mike also created the Facebook group RMS *Lusitania* Association of Relatives and Researchers, which has brought hundreds of people together in their shared passion for the ship and its passengers.

Of course I couldn't have completed this novel without the continued support of my friends and family. A special thank you to Karen Ashbee, Suzanne Boyd, Derick Chetty, Mike Crisolago, Louisa McCormack, Athena McKenzie, Ceri Marsh, Diane Phillipson, Kaye Pollock, Vivian Vassos, Meredyth Young, my mother Carolynne and sister Jackie, and my colleagues at *Zoomer* Magazine.

I also wish to thank my agents, Diana Beaumont and Grainne Fox, who guided me throughout. My editor at HarperCollins, Jennifer Lambert, who managed to "steer the ship" whenever I had doubts—I couldn't have done it without you. I also want to thank the entire HarperCollins Canada team—from copy editor to production to art department to publicity (that's you, Rob Firing)—whose professionalism and support were immeasurable.

And finally, a big shout-out to author, editor and publisher—and acclaimed *Titanic* expert—Hugh Brewster, who inspired me to write this novel in the first place.

SELECTED BIBLIOGRAPHY

Beesly, Patrick. *Room 40: British Naval Intelligence 1914–1918*. New York: Harcourt Brace Jovanovich, 1982.

Churchill, Winston S. *The World Crisis 1911–1918*. New York: Charles Scribner's Sons, 1931.

Denniston, Robin. *Thirty Secret Years: A. G. Denniston's Work in Signals Intelligence 1914–1944*. United Kingdom: Polperro Heritage Press, 2007.

Fitch, Tad, and Michael Poirer. *Into the Danger Zone: Sea Crossings of the First World War*. United Kingdom: The History Press, 2014.

Gannon, Paul. *Inside Room 40: The Codebreakers of World War 1*. United Kingdom: Ian Allan Publishing, 2010.

Larson, Erik. *Dead Wake: The Last Crossing of the Lusitania*. New York: Crown, 2015.

Layton, J. Kent. *Lusitania: An Illustrated Biography*. United Kingdom: Amberley Publishing, 2010.

Preston, Diana. *Wilful Murder: The Sinking of the Lusitania*. New York: Doubleday, 2002.

Sauder, Eric. *The Unseen Lusitania: The Ship in Rare Illustrations*. United Kingdom: The History Press, 2015.

Singer, Barry. *Churchill Style: The Art of Being Winston Churchill*. New York: Abrams, 2012.